CW01086694

First published 2001 by Prowler Books,
part of the Millivres Prowler Group,
116-134 Bayham Street, London NW1 0BA

A catalogue record for this book is available from the British Library

ISBN 1 902644 42 5

Printed and bound in Finland by WS Bookwell

SEX SAFARI

Peter Gilbert

PROWLER BOOKS

Chapter One
Kenya, 1970

Robert couldn't believe his eyes, or his luck. He'd got the right house. "Thirty-four Kenyatta Road. There's no number on the out-side but it's the only house in the street with a basketball ring over the garage doors," Malcolm had said. There it was: a basketball ring and net. And it was in use. Malcolm had said he had two sons, both of whom were at school. Malcolm himself didn't look much more than 35. That meant the oldest couldn't be much older than thirteen and yet...

There were two boys practising shooting a ball into the net. Both were wearing very brief shorts and, apart from footwear, nothing else. One was very young, eleven or twelve maybe. But the other...He was quite tall, with dark curly hair like Malcolm's and the dark shading of hair on his legs. Surely he couldn't be Malcolm's son? No. He had to be a coach of some sort. Robert wound down the window.

"Is this Malcolm Marriott's house?" he asked, praying that they would say it was.

"Yes," said the elder one. "Are you Mr Hall from Kampi-ya-Moto?"

"That's me," said Robert, transferring his gaze from the young man's very hairy legs to his face.

"He's here, Mum!" the younger one shouted in a shrill treble. Robert climbed out of the car just as Mrs Marriott came out of the side door of the house.

"Oh, you're here. My husband has told me all about you. Did you have a good journey? The roads are dreadful, aren't they? It was all so much better in the old days. Now, have you got all your shopping? Oh! In a cold-box. What a good idea! Of course it isn't as hot now as it will be later in the year." She had the delivery of a speeded-up machine gun. She turned to the eldest boy.

"Martin, take Mr Hall's shopping and give it to Ibrahim. Tell him to take the lid off and put the whole thing in the freezer." She turned back to Robert. "Ibrahim hasn't got a clue. None of them has. He put my food mixer in the dishwasher: cable and all. Ruined it of course. Now come in. The coffee pot's on. You'll need one after that long drive."

Meeting Malcolm Marriott had been pure chance. Robert's wife, Pat had gone back to Britain to have a check-up. The baby they had both desperately wanted didn't seem possible after all and Robert was lonely. And meeting Pat had been wonderful. Pat understood him and, for the all too short time they were together, his old "urges" (as she called them) vanished. Both of them were thrilled when his posting to Kenya came through. The President was fearful of a coup from a tribe other than his own and wanted a network of airfields established so that troops could be put on the ground quickly. It was a dream-posting. No uniform; no boring "dining-in" nights. "Just get on with the job and keep your head down," the military attaché at the Embassy had said.

The house, as Pat had said, was perfect: a low bungalow right on the edge of the Great Rift Valley. The view from the verandah was so spectacular that they had both spent hours out there. Fires down in the far distance glittered like little orange sparks. The smell of wood-smoke from the African village up the road drifted in the evening air. There was only one drawback. Kampi-ya-Moto was miles from anywhere. They had to go into Nairobi every weekend for shopping. When Pat was around, that wasn't too much of a snag. The drive home with a car loaded with provisions was fun. After she had gone, the prospect of returning late at night to an empty house was so depressing that Robert took to spending the weekends in a small hotel. It was on one such evening when he was sitting out on the terrace of Plum's Hotel that he had met Malcolm Marriott, an engineer with the East African Railways. They had had a couple of beers together and Malcolm had invited him to spend future weekends at their house.

"It'll save you money," Malcolm had said. "I hope you don't mind roughing it. I've got a couple of unruly kids. They're at school during the week, of course, but the weekends can be murder."

Robert had jumped at the chance to spend every weekend with a proper family and was pre-disposed to get on with the kids, however unruly, right from the start.

Over coffee, he learned that Malcolm was playing golf and due back some time in the afternoon; that Martin and David were both at the same school. Martin was nineteen and should have left school in the previous year. In fact he should have been at university, but there had been some sort of mix-up about certificates – caused almost certainly, according to Catherine, by the presence of Africans in the Ministry of Education.

"It's almost incredible," she explained. "It's not just Martin. Most boys and girls of his age are in the same position. The certificates were apparently sent to the Ministry by the examining board and some fool there lost them. In Martin's case, we are actually quite glad. He's terribly immature and I don't think he's ready to leave the nest yet."

Robert also learned the provenance of almost everything in the room. "That elephant table? It is nice isn't it? We bought it in Mombasa. No. I tell a lie. It must have been Kericho. I must ask Malcolm." So it went on. Strangely enough, Robert quite enjoyed it. It had been a long time since he'd been in European company. He would have liked to have gone out and perhaps talked to Martin a bit, but Catherine Marriott had much to say. There would be other times, he thought.

At lunch, little David monopolised the conversation. The meal was delicious. Ibrahim might not have had a lot of knowledge of electrical household appliances, but he could certainly cook. Robert would have preferred to have eaten his before it got cold, but David fired a question every few seconds; each one in a high voice that seemed to threaten the beautiful thin glasses on the table. What was it like living so far from civilisation? Had Robert seen any wild animals? Was it "frightfully jungly"? Was Robert married? Where was his wife?

"Why has she gone to England to see about having a baby?" David asked. "Africans don't. They have babies all the time. They just crouch down under a bush and it pops out. My friend saw it happen."

"Oh really!" said Catherine in an exasperated tone. "They're quite different, darling. It's not the same at all."

"They should use condoms more. Even Father Cole says that," David added.

Catherine looked shocked. "The things they teach them nowadays!" she said. "I suppose they have to, now that they've got them in the same class as white children."

"Racist," said Martin. It was the first and only word he had spoken since he had sat down. His voice was deeper than the tenor one would have expected and it had a husky quality that sent a shiver through Martin's spine.

Catherine ignored the remark. Robert wanted desperately to involve Martin in further conversation, but David and his mother prevented this. David's questions and Catherine's criticisms of native Kenyans continued throughout the meal. It's probably for the best that Martin and I don't converse, Robert thought. Martin was a very pleasant and good-looking young man whom he would remember and think about fondly on his verandah when he got back. Nothing more.

After lunch the two boys went back to their basketball practice. Robert offered to keep the score, which was hardly worthwhile. Martin's height gave him all the advantage. Robert recorded every one of David's successful attempts to get the ball into the net. With Martin he wasn't quite so accurate. Gazing at Martin's legs and beautifully round behind made him lose count. Robert noticed also Martin's powerful chest and arms...

"How many was that?" Martin asked after one series of shots.

"Oh...er...seventeen."

"I made it nineteen."

"If Mr Hall says seventeen, seventeen it is," said David. "Anyway, it's time to pack up. Daddy's here."

Malcolm's Mercedes swept into the drive. Ibrahim ran out of the house to relieve him of his golf bag.

"You got here all right then?" Malcolm asked. "Looking after you, are they?"

Robert said that he couldn't have been happier which, at that moment, was true. Martin and David were sitting on a raised bank along the edge of the drive. Martin's knees were under his chin, affording a delightful view of long, sun-tanned thighs.

They all went back into the house. Ibrahim rolled in a tea trolley and, for the next hour, Robert sat sipping tea and nibbling cake whilst Malcolm talked golf and Catherine contributed to the conversation by bemoaning the present state of the course and the club which had started to accept Africans as members.

At dinner that evening, David and Catherine once again did most of the talking. Malcolm and Martin just got on with their meal.

"Feel like going down to Plum's for a drink?" Malcolm asked when Ibrahim was clearing the table. Robert said he would like that very much.

"Can I come, Dad?" Martin asked.

"What's got into you?" Malcolm asked. "You never usually come out with me."

"I've got someone interesting to talk to this time," said Martin.

In fact, he hardly spoke a word the whole evening and at one point he left the table and was away for almost an hour. Malcolm seemed unperturbed. "He's almost certainly listening to a sob story from one of the staff," he said when Robert asked where the boy had gone. "He's a quiet lad but his heart's in the right place."

His surmise proved to be correct. One of the waiters had been given notice because his eyesight was failing. Martin wanted a hundred shillings to pay the optician's fee. Malcolm handed over the money. "I'll deduct it from your allowance," he said. "Don't tell your mother. She'll only say the man's lying." Martin left them again.

They got back to the house quite late. Ibrahim, whose working hours seemed to extend throughout the twenty-four-hour day, brought in coffee. "David's gone to bed and we have a minor crisis," said Catherine.

"Oh yes? What is it this time?" asked Malcolm.

"I'm sorry, Robert. I had planned to put David into Martin's room on a folding bed so that you could have his room, but he refused. You know what children are like. Would you mind awfully sharing Martin's room?"

"Not at all. How does Martin feel about it?" asked Robert.

"Okay by me," said Martin.

"Oh, good. That's that worry over. In the old days we had the summer house to put guests up but now the government has decreed that Ibrahim has to be provided with accommodation...He's ruining it, of course. Typical of them. In the old days he'd have been happy enough to live in a chicken shed..."

Martin decided to go to bed early, for which Robert couldn't blame him. Politeness dictated that he had to spend a further hour listening to an account of the country's deterioration and inevitable collapse. Malcolm said nothing.

Finally, Robert was able to drag himself away. He thanked his hosts for a pleasant day and Catherine showed him the bathroom – actually provided with instant hot water. Back in his "bush" home, if you wanted hot water you had to light a wood fire under the boiler at least two hours in advance. He enjoyed a long shower, brushed his teeth and then padded softly along the landing to Martin's room. Very quietly, he opened the door. The room was in almost total darkness. The folding bed had been placed along the window. He took off his underpants and slipped on his pyjamas. They took some finding in the dark and he'd packed them at the bottom of his bag. Finally, he slipped down under the sheet and tried very hard not to think about Martin. The result of doing so under just a sheet would have been immediately visible had Martin woken up.

Glad that the days of paying for a hotel were gone, he was just dozing off when Martin spoke.

"Are you asleep?" he asked.

"Not yet," said Robert.

"Nor me. It's hot in here tonight, isn't it?"

"Do you want me to open a window?" Robert asked. "I can just about reach it."

"No. It'll only bring insects in. Do you reckon I did the right thing paying for Peter's glasses?"

"I'm sure you did. It was a kind gesture. This country needs more people like you." He told Martin about Mr Hanson. Mr Hanson was one of the few big farmers who had stayed on after Independence and now ran his farm as a training co-operative with the Kenyans and provided them with free health insurance.

"He sounds like a nice man," said Martin. "I'd like to meet him."

"You'll have to come up some time," said Robert. Sitting on the verandah with Martin and looking out over the Rift Valley was an attractive prospect. Not that it would come to pass, of course. It was just one of those things one said. It would be forgotten in the morning.

There was a long silence. Robert concluded that Martin had fallen asleep. Suddenly his voice came through the darkness again. "Do you fist?" he asked.

"Do I what?" Robert replied.

"Fist. You know. Masturbate."

The question took Robert off-guard to such an extent that, for a moment or two, he didn't know what to say. "Well, yes," he said finally. "Everybody does."

"Girls don't."

"Yes, they do. They –"

"Don't tell me. I don't like girls."

"What's that supposed to mean?"

"What do you think it means?"

"You like boys?" Martin didn't answer. "Nothing wrong with that," Robert continued. "Quite a lot of people are that way."

"Are you?"

"Yes, if you must know."

"I thought so. Are you going to fist tonight?"

"I don't know."

"I am. It's too hot to sleep. What do you think about when you do it?"

Robert slid a hand under the sheet to restrain his rising excitement. "All sorts of things," he said.

"Me too. People, mostly – and what I'd like to do with them," said Martin. "It's better when somebody else fists you."

"Is that an invitation?" Robert could hardly believe his luck.

"It could be."

"What about your parents?"

"Don't worry about them. They won't disturb us."

"You're sure?"

"Quite sure. They never come up until about two o'clock at weekends."

Robert's cock was already rampant. If he hadn't been alone for so long, he might have thought for longer. He might even have turned the invitation down. Sex with a lad whose parents were downstairs and whose brother was in the next room was risky to say the least. He peeled back the sheet and got out of bed. As if to lead the way, his eager cock stuck out through the gap in his pyjamas. He tucked it back in again and took the few steps to Martin's bed.

"You're hard," Martin whispered, putting out a hand to touch the lump. "I am too," he added.

"Let's see," said Robert, expecting Martin to pull back the sheet. He didn't move. Robert sat on the side of the bed. A conical lump in Martin's sheet confirmed what he had said. It was a temptingly large lump. Robert touched it. Hard flesh waiting to be unveiled. Very gingerly, he took both sides of the sheet and rolled it back.

"What on earth are you wearing?" he whispered. A cloth bound Martin's waist and extended down to his ankles.

"It's a kikoi. It's cooler. The Kenyans wear them."

"Weird," said Robert.

"Better than those silly things you're wearing," said Martin. "More convenient too."

"For this, you mean?" Robert asked. He slid the fingers of one hand down over Martin's navel and under the material. Martin had done it up pretty tight. Robert found the end with some difficulty – largely because his fingertips came into contact with something much more interesting than the corner of a kikoi, something extremely hard and surrounded by a clump of bristly hair.

"Like unwrapping a Christmas present," Robert murmured, as he undid the knot and laid out the material on Martin's left. His cock was still covered. Robert took the remainder of the fabric and laid it on the boy's right. Martin lay naked. Robert reached out for the light switch.

"No. Don't turn it on. It's better in the dark," said Martin. His hand touched Robert's thigh and then moved over the front of his pyjama trousers.

"You're pretty big," he whispered. "How old are you?"

"Twenty-nine."

"I'll bet you look quite nice without those stripey things you're wearing," said Martin. It was just possible to see his grin as he said it.

"Shall I take them off?" Robert asked.

"Of course. I want to see you naked."

That didn't take long. Martin reached out again and clutched Robert's cock in a warm and sweaty hand. "If you lie alongside me, I can fist you and you can fist me," he said, releasing his grip. "Hang on. I'll shift over a bit."

Robert got on to the bed, lay back and then slid a hand down over Martin's belly. He stopped when his fingertips touched hair and then moved them very gently forward until they were in contact with Martin's stiff and eager shaft. Martin's fingers went round his, squeezed them hard and then began to move frantically up and down: an action more suitable for pumping up a bicycle tyre in a hurry.

"Hey! What's the rush?" Robert gasped. "Slow down." He prised Martin's hand away and then returned to the boy's tool. Very gently, he ran his fingers over Martin's silky foreskin. Almost imperceptibly, it slid down over the hard core. Robert touched the tip of Martin's cock and felt the outline of the slit against his fingertip.

"You'll have to do it faster than that," said Martin.

"Wait and see," Robert whispered. He ran his hand up the

inside of Martin's right thigh, delighting in the feel of the sparse soft hair and the cool skin.

"Hmm. That's nice," said Martin in a dreamy voice. Those were the last words Martin spoke for about the next half hour. He sighed a lot. He grunted and he groaned and, as Robert's questing fingertips found his most sensitive places, he began to reciprocate with his own. Robert played gently with Martin's gratifyingly large, loose-hanging balls. Martin did the same to Robert. Robert extended his middle finger and found what he wanted to feel. There were several wiry hairs there, growing from a tiny, soft and tightly pursed dimple of a muscle. It was, as a friend of his used to say, "superbly fuckable", but instinct told him that there was another time and another place for that particular delight, despite the fact that Martin opened his legs wider and lifted his behind. Robert stroked it and tickled it. Martin groaned. He stopped jiggling Robert's balls and put his arms down to his sides.

Robert stopped, too. Martin sank back on the bed and groaned again. Robert ran his hand over the boy's chest and touched his nipples. Martin sighed. Very slowly, Robert used the palms of his hands to explore Martin's torso and abdomen. He had rarely felt a young man so hard. There didn't seem to be a soft spot anywhere on Martin's body. He moved further down. Martin's belly felt like a teak table-top. His cock was like a truncheon of the same wood.

Martin gasped again and reached out in the darkness for Robert's own cock. His hand felt damp and warm. He began to move the foreskin up and down, much more slowly this time. Robert did the same to Martin. The feel of the boy's pulse against the palm of his hand set his brain to work. Seven and a bit inches by one inch, he thought – superbly suckable. Should he? It would avoid the inevitable mess.

Martin's hand squeezed rather more tightly. He was keen, thought Robert. There was no doubt about that. He hadn't needed to be persuaded. He hadn't been seduced. He was enjoying every minute. It was possible that he actually wanted Robert to suck him, but didn't want to say so. For a second or two, Robert kept his hand going. How much nicer those bristly hairs would feel against his lips, he thought. It had been a long time since he had had a cock in his mouth – especially a cock like Martin's. A hard cock waiting anxiously to explode in his mouth, filling it with warm juice. Of course, Martin wouldn't ask him to do it, he thought. He'd be afraid that Robert might think the idea distasteful. Silly lad. There was nothing more delicious. And Martin was perhaps too inexperienced for Robert to ask. Anyway, actions spoke louder than words. He took his hand from Martin's cock, raised his head and then sat up. Martin changed his position slightly so as to continue his hand movements. Robert took the boy's pulsating cock in his fingers, and lowered his head towards it.

He was too late. Martin gave a loud sigh, thrust himself upwards and came. The room was so warm that Robert hardly felt it spattering on his face and chest at first. Martin gave another sigh and let go of Robert's tool. Robert resumed his original position, reached out and found the boy's wrist. His heart was thumping hard. "Carry on. Nearly there," he whispered. Martin started again and Robert lay, thinking of what might have been. He licked his lips.

It didn't take long. He did warn Martin, but the lad took no notice and kept pumping even as the first jets splashed on to Robert's belly. "Christ!" he exclaimed. Martin stopped. They lay together panting. Robert stared up at the ceiling. He was suddenly aware of Martin's breath on his cheek and turned his head to face the boy.

"Where ...did you learn ... to fist ... like that?" Martin asked.

"Years of practice," said Robert. He ran a hand down under his navel. "We seem to have made a bit of a mess," he said.

"No problem," said Martin. "Advantage number two of wearing a kikoi. Stay as you are."

He pulled the cloth from under Robert, wiped himself and then handed it over. "There are several in the drawer," he said. "This one will go in the washing machine. Ibrahim won't say anything. He never does."

They lay talking – about the Royal Air Force, of all things – for some time. Robert hoped that Martin might suggest another session in the morning, but he didn't.

"I suppose we ought to get some sleep," Martin said and Robert returned reluctantly to his own bed. By the time Malcolm and Catherine came up the stairs, Martin was snoring lightly.

"I hope you slept all right. David's so odd about his bedroom. Thank goodness Martin's more sensible. I was worried. I hope we didn't wake you when we came up. There was such a good film on and we both wanted to see it. We kept the sound down as low as possible. Fortunately these houses were built to European standards. Now I don't know if you're a church-going person, but David and I always go to St. Martin's on Sunday morning. There's such a nice clergyman there. British, of course, but I don't know how long he'll last. They're ordaining a lot of them at the moment. Quite ridiculous..."

Both Robert and David tried in vain to stem the flood of words – David protesting that he wasn't odd at all and Robert saying that he had slept very well and wasn't keen on church-going. Catherine took no notice at all and continued whilst Ibrahim impassively served breakfast.

"What are your plans for the rest of the day?" Robert asked Martin, when Ibrahim had cleared the table and Catherine had followed him into the kitchen.

"What time do you have to leave?"

"After lunch some time. I don't want to drive in the dark."

"We could go over to see my friend George. He lives out at Langata though."

"That's no problem. We can go in the car."

"That'd be great," said Martin. "You'll like George. Have you heard of 'Sunshine Safaris'?"

"Vaguely. A posh sort of firm that arranges hunting trips for rich tourists?"

"That's it. That's George's dad's firm. George's actually against hunting, though."

"Sounds like a sensible young man," said Robert.

"You're sure you don't mind?" Martin asked.

Robert smiled. "It will be more interesting than going to church or plodding round a golf course," he said.

Their departure was delayed by some twenty minutes. Catherine deplored the fact that Africans were beginning to move into Langata, one of Nairobi's classiest suburbs and Robert was forced to listen to accounts of smart garden parties she and Malcolm had attended there in the old days. Martin escaped and went to sit in the car.

"My mother infuriates me sometimes," he said when they were finally on the way.

"She probably means well," Robert replied. Privately he thought Catherine's departure would be the best thing that could happen to the country. Unfortunately that would almost certainly mean that Martin would go too and there would be no more pleasant weekends – which, if he played his cards right, might be even more pleasant in the future.

The Glovers' house was enormous and totally incongruous. One doesn't expect to find a typical British country house a few miles from the equator. Built of yellowish stone, it stood on a slight hill surrounded by immaculately maintained lawns and flower beds. The house servant came down the drive to open the wrought iron gates. He seemed delighted to see Martin again and shook Robert's hand enthusiastically when Martin introduced him.

"Bwana Glovers and the memsahib have gone to Meeting," he said. "Only Mr George is at home."

"Is he up yet?" Martin asked.

"Oh yes," said the man. "Mr George is in pool."

"That makes a change," said Martin. Robert parked the car in the drive and followed him across the lawn. He had never actually met anyone with a private swimming pool. Its huge size didn't really register at first. The reason for that was certainly its sole occupant. An extremely beautiful youth was pounding powerfully through the azure water. He was very brown, obviously very fit and strong and his hair was blond. He didn't see them at first. Robert hardly glanced at the diving boards, the pump and filtration plant, the bar in the corner with its striped awning and the luxurious lounge chairs. All his attention was on the rounded, jutting contours covered by the tightly stretched green material of George's swimming shorts.

"George's family are Quakers," said Martin. George, hearing a familiar voice, waved and swam towards them. Robert was still trying to reconcile being a Quaker with decimating the animal population when George climbed out of the water.

"Hi!" he said, shaking his head and showering both of them.

"This is Robert," said Martin. "He's an Air Force officer working up in the bush."

"Hi," said George again and took Robert's hand in an extremely wet one. Not that Robert minded. He forced himself to look at George's face, rather than dropping his eyes to look at something lower down. He was a remarkably good-looking young man. A phrase he'd read somewhere came to mind: "The body of a Greek god and the face of a water baby". It fitted George perfectly.

Martin asked if George had managed to solve some sort of mathematical problem. George said he hadn't been able to get it out, which set Robert's mind racing. Getting it out from the wet, green fabric that covered it could be fun, he thought, but it might be difficult to locate. There was no sign that George even had one. Then he felt guilty at having entertained the thought. He attributed it to the events of the previous night, after such a long abstinence. Anyway, George was a Quaker. Robert knew very little about Quakers, but he was quite sure they didn't go in for that sort of thing.

"Robert's a terrific fister," said Martin. Robert couldn't believe his ears.

George grinned. "How did you find that out?" he asked.

"Last night. I got David to kick up a shindig about moving out of his room, so Robert could sleep in mine. It was great."

"I wish I'd been there," said George. He grinned. He had an extraordinarily wide mouth.

"We could have a session now, if you like," said Martin. Robert's cock, already stimulated by George's good looks, jerked upwards.

"Oh no. Not on a Sunday morning," said George.

Robert was about to make what he hoped would be taken as a humorous remark about religious observances, but Martin got in first.

"But you never go to the Meeting. You said you didn't believe in it," he said.

"It's not that. I always have one on Sunday morning before I get up and I've just had another one under water. Just before you got here, as a matter of fact."

So that was the reason, thought Robert. He glanced at the size of George's fingers. If that was anything to go by, George was a well-hung young man, if caught at the right time.

"Perhaps you'd like something to drink?" said George. Another thought arose in Robert's mind. He settled for orange juice. George pressed a button on the bar in the corner and the servant arrived within seconds. George ordered drinks in Swahili: proper, grammatical Swahili – not the bastardised version used by most

Europeans. They sat on lounge chairs. George, unfortunately, sat on the far side so that he was almost hidden from Robert's view by Martin. That wasn't a huge disadvantage; Martin was in shorts and it was pleasant to lie there and contemplate the flesh that had proved so responsive a few hours previously.

The servant brought the drinks. The two lads talked about school. It was an extremely warm day and Robert was just beginning to doze off when Martin brought him into the conversation.

"Are there any schools up in the bundu where you live?" he asked.

"Oh yes. One. It's a pretty ramshackle affair. A lot of the students end up as agricultural trainees with Mr Hanson. He's the man I told you about last night," said Robert, addressing Martin.

"Surprise, surprise – you found time to talk as well," said George. "Mr Hanson...Is that Jeremy Hanson?"

"I think his name is Jeremy, yes. Do you know him?"

"My dad does. He's a Friend. A Quaker."

"Is he? I didn't know that."

"I've always wanted to go up there. Dad goes occasionally."

"Go with him on the next trip and get him to drop you off at my place," said Robert. "I could do with some company."

"I've got a better idea," said Martin. "It's half-term next month. Why don't we both go and spend the week with Robert? That would be okay, wouldn't it, Robert?"

It was more than okay, as far as Robert was concerned. He said he would be delighted. Martin fell to making detailed plans. Robert would come down to Nairobi as usual for his shopping and take the two boys back with him. George reckoned he could persuade his father to come up a week later on the Sunday afternoon to collect them and bring them back. "That way we get an extra night," he added.

"Provided both sets of parents agree," said Robert. It was a delightful prospect, but he couldn't see Catherine agreeing.

"Oh, they will. Don't worry," said Martin.

"Is there room for both of us?" George asked.

"Plenty. There's my room and there's a spare room. It's unfurnished at the moment, but I can do something about that." Robert went on to describe the house and the area.

"Sounds like fun," said George, and then, addressing Martin, said, "It would give us the chance we've been waiting for, wouldn't it?"

"I was just thinking the same thing," said Martin. Robert was about to ask what that was, but the tent-shaped lump in Martin's shorts rendered the question unnecessary.

Chapter Two

"I'm sorry. I can't shake your hand. Mine are filthy. Gardening, you know. You can't leave it to *them*. They haven't a clue. We'd end up eating weed soup. Good gracious! What have you bought?"

The object on the roof rack was very obviously a mattress, but Robert patiently identified it as such. Catherine wondered why he needed another. Robert had anticipated that question. Up to now, he explained, he had managed with two Air Force issue beds put together. He had got hold of a double bed and he needed a mattress for it.

"You were lucky to get hold of a double bed," said Catherine. "They're like gold dust at the moment. I mean, they get married so early – if they trouble to get married at all. It's all utterly disgusting, but I wonder if you might be more comfortable on that than on the folding bed. David's still playing up. It's all quite ridiculous. He's going off to spend the night at a friend's house and he still won't even contemplate giving up his room. We could put this on the landing or in the lounge for you. It would mean untying it, I suppose, but Ibrahim could just about manage to do that."

This was a possibility that Robert had not thought of. He was perfectly happy on the folding bed, he said, and to untie the mattress would be a waste of time. Besides which, it was sealed in a polythene wrapper. There was no chance of rain, so it might just as well stay where it was. Catherine was not totally convinced. Fortunately, Martin came bounding out of the house at that moment and he, predictably, agreed with Robert.

"Is that for us?" Martin asked when Catherine had returned to her gardening at the back of the house.

"Right first time," said Robert. "Thanks for the call the other night. Was it difficult to get permission?"

"No. No trouble. We both plugged Mr Hanson as hard as we could. George's dad rang my dad and it was all sweetness and light."

"So you'll have to go over to see the Hansons some time."

"Oh sure. I'll be interested to meet Mr Hanson. But if that visit takes two hours, I've worked out that there are still two hundred and fourteen hours for other things."

"You can't have sex all the time," said Robert.

"We'll have a bloody good try," said Martin.

That night Malcolm went off to Plum's by himself. Robert had planned to plead a headache. In fact, Catherine's constant chatter gave him one. Trying to concentrate on the television and on her ceaseless racist comments was enough to give anyone the grandfather of all headaches.

"I'll come up with you," said Martin. "That would save disturbing you later. I can always read."

Catherine protested that she would be all alone and have nobody to talk to, which made Robert feel guilty. Martin was unmoved and suggested that she might care to call Ibrahim in from the kitchen to keep her company. Catherine was not amused.

"I tried to get them both to go to the theatre," Martin explained as he followed Robert up the stairs. "No go, I'm afraid. At least I managed to get David out of the house."

"You're quite a planner on the quiet, aren't you?" said Robert.

"I try to be. Do you want to use the bathroom first?"

"No. You go first. What are your plans for this half-term at my place?"

Martin smiled. "I was always told to fall in with what the host had in mind," he said.

With that delightful prospect in mind, Robert fished in his bag for the kikoi he had bought that morning, undressed and draped it round himself. Pyjamas, he decided, were easier. If he tied it too tightly he felt constricted. If he loosened it, it fell down. He just managed to keep it up in time for a look at himself in the mirror on the wall, but then had to grab it when the door opened and Martin walked in.

"Oh, you got one then?" he said. Robert sat on the folding bed. "I can't keep the bloody thing up," he replied.

"Ah! There's a knack in keeping things up. You taught me about cocks. Hang on while I get undressed and I'll teach you to cope with your kikoi."

Robert sat on the edge of his bed. He had no choice but to watch the undressing process. He felt slightly embarrassed because Martin obviously felt the same way. He turned to face the wall before slipping his briefs down. Such modesty made Robert's thoughts of a night in the near future when his cock would slide between those cheeks seem almost sacrilegious. Nonetheless, it was an exciting prospect. He just had time to appraise their smoothness; their roundness and their whiteness before Martin wrapped the kikoi round himself quick as a flash and turned round.

"Right," he said. "Stand up."

"If I do that, it'll fall down," said Robert, actually more concerned with the state of his cock than with the effect of gravity on a piece of cloth.

"It's got to come off if I'm to show you how to put it on properly," said Martin. Robert stood. It fell. Martin stooped to pick it up. Robert looked down at the vertebral bumps along Martin's brown back. He had strong arms too, a fact which Robert hadn't noticed before.

"If you stand in front of the mirror..." said Martin. Robert's embarrassment increased. Being aware that your cock is hardening fast is one thing. Standing in front of a mirror and watching it rise in little jerks is worse. Strangely, Martin didn't comment. He stood behind Robert and grinned over his shoulder into the mirror.

"Now then, the first thing to do is to drape it so that one edge is in your middle," he said. His arms went round Robert and he hung the cloth so that it just covered his cock. Only just. The feel of Martin's warm arms on his sides made it rise even further. Once again, Martin made no comment.

"Then you take the other end, wrap it round as tight as it will go... like this... and then you join both ends and tuck them in. Voila! One kikoi. How does it feel?"

"Okay," said Robert, not wanting to turn round.

"Now to remove the kikoi, the process is reversed," said Martin, grinning into the mirror. "It goes like this." He stepped forward, put both arms round Robert and joined his hands together just under Robert's navel. His chest pressed against Robert's back. He took another half-step forward. His cock pressed against Robert's buttocks. It felt rubbery and thick.

"To remove the kikoi," Martin continued, whispering in his ear, "is much more fun and best done slowly like you showed me. Like this..." A soft, warm palm slid down Robert's abdomen. His cock pushed upwards against the knotted material as if anxious to meet Martin's hand – which it was. Robert watched in the mirror as Martin slid his fingers in.

"Mmm. Lovely hair," Martin whispered. "I like hair, do you?"

"I like what you're doing to it," Robert replied, huskily. Martin's fingertips were twining in his bush.

"George is quite hairy. Did you notice?" Martin breathed the question. His lips were touching Robert's ear.

Robert caught his eye in the mirror. Martin was smiling. "Now you come to mention it, I did," he said or, rather, gasped. His breath condensed on the glass. Martin's long fingers were round his cock.

"I thought you had. He's rather nice, isn't he?"

"Very nice. Is he a special friend?"

"I suppose he is. There's another one. You haven't met him yet. Raymond. He's nice too. I think I prefer George, though. You're not going to come yet, are you?"

"Not yet."

"Good. Neither am I. I like doing this. Do you like it?" His fingers were slowly manipulating Robert's foreskin.

"Of course," Robert replied. Once again, a patch of condensation formed on the mirror and then disappeared.

"Time for the great unveiling," said Martin. The kikoi dropped on Robert's feet. "There!" said Martin. "The purple-headed python. That's what Raymond says about mine. He's into snakes. This is a nice python. Just about the same size as mine, too."

Rapidly hardening flesh pressed against Robert's arse.

"Shall I tell you about me and George or me and Raymond?" Martin asked. Robert watched the mirror image of the boy's long fingers working on his cock. He had brought it to such a state of hardness that it was almost parallel to Robert's abdomen.

"Why don't we get on the bed and concentrate on each other?"

"Oh no. I want to see you get worked up until you shoot. Fisting people in front of a mirror is good fun."

"Please yourself," said Robert. There would be plenty of opportunities in the future. His heart began to beat faster so he suppressed that thought and replaced it with thoughts of having to manhandle a double mattress when he got back to Kampi-ya-Moto and of how he would explain its purchase to Kiberech.

"I'll tell you about George, as you've met him," said Martin, still moving his hand up and down. "Now George is a Quaker..."

"But not religious?" Robert's voice was getting more and more husky.

"No, I am glad to say. He's a good fister. Not as good as you. How am I doing, by the way?"

"Very ... well."

"Good. Well, George's got a really nice cock. A bit bigger than mine and he's got really big balls. You'd like to play with them."

"He's got ...a nice arse...too," Robert gasped.

"Oh, are you into that? Arse-fucking? We think it's pretty disgusting."

"It's ...not disgusting...at all," Robert protested. "Leave off... for a bit."

"I thought you were getting hot. I'll play with these, shall I?" His fingers went down to Robert's balls.

Robert took a few deep breaths. "That's better," he said. "Make it last a bit longer."

"Is it thinking about fucking George's arse that does it?" Martin asked.

"Not entirely. I mean... not at all. You can't expect anyone to hold back with a beautiful person like you working on his cock."

"Do you really think I'm beautiful?"

"Of course you are."

"More beautiful than George?"

"Definitely," said Robert. Martin's fingers were stroking his balls.

"Does that mean you want to arse-fuck me?"

"Do you want me to?"

"No. It would be horrible. It would make me feel like... well... a sort of object that people do things to. Animals do that sort of thing. Not humans."

"By the feel of that monster pressing against me, I'd have said you were quite keen," said Robert.

"It's covered with a kikoi, so it can't go in," Martin replied. He frowned and took his hand away - which was just as well. If he hadn't, spunk might have obliterated his reflection in the mirror and the conversation might have ended there. As it was, Robert was able to look into the young man's eyes.

"It's a question of love, really," Robert said. "Some things strike us as repulsive, but it's different when the people concerned love each other."

"Like what?" Martin asked. He put his hands on Robert's shoulders and then slid them down his arms.

"Well, what about cock-sucking? Have you ever done that?"

"Ugh! Now that is really gross. You'd have to be a complete pervert to do that!"

"That's what you say now. If you really loved the person, you'd see it differently," Robert said.

"I'm not a pervert!" said Martin, angrily. "None of us are."

"How would you describe yourself then?" Robert was beginning to feel that the conversation was getting them nowhere.

"Well...different. That's it – different. We don't like girls, but we like fisting. Blokes have got more to play with." His right hand appeared and settled under Robert's navel. "Speaking of which, shall we start again?" he asked. Robert nodded. The hand moved downwards. Fingers curled round Robert's still-stiff penis. "Especially blokes of your age. You've got a lot to play with," Martin whispered. He squeezed it and his hand began to move again.

"So have you," Robert replied. Martin's cock felt like a fence post against his arse. "If George is better hung than you are, he must be quite something," he added.

"Oh, he is. And he...Let's stop talking about him." Martin's hand speeded up. A series of little vignettes flashed through Robert's mind like scenes from a badly edited film: all the men he had slept with in the past before he met Pat. For a second he wondered how she was and determined to call her mother's place.

Tomorrow – or maybe the next day. Because the image of George lying face down with his legs splayed out over the still-wrapped mattress was extraordinarily clear, right down to the hissing gas lamp in the corner of his spare room.

Martin's hand speeded up to such an extent that it was impossible to count the strokes. Robert's heart thumped. He would have told Martin to slow down if he'd been able to speak. The words ran round his brain instead, along with images of Martin and George together – with Martin himself as voyeur. He could nearly hear his own voice.

"Slow down, Martin. Let him enjoy it. You're his lover, not a potato-planting machine. That's better." Martin's arse lifting and sinking again slightly more slowly. George moaning softly. Martin snorting with every stroke. It wouldn't be long now...

"Aaaah!" Instinctively, Robert's buttocks tightened and he thrust forwards. The first drops appeared on the mirror as if by magic and began to run down the surface. The odd thing was – and he couldn't be completely sure – it seemed that Martin was pushing, too. Martin's hands were clasped round his waist and the pressure against his arse seemed to increase with each spasm. "Ah!" Another lot appeared.

"Oh!" Martin gasped. His linen-wrapped cock slipped between Robert's thighs.

"Ah! Oh, yeah. Yeah!" It was all over in seconds. The mirror was a mass of translucent, running spots. Some had landed on the upturned hairbrush on the dressing table and vanished slowly between the bristles.

"God! You...made...a lot," Martin panted.

Robert put his arm round the boy's middle. "And so will you," he said. "Bedtime."

"It'll be great on that new mattress," Martin observed as he lay back on the bed. "Why did you actually buy it?"

Robert perched on the edge of the bed. "For you and George, of course."

"But what about you?"

"I was rather hoping you'd say something like that. We'll think of something."

"I can't wait," said Martin.

"So I see." Robert leant over and touched the knot in Martin's kikoi. It was easier to undo this time. Small wonder, with something like seven inches of rigid flesh pressing against the material. There was a small damp patch at the summit of the conical projection.

"You going to fist me?" said Martin. He sounded breathless.

Robert lifted one side of the kikoi and then the other and laid them out on either side. The material had a dark tartan pattern which made Martin's sun-tanned body look quite pale. His cock stood out at such an angle as to remind Robert of a ship's funnel. The foreskin had retracted and the purple head, contrasting with the whiteness of the skin below it, accentuated the fact. Robert put a hand between the young man's thighs and cupped his balls. Martin gasped and instinctively parted his legs.

"Go on. Fist me," he whispered.

"I've got a better idea," Robert replied and lowered his head. He caught just a glimpse of the amazed expression on Martin's face before he licked upwards from the clump of bristly hairs. Martin said nothing but Robert could actually hear his heart beating. He licked again, this time getting his mouth even lower. At the moment when the tip of his tongue touched the crinkled skin of Martin's scrotum and his taste buds reacted to the exquisite flavour of a sexually aroused young man, he knew the truth about himself. He would never change. There had been times in the eighteen months Pat and he had been together when he actually thought he had. He'd been deceiving himself. There was no pleasure in the world, he thought as he licked slowly upwards, like this. Well...there was one thing that was even better, but that would have to wait until both the new mattress and Martin were in Kampi-ya-Moto.

The slick feel and the taste of Martin's cock-head were too much of a temptation to withstand. He hadn't had one anywhere near his mouth for something like five years. Past experience, forgotten until that moment, told him that he should continue licking and kissing until Martin was squirming like an eel in the bottom of a fishing boat, but he couldn't wait that long. He slid his lips over the head and moved down. The ridge slipped past his teeth. Down even further. The long-forgotten scent filled his nostrils and he inhaled it lasciviously. Martin groaned softly and Robert slid his lips upwards again, paused and then moved down, sucking hard as he did so.

That did it. Up to that moment Martin had seemed composed. Now he put his hands under himself and shoved upwards. Robert nearly choked. Martin lunged upwards again, but this time Robert had his palms on Martin's groin and was able to hold him down. Martin kicked out and then, finding upward movement impossible, he began to writhe around and gasp. Only just able to hold him still, Robert sucked steadily and flapped his tongue from side to side against the shaft which filled his mouth.

"Oh! Ah! Oh! It's..." Martin panted and the first flood of semen filled Robert's mouth. It oozed round the back of his teeth and filled the space between his tongue and the floor of his mouth. He just managed to swallow some of it before the next spurt. That was followed by another and he had to take his mouth away to stop himself from choking. It felt warm and delightfully thick in his mouth and he seemed able to appreciate the flavour on his tongue and the scent in his nostrils at one and the same time. He didn't know why, but there was a freshness about it which reminded him of newly mown grass.

He kissed Martin on the cheek. "Thanks," he whispered.

"Did you actually swallow it?" Martin asked, in a tone more appropriate to asking an astronaut if he had actually walked on the moon.

"Sure," said Robert, licking his lips.

"What's it taste like?"

"Delicious."

"Mmm." Martin said nothing for some time. Robert kissed him again.

"What do you reckon George's tastes like?"

"Nice," said Robert, hoping that he might one day have the pleasure.

"He spends so much time in that pool that I should think his cock would taste of chlorine. I wouldn't fancy that much," said Martin. "Now that I know what it feels like, I suppose I could ask him..."

"When you both get to my place," said Robert. "We'd better get some sleep now." He recovered his kikoi, managed to tie it round himself and slipped into his little bed – which creaked loudly.

He slept very soundly that night. He was rather hoping for pleasant dreams, but there weren't any. Yet there was no doubt when he woke up that the young man towering over him was real.

"Wassa...wassa time?" Robert asked, staring up at Martin's stiff cock.

"Six o'clock," Martin whispered. "Do you want to do it again?"

So they did. This time with Martin standing up with his feet astride and Robert perched on the edge of the bed. "The colossus of Rhodes," said Robert. The young man's position was certainly that of the famed statue and the cock which he pushed between Robert's lips was both very large and as hard as marble.

Robert enjoyed this session even more than the one at night. With his hands on Martin's buttocks, he delighted in the rhythmic tensing and relaxing of the muscles and the feel of the cool, smooth skin. Thinking about the delights which lay hidden between the boy's arse-cheeks caused him to come a few seconds after Martin had tensed up and then gushed into his mouth.

He couldn't swallow all of it and drops of Martin's semen fell onto his thighs, to be joined almost immediately by drops of his own.

He let Martin go into the bathroom first and then went in himself and enjoyed a shower. When he came out, Catherine was on the landing waiting to go in. "Did you sleep well?" she asked.

"Yes, thank you. Very well."

"Martin didn't wake you?"

For a moment Robert was at a loss. "He had one of his nightmares," Catherine explained. "We both heard it. It sounded as if he was running a race of some sort. He was huffing and puffing like a steam engine. I wonder you slept through it."

"It didn't disturb me in the least," said Robert truthfully.

If truth be told, Martin became something of an embarrassment after that weekend. He wanted to know what time Robert started from Kampi-ya-Moto for his regular shopping trips. Robert told him and was surprised, the following Saturday morning, to see Martin standing on the side of the road by the Ainsworth roundabout, flagging down the car. "I've come to help you do the shopping," he said.

So they toured the supermarket together. When told that the particular brand of coffee that Robert usually bought was out of stock and that the supermarket's own brand was just as good, Martin said, "We only like the other stuff." Then it was, "Do you think we should get some orange juice?" and "How are we off for pasta? Did you check before you came out?"

Back at the Marriotts' home Martin announced that "we" would be in for lunch and that "we" might go out for a drink in the evening. David might have noticed the way he sometimes touched Robert's hand. Catherine didn't. She'd had her handbag snatched the previous week and, instead of being delighted that it was returned intact by the police on the same day, was convinced that the police were in league with the thief.

"I've always thought that Inspector Macharia was a rogue," she said. "I shall take it further, of course, but I don't suppose I shall get anywhere. I could see from the look in his eyes when I described the thief that he knew who I was talking about."

"But everything was there," Martin interjected. "You never lost a thing."

"A typical trick," said Catherine.

"If your theory is right, they would have emptied it first and then brought it round," Martin persisted.

"They're all thieves!" Catherine said, totally ignoring his observation. "It's born into them. It's their nature. They're just animals, really. I suppose one shouldn't blame them. It's like blaming a lion for stealing a calf. Now in the old days when Inspector Morris was in charge of this area there was no crime at all. You could leave your bag anywhere and nobody would have touched it."

"But the Kenyans were around then. If it's in their nature, why didn't they steal things then?" David asked.

"Because they got a good thrashing. That's what they need. Just as I said, they're animals."

What Ibrahim, who was standing in the corner ready to take away empty plates, must have thought of this conversation Robert had no idea. The man just stood there, staring into space.

After lunch Martin took Robert out for a walk.

"I had to come out," Martin explained. "Mum really gets up my nose when she's in one of those moods." Robert said he understood. By the time they were on the way home again, he understood much more. Martin not only knew most of the native Kenyans in the area, but was obviously popular. Hands slapped his back in recognition. People waved from the other side of the road and came over for a chat. A walk which should have lasted about half an hour took over three hours. One family insisted that they should come in and have a cup of tea. The tea tasted pretty revolting, but Robert drank it. Martin introduced him as "my best friend", but none of the family, consisting of three strapping teenage sons, a daughter and the parents, raised an eyebrow.

"Nice people," said Martin when they had managed to tear themselves away. "Josiah's an accountant and wants to get good jobs for his sons. The school fees are the problem. At the moment, only young Matthew goes to school. It's terribly sad, really."

They walked on. "I spoke to George," said Martin suddenly.

"Oh yes? What about?"

Martin didn't answer, but put his thumb into his mouth.

"And what did George say?" Robert asked.

"He won't do it."

"I wouldn't worry about that too much. It was probably a mistake to ask him outright like that. Wait – he'll soon change his mind."

"I hope so."

"Sure he will. Once you've got him hard and got it in your hand..."

"That bit's easy enough. I love his cock. Since meeting you, I've been dreaming about it."

"With messy results?"

Martin blushed. "Once or twice," he said. "Do you want to suck him when we're at your place?"

"I wouldn't say no. I'd be happy to oblige."

"Are you going to oblige me tonight?"

"You bet I am – if you don't mind."

Martin laughed. "I'll be happy to oblige," he said.

Chapter Three

The weekend before the school half-term holidays came round. Catherine was almost unbearable and one would have thought Martin was nine rather than nineteen. "Don't forget to pack enough handkerchiefs, darling. Maybe I ought to buy you some more. You know what you're like when you're in a car on a dusty road." The whole of Saturday afternoon was devoted to the question of Martin's luggage. Should he take the sportsbag he used for school, or a suitcase? The suitcase, she decided, was the better choice because it had locks. "I'm sure your servant is trustworthy. You wouldn't employ him if he wasn't, but they've all got relations – far too many of them – and they're all light fingered," she explained. Martin said he couldn't really understand why someone would wish to steal his underpants and shirts. Catherine said they would steal anything, given half the chance.

Ibrahim had to leave the washing up to go up into the attic to find the suitcase. Then he was ordered to wipe it with a damp cloth. Finally, he brought it into the lounge. "Hmm. Now I'm not so sure," said Catherine. The suitcase itself, she explained, might easily become the target for a thief's attention. Perhaps the school sportsbag might be better after all. Martin had to use it on the following Wednesday afternoon, but that should have left enough time for Ibrahim to clean it thoroughly.

Robert was inwardly screaming for Martin to step in and make a decision, but he didn't. He just sat there patiently listening. Ibrahim was sent for yet again – this time to return the suitcase to the attic. Travel sickness pills were next on the agenda. Martin had never yet suffered from the condition, but a hundred and something miles on rough roads? One never knew. Catherine would get some in the week. Something for possible diarrhoea might also be a good idea and she'd ask the pharmacist for other recommendations.

She would have certainly gone on for longer, but Malcolm came back from the golf club and that meant tea and sandwiches and she turned her attention to the state of the golf club. Martin and Robert left to go for a walk.

"Mum does get worked up," said Martin. "You'd think I was going to the Himalayas."

Robert tactfully agreed. As usual, they met several of Martin's Kenyan friends and were just about to turn into Kenyatta Road again when a motorcycle approached. The rider waved, slowed down and then stopped. The bike was very dusty but Robert paid no attention to that. The rider was wearing a bush-shirt and khaki shorts which had ridden right up his thighs. Robert had rarely seen such beautifully proportioned legs. The lad's thighs were thick and fleshy. The backs of his legs were exquisitely curved and, although he was covered in red dust, it was easy to see that he was a very hairy young man indeed. He pushed up his goggles and took off his crash helmet to reveal a shock of extremely fair hair. Even that had dust in it. His face was covered in dust and the white patches round his eyes made his face look like a skull.

"Hi!" said Martin laconically.

"Hi, Martin. Got a puff adder – a good one," said the young man, pointing behind him to the pillion on which stood a plastic bucket with a lid held down by two elastic cords.

"Great," said Martin. "This is my friend Robert. The one I told you about."

"Oh, yes. The Air Force officer. How do you do?" The young man extended a dusty hand. He had a remarkably firm grip. Probably from riding the bike over rough country, Robert thought.

"You and George are away in the half-term, aren't you?" the young man asked. Martin said that was right.

"Shame. There's talk of a python in the Ainsworth valley. I thought I might go for it. If it's as big as they reckon, I might need help. Anyway, I'd better get this one home. See you on Monday." The crash helmet went back on to his head. He kicked the machine into a spluttering start and rode off.

"Raymond," said Martin.

"Not 'fisting-Raymond'? The one you told me about?"

"That's him. He's a good bloke, except that he's got this fixation on snakes."

"You'll have to bring him up to Kampi-ya-Moto some time. There's plenty of snakes there. There was a cobra on the road the other day. I thought a car had shed a tyre at first. It frightened me to death when I realised what it was."

"It would scare me too," said Martin. "I hate the bloody things. Ray's got snakes everywhere. He's even got some in his bedroom. He takes them to the snake park eventually. They milk them for the venom, but there's always one or two in the house."

"That must be a distraction."

"Oh we don't do it at his place. He shares his bedroom with his brother."

"Well, tell him that if he wants to get away, he's welcome. He could just about make Kampi-ya-Moto on that bike."

"He goes much further than that," said Martin. "In both senses. We think he's pretty filthy. He sort of keeps on about it."

"Tell him I'd be happy to give him a hand any day," said Robert, visualising Raymond's huge thighs again.

"Or a mouth?" said Martin, laughing.

"Especially a mouth – once he'd had a shower and got rid of the dust," said Robert. "After that he can be as filthy as he likes."

"You'd have a job getting it all in," said Martin. "He's enormous when he's got a hard-on."

That sentence came back to Robert in the ensuing night. Martin's cock was ramming against the back of his throat and his jaw was aching. When he was back in his own bed and had run his tongue round his teeth several times to savour what was left of Martin's spunk, he spoke.

"You asleep yet?" he whispered.

"I'm not ready for another one yet," said Martin.

"Nor me," said Robert. "How old is Raymond?"

"He'll be twenty next month. He had to repeat a year on account of being bitten by a green mamba. He got gangrene in his toe and they had to amputate it. Really, he's in a worse position than George and me. He'll be twenty-one by the time he eventually gets to University. Funny how things work out for the best. We'd both be in England at University if we hadn't cocked things up and I wouldn't have met you."

"If you go to the same university, you'll have something to play with when you aren't in lectures."

"Ha! Raymond would be out collecting bloody snakes and even if he wasn't, I wouldn't be that keen. George and me will probably go together. He's okay."

"He has safe hobbies or something else?"

Martin sniggered. "Mostly something else," he said. "Hang on a minute. Mum and Dad are coming up. They're late."

They heard Malcolm and Catherine pause outside the door. Martin snored lightly. Robert did the same but more loudly.

"Both asleep," said Catherine. "I do hope young Martin will be all right up there in the bush."

"Why shouldn't he be?"

"He's so young and impressionable."

"He's nineteen and he's got a good head on his shoulders. Now come to bed and stop worrying."

"That's me. Young and impressionable," said Martin when his parents' bedroom door had closed.

"Young and beautiful," Robert replied.

"But I'm going to have a good time in the bush. Your bush," said Martin. "Incidentally, you ought to see Raymond's."

Robert was about to say, "I hope to!", but thought better of it and instead said, "I noticed he had hairy legs."

"It's nothing to what's round his cock," said Martin. "You know his hair's blond?"

"Yes."

"That's the funny thing. The hairs on his legs are blond too, but his pubes are black – well, dark brown. Honestly, it's like a coconut mat!"

"Sounds nice," said Robert.

"It is. Not as nice as George's, though. Do you really think he'll let me?"

"Sure he will. It's just that you asked him at the wrong moment."

"God! I hope so. I can't wait."

"And providing you've got the energy after your sessions with George, I can't wait either."

"I'll still have enough for you. I promise."

"In many ways it's a shame that your friend Raymond isn't coming too," said Robert.

"Raymond? That would make three of us."

"So? The more the merrier. That's what I say."

The sheer hypocrisy of that sentence hit him as he said it. He was the fellow who'd considered himself extremely lucky to be in bed with a man more than three times a year.

"How would we work it out?" Martin asked.

"Well, there would be four of us. We could change partners so everybody had somebody."

"But you and me...I mean...we're special, aren't we?"

Robert had obviously made a serious mistake.

"Oh yes. You and I are special. We could have the others when we felt like it."

"Like biscuits. No...what would be even better..."

"What?"

"You might not like the idea. It's only a dream, of course. I mean... It's not for real."

"Tell me about it."

"If they liked the idea, we could keep them in cages, like they do down at the animal orphanage. Then we could walk around in the evening and sort of choose one."

Robert laughed. "What a glorious idea!" he said. "Sadly, there are no cages and there's no time to make any. Would they have clothes on in their cages?"

"Oh no. At least I don't think so. No. No clothes. I want to be able to reach through the bars and feel their cocks. Anyway, I suppose we ought to get some sleep."

"Not unless you're tired. I'm not."

"Nor am I, actually."

"So carry on with your ideas."

"Do you really want me to? I mean...it's daft really."

"Nothing that you say is daft."

There was a short pause. "Do you really mean that?" Martin asked.

"I wouldn't have said it if I didn't."

"It's nice. Well.... I can't really place the cages at the moment, because I haven't seen your place."

"They could go on the verandah or round at the back of the house next to the boiler."

"The verandah would be better. Not so far to go," said Martin, dreamily.

"They'd need some sort of exercise compound, wouldn't they?

To keep them in good condition, I mean."

"They're in pretty good shape already," said Martin. "George swims every day. Raymond goes to the club about once a week with his dad and swims there."

"Money is no object in a dream. We'll build them a swimming pool."

"Oh yeah. That would be good. And you and I could stand on the side watching them and choosing which one we're going to have."

"Watching their arses cut through the water." Robert slid a hand under the bedclothes, undid his kikoi and took his rising cock in his fingers.

"Not much keen on that idea. How about when they've finished swimming and get out of the pool?" Martin whispered in the darkness.

"Okay then. You take over. Tell me what happens." Robert felt his cock-head emerging from the enveloping skin.

"Mmm. Let me see now. Well, they'd be standing there, all wet. Sort of glistening wet, if you know what I mean, and I'd say, 'Which one do you fancy tonight, Robert?' What would you answer?"

"Oh Raymond, without a doubt."

"Really?"

"I'd leave George for you," said Robert, stroking his rapidly awakening cock. Even accounting for the fact that the Kenyan climate wouldn't leave anyone "glistening wet" for more than a couple of minutes, the image of George, naked at a pool-side, was almost overpoweringly exciting.

"Would you like to do it with Raymond?"

"Well, he wouldn't be as good as you, and probably not as good as George, but I'll put up with that."

"Mmm, he'd let you. There's no doubt about that. Raymond would let anyone do anything, So I can have George?"

"Sure."

Martin didn't speak for some time, but the room wasn't totally silent. Robert lay, trying not to breathe too hard, listening to the gentle rustling of Martin's bed-clothes.

"Carry on," he said, after some time. He smiled. Martin was carrying on – even if not verbally.

"I think maybe we ought to get some sleep. It must be quite late. Anyway, it's weird talking to someone you can't see."

"Shall I come over again? Just for talking."

"Er.... Oh. Yes."

Robert got out of bed so rapidly that it almost toppled over. He just managed to hold it upright but the sheets and his kikoi landed in a tangled mess on the floor. He stepped over towards Martin's bed, groped to find the edge and sat down.

"There. That's better," he whispered. "Now then, where were we?"

"Your thing's hard. I can see it," said Martin.

"And no doubt yours is too."

"It is actually. Thinking about George did it."

Robert resisted the urge to say "Me, too!".

"Keep on thinking about him," he said, instead.

"If I do that, I'll come."

"So?"

"It's not good for you to do it too often. I read it in a book."

"George obviously doesn't think so. Didn't he say that he'd had a wank in bed and another one in the pool?"

"That's right, he did. I wish he'd waited for me. God! Just thinking about it...It goes really hard, you know."

"I'm sure it does."

"And when he comes it's like a fire hydrant. It's really powerful."

"That would feel good in your mouth."

"Oh don't! It would, though. You're right."

"I'm sure George thinks the same about yours."

"Hmm. I wish."

"Ever heard of sixty-nine?"

"No. What's that?"

Robert explained. "It sounds a bit gross," said Martin.

"It's fun, though."

There was another period of silence. Then Martin spoke. "So if I was George and you were me, show me how it works," he said.

Robert lifted the sheet, pulled it right out from under the mattress and dropped it on to the floor. The room was dark, but instinct told him not to turn on the light. He could see that Martin's kikoi, like his, had been taken off. He could just make out the dark patch of hair at Martin's groin.

"Lie sideways," he whispered.

"Like this?"

"That's right."

He knelt for a moment with Martin's head between his knees and then leaned forward. It wasn't difficult to find, despite the darkness. Martin's cock flopped against his chin – almost as if to say "I'm here". Once again, he took it into his mouth. He felt Martin's breath on his cock-head, but the reaction he was hoping for didn't take place. He lowered his head and again sniffed the mixture of perspiration and excitement.

Martin gave a low moan as Robert moved his head up and down, feeling the hard veins against his lips. He felt the boy's hands on his behind. One of them moved over and under him and touched his cock.

"Tell me before you come," said Martin. Robert's entire body stiffened with shock as warm, wet tissues enveloped his cock-head and teeth scraped against his most sensitive spots.

It was amusing, he thought – whilst conscious thought was still possible. He had no doubt that he was George as far as Martin was concerned, and there were several moments when Martin also became George in his own imagination.

Martin kicked his legs apart. Robert could just make out the boy's toes at the extreme edge of his field of vision. He managed to get a hand under Martin's balls and Martin immediately recip- rocated – painfully. There was an awful lot the lad didn't know about – but he was a very willing student. The cage fantasy returned. George and Raymond, standing naked in their cages. No...there would have to be more than two. A row of young men, standing at ease, just as they had at the Officer Training School, waiting to be selected for one of Squadron Leader Wilkins' embar- rassing role play exercises. Only these young men would have to be naked and standing at ease. Only their cocks would be at atten- tion. Or would they? Martin would have to be taught how to get one ready for action.

Suddenly, his mouth filled. It was a flow this time, rather than a spurt. Robert felt it running against his teeth. His cock slid, again painfully, out of Martin's mouth.

"I'll...do it...by hand," Martin gasped and grasped Robert's cock. He only just had time to warn the lad before he shot – sur- prisingly hard.

"That was great!" said Martin when he had recovered his breath. "How do you manage to breathe? I was nearly suffocated."

"It comes with practice," said Robert, as he clambered down off the bed.

"So do we," said Martin. "This sheet is soaking. Not to worry. Ibrahim will change the bedding in the morning and nobody will know."

Fortunately, all Martin had said about Ibrahim's tact proved correct. New sheets were on the bed the following day and Ibrahim not only shook Robert's hand when he left on Sunday afternoon but smiled and said he was sorry that the bwana would not be staying on the following weekend.

It was fortunate that Robert was extremely busy during the

next few days. He might well have got even more neurotic if he had had less to do. Nonetheless, he checked provisions three times – adding something new to the shopping list each time. He checked the boiler and the bathroom. Kiberech, his cook, helped. There were more than enough gas bottles for the kitchen stove and the fridge. Nonetheless, he thought, young men eat a lot. He made a note to buy some more. Then there were drinks to think about. What did they drink? He added soft drinks and beer to the list. By the time Wednesday came round, he realised that there was no way he could bring the two lads and all the shopping back together in one journey.

Fortune smiled. A truck had to go down to Nairobi to pick up some equipment that had arrived at the airport. The driver obligingly dropped him in the city centre and promised to be back there in two hours to drive him back with the provisions – and one or two smaller items which he thought might be useful.

The smaller items came first. The assistant in the pharmacy smiled knowingly as he handed over the vaginal lubricant.

Robert felt guilty. He'd phoned Pat a couple of days previously. "I suppose you're up to your old tricks?" she'd said.

He'd denied it of course, insisting that there were no willing boys in Kampi-ya-Moto – unless you counted the local boys. Saying something so racist made him feel even more guilty. Stuffing the purchases in the pocket of his jacket, he made his way to the supermarket. Butter? Maybe it wouldn't be a bad idea. Packets of biscuits? He hadn't thought about those. By the time he was halfway round the shelves, the trolley was full. The assistant, accustomed to bush-dwellers' huge shopping lists, unloaded the lot for him on to a flat-bed truck. Robert signed the chit and went round again.

He was in the soft drinks section, peering at the labels on the bottles when a voice behind him said hello. He turned round. He'd only seen the boy once before, but there was no doubt as to the identity of the owner of that shock of hair.

"Oh! Raymond isn't it?"

"'S right. We met last weekend. I was on the way home with a puff adder."

"I remember. How is he, or she, or it?"

"Fine. Shopping?"

"Actually, you're just the man I need. What should I buy for George and Martin to drink?"

"Tusker beer, loads of coke and a couple of bottles of Jack Daniel's," said Raymond.

"I didn't know they drank whisky."

"They do when they're away from home. They nick it out of George's dad's drinks cupboard."

"Oh yes. I seem to remember that Martin said something about going round to George's house. With you, I thought he said."

Fair skin, however sun-tanned, shows a blush pretty clearly and there was no doubt of the effect of that remark on Raymond.

"I don't go that often," he said.

"In many ways it's a shame I didn't meet you earlier. You could have come up to my place with them," said Robert rapidly thinking of the delightful permutations of four men, two adjacent single beds and one double bed.

"I couldn't. There's a python under the Ainsworth River bridge. It ate somebody's dog the other day. I'm after that. I've never caught a python."

Robert remembered the night-time conversation on the subject of Raymond's "python" and smiled. He said that if and when Raymond had the time, he was more than welcome and added, as an afterthought, the story of the cobra on the road.

"Thanks a lot," said Raymond. "I'd like that. Can I call you?" Robert gave him the number. Raymond said he had to hurry home with the shopping and Robert watched him go through the checkout. As it happened, he was so tall that his groin was level with the conveyer.

There's a python much nearer than the Ainsworth River bridge, thought Robert gazing at the bulge in Raymond's jeans.

"Haven't you got anything smaller?" he heard the cashier ask. Robert smiled and picked up a crate of Coke.

He had to wait under the awning outside the supermarket for some time. Fortunately it wasn't too hot and he'd brought a cold-box for the perishable items. Nonetheless, he was tired and irritable when the truck finally pulled up. There had been problems with the customs, the driver explained. Robert didn't regain his usual happy composure until they crossed the Ainsworth River bridge. He looked down at the river. Despite the snake there were three young Kenyan men standing on a flat rock in the middle of the river. All were naked and one of them was a very well-built young man indeed.

"Very foolish," the driver commented.

"Yes. I heard there was a python down there."

"No chance, sir. No, it's the Europeans – with respect. I know you're not like that."

"Like what?"

"There are men. They stay at the Norfolk hotel and they come down here to look at the boys. You see them with binoculars. They choose a young man and take him back to the hotel. The young men get big money."

"Good Lord!" said Robert. "I would never have guessed."

"It is the parents who are to blame, sir. They are very poor. No son of European parents would do things like that."

"I'm sure you're right," said Robert and, as the truck went off the tarmac road on to the dust of the bush road, he added "Utterly disgusting!" and the driver nodded approvingly.

Friday afternoon came at last. Kiberech had lit the fire under the boiler, so Robert was able to have a shower. "Make sure the fire is kept going," Robert warned. "The two young men will want to shower when they get here."

"The bwana too," said Kiberech. "The road is very dusty today. It was given so on radio."

Robert made a final inspection of the bedrooms. Everything looked to be in order, so he got into the car and was soon speeding along, followed by an immense cloud of red dust. He slowed down to walking pace as he passed a small group of Samburu warriors and they raised their spears to thank him even though they were already so dust-covered that they looked like terracotta statues.

Both Martin and George were waiting for him in the front garden of the Marriotts' house. All hopes of a quick getaway were shattered when Catherine emerged from the side door.

"Oh my God! You poor man. You look as if you've been through a dust storm. Come in and have a shower, for goodness sake. Is it so bad? I heard something on the radio. I wonder if the boys shouldn't have masks of some sort. I suppose I could wet some handkerchiefs. Martin is terribly sensitive to dust. It's different for George, of course. He's used to it from going out with his father. Have you met his parents? Such nice people. Quakers you know, not that I hold that against them. Heaven knows we're all the same. Europeans anyway. Now what about food for the journey? I've got Ibrahim to make up a couple of packets in case they get peckish. That reminds me, I was going to tell you about Martin's dislikes in the way of food..."

He could easily have had a shower, dried and dressed himself and been on the road in the time it took for her to finish. Finally, he got the boys and their bags into the car. Martin sat in front and George in the back seat and they were on the way. Catherine stood at the gate waving until they were out of sight.

"Silly woman," said Martin. "You don't get dust in a closed car."

By the time they got to Kampi-ya-Moto, Robert realised how

wrong Martin was. A dust-tight car had not been invented. Dust blew up through the holes for the pedals. It insinuated itself round the tightly closed windows. Still, neither of the boys seemed to notice it. They were too busy looking at the countryside. They changed places about halfway, which gave Robert the opportunity of a really good look at the area he had previously only seen when covered by green bathing trunks. Under jeans, the shape of his cock was visible and looked extremely attractive. Fortunately, George had spotted a herd of giraffe in the distance and wasn't aware of his host's interest.

It was just after nine o'clock and quite dark when Robert turned into the driveway. Kiberech, dressed in a new white robe, was waiting for them and, when he realised that both boys spoke Swahili, there was no holding him back. Robert parked the car under his primitive thatched shelter and joined them, feeling unwanted as they chattered.

Kiberech, according to instructions, had prepared a salad meal and covered it with a cloth. Robert dismissed him for the evening – in person. He stayed on in spirit.

"Terribly sad about his son," said Martin.

"I didn't know he had one," said Robert. "I didn't even know he was married. He looks too young."

"That's the sort of thing my mother would say," said Martin and went on to explain that Kiberech's young son had been crushed to death under a tractor.

They finished the meal. Robert put the plates in a bucket of water for Kiberech to wash in the morning. He showed them the bathroom and explained the primitive plumbing. "I should have a shower now and then we can sit out on the verandah and have a drink before turning in," he said. He showed them the spare bed-room with its huge bed.

"What about you?" George asked.

"Oh, I'm all right. I've got used to it. I'll have mine later. There should be enough hot water for the three of us."

They were ages in the bathroom. Robert was on his second bottle of Tusker, listening to the sounds of the African night: animals calling to each other and insects chirping over the low bubbling noise of the boiler refilling itself. He went round to the back of the house and threw another two logs into the still-glowing boiler furnace and then went back to his beloved verandah. Doors in the house were opened and shut again. He heard them talking to each other and laughing. Finally, they came out. He turned round. Each was wearing a kikoi. Martin's was white this time and it was George who wore one with the tartan pattern.

"Gosh! That's better!" said George. "I feel like a new man."

"Play your cards right and you might have one," said Martin.

"If you mean what I think you mean, no thank you," said George.

There seemed little doubt as to the meaning of that sentence, but Robert pretended to ignore it. "Get yourselves drinks," he said. "They're in the fridge or in the sideboard."

They both went indoors again and re-emerged with full glasses. There was considerable shuffling round of the wicker chairs and the little circular table but, finally, they were all sitting down.

"When are we going to see Mr Hanson?" George asked.

"Whenever you like. Tomorrow, if you wish. Though won't he be at a Quaker Meeting, as it's Sunday?"

"There's no meeting-house up here. They'd have Meeting for the family and staff early in the morning at home. We could go after that," said George.

"Why not Monday?" Martin asked. "Sunday morning is for staying in bed – unless you happen to have a swimming pool and feel like doing it under water."

"You're pretty earthy sometimes. No. I think we ought to go tomorrow. I wouldn't like my dad to know that I delayed it. Mr Hanson is quite somebody in this country."

"So is the president. So are the ministers – not to mention the district officer. You wouldn't be so anxious to call on them, I suspect," said Martin.

"They're different. No, if Robert agrees, I think we ought to go over there tomorrow. I'm looking forward to it."

"Aren't you looking forward to anything else?" Robert asked. There was no mistaking the lump under that tartan material.

"How do you mean? Oh, that." George must have seen where Robert was looking. "That happens sometimes," he said.

Robert said nothing. A phrase he'd heard during his officer training came to mind. "You must have a plan for everything, gentlemen. I care not if it's an all-out war or a trip into town. There must be a plan." The present situation wasn't covered in the manuals and he was at a loss as to what plans one should make to attract a good-looking nineteen-year-old into his bed. The more he thought about it and the more he looked at George's honey-coloured torso, there was a danger that the disposition of his weaponry would be apparent to the other side.

"I think I'll leave you and go and have my shower," he said. "The water should be just about hot enough by now."

Martin said he should have gone first. They would have been glad to wait. Turning slightly and hoping they wouldn't notice anything, Robert stood up.

"I'll put your beer back in the fridge," said Martin.

"No. Don't worry. I won't be long," Robert replied.

Twenty minutes under a cascade of lukewarm water helped bring things back to normal again. It wasn't possible entirely to forget the fact that they were out there. The thought that he would have to take them to see the Hansons in the morning helped. The thought of spending Sunday morning with a Quaker family had a remarkable effect on his over-enthusiastic penis. He dried himself and then went into his room. If they were each out there wearing a kikoi, he thought, he might as well follow suit.

Provided the conversation and accompanying thoughts were kept under control, there should be no problem.

He had just reached the door and was about to open it when he stopped. The little window next to the door was open but screened against insects.

"His dad's really rich," he could hear Martin saying, dispelling any thoughts that they might have been talking about Robert. "It's absolutely enormous, even when it's slack," he added.

Robert let go of the door handle and moved silently to one side so that he was standing by the window. A cool breeze blew against his face through the mesh.

"I know. I saw it the other day after cricket practice," said George.

"How do we do it? That's the question. He's almost certainly got a swimming pool at home so we can't do what we did with Raymond and my place is out. My folks wouldn't allow it. We'll have to think of something. Just imagine getting that lovely brown flesh in your hand or even in your mouth."

"I wish you wouldn't keep bringing that up," said George. "It's disgusting."

"No, it isn't. It's nice."

"How do you know? You haven't done it...or have you?"

"Of course I haven't. I wouldn't mind, though. Do you feel like fisting?"

"Not now. Robert will be back any moment."

"He wouldn't mind."

"Later on, inside," said George. "I must ask Robert to ring the Hansons when he comes out again."

Robert opened the door and stepped out.

"Oh, there you are! We thought you'd fallen down the plug-hole!" said Martin as he rejoined them.

"I put your beer down on the floor. Here. It's probably too warm now."

"It'll be okay," said Robert as he sank into his chair again. He could hardly believe his eyes. The fleshy lump in the front of George's kikoi had enlarged considerably. Martin looked as if he had a model of Mount Kilimanjaro under his.

"No prizes for guessing what you two have been talking about," said Robert.

"Cricket actually," said Martin.

"I didn't know cricket had that effect." Robert pointed with the beer bottle towards Martin's lap.

"We were talking about the people, rather than the game," said Martin.

"Well, just go ahead. Don't mind me."

"There's this chap in the upper sixth," said Martin. "He's really gorgeous."

"Name of Shah," George added. "He's a really high-caste Indian. His dad's in real estate and owns a sugar factory. They reckon he's worth millions."

"What's his name?"

"Vijay."

"He never pulls the curtain across when he has a shower," Martin said. "He doesn't mind showing off what he's got. Honestly, the thought of fisting him makes us both go weak at the knees."

George picked up Martin's glass and held it over the top of his own. "It's that size when it's limp," he said. "God knows what it's like stiff. Like a giraffe's neck, I should think."

"And you know what we were talking about the other night? He's got a beautiful bottom as well. It sort of juts out from his back. Know what I mean?" Martin added.

Robert laughed.

"Martin gets really disgusting sometimes," said George and then, "Where exactly do the Hansons live?"

"You see those lights right over there in the distance? About a mile beyond them," Robert replied.

"Do you often go over there?"

"Only occasionally. Mr Hanson is the nominal owner of the land that's been appropriated for the Kenyan Air Force. Nominal, because there's no chance he'll ever be able to farm it again. He'll have been compensated, of course. They're good about things like that. I don't think he needs the money, though."

"My dad says he's one of the richest men in the country," said George.

"He's not short of the odd shilling, that's for sure."

"Hmm. With all that money you could have anything you wanted," said George.

"Possibly even Vijay Shah," Robert replied. George blushed.

"You could do so much too," said Martin and, before Robert had a chance to comment on that remark, he added, "like help the Kenyans to be really self-supporting. Open schools and health centres. Things like that."

"Which, in fairness, Mr Hanson does already, as I told you," said Robert. "I suppose if we are going over there tomorrow morning, I'd better call him now."

"It would be a good idea. Make sure you mention my name," said George.

Mr Hanson, as always, was grace itself. He and Mrs Hanson would be delighted to see Robert and his young friends, he said. The name Marriott meant nothing to him but, to George's obvious delight, he said he held Mr Glover in the highest regard and would be delighted to meet George again.

"Ten o'clock tomorrow morning," said Robert as he rejoined the lads on the verandah. If the tensile strength of cotton was anything to go by, they had changed the topic of conversation completely. Robert got himself another beer and settled down for the evening.

George talked of long, tough safaris with his father. After that the theme changed to football and then to their respective ambitions. Martin wanted to do something for Africa. George wanted to expand his father's business into a multi-million-dollar firm arranging tours for people who just wanted to photograph the animals.

"I've just realised something," said Martin.

"What?" Robert's mind was miles away – in England, to be precise, and in his mother-in-law's house. He would have to call Pat in the morning.

"You could do anything out here on this verandah and nobody could possibly see you," said Martin. "The hedge is all round and too thick to see through and the drive is at an angle from the road, so even if somebody stood at the gate he couldn't see the house."

"What are you getting at?" George asked.

"Nothing. It was just a thought. Anyway, it's getting late. I think we ought to turn in."

Robert looked at his watch. It was a little after ten o'clock. "Already?" he asked.

"I am a bit tired after the journey," said Martin.

"I am too, as a matter of fact," said George, draining his glass. He stood up and went inside.

"You coming in too, Robert?" Martin asked.

"Not tonight. I'll leave you to it," said Robert.

"Can I come visiting later?"

"The door is never locked," said Robert, and he was left to enjoy the comparative silence and to think very deeply indeed about his own future.

Chapter Four

There was a group of camels with remarkably human faces. Pat was riding one and her mother was on the other. Strange music came from behind a heap of building rubble. Pat was trying to say something; trying to get some message across to him, but he was too far away and couldn't hear what she was saying. He ran towards the camels, but they started to run too and he couldn't catch up with them. Then Martin appeared, stark naked and he joined in the chase.

"Stupid idiot!" Robert murmured as he woke up. He shook his head. He never usually remembered dreams. The room was dark. He could only just make out the furniture and it took him some time to realise where he was. He picked up the pocket torch from the bedside table and shone it on his watch. It was half-past three in the morning.

He lay there for some time willing himself to fall asleep again. The house was eerily silent. It was difficult to believe that it contained three people. The two lads had obviously done it – whatever it was – and were asleep. Even thinking about them made his cock rise slightly. What had they done? he wondered. If he hadn't drunk so much beer, he might have been able to stay awake and listen. The walls were not that thick. He might have missed Martin's characteristic long drawn-out sigh as the spunk pumped out of him and it would have been nice to hear what George sounded like at such a moment – even if, as he strongly suspected, all they had done was to wank each other.

Even nicer would be the opportunity to hear what either of them sounded like when a cock reamed into their arses for the first time. Martin would probably groan in his habitual husky tone as Robert's well-greased cock pushed its way, inch by inch, into tight, moist, virgin territory.

His imagination had taken over completely. Martin would be good, he thought. Once the initial discomfort had gone, he'd probably be even more enthusiastic. George would be quite different. A boy who wouldn't let anyone suck him would have to persuaded. Robert remembered what George had looked like as he stepped out of the swimming pool. George wasn't as tall as Martin, but his body appeared to be packed with muscles. Just as his cock had strained against the cotton of a kikoi, his muscles had strained against restraining skin. His upper arms had been perfect curves. Robert summoned up the memory of George's pectoral pads, each crowned with a corona and surmounted by a prominent nipple. Then there was his belly, hard and almost concave, in complete contrast to –

"His arse!" Robert said the words out loud, and then wished he hadn't. It was far too coarse a name for anything so beautiful. He lay there for some moments, fingering his by now steel-hard cock and thinking. "Buttocks", "behind" and "butt" – none of them were appropriate. "Rump," he whispered at length. "A well-rounded rump." And what did one do to a rump? One skewered it. Why couldn't George be as accommodating as – what was the lad's name? Robert couldn't remember.

It had been his stag night at the Britannia Hotel. It would have been no surprise if the events of that evening had convinced him to call the whole thing off, but wedding preparations take on an impetus of their own. Pat might have understood, but her mother wouldn't have. She'd have written to the Ministry of Defence, denouncing this queer who had led her daughter up the garden path. She was a terrible, not to say terrifying, woman. Robert quickly concentrated instead on the memory of the kind bellboy who had stayed around in case he'd needed to be helped to his room after the guests had left. He hadn't needed help. He'd drunk one hell of a lot but was reasonably sober.

"Better take the lift, sir." He had had a nice voice too. He'd also been blessed with a beautiful figure, set off to perfection by those bum-hugging trousers and little cutaway jacket. George would look nice in a uniform like that, Robert thought. He moved his fingers up and down his cock - just as the bellboy had done when he'd undressed Robert and helped him on to the bed.

"You've got a nice one," he had said and Robert had said that it wasn't in much of a condition at that moment.

"It could be," the bellboy had said. What the hell was his name? For the life of him, Robert couldn't remember. It started with a P. Peter? No. Paul? Not quite. Something like that.

"Do you feel like it? I could stay all night if you want. I live in, see. Nobody would know."

And then what had happened? Robert couldn't be sure. He remembered the bellboy uniform on a clothes hanger in front of the wardrobe. He remembered the whiteness of the young man's body and the wonderful feeling of warmth and security as he hugged him. Most of all he remembered what the bellboy had said. "I've never done it."

"I'm sure you must have done." Robert's hands had glided over the young man's buttocks.

"No. Honest. I let them wank me or suck me if they want. One or two regulars come here because of me. Commercial travellers, people who come for conferences, that sort of person. I've never done it with an Air Force officer, though. What are you exactly?"

"I'm a Flying Officer." It was only a rank and he only flew as a passenger, but it had impressed Philip – Ah! That was his name! – enormously. That moment was really the beginning of the self-deception that had been going on for so long, he thought. It was fortunate that, by the time the question had been answered, Philip's face had been buried in a pillow and they both had been too far gone to continue the conversation.

Philip had yelled in pleasure. It was odd that he found that so exciting, Robert thought. He let go of his cock and lay for some moments thinking. It was almost the best moment of a fuck. His face flushed as he remembered the exquisite sensation of a muscle-ring riding up the length of his cock and the feel of warm tissues enveloping it. Philip had been good. Martin would be even better and George would be sublime. He took the quilt off the bed and wrapped his fingers round his cock. This, he thought, was going to be a good one. Who to think about – that was the question. Martin or George? Alternatively he could re-run the memories of Philip or – the idea came to him in a flash – how about all three of them together? There had to be a way. Maybe Martin could fuck Philip, leaving him with George.

If it wasn't for the fact that one of the hinges squeaked slightly, he might not have noticed the door opening. He stopped, automatically holding his breath for an instant.

"Are you still awake?" It was Martin's voice. "Oh! I see you are. Sorry."

Robert grabbed the quilt and pulled it over himself.

"I thought you were asleep," he said.

"Not me. What were you fisting yourself for? You should have tapped on the wall or something."

Robert laughed. "You're incorrigible!" he said.

"Not at all certain what that means. If it means 'in the mood', you're right. Can I come in?"

"Sure. Shut the door behind you."

"I mean in bed with you."

"Even better." Robert lifted the side of the quilt. Martin stepped into the room, closed the door as silently as he could and climbed into bed.

"How did you get on with George?" Robert asked, brushing Martin's stubbly cheek with his lips.

"All right."

"Well... let's have the details. Did you fuck him?"

"No chance."

"A shame. It would do him good. So what did you do?"

"I fisted him until he came and then lapped it up. Want a taste? Here." He put his fingers under Robert's nose. A slightly acrid smell drifted into Robert's nostrils. He licked Martin's finger.

"Good, eh?" said Martin.

"Very good." Robert took as much of Martin's finger as he could into his mouth and sucked it. Martin pulled it away. "Don't waste time on a finger. I've got something much better," he said.

"Haven't you come already?"

"Yes. There's still enough for you, though."

Robert reached under the quilt and slid his hand down over Martin's hard belly. He was actually trying to find the knot in Martin's kikoi, but found something else instead.

"I can feel it," he whispered. Martin's cock pulsated in his fingers through the cloth. He found the knot and undid it. Martin took hold of it and pushed it to one side.

"Is George asleep?" Robert asked.

"Unconscious is more like it. He's probably dreaming about what he's going to say to Mr Hanson tomorrow."

"Whereas he ought to be dreaming of something else entirely." Robert insinuated his fingers down under Martin's balls. The skin was warm and slightly damp.

"Such as? Mmm. That's nice."

"Getting fucked," said Robert, illustrating the point by pushing his middle finger even deeper.

"By?"

"You – me – both of us."

"A nice thought, but I don't think either of us has much of a chance with George. You might if you were an Air Marshall or something like that. I might if my dad owned the railway instead of just working on it. George's saving his arse for the right man."

"And what about you?"

"I've found the right man. I'm not so sure that this is the right time though."

"But you don't mind obliging with a refreshing drink?"

"Providing it's in here already. I'm buggered if I want to get out of bed and go to the fridge."

"It's here all right. Don't worry." Robert tried to squeeze Martin. He might as well have tried to compress the local chief's ebony walking stick.

Once again the bed-cover landed on the floor, this time for some hours.

"You never would have thought it." It might seem odd that a man should remember his mother-in-law's favourite saying at such a time, but Robert did.

"You never would have thought it!" He would never have thought that he would be licking the legs he had admired when Martin was playing basketball with David. He would never have thought that the generous young man who had paid for a waiter's new glasses would give himself so willingly.

He forced himself to remember some of his mother-in-law's other sayings. Paradoxically, it helped. He was all too aware of his propensity to shoot early and there was no better inhibitor than thoughts of Mrs Angel. Nobody had ever had a less appropriate name.

"I'll leave you two to enjoy yourselves." She certainly hadn't had this in mind, he thought as he pushed the tip of his tongue into Martin's navel. The skin against his lips was hard but warm and very, very alive. His taste buds detected a faintly soapy flavour. He moved downwards, licking as he went. His tongue touched the first few bristly hairs and Martin gave a slight moan.

So far as he could recall, Mrs Angel had never said anything on the subject of hair, which was hardly surprising. It would have taken a poet to describe the exquisite springiness and scent of youth that became stronger as he moved downwards. Martin moaned again and spread his legs further apart.

"You'll have to go deeper than that if you want a strong root." That was the time she coerced him into planting an apple tree. Well, the root was strong enough, he thought. It was well watered, too. In fact, although it was too close to his eyes for him to focus properly, it seemed to be oozing moisture. Getting down deeper was appropriate though. He shifted downwards slightly and pushed his face down as far as he could. The musty odour grew stronger and stronger. The loose skin of Martin's scrotum felt warm and moist against his chin. He opened his mouth as far as he could, but that didn't work. He sucked hard.

"Pop a couple of these in your mouth and suck them. They'll make you feel better. Not together, silly man! One at a time."

That was the funniest memory of all. A day trip to Hunstanton and Mrs Angel decided that they would have lunch before going on the beach. Lunch, as far as she was concerned, had to consist of at least three courses, so it was hardly surprising that Robert had indigestion when they were finally ensconced in deckchairs. Mrs Angel brought out her knitting as she always did. Robert and Pat sat holding hands.

"There's nothing much here, is there? A waste of time coming," said Mrs Angel over the clicking of her knitting needles. Robert didn't answer. It would have been difficult with a tablet in his mouth and he certainly didn't agree. Some twelve feet in front of them, a blond young man lay face down on a towel. At first it seemed that he had nothing on but, if you looked really carefully

– as Robert was – you could just see a thin cord across the small of his back and another that vanished between two of the most attractive humps of flesh he had seen for a long time.

Pat realised, of course. She squeezed his hand sympathetically. "That young man will know all about it tomorrow morning if he doesn't turn over," said Mrs Angel. Robert had the impression that the young man knew all about it already – and not just the effect of hot sun on a pale skin. His suspicions grew even stronger when, after deliberately turning his head and staring at Robert for a few minutes, the young sunbather did turn over - to reveal, under what must have been the skimpiest swimming costume seen on Hunstanton beach for some years, a definite and very appetising lump.

"Showing everything he's got!" said Mrs Angel in a shocked whisper. Once again, Pat squeezed Robert's hand.

"Not quite everything, mother dear," said Pat and that time Robert squeezed her hand. There was enough to make him forget his stomach problems. The fair hair on the lad's legs caught the sun. Who knew what lay under that little triangle of green cloth? Of one thing he could be sure. Even limp – if indeed if was completely limp – it was thick...fleshy...succulent...

"How's your stomach now, Robert?" Mrs Angel's voice cut right through his thoughts.

It wasn't his stomach that he was concerned about, but something below it.

"I think we'll go off for a stroll, mother. That will help settle it," said Pat. It was as well that she said it then. A few minutes later would have been too late. Somehow or other Robert managed to get out of the deck-chair without it being too apparent.

They talked a lot on that stroll. Pat was certain that he would change. Robert had his doubts, but allowed himself to be persuaded. It was a terrible mistake.

With Martin's scent in his nostrils and a considerable portion of Martin's scrotum in his mouth he knew that now for sure.

Martin groaned and brought his legs together so that his thighs were pressing against Robert's cheeks.

"Yeah! Yeah!" he said. Robert managed to extract his head and looked down at the purple-headed shaft.

"Yeah!" Martin gasped again. Robert lowered his head and felt the silky skin on his lips. He opened his mouth. It didn't seem that he had moved his head downwards and Martin didn't appear to have moved upwards but, nonetheless, the cock glided into Robert's mouth. He flicked his tongue against the shaft. Martin moved upwards slightly, forcing him to lift his head. It pushed against the back of his throat. He wanted desperately to take as much as possible. Martin thrust upwards again. Robert put his hands on the lad's hard nipples to push him down again and slid his lips upwards until they were on the ridge of Martin's cock-head. He breathed in deeply through his nose and went down again. Martin lay still this time. Robert could feel the boy's heart pounding. He slid his hands down Martin's sides until they were in the hollows of his hips.

He sucked hard and then stopped. "Eat it all up. I don't want anything wasted." Another of his dear mother-in-law's favourite sayings. Well, there wasn't going to be any waste this time, he decided. Nothing would be left. Unlike some of Mrs Angel's cooking, Martin's offerings were too delicious to waste. The delightfully cool depressions in the side of Martin's arse seemed tailor-made to hold the boy still. Robert pressed his hands into them and licked up the length of Martin's shaft, playing his tongue over the veins, sucking his own saliva – now subtly flavoured – back into his mouth.

Martin gave a terrific upwards heave. It would have taken more than one man to hold his behind down on the bed. Just what happened at the back of his throat, Robert didn't know. He had a terrifying feeling that he might choke to death and then that subsided. He heard himself gurgling. Martin grabbed his head and pushed it upwards and Robert's mouth filled instantly with warm, sweet-tasting semen. He gulped, which was painful. Another gush came and he managed to swallow that more easily. After that there was just a long dribble – which, if anything, was sweeter and warmer than the first. Martin collapsed back on to the bed, gasping. Robert slid his mouth upwards and then flicked the tip of his tongue over the still-dribbling slit.

"Jesus! That was something else!" said Martin after some minutes. "How did you make it last so long?"

"Thinking about my mother-in law," said Robert, wiping his mouth with the back of his hand. "How did you manage?"

"I didn't have to. That was the second coming. George got the first – all over him!"

"Like I said before, you're incorrigible," Robert said.

"Just healthy. Have you come?"

"Not yet. Feel like giving me a hand?"

"I'll give you something better. Let's change over." Martin threw his legs across the side of the bed and stood on the floor.

"You mean?" said Robert.

"Of course. Lie back and enjoy it."

It didn't take long, but every millisecond was sheer bliss. The feel of Martin's tongue exploring him was almost enough to make Robert faint. When, not a moment too soon, his cock was enveloped in Martin's mouth and Martin's hands were gliding up and down his thighs, he tried desperately to hold back but it was impossible to think of Mrs Angel. It was impossible even to think of Pat. He tried to grab Martin's head but couldn't. He couldn't even give Martin any warning. His back ached. His balls ached and Martin kept on sucking. There was nothing he could do. He came. Once – twice – and then a third time. Martin must have swallowed the first lot. Robert wasn't sure about the rest. Martin knelt upright between his legs and licked his lips. He smiled.

"Sorry. I couldn't hold back," said Robert.

"You were right," said Martin.

"About what?"

"What you said about if people love each other, it's nice."

"Which shows how much I love you. Yours is delicious."

Martin kissed him clumsily on the shoulder. "Yours is nice too," he said.

"And now you've got a taste for spunk?"

"Too right I have. When can I have the next helping?"

"Stick around, as they say. Let's have a rest first. Where's the quilt?"

"Down here."

"Let's snuggle up together under it."

"You won't let me go to sleep?"

"I shall be sure to wake you up at the right time. That's it. Come a bit closer." He put both arms round Martin's still-trembling body. "I love you," he said simply, and kissed Martin's lips gently.

"I love you too," Martin replied and their lips touched again but harder and for much longer.

In fact, and not surprisingly, they both fell asleep and the early morning sun was already turning the white walls pink by the time they lay diagonally across the bed with hands on each other's sweat-dampened buttocks – each of them reluctant to release the slackening flesh in his mouth. Robert's fingers were deep in Martin's cleft.

Martin opened his mouth and released Robert's cock. "I'd better get back to our room, I suppose," he said.

"Must you?" Martin's cock slapped against Robert's chin but Robert's middle finger had found what it had been searching for.

"Mmm! I'd better."

They both froze at the sound of keys jangling and the front door opening.

"Shit! Kiberech!" said Martin.

"You'll have to stay now. Wait till he takes the doormat out. He bashes it against the fence. Go then."

"Looks like I shall have to. Do you reckon he knows?"

"I shouldn't think so."

"When are you going to fuck me?"

"When you're ready and when we've got time."

"I'm ready now."

"I know." What had felt as hard as a knot in a piece of wood a few minutes previously had suddenly turned rubbery. There was resistance there, but something told him that it could be overcome.

"We won't tell George," Martin whispered.

"He'll know. He's bound to if we do it here. You can't have two people in the house and fuck one without the other knowing."

"Wait till he's asleep. Like we did tonight. Last night I mean."

"It's different," said Robert, "especially the first time." He continued to caress and tickle the tightly puckered knot of muscle.

"How?"

"It just is."

"Which means wait and see?"

"I guess so." Not "see", he thought, and pressed a bit harder. "Hear" was the word. It was odd that one could love a person – especially a person like Martin – and yet want to hear him cry out in pleasure.

The front door opened again. "That's it," said Martin. "Let go."

Unwillingly, Robert took his hands away and Martin clambered off the bed. "Now, where the hell is it?" he said and lifted the quilt. His kikoi was crumpled up in a corner of the bed. He retrieved it and wrapped it round himself and then stood by the door. A thump came from outside the house, followed by another. Robert nodded.

"See you at breakfast," said Martin. "Thanks for everything."

"Thank you," Robert replied but, by that time Martin had left the room. Robert arranged the bedding as best he could without getting out of bed and lay back to think.

"You've made the bed. Now you've got to lie on it." That was another of Mrs Angel's sayings. In fact, he thought, he'd made two beds and it was more than unlikely that he'd get the chance to lie on either one of them. Inviting George had been a mistake. Martin was willing enough. Martin actually wanted it. So, for that matter, did he. His exhausted cock gave a tiny twitch at the thought. If it's going to happen, it will happen, he thought, and then gave his thoughts over to how he was going to handle the other difficulty in his life: Pat.

He must have fallen asleep and would probably have slept through the morning had Martin not tapped on the door. He showered, shaved and did all that was necessary at top speed. The lads had finished breakfast and were sitting out on the balcony. Martin was in shorts. George, on the other hand, was dressed in a sort of safari Sunday best: a bush jacket with capacious pockets and immaculately creased long trousers. Robert took a slice of toast and his coffee out to join them.

"Did you sleep well, George?" he asked.

"Yes, thanks. You?"

"He must have done to get up so late," said Martin. He didn't look at Robert. Robert, on the other hand, was looking at him. His shorts had ridden up. If it's going to happen, it will happen, he thought. Thighs like Martin's were irresistible. It was up to Martin to make it happen, but how?

Chapter Five

Eldama, where Mr Hanson lived, wasn't very far but it was a difficult drive. "It'll be easier when we've finished the air-strip. There'll
be a proper road then," said Robert as he negotiated the third ford.
Fortunately it wasn't very deep and he'd learned the art of driving
through water. Finally, they reached the avenue of acacia trees that
led to the house. Like George's house, it was built of stone but it
was much larger. Robert had been almost dumb-struck when he'd
first seen it. A huge, imitation Elizabethan country house so many
miles from Britain might well have been a mirage. Robert parked
the car and they got out and skirted a lawn of immaculately mown
grass surrounded by flower beds to reach the studded oak door.
Robert pulled the rope and a bell could be heard inside the house.

It was an interesting morning. Mr and Mrs Hanson were, as
always, gracefully condescending hosts. It made a change to sit on
chintz armchairs drinking coffee out of expensive china cups
instead of mugs. Mr Peters, the Hansons' British butler and general factotum glided silently in and out of the room and was, as
always, ignored. Robert had always found him easier to get on
with than his employers. Mrs Hanson spoke of a forthcoming trip
to London to buy clothes. Mr Hanson spoke guardedly of the new
air-strip and wanted one or two technical matters cleared up. They
drove out to look at it – a considerable distance from the house –

and then came back to the house for lunch.

Martin was ill at ease the whole time. He fidgeted and hardly spoke at all. George, on the other hand, was completely at home. One would have thought that it was he, rather than his father, who had known the Hansons for years.

"Aren't the boys home for this holiday or do they have different half-terms in England?" George asked.

"Hardly worth it for such a short time. No, they're with their aunt in Devon," Mr Hanson replied.

"I didn't know you had sons," said Robert.

"You wouldn't. They're in England and even when they're here you'd be unlikely to see them. We gave them the bungalow in the grounds. They can play their dreadful music and make as much noise as they like down there. It would drive Dorothy and me crazy if those three were in the house."

Robert interested and wanted to know more. "There's Patrick. He's the eldest. He's at Oxford. Then there's Jeremy and the youngest is Tim. We must make sure you meet them when they are next home. Do you play croquet?"

Robert regretfully admitted that he had never played the game in his life. In fact he had never even seen it played.

"Pity," said Mrs Hanson, perplexed, it seemed, that anyone could lack such a necessary social asset. "We'll have to get them to teach you."

It was after three o'clock in the afternoon when they left for the drive back to Kampi-ya-Moto. Martin had to squeeze himself into the back seat of the car where he sat surrounded by vegetables, pots of homemade jam and pickles and half a cheese.

"You learn something new every day," Robert observed. "I've been there before and I didn't know they had any children."

"I've never met them," said George, "but my dad says Patrick's hoping to be selected to row in the boat race. Jeremy and Tim are at boarding school somewhere in Devon."

"That's interesting," Robert replied. He had no interest whatsoever in rowing, but Pat had taken to the Hansons almost from the moment she arrived in Kampi-ya-Moto. She'd been up to their place umpteen times, spending whole afternoons with them and staying to tea. She'd played tennis with Dorothy Hanson on their private tennis court. It was inconceivable that they had never told her they had three older sons and yet she had never mentioned the fact to Robert. He smiled. He was pretty sure he knew why.

George continued to talk about the family for almost all the journey. Martin was strangely silent. He was obviously tired out, Robert thought. He'd have to let him sleep that night.

The sun was already beginning to sink down into the Rift Valley when Robert pulled in to his driveway and brought the car to rest under the thatched awning. "Wake up, Martin. We're home," he said.

"I wasn't asleep," Martin protested but, by the time he was out of the car, George was already carrying out the stuff they had been given to Kiberech and chatting in Swahili.

Kiberech had worked his usual miracle with the boiler. A long plume of wood-smoke extended out from the chimney into the still evening air. They had dinner. Kiberech cleared the table and said good night.

"Shower time," said Robert. "By the sound of the boiler, if we don't use some water now it'll blow us all to kingdom come."

He went first this time and emerged in his kikoi, took a beer and went to sit on the balcony and think.

"Whatever you're thinking of doing, a plan of campaign is absolutely essential." That was one of the lecturers at the Officer Training Unit's favourite axioms. One had to have a plan of campaign.

Robert popped the top of the bottle, poured the beer and sat back to enjoy the sunset. It was one of those evenings that tourists raved about. The sun hung: a huge, apparently motionless, yellow ball in the haze. The insects had just started their evening chorus and wood-smoke from the boiler scented the air. It wasn't the sort of evening for plans of campaign. The favourite words of a fellow student on the course came back to him again. "I always say if it's going to happen, it's going to happen." They'd teased him at the time, suggesting that he perhaps ought to be a professor of philosophy rather than an Air Force Officer.

"If it's going to happen, it's going to happen," Robert repeated.

"What's that?" George was standing behind him.

"Nothing." Robert turned round to answer him. George was in the same tartan kikoi that he had worn the previous evening.

"Can I have a drink?"

"Sure. Don't bother to ask. You know where everything is."

George went back inside and re-emerged with a drink. He sat down next to Robert. "It's great out here, isn't it?" he said. "I really envy you living out here."

"It has some disadvantages. Is Martin still in the bathroom?"

"Yes. He'll be ages. He's shaving. He's using your razor. I hope you don't mind but he forgot to bring his."

"And you don't shave?"

"Not every day. Especially when I'm on holiday."

Robert hadn't noticed the pale hair on George's upper lip before. It made him look even more attractive and certainly more desirable.

"Do you mind if I ask a personal question?" said George.

"Fire away."

"You've got photos of your wife all over the house, but you never talk about her. Why?"

"I'm probably fearful of boring everyone to death."

"But you love her?"

"Yes, I do."

"That's what I can't get straight. I mean...being like you are...and having a wife. It doesn't add up."

Robert didn't tell him that he had come to the same conclusion. None of the ensuing eulogy of Pat's nature – her understanding and instinctive sympathy – was untrue, but still Robert said nothing about the letter he was already trying to compose. Whether it "added up" at the end he didn't really know. George said he thought he understood. "I hope I can find a wife like yours," he said.

"Perhaps you won't get married at all. You might find a male partner who you're happy with."

George looked aghast. "Not here," he said. "You have to have a wife."

"Maybe things will change. It's an independent country now. The old ideas will go. I sometimes wish the armed forces would move with the times. As it is, I have to live a secret life."

"I think I know what you mean," said George. There was something about the way he said it which made Robert yearn to touch him; to hold on to him. He didn't. "But," George added with a sudden and radiant smile, "it's great to be here and talk about things like this. You can't at home."

"Doing it is even better," said Robert.

"Mmm...Did Mr Hanson ever tell you about the gold cup?" George asked. "My dad told me about it."

"No. What gold cup?"

George was still relating the story when Martin emerged, kikoi-clad and with a bottle in his hand. It appeared that many years before Independence, a one-time rich and race-horse owning friend of Mr Hanson's had turned up at the farm one evening with his prize possession, a gold cup he had won. Fearful, and rightly so, of an ensuing war against European settlers, he'd asked for permission to bury it somewhere on the Hansons' land. Shortly afterwards, he was murdered in the Mau Mau wars and the cup had never been found.

The story sounded most improbable to Robert, but Martin was

clearly fascinated. It seemed hardly possible that the young man who had been wriggling round in ecstasy less than twenty-four hours previously and who must already have been thinking about the forthcoming night could possibly be interested in buried treasure, but he was. Robert tried to interrupt on a couple of occasions. They didn't ignore him exactly but it was obvious that it was going to take more than a few quips from him to change the subject.

"I wonder you don't get the Hanson boys in on the hunt in the summer holidays," he said at last. "They'd have more idea where it might be."

"I'm not sure that's a good idea. They might want to hang on to it," said George.

"Just us two would be best. We could get hold of a tent and camp up there," said Martin. Robert caught just a glimpse of a mischievous smile as he spoke.

"I have enough of camping when I go out with Dad," said George. "That reminds me, if you don't mind, Rob, I ought to ring my dad. Otherwise Mr Hanson will get in first and tell him I was there."

"Sure. Go ahead."

George went inside. Out of politeness, because the telephone was so near the door, Robert closed the door after him. Martin raised his glass and grinned.

"It's a pity Raymond couldn't come up with you," said Robert. "I met him in the supermarket. Did he tell you?"

"That's right. He did. He's catching a snake in the Ainsworth valley this weekend."

"Providing he doesn't catch anything else."

"How do you mean?"

Martin had never heard of the young bathing men or the guests from the Norfolk Hotel with their binoculars. As Robert related the story the driver had told him, he began to realise that George had been right. He had said that Kenya was still in the 1930s – at least as far as the European population was concerned.

That people should come to Kenya and select young men from the parapet of a bridge, that there were actually men who did that sort of thing, was a revelation to Martin. "Gosh!" he said. "I did see a couple of chaps there once. I thought they were bird-watching or something."

"Boys, not birds," said Robert.

"Do they fist them?" Martin asked.

"Or suck them or fuck them."

"Gosh!" Martin said again. "I suppose the lads need the money. It's terrible, really. I don't think I'd fancy doing it to an African, though that's probably my mother coming through."

"Yes," said Robert.

"What's it actually like to fuck another bloke?"

"Great – as I hope you'll see if we get the chance."

"I wouldn't mind trying it. On somebody I knew – not just somebody I met, whatever his colour."

"George or Raymond?"

"George wouldn't. Ray would. Raymond would let you do anything once he was randy enough."

It was apparent that this conversation was having an effect on Martin – not to mention on Robert himself. Raymond might well at that moment be on his python hunt, whilst a hundred or so miles away in the bush, something similar, that he would find infinitely more pleasurable than a reptile, was creeping along Martin's thigh under his kikoi.

"You'll have to bring Raymond up here some time and try it out," said Robert.

"I could do. Are you going to try it with George?"

"That depends on George."

The door behind them opened and George came out again. "My dad sends his regards," he said. "He'll be up here on Sunday afternoon and he says we both have to be ready."

"Not a pleasant thought at the start of a holiday," said Robert.

"Do you mind if I have another drink?" George asked.

Martin stood up. "I'll get it," he said. "I need another one as well. How about you, Robert?"

"Oh...er. Yes, please, but don't open the bottle. I've still got some in this one."

Martin pushed past them and elbowed the door open.

"Yes, it's really nice here," said George again. "If the Hansons can't have us in the summer, can we stay with you?"

"Of course you can."

"What about your wife? When's she coming back?"

"Pat finds the summers here a bit too much of a good thing. I shall have to think about that."

Martin returned carrying a tray. "I must try to do this like that man up at the Hansons' place," he said. "How's this?" He placed the tray gently on the table and stood to one side.

"Not bad. You may sit down, my good man," said George.

Martin sat.

"Robert says we can stay here in the summer if we want," said George.

"Hey! That'd be good. And it's not that far to the farm. Maybe if Robert could drive us there in the morning. Then we can spend the whole day looking for it. Where can we get hold of a metal detector? That's what we need."

It was Robert's turn to sit silently and admire the night-time view. He tried not to look too often at George, but it was difficult keeping his eyes off anyone quite so good-looking and the way George was sitting with one leg crossed over the other, accentuated every glorious curve and the distinct lump at his groin.

"It shouldn't be too difficult to find with a proper metal detector," Martin continued. Robert had no wish to dampen young enthusiasm, but felt obliged to point out that the Hansons' holding was rather larger than the average farm – by many square miles.

"We'll think of a way," said Martin confidently. "There may be some documents somewhere that say where it is."

"I very much doubt it. If you're going to hide something, you don't draw maps or write about it. That sort of thing happens in kids' adventure stories, but not in real life," said Robert. For a few minutes he sat back and let them talk about it. There was, he thought, a lot of truth in what Catherine had said about Martin's lack of maturity. It was true of George too. Robert had spent years working with hard-bitten young airmen, every one of whom would have dismissed the gold cup story as a fairy tale.

He sat, sipping his beer and listening. George remembered somebody at school who had a metal detector and might be persuaded to lend it to them. Martin could lay his hands on at least two spades they had at home. "We need something bigger really," he said.

"You find out where it is and I'll arrange for an earth mover," said Robert.

"Cor! Could you? That'd be great!" said Martin.

"And what will you do with it if and when you find it?" Robert tried not to let his amusement show.

"I thought about that just now, actually. Well, if George agrees, we'll sell it and my half of the money can go towards some project to help the Kenyans."

"And I'll use my half to expand the business," said George.

"But first we'll have to have a ceremony," said Martin.

"What sort of ceremony?"

"We'll get everyone to wank into it and then we'll drink it. That could be a load of fun."

George blushed. "You get more and more disgusting," he said. "You can count me out."

"Robert will, won't you, Rob?"

"If you find the gold cup, I hereby promise to do anything you wish," said Robert.

"Great! What shall we talk about now?"

"Talk about anything you wish," said Robert. "How about talking about this Indian lad at school? Vijay or whatever his name is?"

"Oh, don't! You'll get us both going."

"Get *you* going, you mean," said George.

"Come off it. You wouldn't say 'no' if he offered.

"Which he won't do, so there's no point in talking about him," said George sulkily.

"There's sod-all chance of you having the Ferrari you dream about having, but it doesn't stop you talking about it."

"That's different."

"Not so different. Ferraris look good and so does Vijay. Ferraris are powerful. So is Vijay. Ferraris are fast. I wonder if Vijay is. I hope not."

Robert never found out if Martin had planned the conversation that ensued. To compare a young man with a sports car seemed to him at first to be particularly inappropriate. It was only when George shifted in his chair that he spotted the effect it was having. For a brief moment, the shape of George's tool showed against the tightly stretched material of his kikoi. He shifted position again and the lump vanished.

"I'd fist him into the gold cup," said Martin. "I'll bet it's really huge when it's up."

"It's a pretty big cup," said George. "Dad's got an old magazine with a picture of Colonel von Meinerherzhagen holding it. You'd have a job holding that and Vijay's tool at the same time."

"Then you can have the job of holding the cup and I'll concentrate on his lovely big brown cock."

"Maybe he's not as fast as you think. Maybe you'll have to change over halfway," said Robert – and that remark was deliberately planned to have the effect it did.

"Mmm. Maybe," said George and the lump became apparent again. It was even larger this time. Robert forced himself to look away, only to be confronted by a similar swelling under Martin's kikoi.

"The last stroke must be mine," said Martin. "I want to see his spunk spurt."

"That might be difficult to arrange," said Robert. "A person being wanked by two extremely good-looking young men like you might not be able to hold back or give a warning."

That one went home. He was sure it had. George lay back in his chair and smiled in an almost feline way. Martin smiled at Robert. Silence. Robert made no attempt to break it. He had the impression that both of them were thinking deeply. Finally, Martin spoke.

"You know, it is rather ridiculous," he said.

"I suppose it is," said Robert, "but it does no harm to let your imagination run riot at times."

"Not that. We're sitting here in the dark. There's nobody for miles around and nobody could see through the hedge anyway and yet we're sitting here with cloths wrapped round our middles. Down in the Rift there are African men and women sitting round their camp fires without a stitch on. I reckon we should take them off."

"Suits me," said Robert. They both stood up simultaneously, almost knocking the table over in their enthusiasm. Two cloths fell to the floor and two erect cocks sprang out into the cool night air.

"Come on, George," said Martin. "You can't be the odd man out."

"I can if I want."

"No, you can't."

Robert busied himself retrieving the fallen kikois and folding them up. Anything to keep his patience whilst this banter went on. He was about to say "Oh, for Christ's sake! If he doesn't want to..." when George capitulated.

"I'm not standing up," he said, struggling with the knot at his waist. He undid it and peeled away the material on both sides, spreading it over the arms of the chair.

"There! Happy?" he asked.

"Extremely," would have been the correct answer. Instead, Robert said it did seem more sensible. George's cock was, as Martin had said, huge: much longer and much thicker than his own. Martin had been right about the hair, too. One could be forgiven for thinking that someone had cut out a section of a very thick coconut doormat and slipped it over George's erect shaft. It spread out sideways, to cover the insides of his thighs.

"I just hope there are no mosquitoes," said George. "I don't want to get it bitten."

"They don't bite. They suck," said Martin. He caught Robert's glance and smiled.

"You don't get mosquitoes at this altitude," Robert added.

"You could get sucked though," said Martin. "How about it?"

"What? Out here?"

"Why not? We can't be seen. How about it George? Robert's really terrific at it."

"I'll take your word for it. It's stupid. Childish. You know what you are? You're sex-mad," said George.

"I don't see how it can be childish for a person with a cock like yours," said Martin. "Great hairy thing."

"It isn't hairy."

"Well, all round it is."

"Not so hairy as Vijay Shah."

That started yet another argument. Robert diverted his concentration from the seemingly unending chorus of "You are" and "I'm not" to the objects of the controversy. To his left, George's massive club-like cock still stood upright from its thicket of hair. Martin's, to his right, had gone down slightly – almost as if, like Robert, it had started to realise that all this silly banter was unlikely to lead to anything. It twitched slightly as it subsided.

"You're selfish," said Martin. "The least you can do is let Robert suck it. He gives you a free holiday…"

"Stop that at once!" said Robert. Frustration had given way to anger. "I won't have that said. If George doesn't want to, that's the end of the matter," he said. "Now let's stop all this silly arguing. If anything is childish, that is."

"Well, you can do it to me. I don't mind," said Martin.

"Bloody sex maniac!" George muttered.

"'I don't mind' hardly shows keenness," said Robert. "Anyway, wouldn't it be better and more comfortable indoors?"

"It'll be even better here. George can go inside."

"Don't mind me. I shan't watch."

Even if your knees are resting on a couple of folded kikois, a concrete floor is uncomfortable. Fortunately a pair of balls like Martin's can compensate for almost anything. Martin lay back in the chair with his bottom on the edge and spread his legs. He sighed as Robert's tongue tickled his loose-hanging scrotum. He sighed again as his cock responded to Robert's slow and careful upward licking. "Oh yeah!" he gasped as Robert's lips touched the swollen head and the tip of his tongue pushed against the wide open slit.

It slid in. Robert tried, with extreme difficulty, to forget about the feel of a rock-hard cock in his mouth. He tried to forget the sublime taste of young flesh. He forced himself to think of Martin. After all, he was there to give pleasure to Martin and to forget himself. And...another thought crossed his mind, pausing long enough to impart considerable pleasure... if Martin enjoyed it and gave evidence of enjoying it, that might possibly tempt his friend. With Martin's cock still in place, he turned his head, feeling like a man with a huge cigar in the corner of his mouth.

He blinked and then stared. George was also leaning back in his chair – almost to the point of sliding off it. One hand was on the arm of the chair. The other was buried between his legs. Robert let Martin's cock slip from the corner of his mouth. He restrained it with his lips under the ridge and then sucked as hard as he could. The insides of his cheeks pressed against it.

"Mmm. Mmmm!" Martin murmured. He sucked again. "Go on. Do it!" Martin groaned. Torture was never one of Robert's strong points, but he forced himself to let it slip out. It waved temptingly in front of his eyes, glistening in the pale moonlight.

"Go on! Go on!" Martin gasped. Robert put a hand under his scrotum. Instinctively, Martin spread his legs even further apart. Robert carefully placed the tip of one finger on the hard skin behind Martin's balls. The thought that there was something much more yielding only a centimetre further made him tremble slightly. He didn't turn his head but managed to get a glimpse of George. This time his hand was on his cock – unmoving, but the whiteness of his knuckles said a lot.

Martin tried to slide forward even further and almost fell off the chair. Robert lifted his head again and had to reach up to bring the lad's cock down to his lips again. By this time his knees were hurting badly. In retrospect he thought that might have been a good thing. He might easily have come at that moment. It took a lot of willpower not to make the whole process as short as possible. Once again, Martin's cock slipped into his mouth but, by this time, it was so rampant that he had to straighten up slightly to get as much as possible in. That made the pain in his knees even worse.

Once again, Martin groaned. He tried to heave his bottom up from the chair but Robert pressed him down again. He tried to sneak another look at George, but in that position all he could see was the boy's head on the back of the wicker chair. George's eyes were closed and his mouth was half open. An ache – by no means unpleasant but an ache nevertheless – began to develop in Robert's groin. He hoped desperately that he wouldn't come before Martin. A simultaneous ejaculation would be perfect, he thought, and went to work as carefully as he could on Martin's pulsating penis.

He let it slide between his tightly compressed lips. He savoured the unique flavour of a young man who, by that time, had lost control of his actions. Martin was groaning and trying to heave himself upwards, determined to thrust as much as possible of his cock into Robert's dribbling mouth.

Robert was hardly master of himself. If he had been, he would have thought of the kikois under his knees. Martin gave such a powerful upward thrust that Robert almost choked as his mouth filled with warm, viscous spunk. He managed to swallow most of it but some dripped from his mouth. He swallowed again and then could hold back no longer. Most of it must have gone under Martin's chair but the kikoi under Robert's right knee suddenly felt warm and wet.

"Jesus!" Martin gasped. "That was the best ever."

Robert swallowed the last few drops. Martin's cock slid reluctantly out of his mouth.

For some minutes they stayed in the same positions. Robert's knees hurt so much that he couldn't have stood up without some sort of support. Finally, by grasping the sides of Martin's chair, he managed to get to his feet.

It was then that they noticed George. He was sitting up straight again – so was his cock. A drop of clear fluid formed at the tip and ran down the shaft as Robert watched.

"It got George going too," Martin observed.

"Only a bit."

"Ha! You can't fool us."

"It's very unhygienic," said George. "Anyway, my glass is empty."

Robert and Martin both tried not to show their amusement as George tried to fasten his kikoi again – a job made impossible by something like eight inches of rigid flesh. Finally he gave up the attempt and went into the house, blushing and with his cock pointing the way.

"He'll be ages. He'll have a wank, you see," said Martin. He shifted in his chair. "Daft bugger!" he added.

"Oh, leave him be. If he doesn't want to, that's it," said Robert.

"But he does. Deep down he does. I'm sure of it," said Martin. "Ready for another beer?"

"I've still got this one, but you could bring another bottle out. However, I've got an even nicer taste in my mouth at the moment."

Chapter Six

Robert forced himself to stay awake as long as possible that night. He listened carefully, but no sound came from the next room. Just what sort of sound he expected, he couldn't say. The vibration of bedsprings, perhaps. Even nicer would be an increasingly rapid slapping noise, growing more liquid by the minute, but that was totally impossible. Thin though the walls were, they weren't that flimsy. If he'd been allocated a one-bedroom bungalow, he thought, they'd have had to share his room. That was even more unlikely. They'd have settled for sleeping bags on the lounge floor.

He wasn't nosy. He convinced himself of that. He was just…well…curious. He got out of bed and put his ear to the wall. Silence. He got back into bed and was soon asleep. It was after eight o'clock when he woke. The two of them were in the garden again. He breakfasted hurriedly and then went out to the car. Just as he got to his improvised garage, the telephone rang. He ran inside the house again.

"Mr Hall? Jeremy Hanson." Robert's mind was in such a turmoil from getting up late that he wondered, for a moment, which Jeremy Hanson he was talking to. The voice should have been a clue. "We're giving a little party tonight and I wondered if you'd like to bring your two young guests," said Mr Hanson.

"Oh well… er. I'll ask them," he said. "The best thing would be for me to call in at your place on the way to work. I'm about to leave now." Anything, he thought, just to give him time to think rationally. A party up at Eldama would rule out something else he had planned.

"I don't see how I can possibly get out of it," said George when Robert told him. "My dad would want me to go. He's bound to ask."

"Not for me," said Martin. "I hardly know them."

Mr Hanson was in conversation with one of his gardeners when Robert parked the car. He waved. Already late for work, Robert climbed out and negotiated a couple of flower beds. The gardener picked up his hoe and resumed work.

Robert declined a coffee in the house. To his surprise, Mr Hanson accepted the fact that Martin would not be coming to his party without the slightest show of disappointment. "But you'll be coming with young George?" he said. "Lot of chaps want to meet you."

It was understandably difficult to persuade a man whose own sons were banished to an out-building that Martin would need to be looked after for a few hours.

"He's big enough to look after himself," Mr Hanson protested. "Stay just for an hour or two if you like."

Robert said that that might be difficult and promised to attend another of their parties, if invited, when he had no guests to concern himself with.

It was just as well that he was so busy that morning. Just about everything that could have gone wrong, went wrong. The asphalt-laying machine got clogged. One of the workmen discovered the remains of an old standpipe to the side of the strip and that had to be dismantled right down to subterranean level and then blocked off. Liquid mud was everywhere. He borrowed a pair of Wellington boots from the sergeant, but the squelching noise they made was reminiscent of a sound he would like to have heard at night and began to have an arousing effect. He took them off and left the sergeant to deal with the problem. A telex delivered to the farm and brought down to the site by one of Mr Hanson's men announced that the party who were to install the navigation aids would be there the following week and asked him, as if it was the easiest thing in the world, to arrange accommodation in the area for them. Fortunately Mr Hanson had seen it first and had proposed putting them in his sons' place, it being empty. That was one worry out of the way.

"One thing after another," Robert muttered as he climbed into the car. "I wonder…"

An atmosphere of panic was apparent the moment he got out of the car. There was fresh washing on the line. Kiberech sat on the step polishing a pair of shoes. Martin was attempting to set up an ironing board in the lounge. "Ask him to make sure he washes the socks I've just left off," George's voice called from the bathroom.

"What's going on?" said Robert as he stepped inside.

"Getting George ready for the party," said Martin. "Kiberech has washed his clothes and is about to iron them. George's having a bath. I am trying to keep control, but not doing awfully well." The ironing board collapsed with a crash, causing Kiberech to dash in and pick it up again.

"There! See what I mean. I'll be very glad when he's gone to the bloody thing," said Martin – which was a perfectly ordinary remark, save that he gave one long wink as he said it. That, together with his posture, crouching to position the stay under the ironing board, caused Robert's cock to swell under his trousers. Instead of helping, he had to sit down.

"I'll have to get a new one," he said. "That one was second or third-hand when we bought it." But his mind was not really on domestic appliances. What he was looking at had almost certainly never been used by anybody.

"It's not bad. It's just difficult to get it in the slot," said Martin, suggestively.

"Maybe a bit of oil might help," Robert replied.

"I don't think so. The slot is too small. That's the problem. Aha! That's it. It just needed patience."

"Precisely," said Robert, wondering if he would have enough when the time came.

George emerged from the bathroom wearing just a pair of purple underpants. Robert was extremely thankful to be sitting down, to hide his excitement at this sight.

"Nearly ready," said Martin. "By the time you've done your hair, we'll have your clothes ready." George went into the bathroom. "I'll leave Kiberech to get on with it," said Martin. "I've never done any ironing." He went out into the garden and Robert, allowing a suitable interval during which he concentrated on Kiberech's sweeping movements with the iron, went to join him out there.

"I've told George to find out as much as he can about the gold cup," said Martin.

"Oh good."

"I'm glad I'm not going. Are you?"

"Very glad. Just us two this evening. Any idea what you want to do?"

"In what way? Go out somewhere, you mean?"

"I was thinking more of going *in* somewhere."

"I thought you were. I still don't know about that. I mean...well, you wouldn't tell anybody, would you?"

"Of course I wouldn't."

"Not even George?"

"Not if you don't want me to."

"Part of me says I'd like to try it and the other part of me says it's sort of demeaning and I'd feel bad afterwards. I can't explain it any other way. Do you know what I mean?"

"I know exactly what you mean." Robert put an arm round Martin's shoulders. He had a powerful urge to kiss him but, despite the hedge and the fact that Kiberech in the house had his back to them, he didn't. "If it happens, you'll feel great," he promised. "If it doesn't happen I will still respect you and love you as much as I do now."

"I sort of hoped you'd say something like that. Anyway, it's time we got George ready. How's he going there?"

"I'll drive him up there and come straight back. I just hope that somebody there will bring him home. We'll be too busy, I hope."

"I might as well come with you. Maybe I can ask about the cup as well."

It was just after six o'clock when they left. Robert would have preferred to have sat on the verandah, as he usually did after his shower. George, immaculately attired thanks to Kiberech, sat in the back seat. Martin had put on long trousers for the first time in that holiday and sat in the front. The car, despite having been parked in the shade was like a hot-house – not helped by the fact that Robert had all the windows tightly closed against the dust. Fortunately it was an uneventful drive.

"Ye gods! It looks like a fairground!" said Martin as they drove up the acacia-lined drive to the house. Floodlights lit up the garden and a row of coloured lights was suspended from the eaves. Cars were parked along the end of the drive. Men in white dinner jackets and women in long dresses stood on the lawn whilst white-robed waiters passed among them bearing trays.

"Looks a bit posh," said George.

"Just your scene," said Martin. Mr Hanson detached himself from the group he was with and walked over to the car. "There you are," he said, opening the car door. "You've all decided to come. I'm so glad. Come and let me introduce you to the others."

"Well, actually I..." Martin stammered, but there was nothing for it but for him to get out of the car. Robert did the same and George clambered out.

"We can't stay, unfortunately," said Robert. "Martin's expecting a call from his parents this evening." It was all he could think of on the spur of the moment.

"Couldn't you go home and tell them to ring here?" said Mr Hanson. Robert was obviously pretty low down on the guest list.

"As a matter of fact, we don't actually know that they'll ring tonight. It wouldn't matter much if we weren't at your place. They can always call again tomorrow," said Martin. Astounded, Robert stared at him.

"Splendid, splendid. Now come over and meet the guests. Don't worry about coming up here for them, Mr Hall. One of my men can run them back."

George and Mr Hanson led the way. Robert grabbed Martin's arm. "What the hell's got into you?" he whispered.

"It's better this way. Honest," Martin replied.

"But it's not our scene, Martin. I don't know about you but I'd feel a complete outcast amongst that lot. Besides which, we're not dressed for it."

"I think we ought to stay," said Martin. That seemed the last word on the subject. Resignedly, Robert took a drink from the tray a waiter offered and was soon miserably out of his element, trying to converse with the other guests.

"You're in the Air Force, I hear. I wonder if you know Air Vice Marshall Mason. He's a great friend of ours." Robert had never heard of the man.

The next person to buttonhole him was a lady with the longest earrings he had ever seen. "It must be rather ghastly for you living in KYM," she said. "My husband and I have often been through the place. How on earth do you manage in the long rains?"

Robert looked over to Martin and George. George was talking animatedly to a middle-aged, rather fat man. Martin was just standing there, looking like a fish out of water. Robert took a few furtive sideways steps, bent down to examine a flower and was about to make another surreptitious move in the their direction when he heard Martin's name mentioned.

"...son of some sort of railway-worker, apparently. He's staying up here with the other boy; the one with the fair hair. Now he, my dear, is a bit more like quality. He's the son of Marcus Glover of Sunshine Safaris. Do you know the King-Mastersons?"

"The King-Mastersons at Molo or the other ones?"

"The Molo ones, my dear. The brother is hardly spoken of these days. Well, Jeremy and his wife are keen on introducing young George to their daughter when she comes home for the holidays. It would be such a good match. I really cannot imagine why the Glovers kept George in Kenya, let alone send the boy to a Catholic school. It's terribly difficult for them to meet girls of the right sort out here nowadays, too. Our Hamish is having a wonderful time in England. The school organises dances with the girls' school down the road. It's so much better for them and well worth the expense and Hamish says there are only two blacks in the entire school."

"Not the only advantage," said a portly man by her side. "One hears things about these Nairobi schools, especially the ones run by priests."

"I don't think we need discuss that, dear," said the lady who had started the conversation.

"Oh do tell us what you've heard, Gerald," another woman said. "I like to be up to date with the gossip. It makes my little soirees go with a swing."

"Homosexuality," said the man in a low voice. "I suppose it's to be expected when you take in blacks. It's probably normal for them. I met a chap down in the New Stanley Hotel the other week. He's a teacher and he reckons they're having it off with each other all the time at his place. Has to use a crowbar to prise them apart."

"You do exaggerate, darling, but I must say I'm not surprised. The Glover boy wouldn't do anything like that."

"Probably not, but I wouldn't mind betting that one of them is after him. Blond hair and all that. You know what they're like. I heard..."

Mr Hanson joined the group. "Are you all okay? Glasses need refilling? Mr Hall, come over and meet the Wilburys and the Carsons."

Robert endured the usual introductions. Martin looked over towards him but he was trapped.

"We were just talking about schools, Jeremy," said Mrs Carson. "You were so wise to send your boys to England. Gerald here was saying that the schools here are hotbeds of unnatural vice – positive hotbeds!"

"Heard it from a teacher," her husband explained.

"Oh, I doubt if it's as bad as all that. It goes on in British schools as well, you know," said Mr Hanson.

"Not at Hamish's school!" said Mrs Carson indignantly.

"Possibly not, but my two eldest sons have gone through that stage. May still be going through it, for all I know."

"And it doesn't worry you?"

"Not in the least. Now then, your glasses are nearly empty. Where's Josiah? Aha! There he is."

He beckoned to one of the waiters.

"We were talking about your plans for the Glover boy," said Mrs Wilbury when their glasses had been replenished.

"A nice lad. He and his friend are staying with Mr Hall."

"Oh is he? How nice of you, Mr Hall. It can't be much fun for you."

Robert said he enjoyed their company. Mr Hanson said that he would have to come to the party he was organising in the summer so that George could meet Rosemary King-Masterson.

"Oh, I do hope it comes off," said Mrs Wilbury. It would be such a good match. Their money and if he's inherited his father's business acumen..."

Mr Hanson drifted away and that gave Robert the opportunity

he wanted. He was soon by Martin's side.

"Thank God. I thought you'd never get here. Take me away," said Martin, urgently.

"I thought you wanted to stay."

"Not now, I don't. Tell them I've got a headache or something. Tell them anything, but take me away."

Mr and Mrs Hanson seemed genuinely sorry. Mrs Hanson said that Martin ought perhaps to lie down until he felt better. Robert said that he feared Martin might be sick. Mrs Hanson changed her mind and said it might be better to take him home after all.

"What's up?" Robert asked when they were in the car again.

"They're racists! The whole bloody lot of them. "

"You yourself said the settlers were like that."

"I never thought they were that bad. God! It was disgusting. This country will never get anywhere with people like that. They all ought to be deported back to England."

"Why did you decide to stay at the last minute?" Robert asked later, driving home.

"Well...Oh, I don't know. It's difficult to explain."

"You thought an evening at Eldama might be more enjoyable than what I had in mind?"

"I suppose so. Yes."

"I thought I'd made it clear that I wouldn't do anything you didn't want me to do."

"Yes, you did. I thought maybe you wouldn't be able to..."

"Control myself?"

"I guess so."

"You have the oddest ideas," said Robert.

"How do you mean?"

"I'll explain when we get home. We're nearly there."

"A beer on the verandah?" Martin asked when the car was parked and they were in the house.

"That sounds like an excellent idea," Robert replied.

Martin went towards the kitchen and then turned round again and grinned. "A naked beer on the verandah ?" he asked.

"That sounds like an even better idea," said Robert.

"In that case I'll get ready first and get the beers later," said Martin. He went into his bedroom. Robert went to his.

"That's better. That's much better. This is how one should drink in Africa," said Martin when they were both sitting on the verandah and enjoying the cool breeze on their naked bodies.

"I wouldn't make that a general rule. Some of those people at the party would be pretty repulsive," said Robert.

"Hmm. They were repulsive with clothes on," Martin agreed. "Who were those horrors you were with?"

"The Wilburys and the Carsons. They reckon that schools in Kenya are hotbeds of gay sex."

"I wish they were. We might stand a chance with Vijay Shah."

"*You* might, you mean."

"George's just as keen as I am. He's just got a hang-up."

"A stand-up, from what I saw last night," said Robert.

Martin laughed. "I know. I was watching him. He was having a hell of a job trying not to fist himself. He started at one point, but then he stopped. He must have had a good session in the bathroom when he came in. All I got out of him last night was a dribble. Do you want another beer?"

"Just one more," said Robert. Martin stood up. His cock wasn't much bigger than his thumb.

"What time to you reckon he'll get back?" he asked when he returned with the two bottles.

"Pretty late, I guess. Did you know the Hansons are planning to marry him off to some girl from Molo?"

"Much chance!" said Martin. "Why is it that the older generation is always planning things for young people? Why can't they leave us alone to run our own lives? I mean...you're just as bad, really. You just invited us here because you were planning to fuck us."

There was an aggressive tone to his voice which Robert hadn't heard before. It must have been the drink he had had up at the Hansons' place, he decided.

"I've already explained that that particular plan depends on the co-operation of the young men involved," he said. "Same as the proposed marriage for George. If he doesn't want to, he won't. It's as easy as that."

"Yeah. Well, we shouldn't be put under pressure!" Martin muttered and then fell silent again.

Robert put out a hand and placed it on Martin's thigh. "There is no pressure. Honestly, Martin," he said.

"Oh, I'm sorry. I'm still in a mood after listening to that lot up at Eldama. When people compare intelligent human beings to monkeys, I get worked up."

"It's much nicer being worked up in another way," said Robert. He moved his hand up the smooth skin. "Do you want me to stop?"

"No...I like it. Go ahead if you want. Make me forget them."

Robert shifted his chair sideways without getting up and slid his hand right up Martin's thigh until the tips of his fingers were buried in bristly hair. "There is some similarity with apes," he said, eyeing Martin's rapidly rising cock. "So I would say a gorilla rather than an monkey."

Martin laughed for the first time since they had sat down. "You're only saying that because gorillas have bare behinds," he said. "That's what you're really after. Shall we go inside?" He stood up. His cock waved from side to side.

Robert went first. It seemed the right thing to do. 'In unfamiliar situations, the officer must always lead.' Again, the lecturers wouldn't have had this particular situation in mind, he thought.

"Our room or yours?" Martin asked.

"Mine," said Robert, opening the door and this time Martin went first.

Robert opened the drawer in the bedside cabinet to make sure that what he might need was to hand. It was. "Come on then," he said, as he lay on the bed. Martin followed suit. Robert put his arms round the boy's waist and kissed his cheek. Martin's cock, by now rock-hard, pressed against his thigh. Desperately forcing himself to stay under control, Robert kissed his chin and then moved down to his nipples. Feeling Martin's heart beat against his lips was an extra-ordinary sensation that induced a tenderness in Robert that he had-n't felt on any of the previous occasions.

Just what words he murmured as he moved downwards, he did-n't know. They were probably platitudes he'd picked up from books. No words came from Martin's lips: just low, contented moans. Robert's tongue played in his pubes, licked his cock up to the head and then down again, lower and lower each time until it was in contact with the soft skin of his balls. For a moment, Martin seemed to hesitate and then he suddenly spread his legs so wide apart that one of them overlapped the edge of the bed. He shuffled towards the centre but Robert didn't let up. It would be untrue to say that he couldn't have. If Martin were to tell him to stop, he would've stopped, but Martin said nothing. Robert pushed his face as hard downwards and forwards as far as he could and the tip of his tongue found the place immediately. Martin spoke.

"Do it if you want," he said. Robert lifted his head and looked forward along the boy's body to his face.

"Sure? Remember what I said?"

"I'll come if you don't."

Robert smiled. He reached out for the things he wanted. Then, being careful to keep a well-greased finger out of the way, he lift-ed Martin's legs on to his shoulders. Martin looked puzzled but only for a moment. The finger found its target as quickly as had Robert's tongue.

"Loosen up a bit," he whispered. "My promise still holds good."

Just what he would have done if Martin had told him to stop, he didn't know. Fortunately Martin didn't. Getting the finger in was difficult, probably because Robert was being extra careful. Martin grunted once or twice. Robert watched his face the whole time. Martin's eyes were open to start with, then closed and then tight, as Robert's finger screwed into the tight opening. It was a strange sensation – not a new one, but it had been a long time since he'd felt that warmth and tightness. He pushed in a bit more and then stopped. Martin said nothing but gave a sort of nervous gulp. Robert pushed again and this time the whole length of his finger slid in. Fearing that Martin might yet change his mind, he didn't say anything, but stayed quite still and waited.

Then, suddenly, Martin spoke. "It's funny," he said.

Such a statement at such a time made the scene seem surreal. "What is?" Robert asked.

"It doesn't hurt nearly as much as I thought it would. It's actually a nice feeling."

"I told you so." Very, very gently, Robert rotated his finger. The silky membrane tightened slightly and then relaxed again. He moved his fingertip. Martin gasped. Robert did it again and there was hardly any reaction. He waited for as long as he could and then withdrew the finger, turning it from side to side as he did so.

"Are you going to...?"

"Not quite yet." One greasy finger was joined by its partner.

"Ow! Christ! Oh!" Martin yelled.

"It's okay." Robert stopped. Martin had clutched the sheet covering the mattress so tightly that it had pulled away at one side. His knuckles were white. It wasn't until his grip had relaxed again that Robert began slowly to part his fingers.

"You're beautiful," he whispered. In that position Martin was even more attractive than usual. His nipples seemed redder and more pronounced than they had been before. His belly was tight and flat and the soft warmth inside him made Robert's spine tingle. As carefully and as slowly as he could, he pulled the fingers out. Martin stared at him with eyes wide open.

He had Pat to thank for his skill in applying yet more jelly. Even with Martin's legs pressing on his shoulders, he managed it in seconds. He shuffled up a bit. Martin's behind lifted. His cock touched the right place almost immediately. Putting his hands on Martin's hips he moved forward.

"Ugh! Ah! Ah!" Martin gasped as Robert's cock-head pushed past the sentinel muscles. "Ah! Ah! Ah!" he panted as, centimetre by centimetre, the rest followed, disappearing into him in almost imperceptible jerks. Robert moved his hands to Martin's cock, rolling it between the palms as one would roll dough – save that it felt more like a piece of warm steel than dough. A tiny drop of moisture appeared at the slit. He gave the first thrust forward. Martin grunted. He gave another grunt – "Ugh!" – and then another – "Ugh!"

There had been a lot of blissful times in that bedroom, but the ecstasy of fucking a young man as beautiful and willing as Martin beat them all. He felt the hardness of Martin's prostate; viscous fluid oozed from the boy's cock on to his fingers and Martin gave a low moan. Opposing thoughts flashed through Robert's mind. 'Go slowly now. Make it last.' That was countermanded by 'Go on. He's loving every minute of it. Give him a fucking he'll remember.' The latter won. Beads of sweat dropped from his forehead on to Martin's heaving torso. 'Go on. Further in. Harder...'

"Ah! Ah! Harder!" That was not an imaginary voice. That was Martin, seeming to yell at the top of his voice. He said something else too but Robert didn't catch the words. He came at that moment. His cock swelled for an instant. The grip on his cock tightened and a jet of Martin's semen shot into the air. Another tightening and the second spurt splashed against Robert's forehead. His own libations felt like weak dribbles in comparison. Martin shot again and then fell back, panting for breath.

"Christ!" he said after some moments.

Robert lifted his long brown legs from his shoulders.

"See?" It was all he could manage to say. Martin looked up at him and grinned.

"It was like…," he said.

"Like what?"

"Indescribable," said Martin. "Shall I tell you something?"

"What's that?"

"George's not going to be the odd man out."

"Meaning?"

"George's going to get fucked this holiday. Fair's fair and all that."

Robert leaned forward to kiss him. "What a nice idea," he said.

Martin put his arms clumsily round his neck. "You or me?" he whispered.

"Both," Robert replied and their lips met.

Chapter Seven

"What were you doing when I came in last night?" George asked. He hadn't wanted any breakfast but Kiberech persuaded him to have half a paw-paw. That, he said, made him feel a bit better.

"Nothing," said Martin – which, in his case was true. Robert, whose head had been covered by the quilt with his mouth full of eager cock, hadn't even heard the car draw up outside.

"You must have been doing something. Why were you in Robert's room?"

"Guess," said Robert. "Tell us about the party first."

"It was good. I enjoyed it. I met a lot of Dad's friends. I must ring him later and tell him."

"But not that you had far too much to drink," said Martin.

"Oh, it was just the once. He'd understand. Anyway, it was cocktails and gin and lemon. Things like that. You have to have drinks like that with those sort of people." If the look Martin gave him was anything to go by, prussic acid or cyanide would have been more suitable.

"You can always have gin and lemon here if you want," said Robert. "It's Pat's favourite tipple. I think we've got a couple of bottles of gin still unopened." Martin stopped glaring. A slow smile spread over his face. "Why not?" he said. "Upper-crust drinks for upper-crust people."

"We're not actually in their class," George explained. "Mind you, Mr Carson said he has a great respect for Dad."

He was still extolling his newfound friends when Robert left for work and when he returned, some six hours later. A Mr Peter Hardwick, who had apparently insisted that George call him by his first name, was a private pilot and already in touch with the Government about permission to use the new landing strip.

"He says he'll take me up when I am next here," said George proudly.

"That might help us find the gold cup," said Martin enthusiastically. "You know – archaeologists do it. They take pictures and can tell whether the earth has been dug up. I read about it."

"Yeah. Maybe. Peter's actually more interested in the game."

"Very sensible of him," Martin replied. For a moment Robert was taken aback. Martin's views on hunting had been made very clear. Martin looked across to him and smiled. He turned back to George. "What does he do? Fly round the animals to round them up and then land and shoot some?" he asked.

"Of course not. He just likes to find out where their favourite watering places are so that he knows where to look on his next trip."

"Mmm. Find out their drinking habits and then go for it, eh?" Martin looked over to Robert and, almost imperceptibly, he nodded. He did it again at dinner: a slight, almost imperceptible lowering of his head and a half smile which would have delighted Leonardo da Vinci but which made Robert feel slightly uncomfortable. He became more and more aware of a sort of tension in the air.

"So, tell me what you've been doing today," Robert said.

Martin said that they'd been exploring the village and had been invited into the school. Robert had only a vague idea of where it was. He listened attentively to Martin's indignant account of the lack of facilities there. George said very little. Kiberech took away the empty plates and brought in the coffee.

"What's so awful is that there are some rich people round here – really rich people – and they don't lift a finger to help," said Martin. George glared at him, obviously taking this as an attack on the Hansons and their circle. Robert could feel the tension rising again.

"I think I'll have my shower," he said.

"You haven't drunk your coffee yet."

"I'll have it later."

Something was up, he thought as he soaped himself. He'd been a fool to invite both of them together. They were so totally different. Class distinction obviously played a greater role in Kenyan society than it did at home and their interests were different, too: very different. One could hardly expect a lad with a background like George's to sympathise with Martin's crusading zeal to improve the lot of the Kenyan Africans. Then, of course, there was the other factor. Martin alone would have been a much more sensible idea. He could have given Kiberech the week off. His own cooking wasn't up to much and he was fairly sure that Martin didn't even know how to boil an egg, but they would have survived somehow – getting out of bed to eat and then going back. Martin would be even more lascivious without George.

"You've been an idiot," he told himself. A mental image of what might have been formed in his mind. Coming home from work and finding Martin, sitting there naked waiting for him. Martin saying something about having made a salad. Sitting at the table eating it with one hand and fondling Martin's already erect cock with the other.

"So what have you been doing today, Martin?"

"Waiting for you to come home." That Mona Lisa smile again.

"I've been thinking about that all day."

"Not half so hard as I've been thinking about it – and I mean 'hard'. Come on. Let's finish this later."

"You going to be long?" Martin's real voice shattered the illusion.

"Why? Are you waiting to come in?"

"No. We showered when we came back. I've put the chairs out on the verandah. Shall I get your beer out now?"

Robert turned off the water. "Might as well," he called.

It was odd, he thought. A couple of days ago he'd have been out of the bathroom much more quickly. A couple of days ago his cock would have been straining out in front of him, not dangling loosely like a bit of spare flesh. It was all George's fault. No. He corrected himself. Not George's fault. His fault for inviting the lad. He took a towel from the rail, and began to dry his hair.

"Be thankful for small mercies." That was one of Mrs Angel's favourite sayings and, suddenly, he realised how appropriate it was – in one sense. Martin was hardly small.

He suddenly realised that the pattern at the edge of the towel was unfamiliar. He didn't have one like that. He peered at it more closely. The letters "GG", faded but still legible, had been written in the corner. George's towel! He put it to his nostrils and inhaled deeply. It felt warm and damp and the scent was only just perceptible, but it was there and had an almost immediate effect. He felt his cock beginning to swell. He draped the towel over his hands, trying to mould it into the contours of George's backside. A bit too flat...make it rounder...Hmm. That was more like it. Not a perfect likeness. One needed an extra hand to make the cleft. George had almost certainly wrapped it round his waist at some time. It was a pity that towels didn't retain the shape...

Suddenly realising that he was making a fool of himself, he started to dry himself again, but the train of thought, once started, continued on the same lines and wouldn't be diverted. Snobbery was probably the reason for George's refusal to oblige, he thought. It had to be that. Junior Air Force officers didn't stand a chance.

"How much longer are you going to be? Your beer's getting warm." Martin's voice again.

"Just coming." He dried his legs. Keep thinking like that and you will be, he thought to himself. The boys had seen him in that state before, so what the hell. He wrapped a kikoi round his waist and left the bathroom. He realised that he hadn't dried his feet and had left wet marks on the floor.

Martin and George were ensconced in the wicker armchairs on the balcony. George was wrapped in his kikoi. Martin hadn't changed. "At last!" he said. "You don't usually take that long."

"I'm sorry. I thought you said you'd had a shower. I didn't know you were waiting to get in there."

"I wasn't."

"Why no kikoi then?"

"I thought I might go for a stroll later."

"At night? Is that wise?"

"Oh, I shall be all right. Here's your beer. It's already lost the condensation. If it's too warm, I'll get you another one."

Robert poured it and took a sip. "Perfect," he said.

Something, he decided, was wrong. There was something in the air. "Not much more of your holiday left," he said.

"No. The day after tomorrow," Martin replied. "Holidays always go too quickly."

"I shall miss you both."

"We shall miss being here," said George. Not "we shall miss you", Robert noticed. There was another period of silence.

Martin took rather too much of his drink and choked. He put the half-empty glass on the table and stood up. "I think I'll go now before it gets too late," he said. "Can I take your torch?"

"Sure, but I still think..." said Robert but, by that time, Martin was inside the house.

He emerged with the torch. "Have fun," he said – and was soon out of sight.

"That's got rid of him," said George.

"Do I gather that you two have had a row?" Robert asked.

"No. Why should we have?"

"Well, to quote my dear wife, it's obvious that something is up."

George laughed. "You are, for a start," he said. Robert looked down at his groin. It would have taken more than a couple of layers of cotton to disguise that bulge.

"And you're not," he said. George might well have been one of those sexless dummies one sees in shop windows. The material stretched tightly between his thighs was totally flat.

"No. Can I get myself another drink?"

"Of course you can."

George stood up. In that position it was just possible to make out the shape of his cock. He turned to go indoors. Robert stared ahead of him, trying to imagine how far up the hill Martin had got to, but it was impossible not to cast a sidelong glance to admire George's cotton-clad backside. There was, as Pat often said, "no harm in admiring something even if you couldn't have it". The fact had to be accepted. The ultimate pleasure wasn't going to come Robert's way. He became aware of the "chink" of bottles in the drinks cabinet. There was something comforting in that sound. In a few days' time he would be alone again with only the sounds of the African night. The boys would be back in Nairobi. Pat would be in England. One place set at the table. One towel on the rack in the bathroom...Of course there would be the weekend visits to Martin and that was something to look forward to.

"I got myself a gin and lemon. I hope you don't mind." Robert had been so deep in thought that he hadn't even noticed George return to his chair.

"Not in the least."

"Father Francis would have a fit," said George.

"Who's he?"

"One of the priests at school. He's got a hang-up about drink. If any of the boarders come back smelling of drink, they get belted. No matter what age. One beer gets you three whacks. God knows what the reward for gin drinking would be."

"That's ridiculous. I wouldn't be in favour of letting little kids drink, but if a person is over eighteen and it's legal anyway..."

"Try telling that to Father Francis. He's a nutter. Thank Christ I'm not a boarder and Dad doesn't keep the drinks cabinet locked. I'd go barmy if I had to live in."

"So would I. Thank God for King Henry's Grammar School."

"Is that where you went?"

"Yes."

"What was it like?"

Robert hadn't spoken about his school career for ages and wondered several times in the next quarter of an hour or so if George was really as interested as he appeared to be. It was odd how one memory acted as a key to others. The names of long-forgotten teachers emerged as though from a mist. Friends too.

"Who did you knock around with most?" George asked.

"Oh, they changed as I got older."

"Did you fist any of them?"

"One or two. I think that happens in every school."

"How about sucking or arse-fucking?"

"Sadly no. There weren't any opportunities."

"But there must have been someone you wanted to do it with, surely?"

"Some dozens would be more like it, but I don't think I would have got very far."

"Can I have another of these? Do you want one?"

"You can get me a beer, please."

Once again, George stood up. Possibly because Martin wasn't there, Robert noticed how different the two of them were. Martin seemed to struggle out of a chair and then pushed it aside, scraping it on the concrete floor. George was as silent and graceful as a cat. He went indoors and came back a few minutes later with an opened beer bottle and a very large drink for himself. Pat always used a wine glass for her gin and lemon. George's was in a half-pint tumbler.

George sat down again and raised the glass to his lips. "This is the way to live," he said and then, "Go on with what you were saying."

"About school?"

"Yes. All these boys you wanted to fuck. How would you have gone about it – if you'd had the chance, I mean."

"Oh heavens, George. That's one of those hypothetical questions."

"Try."

"Well, I suppose I'd tell him how good looking he was and how I loved him to bits."

"Which would have been a lie. You can't love dozens of blokes at the same time."

"I think you can. In different ways. It's difficult to explain. There was one boy, for instance, who was always shooting his mouth off about his sporting achievements but he was so beautiful that I used to lie awake for hours just thinking about him. Another was quite the opposite. He was shy and, to tell the truth, nothing much to look at, but there was something about his personality that got to me."

George sipped at his drink reflectively and then put the glass down. "That's what I don't really understand," he said. "You love your wife."

"Yes."

"And Martin?"

"Yes."

"Weird," George commented and took a long swig from his glass. He coughed slightly as he put it down. "Good drink, that," he said.

"Don't overdo it, though."

"I won't. You fucked Martin last night, didn't you?"

"I'm not prepared to say."

"I'm sure you did. Was it good?"

"Again, I'm not prepared to say."

"I wouldn't do that. I might do something else, though."

"Such as?"

"Well, I don't mind Martin fisting me, but he's not here."

"I see."

"Nothing else though," said George, "and you mustn't tell Martin."

"I wouldn't."

"Hang on. I'll move my chair."

He stood up and moved the chair so that it faced Robert's. "How's that?" he asked.

"Perfect. Hang on, I'll get this off."

"I think it would be better if you kept it on. I'll just...Oh shit! Who's this?"

Robert retied the knot in his kikoi and moved the chair back as the headlights of the approaching vehicle picked out the gate-posts and then swept into the drive. It was Mr Hanson's car. It stopped about six feet away from them and, for a moment, Robert was blinded by the light. Mr Hanson climbed out.

"Sorry to call at an inconvenient time," he said. "Are you going native or going to bed?"

Robert explained that they found it more comfortable to sit out like that.

"Every man to his own, I suppose. I actually came to find out how the Marriott lad is. I see he's not with you. Is he still ill?"

"He felt much better last night," said Robert – and the thought that crossed his mind as he said it was that his response had very little to do with Martin's health.

"I'm so glad. We weren't worried about him. We knew he was in good hands..."

'Arms actually,' Robert thought. "Would you care for a drink?" he asked.

"An orange juice or something like that. Nothing alcoholic," said Mr Hanson.

George got up. "I'll get it, sir," he said. His cock had swelled slightly in the last few minutes, Robert observed. There was a definite shape of something under the material.

"Nice lad," said Mr Hanson when he was out of earshot. "Pity the parents didn't take our advice about his schooling, though. If he'd gone to a good school in England he'd have been at university by now. The Ministry of Education is one great lash-up from top to..."

He stopped as George re-emerged with a glass of orange juice, topped, Robert couldn't help noticing, by a slice of orange.

"Ah! Thanks, George. Just what I needed," said Mr Hanson. He sat in Martin's chair, on Robert's right.

"Now that you're here, sir, can I ask you about the gold cup?" George asked.

"Oh that! You can ask, but I can't tell you a lot about it. It doesn't exist, you see."

"My dad says –"

"Oh, everyone says. Nobody has seen. Patrick and Jeremy were after it at one time, but even they gave up. No. It's a myth, old lad. A total and typical von Meinerherzhagen myth."

"It would be interesting to hear about it though," said Robert. George said nothing and was looking very glum indeed.

"Well, I was a very small boy when he died, so I don't remember the man very well. He used to hang around my grandfather a lot. He lived a few miles down the road. The house has been demolished now. Originally he was a very successful race-horse owner. That was when he won the cup. That bit is true."

"Yes. Dad's got a picture of him with it," said George.

"Well, after that he seems to have invested in a series of animals more suitable for milk-carts than the race-course and he got poorer and poorer. But, you see, he was a pathological liar.

Everybody knew about it but he wouldn't accept any help and kept on about money he was getting from the German government. That would have been just before the end of the war. I doubt if the German government had any at that time. Apparently he used to go on and on about Germany taking over the whole of East Africa. I doubt very much whether von Meinerherzhagen was his real name. Apparently, he claimed to be a Count of some sort."

"A very odd person," said Robert.

"Very odd. Very odd indeed. By the time I came into this world, he was as poor as a church mouse and living in one room of the house. Obviously he'd sold the cup. He must have done. Nobody would live like he did with an asset like that tucked away in a cupboard. He used to come up to the farm for his meals. All I can remember is his disgusting table manners – quite untypical of a Count – and how he used to go on and on about the war."

"What did he say about the cup?" George asked.

"Oh, he said nothing at all. Not that I can recall anyway. My father told me about it. We knew that the Mau Mau was forming. That would have been in the 1950s. Friend von Meinerherzhagen was convinced they would come after him and asked my father if he could hide his possessions – he insisted that they were immensely valuable – on the farm. Father said yes. That was the last we heard of it. Some days later von Meinerherzhagen told Father that it had been done. One of the Watu said he'd turned up in the dead of night with a lorry. That doesn't ring true, for a start. He hadn't got a lorry and there was nowhere round here where he could have got one."

"He could have hired one from Nakuru or Nairobi," said George.

"Dear man, he hadn't the money to hire a bike. Well, the Mau Mau did for him, as you probably know. That really didn't surprise anyone. He had dreams of becoming a sort of German ruler of the whole of East Africa. As I said, the man was a pathological liar. He's buried down in Gilgil somewhere. I know that my father was one of the people who went down to clear out his house. The condition of the place made him sick."

"Weren't there any papers or things like that?" George asked.

"Not that I know of. No... I should forget about it. You can be absolutely sure that cup was melted down years and years ago. It would certainly have turned up by now. Patrick and Jeremy haven't found it and they're not the sort of lads to give up easily."

Mr Hanson's glass was empty. George took it and went indoors. "You can bring me another beer, George," Robert called after him. By the time he came out again, Mr Hanson was well away on the subject of his sons. Patrick had good hopes of rowing for Oxford. Jeremy was doing extremely well at a school in south England. Young Tim was beginning to show considerable promise in football and cricket.

"An Oxford man. That's very impressive. I look forward to meeting Patrick when they are home again," said Robert.

"Me too," said George. "And Jeremy and Tim, too."

"You might, young George. Do you play croquet?"

"I'm not awfully good."

"Neither are they, but I'll make sure to let your father know. Anyway, I'd better be off. Busy day tomorrow. My best regards to your father, George and oh! – give my best wishes to the other lad."

"He's wrong. He's got to be wrong," said George as they watched Mr Hanson's rear lights disappearing up the hill.

"About what?"

"The cup. It's got to be still there."

"I doubt it. Why don't we return to something that is real and hidden at the moment," said Robert.

"What?"

"Guess."

"I can't."

"This." Robert tried to reach over the arm of his chair to touch it. Unfortunately he couldn't reach that far.

"Oh that. I'm not in the mood anymore. I'm still thinking abut the cup."

"Which Mr Hanson says doesn't exist anymore and which other people have failed to find."

"But they didn't go about it scientifically. We'll have a metal detector."

"George, have you any idea how big that place is? It would have been even bigger before Mr Hanson started his farm training school up there. It would take a thousand years to go over that place – even with an army of men with metal detectors. Be realistic."

"I am. If I can get Peter Hardwick to fly over the place, that will show if the ground has been disturbed. That way we shall know where to look, see?"

Robert tried to point out that a necessary feature of farmland was that it was disturbed at least once a year by ploughing. George rejected this. "It would be a different sort of disturbance," he said. "It's in this book on archaeology Martin's got apparently. He says you have to look for spoil heaps or some name like that. They get left when people bury something. Peter would know more about it, I'm sure."

"Mmm. I can't remember seeing any in our local cemetery at home. Maybe they use a different technique," said Robert. At that moment Martin returned – so quietly that they might not have noticed had a momentary spot of light on the gatepost not given him away.

"Have a nice walk?" Robert asked.

"Yes, thanks. Did you have a nice evening?"

"Mr Hanson called. He sent you his regards," said Robert.

"How do you mean – 'called'?" he asked.

"Just that," said George. "He came, he spoke, he went."

"And you were – like that? Christ!"

"It didn't seem to worry him," said Robert.

"It worries me. What were you doing?"

"Nothing, as it happens."

Martin put the torch on the table and sat down. "That's the end of night-time moon-bathing," he said. "Thank Christ he didn't call last night."

Up to this moment, George had sat with a slightly puzzled expression on his face. "I hadn't thought of that," he said.

"Why didn't you tell us that he sometimes visits?" Martin demanded.

"He doesn't – or he didn't. When Pat and I got here, he sent an invitation down by Mr Peters. That's the only time anybody from Eldama has been here." Either a sudden cold breeze or the realisation of a narrow escape made Robert shiver slightly.

"So. No more sitting out here in kikois," said Martin firmly.

"No more anything," said George.

It wasn't an entirely accurate forecast. Twice in the following nights, Martin padded into Robert's room and waggled spunk-soaked fingers under his nose to wake him up. Twice more, Robert's head was buried between the young man's thighs, but Martin – to quote his own words – was only charged up once.

It was an extraordinarily apposite metaphor. Martin's sudden upward heave and the rigidity of his body as his spunk pumped into Robert's mouth were reminiscent of the films Robert had seen of electrical resuscitation. After a few whispered endearments, Martin would tiptoe out of the room, closing the door behind him as quietly as possible, and return to his sleeping friend.

Evenings on the verandah were spent fully dressed. Nobody called. Nobody was expected. George said that it was probably better that way and Martin didn't argue the point as Robert had hoped he might. The topic of conversation changed, too. Now it was all of the gold cup; of how they would find it and what they would do when it was found. Robert found their youthful self-confidence quite amusing.

Mr Glover arrived on Sunday afternoon. They had just finished lunch when the vehicle, painted in zebra stripes and emblazoned with the words "Sunshine Safaris" drove in. He was a cordial enough man, Robert thought. He listened with interest to George's account of the Hansons' party and of the people he met there – most of whom he seemed to know.

"And there's this chap called Peter Hardwick, Dad. He's got his own plane and he says he'll take me up," said George.

"Hardwick?" said Mr Glover. "Can't say I can place him at all. Where does he live?"

"I think he said Mombasa. Yes. I'm sure he did," said George.

"Mmm. Long way to come out to dinner. Invite him to the house when he's in town next. Now, are you lads ready? I'd like to pop in and see Jeremy Hanson whilst I'm up here."

That made George bustle around much more energetically. Finally, their bags were loaded. Mr Glover shook Robert's hand and climbed in.

"Thanks ever so much. It's been brilliant," said George – and he got in.

"Thanks for having me," said Martin with a mischievous grin. "Pity about the other one."

"You can't have everything, you see. A bird in the hand is worth two in the bush, as my dear mother-in-law is fond of saying," Robert replied.

"There were two of us in the bush, but you only had one in hand," said Martin. "Next weekend we shall be back in town. It's funny, really. Without George, it's going to be easier. You know something?"

"What?"

"I can't wait," said Martin. He said something else.

Robert, assuming it to be Swahili for goodbye, said "Cheers".

"*Tyfma*," Martin said. "T-Y-F-M-A."

"What does that mean?"

"Till you fuck me again," Martin whispered – just as Mr Glover shouted for him to get in.

Robert stood on the verandah with Kiberech as the vehicle lumbered up the hill.

"*Tyfma* – or *tifya*," Robert murmured.

"Bwana?"

"An old English word," Robert explained. "You can take the rest of the day off."

Chapter Eight

Tyfma and *tifya* became part of their vocabulary in the ensuing weekends and were used in the most unlikely places. In the supermarket, for example. Martin reached up to get a packet of cereal. He placed it in the trolley and then said *"Tyfma?"*

"Tifya," Robert replied and his cock, already stimulated by the tautness of Martin's arse-cheeks as he stretched, twitched in anticipation.

On another occasion they were having tea with some of Martin's Kenyan friends and Robert was finding it difficult to express his gratitude for a chipped mug of black tea with globules of condensed milk floating on the surface. *"Tyfma?"* said Martin, suddenly.

"Tifya," Robert replied and that made the drink taste much better.

Martin didn't say it every weekend. There were quite a lot of occasions when Robert had to be content with the young man's throbbing tool in his mouth. For a long time he didn't know why or how Martin made the decision to "go the whole way" on some weekends and not others. Mrs Angel had always said that one should be grateful for small mercies. Robert was more than grateful for a large one and even more thankful when the magic word was spoken.

Martin was a master of planning. David was only in the house for one weekend and that was because he was confined to bed with tonsilitis. Otherwise he spent the weekends with various friends.

There was one occasion when Martin, Catherine and Robert were sitting in the lounge and Catherine, as usual, was holding forth. "Are you quite comfortable on that sofa, Robert? It sinks dreadfully at one side when two people are on it. Maybe Martin could bring in another chair for himself."

"I'm all right, mum," said Martin, who was reading the week-end supplement.

"We'd buy another, but one never knows from one day to the next what the future holds for us out here. You read about Mr Simmonds, I suppose?"

"No. Who's he?" Robert asked. He was dying for Martin to suggest a walk, but the lad was engrossed in his reading.

"A charming man. He did so much to help them, that's the ironic thing about it. He planned the park and all those flowers along the highway are his work. Well, apparently he was at the theatre the other night and fell asleep so he didn't stand up for the national anthem. Not that it's anything special, but they had him out of the country. Forty-eight hours' notice and out. They are so stupid. And they stopped the Women's Institute from singing 'Jerusalem'. They want us to sing something about Kenya instead. I should think so. We're all leaving in protest. And there was a man who works with Malcolm. He –"

Martin put down the paper. "*Tyfma*?" he said.

"Oh. Ah. *Tifya*."

"I do wish you wouldn't use Swahili in the house, Martin darling. Apart from when you have to speak to Ibrahim, that is – though it's high time he learned a bit more English. It's not a pleasant-sounding language."

"Some of it is extremely pleasant," said Robert, casting a sidelong glance at Martin's long, sunburned legs.

"Not in my opinion. I see no reason why European children should have to learn it in school. It's a total waste of time. They'll never need it."

"Unless they decide to stay here and work to get the country on its feet," said Martin.

"That would take a miracle," Catherine replied and Martin stood up.

"Feel like a walk, Robert?" he asked.

"Not a bad idea. Will you excuse us, Catherine?"

They left her doing her embroidery, sticking the needle in with more vigour than necessary.

They walked, and met a number of Martin's African friends. "How's George?" Robert asked.

"Oh, he's fine."

"You still see him, then?"

"Of course. Every day at school. They're doing a special pre-university course for us now, so it's more worthwhile going. I see him in the evening sometimes when we haven't got too much work on."

"And you still oblige him?"

"Fist him, you mean? Of course. Twice last week, as a matter of fact."

"I haven't seen the lad since you left my place." An enjoyable vision of George climbing out of his pool formed in Robert's mind.

"He's not at home at weekends now. He's down at the coast with Peter Hardwick."

"The pilot?"

"That's right. George's got him into the search for the gold cup in the summer. He's got metal detectors arranged and everything."

"Another cut of the profits gone, if you find it," said Robert.

"Essential, if we're to do it properly. Are we going to Plum's with Dad tonight? What do you think?"

"That's up to you."

"We could. We need to be back at about nine, though."

"Why's that?" Robert's heart-rate quickened.

"There's a thriller on TV that starts at nine-thirty. Mum will want to watch that and Dad will watch it with her. Then there's the golf series that Dad likes to watch, so we go to bed just after the thriller kicks off."

"Devious bugger!" said Robert – and Martin laughed happily.

Not even Martin could take the credit for the black clouds that formed over the terrace to Plum's Hotel that evening, but everything else went according to plan. The first heavy drops of rain fell as Malcolm drove into the garage.

"Oh good!" said Catherine as they stepped into the house. "You remember that film, *Ultimatum*? We saw it years ago at the Belle Vue?"

"Can't say I do," Malcolm replied.

"Oh darling, you must remember it. The one where the man lived on the top floor of that apartment block and the old woman who lived below him?"

"Oh, that one. Not much point in seeing it again."

"Of course we will, and there's the golf programme afterwards."

That was all it needed. Ibrahim was set to work making sandwiches. "I think I'll go to bed," said Martin.

"At this hour?"

"Why not?"

"And I'll turn in too," said Robert. The Marriotts, used to these early bedtimes which Catherine attributed to the stress of building air-strips and having to keep to a timetable so that everything was ready for visiting experts, nodded their understanding.

It was, in fact, a time of immense stress, but it had nothing to do with the Royal Air Force. Robert felt horribly guilty about letting Pat down. For weeks after his two young guests left, he'd wondered what he ought to do. He'd written two letters, hoping that Pat would understand but, in her replies, she never mentioned receiving them. 'It isn't going to work out. It can't work out.' Robert murmured these sentences to himself time and time again but he shelved the problem and did nothing more about it. He worked as hard as he could, eagerly looking forward to his weekends.

Robert was particularly concerned that weekend because Pat's usual chatty letter hadn't arrived. Night after night the previous week, he'd thought of calling her but had put it off, knowing that his mother-in-law would pick up the phone first.

His worries decreased as he undressed and they vanished when it was time to do the same to Martin. As always, they lay on Martin's bed fingering each other softly and listening to the sounds from downstairs. First Catherine would use the toilet, then Malcolm. Then came the squeaking of the trolley as Ibrahim wheeled in the sandwiches. "Any minute now," Martin whispered – fortunately not in reference to his nearing orgasm but in expectation of the back door being locked as Ibrahim went to his little house in the garden.

"There!" said Martin as the door slammed. "Two hours."

It took all that time. First came the ritual of applying newly bought lubricating cream to Martin's eager but instinctively resistant muscle-ring. As always, he wriggled and gave out a series of little groans and grunts as Robert slowly increased the pressure. They could just about hear the television downstairs and, as always, Robert stopped for the commercials but there were no sounds of movement from Martin's parents. His finger vanished from sight just after the second break. Again, he stopped. They both lay there panting until the familiar music which introduced the golf series started. Whilst Martin's parents watched golf, a ball game of a quite different sort was taking place above their heads. In this case, though, neither player was attempting to beat 'par for the course' Neither of them had the slightest idea what it was. Robert achieved a 'hole in two'. Martin always tensed instinctively when Robert's latex-sheathed and well-greased cock-head sought initial entry. As always, Robert forced himself into a state of patience and waited. A jingle advertising chocolate drifted up the stairs.

"I think it's...okay now," Martin panted. Robert clasped the young man's broad shoulders. At first the feeling was of tiny, hard lips parting reluctantly to admit him. He pushed slightly harder and the lips encompassed his tool. Tight, warm tissues clamped against his rigid shaft as he sank further and further in. On that particular night, Martin came slightly before Robert. Not that it mattered greatly. It was almost as if his youthful body had a built-up momentum which kept his sweating buttocks moving even after his violent ejaculation. A few seconds afterwards, Robert's cock spilled out too.

"Jesus!" said Martin as he always did.

"Christ!" Robert added. They lay there for some moments. Robert kissed the back of Martin's neck.

Catherine and Malcolm came up the stairs and, as usual, Catherine paused by the door. "Both fast asleep," she said. "Poor Robert looked terribly tired this morning. He seemed to perk up a bit this afternoon, though."

"Martin cheered him up, I expect," said Malcolm.

"Very true," Robert whispered. "Are you tired?"

"Of course not."

"Good. Then I'll keep it in for a bit longer."

"Make sure you're not too tired for tomorrow morning, either," said Martin.

The following week was, without doubt, the worst ever. Three technicians had flown out from England to fit the various navigation aids. The caravan in which the various instruments were to be housed had to be towed all the way from Nairobi – not an easy journey. Predictably, it arrived a day late. The technicians were somewhat over-awed by the Hansons and with their accommodation.

"It's bloody amazing," said one. "It's like three self-contained flats in there. When I think my two kids have to share a room, it makes me think."

They left on Friday morning. Early the following day, Robert's car followed the same route across the Rift Valley and up the escarpment into Nairobi. Hoping very much that it would be a "*tyfma-tifya*" weekend, he decided to go to the pharmacy first to stock up with necessities and, in case this might embarrass Martin, he took a roundabout way into the city, got the things he wanted and then drove back to the Ainsworth roundabout. No Martin. He looked at his watch. He was slightly early. He drove into the city, turned at the roundabout near the airport and drove back again. There was still no trace of Martin. He went to the supermarket, did the shopping and went back again. Again, no trace of Martin. He gave up and went to the house.

"But he wrote to you," said Catherine. "I know because I posted the letter myself. Let me see, that would have been on Monday afternoon. It must have got to you. I mean, I know things have got bad but a letter shouldn't take six days. Of course in the old days..."

It hadn't reached him for a very good reason. He hadn't been near his post box for over a week. There had to be a letter, a horribly recriminatory letter – from Pat. Maybe even one from his mother-in-law in there. Twice he'd set out for the short walk up the hill to the post office and twice he had turned back halfway.

"So who's he with, Catherine?" he asked.

"This new friend of George's. A Mr Hardwick. Malcolm spoke to him on the phone of course. A most charming man it seems and one of the old school. Both of the boys are there, planning some sort of expedition for the summer holidays. It's awfully nice of Mr Hardwick and he seems to go along with their little games. A treasure hunt or something. It'll be their last holiday from school here. They'll be coming back for holidays from University, of course, but it won't be the same somehow. I suppose they'll be wanting to bring their girlfriends back with them."

"Hmm," Robert replied, taking advantage of her pause for breath.

"Still, his being away has its advantages for you," Catherine continued. "You can have a room to yourself. Ibrahim's changed the sheets on his bed and you can use that rather than that silly folding thing. I cannot imagine how anyone could get a good night's sleep on that. Now, let's get your things in the fridge. Where is that man? He's never around when you want him."

Ibrahim emerged from the kitchen, wiping his hand on his apron. "I'll take that," said Robert, indicating the paper bag from the pharmacist's. Ibrahim nodded and carried the rest into the house.

Without Martin, Catherine was even more insufferable than usual. Malcolm was playing golf. Robert endured an account of the lamentable state of the postal service over lunch. They adjourned to the lounge to let Ibrahim clear the table. Catherine had heard of several people whose post office bank deposits had been plundered and their books altered. "Oh my dear, they get up to anything," she said when Robert said he couldn't quite see how that could be done.

He decided to go for a walk. For a ghastly moment he thought Catherine might decide to keep him company, but she didn't. He strolled along the road. One of Martin's friends waved. He waved back, feeling more and more lonely and worried about that letter. It was going, he thought, to be a thoroughly miserable weekend. He found himself at the Ainsworth roundabout – the place where Martin should have been waiting for him. He turned left in the direction of the city centre and came to the Norfolk Hotel. Several people were sitting out on the terrace and a cool beer was an inviting and cheering thought. He climbed the steps, looked at the old rickshaw on display there and took his place at an empty table. Two men, whose pasty faces, white legs and immaculately pressed khaki shorts proclaimed them to be new arrivals or tourists, were at the next table. A waiter took Robert's order and there he sat, staring out over the road.

"Absolutely marvellous!" one of the man near him said. "Well worth every penny."

"They don't have pennies here," said the other in a petulant tone.

"Well, whatever they have. It's a superb hotel and they looked after us so well. You'll have to go there and of course, quite apart from anything else, if you know what I mean, you can sit out and watch all the animals come in to drink. Oh, it was quite exquisite. Everything was."

Robert tried not to listen. He would have been much better off, he thought, if he'd seen Martin's letter and gone to a hotel himself. Unfortunately, it was too late to change arrangements.

"Didn't he feel a bit out of place?" asked one of the men.

"They don't. They can speak the language and get on with the staff and, of course, I bought him some clothes. He was thoroughly spoiled all the time we were there."

In irritation, Robert looked up, perhaps to make a comment. Someone's head was visible over the low wall but there was no mistaking that shock of straw-coloured hair.

"Raymond!" Robert called. The young man walked on. Maybe it wasn't Raymond after all. Robert shouted again – much louder this time – and the young man stopped and turned round. Robert stood up and beckoned. Raymond turned round, walked back, and came bounding up the steps to the terrace.

"Hi!" he said. As always, his khaki shorts and shirt looked overdue for the laundry.

"Fancy a drink?" Robert asked.

"Yes, please. A beer, if I may."

The waiter came over with Robert's beer, and accordingly Robert ordered one for Raymond as well.

"No motorbike today?" he asked.

"No. I've been up to the snake park and the museum. I never like leaving it outside for too long for fear it will get nicked." The waiter brought his beer. " Ah! Thanks a lot. I needed that!" he said, taking a considerable mouthful. "Martin and George seem to have a good time up at your place," he said.

"I think so."

"They seem excited about something."

"Oh, that's probably –"

Raymond didn't let him finish. "They're both like kids some-times," he said.

"Which you are not," Robert observed. It wasn't an empty compliment. Quite apart from the massive chest and hirsute legs, there was something completely relaxed about Raymond. It was a quality that the other two didn't have. Robert had come across it mostly in connection with very senior officers who seemed com-pletely "at home" with just about everybody, however they were dressed.

He took another gulp of beer and leaned back in the chair. "So – what have you been doing since we last met?" Robert asked.

"The usual, really. They've got a pre-university course going at school, but it's sod-all use to me. I want to read zoology and the course is designed for the sociology and African Studies blokes, so that's a waste of time. And I've been snake-hunting of course. I got a couple of good puff adders the other day and a boomslang the week before, so that's worthwhile. I sell them to the snake park. Every little helps."

"And what about the python you were after?"

"Ha! I think that python is imaginary. It was a totally false rumour."

"A pity that you didn't know that before. You could have come up to my place with the other two."

"No, thank you. I would like to come up on my own sometime, if I may."

"Of course you can. I've told you. Just give me a call."

"I do have certain disadvantages as a guest."

"I can't imagine what they might be," said Robert, trying to keep his eyes off Raymond's legs.

"There'd be snakes all over the place."

"Providing they were in boxes and couldn't get out, I can't see that as being a problem."

"Aha! You're a married man. What about your wife? A lot of women have the screaming ab-dabs if they so much as see a slow-worm."

"Pat's not with me at the moment and I don't think she'll be coming back." An uncanny feeling of relief swept over Robert as the words came out. It was so strong that he suddenly felt exhausted and had to put his glass on to the table to recover his senses.

"I rather guessed that from something George told me. Do you want to talk about it?"

"Not now, no, but thanks for the offer." This, he thought, was extraordinary. Raymond was only twenty and technically still a schoolboy. Anxious to return to some sort of equanimity, he turned the subject back to snake-hunting and, for the first few minutes, listened intently to Raymond's accounts of various expeditions, some of which were quite exciting. The two men at the next table obviously didn't think so. Robert had been aware that they were listening intently during the first part of the conversation. Now they started up again.

"He should have been here by now," said one.

"Maybe he's working himself up for you," said the other. "He'll be here. Don't worry. You can hardly expect someone who's never owned a watch to be punctual."

"Hmm. Maybe I'll get him one – if he shows up. It might be worthwhile. Ah! Speak of the devil! I'll see you later."

He got to his feet, almost ran down the steps and crossed the road where a young Kenyan man with the briefest cut-off shorts Robert had ever seen stood waiting for him.

"The Ainsworth bridge brigade," said Raymond, turning to watch as they shook hands.

"Oh! Somebody told me about that," said Robert. The man and his young companion set off at a brisk rate towards the town centre. "They don't do it here in the hotel, then?" he whispered, conscious of the remaining man's presence.

"No. Not in the Norfolk. This place is old-fashioned like that. They go to a doss house in the Godown area. Now the word's got round, there are more and more of them. I counted fifteen of them on the bridge at one time when I was down here after the legendary python – all with their binoculars stuck to their faces. I even got an offer myself, would you believe?"

"Easily," said Robert, looking deliberately at Raymond's outspread legs. "You didn't accept the kind offer?"

"No way! Those blokes are probably carrying more diseases than you'd find in our cess-pit. They pop in here on their way from Thailand or some such place to have a final fling before they go back to their offices in London."

There was no way of telling if the man at the next table heard this remark. He stood up rather suddenly and strode into the hotel, leaving his unfinished drink on the table.

"Gone to get his binoculars," said Raymond with a laugh. "If he puts his skates on, he'll just about catch a glimpse before it gets too dark."

More snake-hunting reminiscences followed. Raymond declined another drink. "I'd better go," he said. "Where will you be this evening?"

"Well... I could be anywhere that suits you," said Robert.

"With Martin?"

"No. He's away this weekend."

"Is he? Where?"

"With a character called Peter Hardwick. Mr Hardwick is a pilot, apparently."

"Hardwick, eh? Let's hope he lives up to his name, for Martin's sake."

"And George. He's there too."

"He won't get much out of George – except maybe in a liquid sense. Anyway I'd better be off."

"I'll be at Plum's Hotel with Martin's dad at about eight o'clock, if you're interested," said Robert. There was something about this extraordinarily mature young man that had got to him. He was reluctant to let him go.

"I'll have to see. I might have to babysit my brother if the folks want to go out. Here. Let me pay for my beer."

Robert, of course, wouldn't hear of it and sat there watching Raymond until he was out of sight. The nine-year age difference made no difference at all, he thought. He had found a friend at last.

Dinner at the Marriotts' wasn't quite so tedious as he'd feared. He managed to keep cheerful, despite Catherine's torrent and Malcolm's occasional interjections. Ibrahim had been to the mosque without asking her permission to leave the premises. Oh yes, she agreed, dinner had been cooked on time and he had mown the lawn before being told to do so, but that wasn't the point. "You have to be firm with them all the time. Give them an inch and they'll take a yard."

"Yes, dear. You'd better speak to him," said Malcolm.

"I already have. He won't do that again."

"Yes, dear. Plum's tonight, Robert?"

"Sure. Good idea," Robert replied.

"Don't be too late back. There's a good film on."

"We won't," said Malcolm resignedly. "We'll miss out on coffee tonight."

"Probably just as well. I doubt if Ibrahim's even thought to put the coffee pot on. He's been in a mood ever since I spoke to him."

In fact, Ibrahim pushed the trolley into the lounge just as they were leaving the house. Robert's depression returned when he was in the car. He missed Martin badly. Martin usually sat in the front seat and it seemed wrong that Robert should occupy it. He cheered up slightly when they got to the hotel – or put on a pretence of having done so.

"I can't thank you enough for having Martin. It did him the world of good," said Malcolm. "Was it hell on earth?"

"Far from it," Robert replied.

"I can't think of much worse in this world than having those young men billeted on you. That George is a nice lad though and – fair dues – Martin's a kind-hearted soul, even if he is a bit green at the moment."

"People mature at different rates," said Robert.

"True. I suppose I was very much the same when I was his age."

Robert suddenly had a frightening mental image of Martin in twenty years time. Martin with a beer-belly. Martin in a grey suit. Martin saying 'I was very much the same when I was his age.' He shuddered. "Not cold, are you?" Malcolm asked.

"No, no. I'm okay."

"Any news as to when your wife will be coming back?" The question made him shiver again which, fortunately, prevented him from answering.

"I hope you've not got malaria coming on," Malcolm said. "You sure you're all right?"

"Yes. Yes. Really."

"It starts like that," said Malcolm. "Now where was I?"

For the next twenty minutes or so, the conversation was of Martin and Martin's plans for the future. Malcolm doubted Martin's ability to get into a medical school. "He's not got it in him," he said – causing Robert to experience a much more pleasant mental image. Catherine, it seemed, was absolutely determined that Martin would be a doctor and was already writing off to medical schools for their prospectuses.

"She can – I suppose I shouldn't say this – but she can get very difficult if her plans are frustrated," said Malcolm, and Robert was working out a suitably diplomatic reply when Raymond appeared at the end of the terrace, dangling his crash helmet from one hand and straightening his hair with the other. Robert waved.

"Aha! The snake lad. You've been to our place once or twice," said Malcolm, standing up to shake Raymond's hand.

"That's right," Raymond confirmed.

"This is Flight Lieutenant Hall. A friend of ours," said Malcolm.

"Yes, I know. We've met. Hi!" said Raymond.

"What will you have?" Robert asked.

"No, no. Let me. You, Mr Marriott?"

Robert and Malcolm exchanged a smile at the waiter who served them. He was wearing enormous spectacles with lenses that looked as if they'd been fashioned from the bottoms of wine bottles. As one totally accustomed to the premises, Raymond ordered the drinks and then, turning to Robert, said, "I've got a bit of a shock for you."

"What's that?"

"Big decision on the home front. Mum and Dad have decided to put little brother into a prep school in England. She flies off with him tomorrow. Dad will be alone in the house, but he's quite happy that way. Could I go to Kampi-ya-Moto with you tomorrow? I could hitch back if you're not coming to Nairobi next weekend."

"I will be. No problem at all," said Robert.

"What about your studies?" Malcolm asked. "It's term time."

"There aren't any for me. I'm fed up with hanging around the place and doing nothing. I can take the books I want to read with me," said Raymond.

"You're sure your parents agree?" Malcolm asked. Robert felt annoyed. It was nothing to do with Malcolm.

"Absolutely. Anyway, I make my own decisions."

"Legally yes. So can Martin, for that matter, but there are some things..."

"Well, it's perfectly okay as far as I am concerned," said Robert. The waiter returned with the drinks and felt for the edge of the table before he put them down.

"What will you do when you're not studying? Robert will be out at work," Malcolm continued.

"That's okay. I'll be out snake-hunting," said Raymond. "Cheers!"

It was a pity, Robert thought, that Raymond had put long trousers on. If Malcolm had seen those hairy legs he might have realised that Raymond was not a little boy but a man of twenty. Then there was the matter of what Raymond would do if bitten by a snake. Raymond explained that he already had been – three times – and carried anti-venom with him all the time. It was all too easy to get lost out in the bundu, said Malcolm. Raymond had been further into the bush on his motorbike and on foot than Malcolm had ever been. What would happen if he were to break a leg or something? He would light a fire and lie there waiting for help, said Raymond.

"I don't know," said Malcolm, shaking his head. "You'd be much better off to have someone else with you. Martin had George. All due respect to Robert, but he can't be expected to look after you all the time."

"I don't think Raymond needs any looking after," said Robert.

"Where and when shall I pick you up?"

Raymond said that he lived in Eastchurch Road opposite the Agip petrol station.

"That should be easy enough to find."

"Very easy," said Malcolm. "It's one of the oldest houses in the city, but I'll draw you a map when we get home. I must say that I think your parents are right in one thing, young Raymond. It's a very good idea to send your brother to England. What does he think about it?"

"I think he's looking forward to the idea. He's lucky. He'll get his certificates on time, not like us. And he'll get away from my snakes and Dad's clutter."

The rest of the evening passed pleasantly enough. Very pleasantly as far as Robert was concerned. All three men left at the same time.

"I just hope you know what you're taking on," said Malcolm, as they watched him speed away.

"He'll be all right," said Robert. The thought returned no less than three times that night. He felt more at ease in Martin's bed than he had in Martin's place in the car.

"He'll be all right," he muttered with his fingers wrapped round his cock. He lay still for a few moments thinking. Hairy legs possibly meant a hairy chest. Well, it might add to the pleasure. There was certain to be a lot lower down. In fact, he remembered Martin saying something to that effect. Slowly the image he wanted formed in his mind. He wished he'd thought to put a rubber on, but by that time it was too late. Ibrahim, poor man, would have extra washing to cope with, but he'd have to wash the sheets anyway. "He'll be all right," Robert murmured again. "You'll be all right, Raymond," he muttered – and he was away.

Chapter Nine

Just what Raymond had meant by "clutter" was apparent the
moment Robert pulled into their drive. A broken swing stood in
the garden, together with three rusty bicycles. There was a bathtub
covered by a black plastic sheet. A row of wooden boxes almost
hid the rusting bathroom boiler behind them.

Raymond came bounding out of the house before the car had
even stopped. "You'd better come inside and say 'Hello' to Dad,"
he said. "I'm all ready." He was wearing the same grubby shorts
and shirt that he had worn at the Norfolk Hotel. Robert followed
him into the house. It must once have been a rather small, neat
little place. Someone had built on so many extensions that the
original plan had been entirely lost. Steps led from one room to
other. The furniture was old and comfortable-looking but, in order
to sit down, one would have to shift the books. He had never seen
so many books. They were everywhere – even on the steps
between the rooms. An old upright piano – or perhaps a harmoni-
um – was covered with books. There were books on the window
ledges and books on the floor. Stepping extremely carefully, for a
broken leg was far more possible at Raymond's home than in
Kampi-ya-Moto, he followed the young man through the house.

"He's here, Dad," said Raymond, opening a door.

His father was much older than Robert had imagined he would

be. He was sixty if a day, thought Robert as they shook hands.

"Very good of you to take the lad off my hands for a week," he said. "I need the time to finish a piece of work I'm engaged on."

Robert said it was a pleasure.

"Dad's a lecturer at the university," Raymond explained. "For my sins," his father added. "Now, you're sure you've got everything you need, son?"

"Quite sure," said Raymond and, to Robert's surprise he leaned over his father and kissed his bald head.

"Bye, Dad. Look after yourself," he said.

"Oh, I shall be all right. Don't worry about me. You've got rid of the last of the collection?"

"All gone to the snake park," said Raymond.

"Just as well. I just hope their relations don't come around to look for them."

"Snakes don't, Dad. Bye."

Once again Robert shook hands and gingerly followed Raymond through the house again. "I've just got the rucksack and this bag and some sacks for the snakes," said the young man. "And the famous catching instrument, of course."

The "famous catching instrument" was a long pole with pincers at one end, operated by a cycle brake lever at the other – and had to be tied to the roof rack. Fortunately there was no shortage of rope in the house. The rest of Raymond's stuff had to go in the boot, as the back seat was loaded with provisions. Soon they were on their way.

"Martin and George were telling me about Vijay Shah," Robert mentioned.

"That's the one."

"He's crazy about them both. He even showers with the curtain back when they're around, but will they take up the offer? No chance. They hang around with their eyes and cocks practically popping out, but that's all. In George's case, I guess his mum and dad being Quakers has a lot to do with it. And you know what they call wanking?"

"Fisting,"

"That's it. I ask you. One day somebody's going to misunderstand and one of them's going to get properly fisted. That'll teach him. I'm sorry. I know you're fond of them but their hang-ups drive me crazy sometimes."

"They'll probably change a lot once they're at University in England," said Robert.

"They'll have missed one hell of a lot of good chances," said Raymond. "When I think of Vijay's cock! God! That bloke's got more meat than a butcher's shop. It's free too. It doesn't cost a cent. His old man owns a sugar factory."

"A sweet young man," said Robert.

"And how! Plenty of it too. Anyway, let's stop talking about him or I'll get a hard-on before we get there."

Several times during the journey, Robert became aware that he was driving faster than he normally did and had to let his foot up. He did it again when they were on the dirt road and that really was stupid and dangerous. At one point he nearly lost control and that forced him to slow right down. It would be ironic, he thought, if they both ended up in separate hospital beds.

The sun was just beginning to sink when they finally drove into the house. As usual, Kiberech was waiting in the verandah. He ran out to open the car door.

"Mr Raymond. Friend. Er...Siddick yangu..." said Robert. Raymond saved him the effort of more Swahili by shaking Kiberech's hand enthusiastically and introducing himself. Once again, Kiberech was delighted to speak to somebody in his own language. Once again, Robert thought he really should make an effort to learn Swahili. That was even more important now that he had made the great decision...

"He's putting my snake-catching stuff round the back of the

house. Is that all right?" Raymond asked.

"Eh? Oh sorry. I was dreaming. Yes, that's the best place."

"And he says if you don't mind waiting a bit, he can do a couple of steaks for dinner. I said we didn't mind at all."

"Sure. Good idea. I rather enjoy sitting out on the verandah with a beer. We can do that while we're waiting. Now, as to sleeping arrangements..." They left Kiberech to unload the car and went inside. "There's this room and my room and the bathroom is here," said Robert. "I leave the decision of where you're going to sleep to you."

"Well, I'll sleep in here," said Raymond, opening the spare room. "Sort of base camp if you know what I mean. I've only got to go next door to achieve the summit."

Robert laughed. "I don't want you getting out of breath on the journey," he said.

"No fear of that," Raymond replied. "Let's have that beer you mentioned."

Any thoughts of a long and interesting conversation out on the verandah were very quickly dampened. Raymond was obviously one of those young men who could not stay in one place for more than a few minutes. He opened the bottle of beer Robert gave him, poured it into a glass, took a sip and stood up again.

"Magnificent view!" he exclaimed.

"I like it."

"I suppose one day there'll be a bloody great hotel up here."

"That sounds a bit like George. He's all for opening up the country to tourists."

"He would be. He's got no soul at all. This is the real Africa and the awful thing is that they're spoiling it."

"And that bit sounds like Martin's mother."

"Dreadful woman! No, I don't mean to criticise the Kenyans. They'd be better left on their own. It's the money-grabbing Europeans who are at fault and the Kenyans need the money, so they let them get away with it. Do you know the coast well?"

"Hardly at all. We went there one weekend but didn't much like it. Hotels and tourists everywhere."

"Exactly. When I was a small boy you could walk for miles along those beaches and never see a soul. It's a shame." He took another sip from his glass and then, to Robert's surprise, climbed up – or, rather, leapt up – on to the low wall at the side of the balcony and stood there gazing out over the Rift Valley.

"Utterly magnificent!" he exclaimed. "You must be able to see twenty-five miles at least."

"Beautiful," Robert agreed. What he was admiring was only three or four feet away. Two massive hairy legs surmounted by equally large, tense hemispheres of muscle.

"In many ways, it's a shame about that hedge," said Raymond. "The view would be better without it."

"It has certain advantages, as George and Martin discovered. We could sit out here in the nude."

"I'm surprised you got George to go that far. You must be a good influence."

"I don't know about that. Hadn't you better get down and finish your beer?"

Raymond jumped down, sat down and picked up his glass. Robert just had time to enquire when the great snake hunt would begin and to find out that snake-hunting, as far as Raymond was concerned, was a twenty-four hour per day activity.

"That long grass in the corner looks a likely spot," he said – and Robert was left alone again. He finished his beer and got another bottle. By the time Raymond came back, he'd knocked back a considerable quantity from that.

"I would say you've got a mamba of some sort there," said Raymond.

"Oh God! Don't say that."

"It won't hurt you if you don't disturb it. I'll ask Kiberech. He'd

143

know," and Raymond was off again. Robert was wondering if it would be worthwhile opening a third beer when he returned.

"I was right. Kiberech has seen it. A black mamba by the sound of it. They're not black, actually. They're a sort of olive colour. Beautiful things."

"Why don't you sit down and finish your beer? It'll be warm."

"Can you finish it for me? I think I'll go for a little stroll. Kiberech says dinner will be ready in about ten minutes."

Robert watched him stride along the drive. He was a really striking young man, he thought. He lacked George's compactness and Martin's strength, but he was undeniably good-looking and distinctly promising – if only he would keep still. Robert smiled at the thought. Raymond wouldn't have to keep still for too long, he thought. Once he was in, Raymond could move about as much as he – and Robert – liked.

Raymond even got up twice during dinner. Once to shuffle through Robert's few books and once to admire the view from the window. Kiberech came in to clear the table. Raymond said something. Kiberech smiled and shook his hand.

"I said I'd do the washing up," Raymond explained.

"There's no need to. He gets paid to do it."

"It's something to do," Raymond explained.

"Well, in that case I'll have my shower and wait for you on the verandah."

"Another beer?"

"Why not?"

"It's not a good idea to drink as much as you do. Is it the business with your wife?"

"Deep down, I suppose it is," Robert admitted.

Deep down he knew it was. He showered, put on a kikoi and went outside. From the kitchen came the clattering of dishes and snatches of a song of some sort. Robert could only make out a few words. "Hey Ho...silver."

Robert had made the decision. The problem – the huge and insurmountable problem – was how to go about it without hurting Pat. It was all his fault; not hers. Somehow it would have to be done so that she didn't suffer. The awful Mrs Angel would go berserk. He knew that. His name would be mud. So...Stay in Kenya somehow? Would the Ministry of Defence allow that? There must be a vacancy of some sort. Possibly leave the Air Force altogether? He could resign his commission and then stay on in Kenya forever. But Martin and George and Raymond would be at university and then go off to follow their respective careers. Sunday afternoons on the Ainsworth bridge? He didn't think so.

The door behind him opened. "I haven't put anything away because I don't know where he keeps things," said Raymond. "Can I have a beer?"

"Sure. You've earned it."

"I'll have a shower first, I think. Sitting outside like that is a good idea. I wish we could do it in Nairobi. Mind you, the view from up here is rather better than ours."

Remembering the boxes, bikes and bathtub in Raymond's garden, Robert sympathised and agreed.

Once again he was left alone. He would do it – whatever he decided to do – as soon as Raymond had gone back to Nairobi, he decided. It would have to be a letter, not a phone call. He'd explain everything in a letter and then, perhaps, they could meet when he was next on home leave and thrash out the details.

He stood up. By standing on tip-toe, he could see the flickering little orange fires in part of the Rift Valley. The Kenyans were lucky, he thought. From what little he knew of them and had heard from Martin, they didn't seem to suffer from marital problems. Though he supposed they had them, like anyone else.

He sat down again. The boiler was bubbling and the drain was running waste water out into the back of the garden. Cicadas were scissoring away happily. Far away in the distance, someone was hammering something. It was surprising how soothing the sounds of a Kenyan night could be. The place had so many advantages – not the least of which was a man of just twenty years old who, at that moment, was...what was the phrase that man had used? Working himself up. It was a nice turn of phrase that suited Raymond. A lad with hairy legs would have hair on his chest and he'd also have well-developed nipples...

Robert forced himself to stop that train of thought and concentrated on the distant hammering instead. A new table maybe – or a bed for the new wife? No...that wasn't wood. It was more likely to be the sound of someone hammering out a dent in his car. The torrent of waste water turned into a dribble. Robert pulled the vacant chair over towards him and waited.

Not for long. The door opened and Raymond appeared, looking very different with wet hair and dressed in a striped kikoi. The other surprise was his chest. As far as Robert could see, it was completely hairless. He'd been right about Raymond's nipples, though. They were absolutely enormous, each one surrounded by a dark halo the size of a penny.

"I thought I'd better follow the local customs," the young man said. He sat down. "You haven't started your beer yet," he said.

"Oh! That's true. I was thinking."

"About your wife?"

"How did you guess?"

"Tell me."

And so Robert started. Once or twice as he went through the saga of Mrs Angel and of Pat and the baby which was so reluctant to start life, he thought how weird the situation was. Raymond at twenty was really little more than a lad, with no experience whatever of such matters, but he listened attentively, punctuating the narrative occasionally with a question, or 'I see' or 'Mmm'. Once or twice, when he was describing the good times, Robert was near to tears. Raymond sat, unmoving and apparently unmoved, until he had finished.

"The first thing we have to do is to see what's in the post box," he said. "You can't shut things out. That's being like an ostrich. After that, I agree with you. You'll have to sit down and put all that you've just told me into words on paper. You'll get through all this."

"You should have been a priest," said Robert, with a somewhat watery smile.

"How long do you reckon to sit out here tonight?"

"Meaning?"

"I wonder if I have time for a beer, or whether you'd prefer something else."

"Have a beer, if you want."

"What do you want?"

"Silly question."

"Then I suggest we go indoors," said Raymond.

What was so nice about that night – and succeeding nights – was Raymond's maturity. What he had said in the car about "doing anything and letting anything be done" was true. What was more, it was done so happily. With all due respect to Martin and to George, neither of them had much of a sense of humour when it came to sex. On that first night, Raymond laughed when his luxuriant bush got snagged in Robert's teeth, although it must have hurt him. He laughed again when his enormous cock – or most of it – was throbbing in Robert's mouth. Robert let it go to ask why.

"I just thought it was an odd position for a potential priest to be in," Raymond explained. "Don't stop again."

The grunt he gave when he finally came was so similar to a laugh that, for a moment, Robert was fooled, with the result that the new bedding was spotted with spunk. Most of it ended up in Robert's gullet, though.

"And now it's your turn," said Raymond. "If there's one thing that turns me on, it's sucking the cock that's going to fuck me."

"Getting the dimensions, eh?" Robert said, as they changed places.

"I suppose so. I've never really thought about it. I know one thing. I'm really going to enjoy this one."

"I'm not sure I could enjoy your monster," said Robert. It still looked formidable in its shrinking state. Raymond didn't answer and Robert was in no mood to pursue the point.

For some hours after Robert had come, they lay caressing each other's heads and kissing. Raymond's hair was still damp. Robert ran his fingers through it, separating the individual strands as well as he could with Raymond's lips pressed against his and Raymond's tongue exploring his mouth.

They slept for a short time. Robert had no idea of the precise moment he slid into the young man's cleft and penetrated his welcoming opening. A hyena howled and Raymond grunted simultaneously.

"Oh yeah," Robert murmured.

"Oh yeah!" Raymond echoed. "Ah! Ah! Ah! Oh yeah! Go on. Fuck me!"

Robert would have liked to have said something like, "As a matter of fact, that's what I am doing," and Raymond would undoubtedly have laughed, but there are times when jokes and laughter are totally inappropriate and high on that list is the moment when a young man is lying on his front with his hands clutching a pillow, whilst the person on his back threads a steel-hard cock into his nether-eye.

Raymond's balls jiggled against Robert's. They felt cool. So did the cheeks of his arse pressed against Robert's groin. They were much softer than Robert had thought and seemed somehow not to be connected with the rest of Raymond. When Raymond's long back was squirming, his buttocks were still. His legs were spread wide open. Once or twice Robert would give another thrust and feel Raymond's hairy legs against his own.

"Go...a bit...slower. Try to...come...together!" Raymond panted. It was difficult to comply but Robert must have achieved it. Just as he pushed in with all the force he could muster and could feel the burning sensation as his cock swelled and pumped his semen, Raymond gave a sort of lurch, cried out and then lay still. Robert buried his face in the young man's lank hair.

"Beautiful!" he whispered.

"I'll bet you say that to them all," said Raymond with a laugh.

"There haven't been that many."

"We'll have to see about that, won't we?" said Raymond.

Robert had no idea when Raymond left his room. When he woke the next morning, it took some time to realise that Raymond wasn't with him. He showered and, just as he turned the water off, he heard Kiberech and Raymond talking in Swahili. He wrapped his kikoi round his waist and stepped out of the bathroom. Raymond was laying the breakfast table. Kiberech was plying a broom at the corner of the ceiling where a particularly persistent spider had been trying for weeks to construct a web.

"Paw-paw and coffee? Is that all right for you, or would you rather have a cooked breakfast?" Raymond asked.

"Perfect. Anyway, there's no reason why you should take over Kiberech's job."

"I like doing it. I do it at home sometimes."

"Well, I'm sure Kiberech won't object."

"Bwana?" said Kiberech from the corner.

"Nothing," Robert replied. Raymond spoke in Swahili and Kiberech laughed.

"I won't do a Malcolm Marriott on you, but do be a bit careful today, Raymond," said Robert, as he took a final look in the mirror and adjusted the position of his uniform hat.

"Don't worry about me. I will. When will you be back?"

"It's difficult to say. Between four and five, if I'm lucky."

"I'll be here. With luck I'll have a snake to show you."

"There's only one I'm interested in."

Raymond laughed. "You're aiming to have your wicked way with me again, aren't you?" he asked.

"You bet I am."

Work that day was pleasant. Quite apart from the extremely pleasant thoughts of Raymond which intruded from time to time, it was nice to be up and running at last. The British Royal Air Force aircraft which had been waiting down in Nairobi for some days to test the navigational aids did fifteen circuits and aborted landings. The pilot pronounced everything to be "spot-on". Robert left the caravan when the test was finished and stood blinking and watching the aircraft as it climbed away out of sight. The crew would probably be in England the following morning, he thought. It was even possible that Pat would be standing in the garden as it flew over. It would be a shared experience, even though they were thousands of miles apart.

"Close down, sir?" his Kenyan sergeant asked.

"Sure, sergeant. Stand everybody down. I'll hang on till he's right out of range."

"Kwaheri, sir."

"Kwaheri, sergeant. Thanks a lot."

Kwaheri, he thought as he climbed the steps back into the caravan. "Good-bye". It was an easy enough word to say, even in Swahili, but it wasn't so easy to put it into effect. He sat watching the cursor line revolving round the screen. The little blip it picked up on every sweep was an aircraft with seven people on board. Seven people, some of whom might well have marital problems themselves but who now appeared as a tiny spot of light that moved slowly towards the top of the screen. Maybe human problems weren't so significant after all. Thinking that way made him feel better. The thought of Raymond waiting for him was an even greater stimulus to happiness. He found himself humming as he drove home.

He realised that things were not exactly normal when he reached the top of the hill. A plume of smoke hung over the garden, mingling with the wisp he associated with the boiler. He stopped the car just inside the drive and stared round in astonishment. The top and the inside of the hedge had been trimmed – expertly, it seemed. Instead of a tangled mass, the inside was vertical. What had been a tangled mass of tall grass in a corner was now a beautifully rectangular patch of freshly dug soil with not a weed to be seen. Out of reach of the smoke, washing hung on a line.

Kiberech came out of the house. "All okay, bwana?" he said.

"Ndio. Okay. What's this?"

Kiberech laughed. "Bwana Raymond. Much hard work."

"So I see," said Robert. He drove the car forward a few feet into the lean-to and climbed out.

"Bwana Raymond is in house," said Kiberech and laughed again.

The reason for the laughter was apparent as soon as Robert stepped in. Raymond was wearing just his underpants. One couldn't have had a better welcome, thought Robert, once again feasting his eyes on the young man's enormous legs.

"My God! You're keen," he said.

Raymond laughed. "You could say that," he said. "I am, but the truth of the matter is that Kiberech confiscated my shirt and shorts."

"What on earth for?"

"Just to wash them. I got them a bit grubby. They'll be dry soon. I've been doing a bit of gardening."

"So I see. It's amazing. How did you manage to do the hedge?"

"I borrowed a step-ladder from the man up the road and Kiberech had a panga."

"A what?"

"A machete, I suppose you'd say. A bloke at school taught me how to use one. If it's sharp, it's much better for hedge-cutting than anything else."

"So you haven't had time for snake-catching today?"

"Oh yes. It was that that led me to cutting the hedge as a matter of fact. I got sixteen green snakes out of that hedge."

"My God! Are they dangerous?"

"Green snakes? Philothamnus irregularis. No. Not at all. They're tiny little things. I'll show you later when I've got some clothes on."

"Hmm. If Kiberech wasn't around, there's another I'd rather see. That would require the opposite."

"It's all yours whenever you want. You know that, but hadn't you better go up and get the post first?"

"Oh, it can wait till tomorrow."

"That way, tomorrow never comes. Go and get it. It's not far."

At that moment Kiberech came in again to ask when they wanted dinner.

"Early," Robert answered. "I suppose you're right," he added to Raymond. "Back in a few minutes."

It was more than a few minutes. His post box was crammed tight with accumulated mail. He sat in the car to go through it. There were two from his parents, the usual Air Force "bumf" and a mass of leaflets advertising everything from car accessories to carpets. There was one addressed in childish scrawl to Kiberech c/o "Airforce Rob" – one long official-looking envelope and two from Pat. He read the letters from his parents in the car. Everything was well. The dog had been ill, but was all right now. Two pages of one letter and one page of the next were full of news of people he didn't know. It was the end of the second letter which worried him. "We both hope you will be able to work something out. We are both worried about you. Much love, Mum." Obviously they had been in touch with Pat or she had seen them, he thought. He put all the mail on the passenger seat and drove back down the hill.

Raymond, still in his underpants, was sitting on the low wall of the verandah. "Anything interesting?" he asked.

"I'll tell you when I've read them. How about a beer?"

"What a good idea. I'll get them."

Robert sat down. They had to be read sooner or later, he thought. Bracing himself, he opened the large brown envelope first. Raymond came out, placed an opened bottle and a glass on the table and sat down to sip his beer.

"Solicitors?" said Robert, as he withdrew the contents. "What the hell do they want?"

He had to read it twice before it sunk in.

"Bad news or good news?" Raymond asked.

"It's...it's Pat. She wants a divorce."

"Oh dear. That could be expensive. Mum is my dad's second wife and he's still having to pay the first one."

"No, no. She doesn't want anything. 'Amicable arrangement', it says here."

"And is that good news or bad news?"

"I don't know. It's a shock."

"The good news is that you can lead your own life again, the life you were intended to lead. The bad news is that you're scared stiff of a lonely old age, is that it?"

"That's it exactly."

"Well, I should stop worrying about the latter. You've got good looks and a smashing personality. You'll never be lonely."

"I wonder. Well, I suppose I'd better read what Pat's got to say. Which is the first one now? Ah! This one."

Once again, Robert sat in silence. It felt as if the words were jumping off the paper, hitting him one by one. "Tom" – "a dentist" – "known him for years" – "three small children".

The second letter made him feel even worse. Pat well understood why he hadn't replied to her first letter. She knew how bitterly upset it must have made him. 'Please, my darling Robert, try to understand how I feel,' she wrote. 'It was all my mistake and it is all my fault. I know that.'

"No hard feelings?" Raymond asked, when Robert had put them both down.

"None at all."

"So what will you do?"

"Write back and say I agree, I suppose."

"Very sensible. Incidentally, dinner will be ready soon. Are you going to have your shower?"

"I suppose I'd better. What about you?"

"I've had mine. It seemed the most sensible thing to do in the circumstances. I wish I'd thought to pack a spare pair of shorts and a shirt."

Robert stood up. "I'll read the rest after dinner," he said.

"Mmm. There might just be time to do that. I've already told Kiberech that I'll do the washing up," said Raymond.

"There's no need to, Raymond."

"We don't want him hanging around, do we?" Raymond smiled. "Go and have your shower," he said.

Chapter Ten

They sat out on the verandah. Whilst Kiberech busied himself laying the table and singing a song in Swahili, Robert went through
the various official letters, reading each one by the light of a small
gas lamp.

"What are they actually?" Raymond asked.

"These? These are what is known as 'bumf'. They get sent out
to people like me who don't have the privilege of reading notice-
boards. I can thus tell you that so many people are losing their
identity cards that it is now to be regarded as a 'prevalent offence'.
The Air Training Corps is looking for officers to give up their spare
time to instruct kids in aircraft recognition. The station barber's
shop at my parent station – thousands of miles away – will be
closed on Wednesdays in future. Fascinating stuff."

"Can I look at some?"

"Good heavens! This stuff is marked 'Restricted'. It would be a
severe breach of security. Here, you can have the lot with my com-
pliments."

Raymond was still reading when Kiberech sounded the dinner
bell. When the meal was over, Kiberech said, "Bwana Raymond say
I can go home, bwana. This okay?"

"If bwana Raymond says so, of course," Robert answered.
Kiberech smiled and put a hand on Raymond's shoulder and said

something in Swahili before leaving.

"He says you're a good boss," said Raymond. He stood up and began to collect up the empty plates. Robert helped. "He's done all the pots and pans," said Raymond. "Now then, is there an apron? I don't want to get these clothes mucky again."

There was one hanging behind the door. Robert reached for it. "You still could get splashed. Wouldn't it be a good idea to take your shirt and shorts off?" he said, grinning.

"What a thoughtful host you are," Raymond replied with an even wider grin. "Back in a minute."

"I'll join you. I don't want to get dirty either," said Robert.

"I rather think we're both going to get dirty," said Raymond. He went into the spare room. Robert went into his. Both emerged almost simultaneously – both naked and, predictably, with cocks already risen.

Back in the kitchen, Raymond filled the sink and put the first plates in. "I'll wash. You wipe," he said, and then, "Actually, the apron might be an idea, if it doesn't hamper your plans."

"Not in the least." Robert put it over the young man's head and tied the strings behind him.

"Thanks. Here goes."

The first plate went on to the draining board – and stayed there, dripping for some moments. The wiper-up was occupied. Both hands were around Raymond's waist, under the apron, and they soon found what they were feeling for.

"Gorgeous!" Robert whispered. His fingers found Raymond's balls. Raymond took his hands out of the water, dried them on the apron and put them behind him. He found Robert's waist and drew the man in towards him. Then, staring out of the window, he fumbled for a few minutes, found Robert's cock and slowly slid the foreskin backwards and forwards. Robert did the same to him.

"Mmm. That feels nice," said Raymond. Robert didn't know which of their respective tools he was referring to. Not that it mattered. He speeded up slightly. Disappointingly, Raymond didn't, but instead took his hands away and placed them on the edge of the sink.

"Mmm. I've been waiting for this all day," he said.

"When you weren't digging or snake-hunting?"

"You can think of one thing whilst you're doing the other," said Raymond. "Oh God! That feels so good. Go a bit slower. Make it last. Oh, yeah!"

Robert took a step forward. His cock rubbed against Raymond's buttock and then, as if it had a mind of its own, found the cleft. He pressed forward and kissed the back of Raymond's neck.

"Going to fuck me?" Raymond gasped.

"In a kitchen? What about...?"

"How come you're so ignorant?" said Raymond. "Got any groundnut oil?"

"I think so. I remember buying some."

"That's the best. Frying oil is okay, and arachis oil. Soap works. So does washing up liquid. One of the best fucks I ever had was on mayonnaise. I must tell you about that one day. Found it?"

"Yes. Here," said Robert as he took the bottle from the cupboard.

He undid the knot in the apron cord with trembling fingers. Raymond put his feet apart and leaned over the sink. "Use a fair bit," he said. Robert poured the oil into the palm of his left hand and rubbed two right-hand fingers in the pool.

"Stay still now," he said and put his oily left hand round Raymond's waist to grasp the young man's penis again.

"I'm not going anywhere. Mmm. That feels nice."

"This will feel even better," said Robert, as an oily finger slid between Raymond's arse-cheeks, made contact with the tightly pursed muscle and pushed. Raymond gave a slight yelp as the muscle yielded but, as the finger began to progress inside him, the exclamation became more drawn out; a sound distinctly reminiscent of a pigeon's cooing.

"Oh yeah!" Raymond exclaimed. Another finger came out to join its colleague. Both waited patiently for a signal to enter further. "Mmm. Yeah!" Raymond gasped. The ring slackened and in they went, to the accompaniment of a long groan from Raymond who grasped the taps to support himself. Robert's left hand still held the young man's cock, now pressed uncomfortably against the edge of the sink.

"Do it. Do it!" Raymond panted - and Robert felt something other than groundnut oil on the palm of his hand.

The fingers came out with a slight plop. Robert didn't wait. Another step forward and a flinch from Raymond, as his cock was squeezed against stainless steel.

It was a fuck like no other. Raymond was entirely different from Martin. There were no ecstatic yells, no writhing around – but Raymond's face, reflected in the window, was enough to show that he was enjoying it. His eyes were closed and the tip of his tongue had flopped out of the corner of his mouth. With both hands free, Robert managed to liberate Raymond's cock. It sprang back and slapped against his belly. That seemed to make it possible for Raymond to tighten his arse-cheeks even more than if he were on a bed. Each contraction drove him further in. Their balls touched. Robert felt Raymond's cool buttocks against his groin. He pushed hard. Raymond groaned. Robert pushed again. His panting breath stirred the young man's long hair.

Groundnut oil, squeezed out by his intruding cock, made the slap of his flesh against Raymond's seem even louder, until even that pleasant sound was drowned by Raymond's loud gasps.

An all-too-familiar ache developed in Robert's groin. It was going to be any minute now, he thought. Why, oh why couldn't the whole of life be one long fuck? But then...it might be. It wasn't the words of Pat's letter that he envisaged at that moment. It was an image of the paper itself: the thin "onion skin" airmail paper that she always used. Onion skin – skin – Raymond's skin –

soft, smooth, cool...Robert ran his fingers up and down Raymond's pulsing cock. And silky, Robert thought – and at that moment he came. At first he thought it was awareness of that which caused Raymond to sigh loudly. The sticky feel in his fingers soon disabused him of that idea.

"Aaah!" Raymond sighed again and then, after a few seconds during which he managed to get his breath back, he said, "We must do it that way again some time."

Worming his cock out of an arse was usually an anti-climax. On this occasion, it didn't seem so bad somehow. Robert didn't know why.

"Look what you've made me do," said Raymond when he was out.

"What?"

"I've shot into the washing up. Oh well, away with the water and I'll have to do them again."

The washing up took longer than it might have done, but neither of them objected. Raymond seemed to radiate happiness and Robert probably had the same effect on Raymond, who even began to sing as he scrubbed the last few plates.

Finally, they were finished. Raymond lifted the apron over his head and hung it behind the door. "Verandah time?" he asked.

"Why not?"

"There seems no point in putting anything on," said Raymond. "Nobody can see us – even though the hedge is a bit thinner than it was."

They took a beer each from the fridge and Robert followed what must surely have been the most perfect and powerful young arse in all Kenya out on to the verandah. It was a sort of haven, he thought. The next few days were going to be difficult, to say the least, but, when the day was over, there would always be Raymond's arse to welcome him; to let him wrap his cock in its warm soft tissues – almost as if it wanted to engulf all of him and hold him tightly, secure against everything the world might throw at him.

"When are you going to write to your wife?" Raymond asked. It was as if he could read Robert's thoughts. Robert opened his bottle and poured the beer.

"Not tonight. Tomorrow maybe," he said. The beer tasted wonderfully cool.

"Tomorrow definitely," said Raymond. "She must be in a hell of a state. I mean, her happiness is at stake. She'll want to hear from you. Couldn't you call her now?"

"I'd rather not. Her mother would answer the phone and she is one woman I do not want to talk to."

"A dragon?"

"A fire-breathing one at that," said Robert.

"Mum's mum is the same, apparently. She treats me okay, but she's the reason why Dad came out here. He would have been happy to stay at Durham all his life. He says the work's not much different here. In England it was world wars and politics. Out here, it's civil wars and politics."

"What does your dad do?"

"You don't know? He's a professor of modern history. He's actually quite famous. He'll be even more so when he retires and we go back to England to live."

"Why's that?"

"Breathe not a word, lest the Philistines hear. Out here, you see, he has to toe the party line. Mustn't let the Kenyans know their politicians are corrupt and letting the country slide down fast while they feather their own nests. Dad's working on the authentic history of what happened here this century and it'll be published in England. He reckons it might even spark off the revolution they need to purge the country. However, that, oh wise one who screws better than anyone I've ever known, is between ourselves."

"Sure." Robert sat silently in a glow of contentment. "...who screws better than anyone I've ever known..." That was nice of him. He was a really nice person. Martin was nice, of course, and George was okay, but Raymond...

"Mind if I look at your RAF bumf again?"

"Sure. Go ahead. It's not very interesting."

Robert had just a glimpse of the young man's generously proportioned tool and the thick mat of hair round it before it was covered by a sheaf of papers. A man couldn't be much more lucky, he thought. Raymond would be with him for some days more. Maybe he would come up to Kampi-ya-Moto more often. In fact... if he could persuade the Hansons to have the other two in the summer holiday, Raymond could stay with him. Martin would be invited to the house, of course. He couldn't be left out. In fact, maybe Raymond and Martin could get together and he could watch. That would be fun. Raymond's cock was bigger than his. Considerably bigger. He looked down again but it was still covered up. Martin would enjoy it. That was for sure. Of course it would be even better to watch George on the receiving end. A cock like Raymond's would work like magic. Amazingly, Robert's cock twitched into life at the thought. He grabbed the rest of the letters. The one from "Simmonds, Simon & Simmonds, Solicitors at Law and Notaries Public" was big enough to cover it and the contents sufficient to quieten his rising flesh.

"Have you got a university degree?" Raymond asked suddenly.

"Yes."

"What in?"

"Physics, actually."

"What branch of the Air Force are you in?"

"Ops. Operations. I'm only in this job because I worked in a civil engineering firm before I went to university."

"Then you're the ideal man."

"Now what have you in mind?"

"It's here. 'Officers holding university degrees, preferably in the sciences...'"

"Don't tell me. '...are commanded to attend some dinner or lecture because they can't find enough volunteers.' Fat chance, thank God. I'm out of all that nonsense."

"No. They're short of education officers. You can...what's the word? Ah, here it is. You can request to be re-mustered. You have to go to university again for three years to get an education degree. How about it?"

"Let me have a look."

Raymond passed over the paper.

"I don't know. It would mean leaving here," he said.

"So? So am I. So is Martin. So is George. How about starting university at the same time?"

"With the three of you?"

"I'm not going to the same one as they are. I'm not pressing you or anything, but two live more cheaply than one and you won't have a wife to worry about."

"What's the last date? Ah here. Next month. I could make that."

"So that's another letter that has got to be done tomorrow. What do you think?"

"I think you've solved a problem. That's what I think. Another beer?"

"Might as well. I'm not ready for another session yet," said Raymond.

For the rest of that evening they made plans. Some were practical. Others not so, but Robert let Raymond carry on. They would find a flat. It would have to have two bedrooms for the sake of respectability. Each would be able to invite friends by prior arrangement with the other. Raymond thought his music centre was slightly better than Robert's, so his could go in the lounge and Robert could keep his in his room. As for the inevitable snakes, they could be housed in a cupboard somewhere until Raymond sold them off.

"Talking of cupboards, I suppose one of things I ought to do is to turn out Pat's stuff and pack it off to her," said Robert.

"No, you won't. That would be stupid," said Raymond.

"Don't tell me you're into drag! I doubt if any of Pat's things would fit you."

"Of course not, but the very last thing you want to do out here is let people know you're divorcing. It would be social death. It comes just one point on the scale above being queer. Bloody hell! Divorced and gay? They'd drum you out and dance on your grave."

"George said something of that sort when he was here."

"He was right. Outside of the family, no one but you knows about Mum and Dad. It's something you never talk about. Being gay is the same. You can screw and suck as much as you like, but afterwards you keep your mouth shut. The Ainsworth Bridge mob are different. They're just visitors."

"I suppose it is just possible that George is having it off with someone after all. Maybe this Peter Hardwick," said Robert. The twitch at his groin returned.

"Possible – or maybe Martin is having it off with Peter Hardwick. He'd be more likely to oblige."

"Oh no! Not Martin. I'm sure of that," said Robert. The thought came as a shock.

"Isn't this bloke a pilot?""

"That's right."

"A flight in a plane? The sort of thing everybody dreams about but can't afford. It's not a long step from 'This is the joystick. How about if I feel yours?' I'll bet he does. Good luck to him."

"Not Martin," Robert repeated.

"Please yourself. Anyway, returning to our central theme, I've put down for Durham because it's Dad's old place and we've got friends there. How does that suit you?"

"Then Durham it shall be. Now, how about returning to another central theme?"

Raymond chuckled and put the papers on the table. "This one?" he asked, fingering his cock.

"You've got it in one – or rather, two," said Robert. "Come on."

During the following days, he thought a lot about sharing a flat with Raymond in Durham. The more Robert pondered it, the more practical it seemed. He had been happy with George and Martin for company. Being with Raymond was completely different, but he wondered several times if his anxiety about Pat had cast some sort of cloud over his relationship with the other two. Now he had written to Pat and to the solicitors and that particular cloud had been dispersed. There was still a minor one, but it wasn't so black and ominous. The military attaché at the British High Commission was far from happy to receive his application but, as he admitted, there was nothing he could do, save pass it on to Ministry of Defence.

Raymond was the most active person Robert had ever met. He spent the days digging the garden and catching snakes and, when they'd had dinner, he still had plenty of energy for other things. The pile of writhing sacks at the back of the house grew. Fortunately, Raymond explained that it wasn't necessary to feed the collection: they went into a state of torpor after their initial struggles to be free. Kiberech kept well away from them – so Raymond was forced to tend to the boiler. That was yet another job he took on quite happily. Robert got used to driving home to find Raymond, stripped to the waist and with soot stains all over his torso, singing happily to himself as he fed logs into the furnace. Once or twice, if Kiberech had to go into the village to get something, they showered together. There wasn't a much better homecoming than to stand in a shower with a young man of

Raymond's muscular build and generous proportions. On one occasion, Raymond came and they just had time to wipe the spunk from the plastic shower curtains before Kiberech returned.

Dinner, washing up, a long talk on the verandah and then bed. It was a perfect routine and Raymond was a perfect partner. He groaned with delight when Robert's cock was inside him and, even after he had shot his load and lay there sweating and panting, he was more than happy for Robert to hug him. The feel of the young man's warm and powerful body in his arms sent Robert into raptures of new delight. Then, after they had both dozed off and woken up again, he'd take Raymond's cock – beginning again to show sign of life – into his mouth and suck on it greedily until the juice flowed again.

In the morning when Kiberech came in, they were in their respective beds. In Swahili, Raymond explained to Kiberech that the bwana's wife had been taken ill in England and would not be returning for some time. No…not terribly ill…just ill. No, she wasn't in the hospital, but at home. She would be delighted to receive Kiberech's best wishes. The little packet of what looked and smelt suspiciously like dried animal dung which Kiberech brought in the next day and which he said was guaranteed to cure anything was duly packed into a padded envelope and addressed in his presence, but once he got to the air-strip Robert threw it surreptitiously away the following morning.

They were on the verandah on Friday evening when the telephone rang. It was Martin. He wanted to know if Robert would be coming into Nairobi on Saturday.

"Of course. I'm bringing Raymond back."

"How is he?"

"Oh, fine."

"Can I speak to him?"

"Just a second." Raymond turned round and shook his head vigorously. "He's out at the moment, Martin. Catching snakes."

"Funny time to catch snakes."

"This is a special sort of snake. A night snake, he said it was. Something nocturnalis."

"Then it could be poisonous. Has he caught any others?"

"Enough to stock a zoo, I should think. We've got horned vipers, green and black mambas, two cobras, green snakes, yellow snakes. You name it – he's got it."

"What about you? Have you caught a snake – notably one he carries with him all the time?"

"Martin! Why go after an ordinary specimen already in hand when you know of a much better one?"

"Oh, I don't know about that. It's certainly bigger. He'll get it out for you if you ask him. Tell him I'll fist him if he's back at school next week."

"I will. And how about you? Did you enjoy the weekend with Mr Hardwick?"

"It was great!"

"You're not thinking of going there this coming weekend, I hope."

"Not me. George is. Peter seems to like him a lot. They get on really well."

"Oh, good."

"Give my regards to Raymond when he gets back."

"I will."

"And tell him what I said about next week."

"Sure." Robert put down the receiver.

"'Why go after an ordinary specimen!' Cheeky sod," said Raymond. "I guess I know what you were talking about."

"I apologise. It is far from ordinary." Robert leaned over Raymond's chair and took it between his forefinger and thumb. "He says if you're back at school next week, he'll fist you – though I doubt if you'll have the energy after a week with me."

"Mmm. It might be as well if this 'snake' goes into torpor. I'll have to see. Don't stop. That was beginning to get me going. What was that about the weekend with the Hardwick man?"

"Oh, they had a good time. George's going back there this weekend. Martin isn't."

"Hmm. Although they'll be in different places, they're both going to get fucked. Maybe you and Hardwick will be in them at the same time. That would be a laugh."

"From what you say and from what I know of him, George will come back as pure as a mountain spring."

"Don't you believe it. Class makes all the difference to George. Class and money. He'll have Hardwick's hard wick in his arse within minutes of getting up there. Mmm. That's a really nice feeling. Keep doing that for a few minutes and then suck it."

"I don't want to put you off something later."

"Don't worry. You won't."

In fact Raymond was better that night than ever before. So was Robert. Robert knew the reason for his own surprising lust. It was amusing to find out afterwards that the same thoughts had been occupying Raymond's mind.

"Just think. George's been had at last," said Raymond when they were lying together wrapped in each other's arms. "It's taken long enough, but he's lost his cherry at last."

"As a matter of fact I was thinking just the same thing," Robert whispered.

"I know. You called me George."

"Did I?"

"You did. I don't blame you. Do you reckon he let Martin watch?"

"Maybe Peter Hardwick hasn't done anything yet. Maybe he's waiting for this weekend when George is up there on his own."

Raymond didn't reply to that one for some time. He couldn't. His tongue was deep in Robert's mouth. Finally he rolled off again.

"Ha! That was good. What was that you were saying?"

"I said maybe he hasn't done anything yet. Maybe he's going to wait for this weekend when George is there by himself."

"Don't step on my dreams. No. He got Martin to watch. I wish it was me. Just think. George with a cock in him at last. I bet he loved it. Do you reckon you can ask Martin when you see him?"

"I'll try. We're couple of nosy devils."

"We're a couple of randy devils. Noses don't come into it."

"I'm going to miss you after Saturday," said Robert, sliding his fingers down Raymond's sweaty front.

"Not so much as I'm going to miss you – or this," said Raymond.

Despite the presence of 28 snakes in the boot of the car, the journey to Nairobi on the following morning was uneventful. Raymond had special stickers – "Live Snakes" – in English and Swahili which he fixed to the car and which drew attention every time they stopped or slowed down.

"Martin will probably be at the roundabout waiting for us. He usually is," said Robert. "If he isn't, I'll drop you off first and then come back for him."

They both spotted him simultaneously. He was standing on the edge of the road, shading his eyes from the sun and peering along the road. Robert pulled up. "Welcome to the snake park," he said as Martin opened the car door. "Don't worry. They're all in sacks in the boot."

"Just as well," said Martin. "Did you have a good time?"

"Brilliant," said Raymond. Robert drove deliberately slowly and listened to their conversation. Snakes, snakes, snakes. Raymond described exactly how he'd caught them all.

"Ugh! I'm glad I wasn't there," said Martin.

"And what about your weekend with Peter Hardwick? Tell us all about that," said Robert.

"Nothing much to tell, actually. Everything's going well for…"

"For what?" Raymond asked.

"Oh, nothing." By that time, Robert had turned into Raymond's road. There was no sign of his father. They unloaded the car outside the house, leaving Raymond to carry in his sacks whilst Robert untied the "catching instrument" from the roof rack and Martin took care of the rucksack.

"Thanks a lot. It was great!" said Raymond and shook hands with a mischievous smile.

"It certainly was," said Robert. "Is your mother back? It doesn't look like it."

"Probably not. Dad will be in though. Will you be in Plum's tonight?"

"Well...er...I suppose so."

"I might see you there, then. Cheers and thanks again."

He stood waving on the side of the road. "Sorry about the Plum's business, Martin," said Robert. "He went there last weekend."

"No matter. He's all right. Only don't mention the gold cup. Peter says the fewer people who know about it, the better."

Robert couldn't remember if he had mentioned it or not. Not that it mattered, he thought. It might, if it really existed.

They did the shopping and drove back to Martin's place. Catherine, of course, was there. She seemed worse that weekend than ever before. Robert began to think of her as a spider, wrapping Martin in sticky threads to bind him tightly to the centre of her web.

"He really is far too immature for university," she said. Martin, at that time was in the garden, but she carried on when he came in again. "It would be so much better for him to get a job here," said Catherine.

Martin said it would be a dead end. "Daddy didn't go to university and he's happy enough. Just because George is going. It's so silly. Mind you, I don't think he's mature enough either, but that's not my problem. Living in a country you hardly know for three years..."

"As a matter of fact, I think I might be in England myself then," said Robert. "I could keep an eye on him."

"Dear man. You've got your wife to think about, and anyway you might be miles and miles away."

Some instinct told Robert to say no more. Malcolm returned from the golf club. They had tea.

"Now you'll have to excuse us. It takes ages to get ready." She turned to Malcolm. "I tried on that dress, but it was a bit too tight. It'll have to be the other one," she said. Malcolm continued to nibble his cucumber sandwich.

"Mum and Dad are going to the golf club dinner and dance," said Martin, with what might have been a wink.

"Oh yes?"

"I used to look forward to these things at one time," said Catherine. "Fortunately not many of them go which is hardly surprising. They're more used to dancing to drums, waving their silly spears."

"Robert and I are going to Plum's," said Martin.

"Oh, must you, darling? I don't like the thought of leaving Ibrahim alone in the house."

"Robert's already arranged for us to meet Raymond there," said Martin. "So we have to go, but we won't be late back."

"Nice lad, that Raymond," Malcolm commented.

"Yes, but tonight of all nights," said Catherine. "I don't often go out. Couldn't you ring Raymond and put it off, darling?"

"That would seem to be the best idea," said Robert – for reasons that had nothing to do with the security of the house.

"No. I think we ought to go," Martin said.

"So do I," said Malcolm suddenly. It was the first time Robert had ever heard him contradict Catherine. "You can't expect young people to stay at home on a Saturday night," he continued. "He'll be away next year, so you'll have to get used to leaving Ibrahim in the house."

"We'll cross that particular bridge when we come to it. I'll talk to you later about it," said Catherine, very firmly indeed.

"Do you think I'm doing the right thing?" Martin asked when they were on Plum's terrace.

"Hunting for the cup?" Martin had prattled about that throughout the journey.

"No, no. Keep your voice down. About going to university."

"Of course you are." Robert lowered his voice and continued. "I'm not so sure about this treasure hunt though, Martin. Finding treasure is all right in books, but in real life the chances are pretty slim and it seems to be the general opinion that the cup doesn't exist any more."

"But it does!" said Martin. "It does. I think so, George thinks so and Peter thinks so. Peter's done some research on Colonel von Meinerherzhagen already."

"And found out...?"

"Well, very little actually."

"Precisely. Look, Martin. I'm very fond of you. You know that, don't you?"

"I suppose I do."

"Well, come down to earth. Concentrate on the things that matter, like going to university."

"But finding the cup would make so much difference. Can't you see that? Oh. Change the subject. That's Raymond's bike."

He must have had extraordinary hearing. It was at least five minutes before Raymond appeared on the terrace.

"Sorry I'm late. I took the snakes down to the snake park," he said, placing his crash helmet on a vacant chair.

"On a motorbike?" said Robert, envisaging the pile of sacks.

"No. Dad let me borrow the car. What are you having? I'm flush at the moment."

Martin's short-sighted waiter friend took their order.

"So. How did you like Kampi-ya-Moto?" Martin asked.

"It was great. More to the point, how did you like – Mombasa, wasn't it?"

"Near there – not in the town."

"Well, tell us all about it, then."

What should have been a pleasant evening turned out to be extremely frustrating. Not in the sexual sense. In fact, as Robert sat there listening to them, he glanced from side to side occasionally and smiled. He wondered how the staid citizens of Nairobi who were sitting out on the terrace would react if they knew that both of his young companions had been well and truly fucked.

The frustration emanated from Martin, who was obviously bursting with enthusiasm for his treasure hunt but keeping it bottled up. If the poor lad only knew it, almost every sentence he uttered stoked the fires of Raymond's suspicion. Robert wanted to say, "Look, if you must go on believing this fairy story about hidden treasure, tell Raymond all about it." He didn't, of course.

"It beats me why you went down there at all if, as you say, he's George's friend," said Raymond, with a slight stress on the word "friend".

"Oh, he wanted us both to go for that weekend. George is there by himself this time."

"By himself? Hasn't this Hardwick man got a family or servants or anything?"

"He's got servants, but he gives them the weekends off to dig their shambas. He likes cooking. He's very good at it too."

"Did you do any fishing? I imagine a man like that would have a boat."

"Well, no. We didn't go out at all. There was so much to do, see."

"Washing up, I suppose? I did it up at Robert's place."

"Well, no. Oh look – see that lady over there, Robert? The one with the red straw hat?"

"What about her?"

"She's Dad's secretary. Excuse me. I'd better go over and say 'Hello' to her."

"There was so much to do!" said Raymond when he had gone. "I'll bet there was."

"You're wrong, Raymond. I'm sure you are," said Robert.

"I'll bet all the money I made with the snakes today that I'm not. It's as plain as a pikestaff. The guy fancies George, for which neither of us can blame him. He knows that George's folks are a bit chary, so he invites Martin as well. Let's face it, you wouldn't have got either of them up at your place alone for the first time. Both sets of parents would have smelt a rat."

"Yes. I give you that," Robert replied, thinking of Catherine Marriott.

"So it's 'Come up to my place but do bring a friend,' and off they go. The chances are that he had it off with Martin, just so he can tell George, 'Your mate likes it. Don't knock something you haven't tried.' Why, at this very moment he's probably giving George the fucking of his life."

It was such a perspicacious summary of Robert's own motives that he felt himself blushing. To his great relief, Martin returned. "Sorry about that," he said. "Tell me more about the snakes, Ray."

Robert ordered more drinks and sat there listening with increasing horror. Harmless snakes in his hedge were not a great worry. Cobras in his compost heap were another matter. Raymond had found two.

"Two? In my garden?"

"Oh, they're just about everywhere," said Raymond airily. "Actually, there are loads of them in the Mombasa area."

"We never saw any," said Martin.

"That's hardly surprising if you didn't go out. Actually, I wouldn't mind meeting this Mr Peter Hardwick. Does he fly into Nairobi often?"

"Every week, I think, but I don't think he'd want you up there. I mean... he's got a lot on his plate."

"I'm sure he has and I wouldn't want to gate-crash on your special friend. I could give him some sacks and he could put the word out among the locals that I pay for snakes and fly them to Nairobi when he comes. Ask him."

"You could ask him yourself. He's coming up next Saturday afternoon with George to collect a camera he's ordered."

"Flying all that way to pick up a camera?"

"Oh, it's a special sort of camera. Excuse me. I need a pee."

"'Special sort of camera.' I'll bet it is. It'll be one of those super Polaroid jobs so he doesn't have to send the films in to be developed," said Raymond. "I'll bet he'll get more from shots of George in the nude than I make from snakes."

"I'm sure you're wrong," said Robert – but he was beginning to wonder.

Chapter Eleven

The bedroom was completely dark and Martin, sweaty and still breathing heavily, was wrapped in Robert's arms. Robert had no idea of the time. Catherine and Malcolm still hadn't returned, which had made a great difference to their performance that evening. It was quite possible that Ibrahim in his little shack in the garden had heard them but that didn't matter – Ibrahim had to wash the sheets and must have known anyway.

"What sort of camera is Peter Hardwick buying?" Robert asked.

"One for aerial photography," said Martin. "He's going to fly over the Hansons' land and photograph every inch of it."

"Oh. Raymond thought it might be to take photographs of George."

"Why would he want to do that? George's not that good looking. They used to call him frog-face when he was a kid."

"He has certain other attributes. You said yourself that he's got a nice cock."

"That's true. I don't think I'd want to buy a photo of it, though."

"Because you have access to the real thing. Does Peter, do you think?"

"Course not. Peter's not like that!"

"But how do you know? Raymond has a theory."

"Raymond's got theories about everything. What did he say?"

Robert waited for a few seconds to get his breath back and then related what Raymond had said.

"He never tried anything on me," said Martin.

"He wouldn't. He wanted George to come back and he would have found out that George has got a bit of a thing about going as far as I did."

"I suppose it's possible. Anyway, it's nothing to do with us, and Peter's as keen as mustard on finding the cup."

"Or he's pretending to be, just to get George up there most weekends. You're both in the hunt together. Why is George the only person who gets invited?"

"I said I couldn't go."

"Why? Your mother again?"

Martin put his hands on Robert's ears and kissed him. "Because I look forward to your weekends here so much," he said. Understandably, neither of them spoke again for some considerable time. Finally, they had to break apart – if only to breathe.

"Can I ask you something?" said Martin.

"Sure."

"You might think it's dirty. You can always say 'No'."

"What is it?"

"Can you lick my arse? It's called 'rimming'. It's supposed to be a great feeling."

"Who told you that?"

"George, actually. He read about it in a book."

Or says he did, Robert thought as he gently turned Martin on to his front and placed his hands on Martin's soft bum. Martin spread his legs. The insides of his arse-cheeks felt even softer against Robert's bristly cheeks. It would have been better for Martin, he thought, if I had shaved before doing this. The tip of his tongue touched the spot. It would also have been better to have done it before fucking or to have bought a tasteless lubricating gel. Robert had never done it before. He licked along the hard skin between Martin's balls and the spot where wiry hairs were.

"It's quite nice," said Martin in a conversational tone. "Oh shit! Stop a minute. Mum and Dad are back."

Once again, Robert was amazed at the young man's hearing. He hadn't heard a thing and didn't until the car door slammed. The front door opened and Catherine's voice drifted up the stairs.

"... such charming people. I'd invite them to dinner one night, if I thought Ibrahim could be trusted to cook something without burning it. Of course, up there they'd have the pick of domestic staff. I thought Lady Norris was particularly pleasant tonight, didn't you darling?"

Malcolm's reply was inaudible – probably even to Martin – not that it made any difference.

"You don't want a drink or coffee, do you?" asked Catherine. "I thought not. You had far too much again. We both did, I suppose. Did you hear what Mrs Hill said about her? Well, she has such a thing about their lack of hygiene, for which she can't be blamed, that she soaks all her vegetables in bleach before cooking them. Mrs Hill says everything tastes like it's come out of their swimming pool!" Catherine giggled and, still chuckling, she and Malcolm began a rather unsteady ascent of the staircase.

"Pissed out of their minds," Martin whispered. Robert raised his head. The footsteps stopped outside the door.

"Fasht... fast asleep," said Catherine.

"So I should think. It's two o'clock in the morning. Come on. Let's get to bed," said Malcolm.

"I suppose he'll be up and about at this time of night next year. Going out dancing and I don't know what else. It's the drugs I worry about. Boys are so innocent and impressionable at that age..."

"We've dealt with that. He's going to university in England. Full stop. End of the matter. Now come to bed, for God's sake."

"That's one good thing," Martin whispered. "Now for another.

You know, I think it might be better if I were to lie on my back. Get off for a minute. Look, like this. You can get at it easier." He lay on his back, put his hands under his knees and lifted his legs. "Try that," he said.

It was infinitely better – for both of them, it seemed. Even if your face is buried deep between somebody's thighs, it's impossible to ignore a cock which, a few minutes before, was hanging damp and limp but which now had swollen and grown in a matter of seconds. Impossible, too, to overlook Martin's balls jiggling in time to his ecstatic squirms. Truth be told, Robert would have much preferred to exercise his tongue further up but every time he stopped, Martin gave an impatient wriggle – once even letting go of his legs to grab Robert's head and force it further in. Twice Robert had to stop to try to quieten his loud groans.

He never really knew if his tongue actually went in. It felt as if it had. There was a moment when something pressed hard against his tongue. Martin sighed very loudly and Robert felt something warm running down his cheek. He stopped and extricated his head from the young man's clamping thighs. Spunk was cascading out of Martin's cock and running down the shaft. Martin let go of his knees and lay flat on his back with his legs spread out.

"That was great! Really great!" he gasped. Robert wiped his mouth with the back of his hand.

"Looks like it got to you too," said Martin, reaching over to hold his cock. "You could say that," Robert admitted.

"Then I'd better do something about it for you, hadn't I?" – and the young man who had once described sucking a cock as "gross" bent over to engulf Robert's. It was just as well that he wasn't able to read Robert's thoughts at that point. He was quite sure that the book George had mentioned was as imaginary as the gold cup. Robert stared down at Martin's head rising and falling and watched the deep dimples in the young man's cheeks fill and form again as he sucked.

Had Peter done that to George? Had George writhed as ecstatically when Peter's tongue explored his virgin orifice? More than likely. The image of George with his knees in the air became more and more vivid. He could visualise George's thick cock standing up proudly from its hairy base. Maybe the woman Catherine had met was right too. Maybe Peter had a hang-up about hygiene and preferred the taste of young men whose cocks had been chlorinated in private swimming pools –

"Aaagh!" he gasped. He couldn't stop himself. For the second time that night he shot his load. Martin sprang into an upright kneeling position and grabbed for his kikoi. He held it to his lips for some minutes and then grinned.

"We'll have to do that again," he said.

"Maybe George has more recommendations. You ought to ask him," said Robert.

"Yeah. I might well do that. I guess we'd better get some sleep. Night, Robert."

"Good night, Martin." Robert kissed him on the forehead and went over to his little bed. Not to sleep, but to think. The more he thought, the more reasonable Raymond's theory seemed. Raymond, after all, was a very intelligent young man who had known both Martin and George for longer than Robert had.

By the time he woke up next morning, Robert was convinced. He looked over to Martin's sleeping form. It was odd how thoughts like that started him off, he thought. He reached under the covers and gave his cock two or three strokes.

"Wassa time?" Martin's voice sounded sleepy.

"Early yet. Go back to sleep."

"No. Come over here. I feel like fisting you."

"Did you fist George up at Peter's place?" Robert asked when he had shot – which didn't take very long.

"We didn't get the chance. We were in separate rooms."

"You could have paid him a night-time visit. You did with me."

"Not really. It would have been a bit difficult."

Robert asked no more questions, but his brain was working over-time on the drive back to Kampi-ya-Moto. It was as if the car were on some sort of autopilot and able to find its own way back. For almost the whole of the following week he couldn't stop thinking about Peter Hardwick and George, imagining who had done what to whom and in what circumstances. Some of the imaginings were a bit over the top, it was true, but they acted as a powerful night-time stimulant.

He tried to analyse his own feelings but couldn't. He wasn't jeal-ous. Of that he was sure. It was just curiosity, really – curiosity spiced with a sense of anger that Martin hadn't told him the truth. He wouldn't have minded so much, if only Martin had been honest. Or would he? Maybe he would. George, after all, could be forgotten, but Martin was his partner. So, for that matter, was Raymond. It was all too complicated.

On Thursday evening Robert rang the Marriotts' number and, after a ten-minute monologue from Catherine, was able to speak to Martin.

"You said Peter Hardwick is coming down to Nairobi this week-end?"

"That's right. He and George are collecting the camera."

"I'd like to meet him. Do you think that might be possible?"

"I should think so. I'll ask George in the morning. Shall I call you?"

"No, there's no need to. It's not that important. I just thought it might be a nice idea. It would be nice to see George again, too."

"I'll tell him. Same time on Saturday morning?"

"Same time. Till then," said Robert.

So, he thought, Martin obviously had no objection to his meet-ing Peter. That made him feel better.

In fact, Robert was early at the roundabout. He had done one com-plete circuit, returning the way he had come, circling the roundabout and driving more slowly. He spotted Martin coming down the hill and drove up to him and opened the car door.

"And how are we this morning?" Martin asked and planted a quick kiss on his cheek.

"We are very well. Did you speak to George?"

"I did. We're meeting them at the Thorn Tree at three o'clock this afternoon. It can't be any later, because Peter's got to fly back and he can't fly in the dark."

"No NFR, then."

"What's that?"

"A special sort of licence for night flying. Shopping first?"

"Sure."

Catherine was at her worst that weekend. There were so many things about the dinner dance that she hadn't had time to tell Robert on the previous Sunday morning. From the number of times Martin and Robert looked at their watches, it was almost as if they'd never worn one before.

The afternoon came round at last. At two-thirty, Robert was all set to leave. Catherine had other ideas.

"You can't go to the Thorn Tree in shorts, darling," she said.

"Why not? Everyone wears shorts at this time of year," Martin replied.

"Robert isn't and Daddy doesn't."

"Only because I haven't got the sort of legs that Martin has," said Robert, glancing admiringly at the limbs in question.

"Well, not those shorts anyway. Ibrahim's washed and pressed your long trousers. Put them on."

"No. I want to wear shorts."

Another pair had been washed, but not ironed. Robert suggested that Martin might do that job himself. Martin had never used an iron in his life. Catherine wouldn't hear of him trying. She said it was Ibrahim's job and should have been done hours ago, so Ibrahim was taken off the washing up to iron a pair of shorts.

Martin might have regretted not taking his mother's advice when he got into the car. It had been standing out in the drive in the glare of the sun for some hours. The hot leather burned Robert through his trousers. Martin literally hit the roof.

"Go inside and change," said Robert. "It won't matter if we're a bit late."

"I'll be okay. I can sit on your road map," Martin replied.

Robert had never been to the Thorn Tree, which was actually the restaurant of the New Stanley Hotel and thus named because of the thorn tree which stood in the centre of the patio area. It had the reputation of being the haunt of the rich but hard-working settler community and the equally rich, idling and sponging parasites they attracted.

He had to park the car some way down the street.

"There they are. Here already," said Martin.

"George's mother obviously doesn't agree with your mother's dress code," said Robert. George's shorts had ridden up to the top of his thighs. He was sitting at a table in the thorn tree's shade, delicately devouring a very tall glass of ice cream. His companion – the person who interested Robert most – was perhaps thirty to thirty-five, dark haired and had the bony sort of face one associates with someone who has been – or is – very ill. He was pale, too. Seeing them approach, he stood up.

"Flight Lieutenant Hall, I presume?" he said.

"Just Robert. How do you do?"

"How do you do? Peter Hardwick. George's told me all about you."

George put down his long spoon, wiped his mouth and gave a wicked-looking grin. Robert and Martin sat down.

"Sorry we're late. Slight argument at home about wearing these," said Martin.

"All young men should wear shorts all the time in my opinion, don't you think so Robert?" said Peter.

"Not all young men. No. It would be bloody uncomfortable if you lived in Alaska."

"And when you get into a black car with black seats," said Martin, rubbing the backs of his knees.

"Poor you. What are you going to have? And what about you, Robert?"

"No, no. Let me."

"No, I insist. Now then, I think I know what Martin likes best."

No truer words were ever spoken, thought Robert.

"The same as George, please," said Martin. Robert settled for an iced coffee.

"I've been wanting to talk to you since I first heard about you, Robert," said Peter.

"Oh yes. What about?" Robert put down his drink. There were some things which one did not discuss in the most expensive restaurant in town.

"You've heard about my aerial photography plan?"

"Yes," Robert replied, with considerable relief.

"I need your help. Part of the Hansons' land is prohibited air space."

"Yes, it would be. There's an Air Force unit based there now."

"So, how do I get round that?"

"I don't think you can. They'll have you on the screen as soon as you're within radar range."

"And then?"

"If you don't clear off, they'll shoot you down. They don't muck about." George turned visibly pale.

"There must be some way."

Robert thought for a few moments, visualising the chart in the caravan. "The only way I can think of is a bit devious, but it would work," he said, after he'd thought it out. "You could visit the Hansons. They've got a grass strip near the house. What sort of aircraft are we talking about?"

"A Cessna Skymaster. It's ideal for this job, because of the high wing."

"The strip is adequate for that. You'd have to wait till the wind was in the right direction and then pay your visit. That would take you right over our bit. They won't like it one little bit, but it's in the lease. Mr Hanson insisted on that. The only thing is that you'd have to keep very quiet about the camera."

"I didn't want to involve the family at all," said Peter. "The less other people know, the better."

"You can't do aerial sweeps over the man's land without telling him what it's all about, for God's sake," Robert protested.

"I thought of a way round that," said George. "Dad says they always spend about three days in Nairobi when they come down to meet the boys and Mr Peters takes his holidays at that time, so for three days there'll just be the farm workers up there."

"I thought the idea was that you and the Hansons' sons would hunt for the treasure together."

"Not a good idea," said Peter, firmly. "They'll want a share of the proceeds."

"I would have thought they'd be entitled to that anyway, if it's on their land."

"No. It's better just the three of us. Anyway, although I haven't had the pleasure of their company, I imagine the Hansons' sons are heavy going. Some Quakers can be boring. Not all, by any means," said Peter and he reached down and patted George's leg.

At that moment there was a sudden squeal of brakes and the unmistakable sound of two vehicles in collision, by no means unusual in Nairobi at that time. Martin and George jumped to their feet.

"Back in a minute," said Martin and they were off.

"Leave it. You'll only get in the way..." said Peter but he was addressing their backsides and from a distance. "They're like a couple of kids sometimes," he said, turning to Robert.

"That's true. Martin's parents are worried about how he'll manage on his own next year at university. I begin to see their point. He can't even iron his own shorts. He'll have George with him, but I can't see him being much help."

"I don't think George will go. He's changed his mind," said Peter. "We have a plan, you see."

Robert was quite sure that the plan involved more than Peter had described. That pat on George's knee had been more eloquent than Peter probably realised. The official plan, though, was to establish a reserve for rare animals on Peter's land under George's management. George's father's firm would send busloads of tourists to photograph the animals.

"It'll cost a mint but it will be worth it – even if only to save the animals," said Peter. "If we find this cup, it'll be a great help."

"The operative word being 'if'," said Robert. "Do you really believe it exists?"

"I don't know. They do. That's the main thing," said Peter.

They talked of aircraft and flight paths and "Notices to Airmen" after that, but only half of Robert's concentration was on flying. Peter wasn't a person he took an instant dislike to. After all, Peter was just like him.

"You're not taking Martin on these photographic sorties, then?" Robert asked.

"I asked him, but he said he didn't want to. Between ourselves, I think the parents discouraged him. George's folks are different."

"I see. So what's the plan?"

"George's father will get the dates of the Hansons' trip to Nairobi. I fly up from Mombasa, pick George up here and off we go. It'll probably take just about three days. I have to train George to use the camera. It's one of these special jobs that superimposes a grid. Ah! Here they are."

The accident, they said, had been rather tame. Just a shattered windscreen and a smashed headlight. By that time their ices had melted. Discarding the spoons, they drank them. "Well, George and I ought to be pushing off," said Peter, summoning the waiter with a click of his fingers.

"See you on Monday morning, Martin," said George as he stood up. Martin was still slurping ice from the bottom of his glass, so didn't see what Robert saw. Peter shepherded George out of the restaurant with his arm round the young man's shoulders.

"He's a really nice chap, isn't he?" said Martin, putting down the glass.

"He's okay," said Robert.

"He's fabulously rich, too."

"Wealth is not everything," said Robert. "What do you want to do now?"

"Silly question, but we can't do it here. It's too early to go to Plum's and anyway, the folks will be expecting us back for dinner. I suppose we could have a little walk or something."

It was more than a "little" walk and there was no "something" – save meeting the famous Vijay Shah. Everything Martin and George had said about the lad was true. Robert spotted him before Martin, which was surprising, but Martin was enthusing about the treasure hunt at the time.

A very tall, very dark lad with glossy black hair was bending slightly to examine something in a shop window. Robert, with only half a mind on metal detectors and spades, admired the young man's remarkably slim waist and very attractive, neat little backside when he straightened up and saw them.

"Hi, Martin," he said languidly, and waved a hand in the air, revealing a glittering wristwatch of enormous proportions.

"Hi ,Vijay." They stopped and for some minutes, Robert stood by like a spare part as they talked about cricket and people he had never heard of. Finally, Martin remembered his presence.

"This is my friend Robert Hall," he said.

"Pleased to meet you."

"Pleased to meet *you*." Did Robert live in Nairobi? No? Did he like Nairobi? Where did he live? Predictably, Vijay had never heard of Kampi-ya-Moto.

"It's a smashing place. Right out in the bundu," Martin explained. Vijay gave no flicker of recognition. Robert was looking closely, mostly because he had never seen such long eyelashes or such brilliantly white teeth. Raymond, it seemed, had said nothing – which was just as well.

The conversation turned back to cricket. Then Vijay said he had to meet his father and he strode off. Martin turned round to watch him.

"Isn't he the most beautiful person you have ever seen?" he asked.

"After you, maybe," said Robert, but in fact the memory of Vijay stayed with him for a long time and not, he thought, just with him. Martin was just that little bit more energetic that night. There came a point in the early hours of the morning when Robert was lying on his back with Martin's considerable weight on top of him and the young man's cock thrusting between his thighs. He couldn't help noticing that Martin kept his eyes tightly closed the whole time, nor could he fail to notice the force with which Martin, who had already ejaculated earlier that night, shot his load before rolling off and lying panting next to him.

He let Martin get his breath back before speaking. "Is Vijay going to university in England?" he asked.

"Ha! You're a thought-reader."

"Is he?"

"Yes. Not this year, though."

"When your papers come through, I wonder you don't tell him where you're headed. He'd be good company."

"That's about all he would be. There's no chance there at all."

"Faint heart never won fair lady and it certainly never won a dark boy," said Robert. "It would do no harm to tell him. Let him make up his mind."

"Do you think there might be a chance?"

"It's possible. Shall we go to sleep?"

"Let's talk about Vijay for a bit. Did you notice his eyelashes?"

"Yes I did, as a matter of fact."

"George says he looks like a film star. Do you think so?"

"In a way, I suppose."

"You should see what's lower down. It's beautiful. It's really black and shiny and his cock is out of this world. It's funny, actually."

"Why?"

"Not his cock. It's me. I mean, with other people I dream about fisting them. When I think about Vijay I dream about fucking him. Even when you first came here and I said I didn't go much on it, I was having fucking dreams about Vijay."

"Quite understandable. All you need to do now is convince him that he needs a friend when he's in England and then you never know…"

"Oh, if only." Martin yawned. "I suppose we really should get some sleep," he said. "I don't much feel like it, but you've got a long journey."

"It's not that long," said Robert – and he reached out in the dark, found what he was looking for and took it between his thumb and forefinger. "Now, this is long," he said, "and just right for Vijay."

Incredibly, that had an effect.

The cold draught woke Robert as Martin pulled the bed cover off him.

"Watch out. This thing isn't strong enough for two people," he said, staring up at several inches of very rigid cock.

"It is for what I want to do." Martin knelt at the side of the bed. Robert turned on to his side. Martin's hand ran up and down the outside of his thigh and then Martin's mouth went to work. For a lad who, not very long before, had professed to abhor the idea, he had certainly changed his mind.

Chapter Twelve

In the distance, the aircraft seemed a small dot in the sky. Robert stood outside the caravan and watched it bank and turn in towards the farm. He had been waiting for weeks, but hadn't expected it to happen quite so early.

"Bwana Hanson is still here, isn't he?" he asked his Kenyan sergeant.

"He was here yesterday, sir. I saw him."

"Good. That's Mr Hardwick coming to visit him." Something had obviously gone wrong with Peter's deception plan. The moment the Cessna got into his circuit, the phone rang in the caravan. By the time he'd got to it and been told that the Cessna at present on its way to him had special permission to overfly, the noise of the aircraft low overhead must have deafened the man at the Air Traffic Control Centre. Robert wondered what they would have wanted him to do if it hadn't had permission – but that wasn't his problem. He went outside again and was just in time to see the aircraft dip down behind the distant buildings.

Reassured that Peter had taken notice of his advice after all, he settled down to work – not that there was a lot to do. The air-strip had been built and tested and most of his days were spent in accounting for various items of equipment – many of which had vanished. Catherine Marriott would have had a field day if she'd known about the seven pick-axes, the portable generator and the cement mixer, all of which had been issued, used and then disappeared.

"How many industrial gloves have we got left, Sergeant?" he asked.

"All worn out and discarded, sir."

"A hundred pairs?"

"Very heavy work, this," said the sergeant with a huge grin.

"What about the tarmac-layer? I know that went back, because I watched it being loaded on to the truck but it hasn't reached Nairobi yet."

"Maybe he had a breakdown. The road is very bad," the sergeant replied.

"And no doubt our tarmac layer is being used to re-surface it. Make a few enquiries, would you? They're not likely to let that one go the way of all the rest."

A vehicle drew up outside and there was a loud knock on the door. "Can we come in?" It was George's voice.

"The door's open," Robert called and in they came: George, followed by a young man of such huge proportions that Robert just gaped. He was well over six feet tall and had to bend almost double to get through the door and was forced to stoop when he was inside. One look at his curly hair and his face made George's introduction unnecessary.

"This is Patrick Hanson," he said.

Robert's sergeant slipped out behind them, only just managing to squeeze between Patrick's bulk and the wall. George sat in the vacant chair and that made the van seem a little more roomy.

"I was going to come and see you this afternoon anyway," said Patrick. "Father told me you were here. I only got back yesterday."

"So I brought him down to see you," said George.

"That's nice. Where's Peter?"

"Oh, he's back at the house talking to Mr Hanson. We had a

good flight." He gave Robert what might have been a wink but might equally have been a tic.

"So you're at Oxford, I understand," said Robert, craning his neck to address Patrick.

"That's right."

"And he's a rower. He might be in the boat race," said George.

"I'm not a bit surprised. I wonder they need any more people in the boat. You look strong enough to row it by yourself."

"I do a bit of single sculling, as a matter of fact, but I'm not awfully good at it. It's the team thing, I suppose," said Patrick.

"Things worked out brilliantly," George interrupted. "Mr Hanson drove down to pick Patrick up at the airport and called on Dad in the office. I thought I'd like to meet him at last, and Peter brought me up here. Anyway, have you got time to show us all this stuff?"

"Sure," said Robert, and for the next hour he demonstrated almost everything. By British standards, it was pretty primitive but Patrick seemed impressed and George, who must have picked up quite a lot of knowledge from Peter, asked some very intelligent questions.

"We have to get back for lunch," said Patrick, abruptly. "Are you here every day?"

"Every weekday," Robert replied. "Weekends only if the Air Force want me here."

"That's great! Can I come and visit occasionally?"

"You'd be more than welcome. At the moment I feel I've got the most boring job in the world."

He watched them leave until the Land Rover was hidden in a dust cloud. He had quite a lot to think about and the more he thought, the angrier he became. He had a definite feeling of being a second-class citizen. In the first place, why hadn't he been invited to have lunch with them? He knew Mr Hanson. He knew Peter and he knew George. What did they have in common? Money. It was all very well for good-hearted people like Mr Hanson and Martin to try and bridge the gap between black and white, but neither seemed to realise that there was another problem in the country: the huge divide between the very rich and people like him.

As for George's obvious lie about wanting to meet Patrick, a person would have to pretty green to believe that! Patrick, whether he knew it or not, was being used. He was the ideal excuse for the low overfly. Seething with anger, Robert munched the sandwiches Kiberech had made for him. He tore a terrific strip off his sergeant about the missing equipment. The poor man looked puzzled, as well he might at the change between humorous acceptance of its loss and the sudden threat of an official enquiry.

The two young men didn't even come down to say "Goodbye". They took off again about an hour before Robert went off duty. Again, he stood outside and watched the Cessna ascend, do a circuit and then climb further and then head east.

"Sod you!" he muttered.

"Sir?"

"Not you, sergeant. I'm sorry about this afternoon. I didn't mean it. Things were getting on top of me."

"You'll feel better when your wife comes back," said the sergeant. "All men need a wife."

"Maybe," said Robert. He looked up at Pat's photograph on the noticeboard on the wall in front of his desk. Bearing in mind George's advice, he hadn't taken it down. It wouldn't have made any difference if he had, he thought. A divorce in the society George inhabited might be a scandal, but this lot couldn't care less about a mere Flight Lieutenant getting one.

That night Robert sat alone and miserable on the verandah and, truth be told, he drank far more than was good for him. It was just as well that Kiberech wasn't around when he stumbled into the house and put himself to bed. It was also a good thing that he had very little to do on the following morning. The sergeant thought he might have heard where the low loader carrying the tarmac layer was stranded and Robert managed a faint smile as he despatched the man in their one and only Land Rover to locate it. He signed a fuel chit, knowing damn well that the sergeant would use the vehicle for a family outing that evening.

That having been done, he settled back to eat his sandwiches. He had told Kiberech at least three times that he hated hard-boiled eggs in sandwiches. The smell alone was enough to put him off. However, he had to eat something. He also had to do something. There was nothing in the caravan worth reading, not that he felt like reading.

Boredom can send the mind in the oddest directions. Idly, and not thinking of anything in particular, he reached for a writing pad and a pencil and began to doodle. A couple of lines – a bit of shading here and there, but what was it? Some sort of bomb or torpedo perhaps? No! Of course! It was George's cock. If one turned the paper so that it was upright...even better, turn the paper at an angle... Yes. That was it – just how it had been when he last saw it. He put in a bit more shading and added the little eye at the top. Amazing. The size was right, too. He couldn't have made a better sketch if he'd wanted to. It was perfect. He tried to sketch Martin's. That was a failure. Raymond's might have been recognised by someone who knew him as intimately as Robert did. Cocks, he reflected, were as individual as fingerprints. He wondered about some of the other young men he'd met recently. There was Vijay Shah, for instance. Martin and George had said his was huge, so it must be bigger than theirs. How much bigger? That was the question. And what about Patrick? What sort of cock hung between those huge legs? More to the point, what sort of cock stood out from a body like his? A towering mass of muscle like Patrick would have to have a cock in proportion. It would probably go right off the edge of the paper...

The sound of a vehicle drawing up outside made him jump.

Hurriedly he tore off the page, crumpled it and threw it into the basket. He should have said, 'Take the Land Rover, sergeant. I don't expect to see you until tomorrow. I'll give you a fuel chit so that you can take the family out.'

There was a light tap on the door. Robert didn't look round. "No luck?" he asked.

"Sorry?"

Robert swung round.

"Oh, it's you, Patrick. I thought it was my sergeant. He's gone off to find a tarmac layer that's gone missing."

"I'm not disturbing you?"

"Not at all. Sit down."

The caravan seemed more roomy as Patrick took the other chair. "You must get a bit bored here, don't you?" the young man asked.

"In a word, yes. You couldn't have come at a better time."

"How long will you be here, actually?"

"They'll do a full-scale exercise here to make sure everything's up and running. Then, presumably, the Kenyans will take over."

Patrick's arms were surprisingly hairless, he thought.

"Will you be sorry to leave this area?"

"In many ways, I think I will," said Robert. They were beautifully sun-tanned too, he thought.

"You don't find the life lonely, then?"

"Sometimes. My wife is in Britain, as you probably know, but George and a couple of his friends have been up to stay recently. They've been good company." The recollection caused a little shiver to run down his spine.

"Oh yes. Father said something about that. George is a really nice chap, isn't he?"

"Yes. I'm very fond of him," said Robert, glancing at the paper ball in the waste basket.

"Do you know this Peter, the man who flew him up here?"

Patrick asked.

"Not really. I've only met him once."

"Once would be too often in my view. I don't like him at all," said Patrick. "Father seems quite taken with the man, but then my father is a notoriously bad judge of character."

"What have you got against him?"

"Oh, nothing. I just don't like him. I think he could be a bad influence on George."

"In what way?" Robert asked. Patrick surely couldn't have realised what was going on, unless perhaps one of them had said something injudicious. They could hardly have done anything in his presence.

"It's difficult to explain. European teenagers out here are completely different from the ones at home. They're mollycoddled from the cradle onwards. I was the same till I got to Oxford. You never get a chance to stand on your own two feet. Apparently, this Peter person has put George off going to university."

"I heard something to that effect," said Robert.

"It's ridiculous! Even Father thinks that, but Peter will persuade him – you'll see."

"Maybe you ought to talk to George – away from Peter," said Robert.

"That would be just about impossible. He doesn't seem to want to let George out of his sight. When we got back to the house yesterday, he was standing outside waiting for us. I reckon there's something unnatural about him. Still, I shouldn't moan. He's promised to make me a giant aerial photograph of the farm and the estate. Not your part of it, of course."

"Of course."

"If I'm to take over running the place one day, it'll be very useful. It hasn't been properly mapped since 1913 and a lot's changed since then – except how to bring up children."

"That's interesting," said Robert and, for the remainder of that afternoon, he listened to Patrick's very well-thought-out plans for the future of Eldama. Much of what he said Robert didn't understand and a lot sounded too altruistic to be practical anywhere other than heaven, but when Robert occasionally queried something, Patrick had the answer. It was actually a relief to listen to someone whose humanitarian ideas were based on calculation and not on the finding of mythical treasure.

It was long after Robert's usual closing-down time when Patrick stood up – or tried to. Due to his height, he had to stoop. "I've really enjoyed meeting you," he said. Robert said that he felt likewise.

"It was a shame you couldn't have come to lunch yesterday," said Patrick, "but Peter explained that you had to stay down here all the time."

"Oh, I can get away when I want."

"Can you? That would be great. Why don't you come up for lunch – every day? Father won't be around, I'm afraid. He's out working all day, but Mother and I will be there."

"That would be very nice. Thank you."

"Shall I come down for you?"

"There's no real need. I have my own car and we possess a Land Rover – currently being used for a family excursion or transporting livestock no doubt, but it should be back tomorrow. Another thought. Why don't you come down to my place some evenings? The view from my verandah is quite spectacular and there's always plenty of beer in the house."

"I don't drink too much, but it would be a nice idea. Even at my age, parents can be trying at times."

They left the caravan together. The early evening sunshine threw their shadows on to the grass. "If you don't mind me asking, how tall are you, Patrick?"

"Six foot three."

"Grief!"

"Grandfather was even taller, apparently. See you tomorrow for lunch. Say twelve-thirty for one o'clock?"

"I'll be there," said Robert.

That evening he felt much happier. He sat on the verandah, watching the sun growing in size and reddening as it sank, and listening to the sounds of Africa. It really was a beautiful country, he thought. With people like Patrick and Martin, it had a great future. It needed practical people like Patrick and dreamers like Martin.

"Six feet three inches," he murmured – and fell to thinking about certain other dimensions.

"I'm so glad you could come. We've never liked to disturb you before and Peter said you had to stay down there all the time, especially when there was a plane here. Another orange juice?"

"Thank you. No, he was under a misapprehension. I would have to stay if it were an Air Force aircraft on our strip. Private aircraft on your private strip are not my responsibility, Mrs Hanson," Robert replied. Misapprehension, indeed! he thought.

"Oh, call me Dorothy, please. How is your wife?"

"Not terribly well at the moment, I'm afraid."

"Oh I am sorry. I thought she looked a bit pale the last time she was up here."

"Yes, we think it might be better for her not to come out in September. Actually, I've applied to go home."

"Oh, that would be tragic for us, now we've got to know you, but I understand of course. Now you'll have to forgive us. Luncheon is very much a makeshift affair during the week. Jeremy's out all day."

The "makeshift affair" was served on hand-painted plates with gold edges and consisted of no less than three courses, a considerable step up from a packet of hard-boiled egg sandwiches.

"When do your brothers get back, Patrick?" Robert asked, wondering if they were giants too.

"Not till July."

"Goodbye peace and quiet," said Dorothy Hanson. "We love to see them, of course, but the exuberance can be wearing. Don't worry. We'll keep them well clear of you. Your wife said you didn't get on with young men."

"Did she?" Peter Hardwick was obviously not the only one who could be devious, thought Robert.

"Oh yes. That would be last summer soon after you got here. Your Pat said it would be better not to ask you over."

"You haven't struck me that way," said Patrick. "Quite the opposite in fact, and didn't you say that George and a couple of friends stayed with you?"

"Yes, you did, didn't you?" said Dorothy. "That must have been terrible for you."

"Not at all," said Robert. "I enjoyed their company."

"Ah. One has to say that, of course. George said something about you staying with the other boy's parents at weekends, so I suppose you had to. Mind you, that George is a nice lad. The more I see of him, the more I think so. You liked him too, didn't you, Patrick?"

"Yes, he's a nice chap."

"You must let me take the picture to show the King-Mastersons when I next go down to see them. They'd be interested."

"No way. It's not good enough."

"I thought it was excellent."

"It's not finished yet. I need to see him again and get him to sit properly."

"Picture?" Robert asked.

"It's only a hobby. I'll show you after lunch."

Aware that he really ought to go back to the caravan, Robert sat through coffee in the lounge. Finally, he thanked Dorothy for an excellent lunch and her hospitality. He walked with Patrick through a succession of beautifully mown lawns and a rose garden to the boys' bungalow.

"You've been here before, I think," said Patrick as he unlocked the front door.

"No. Your father put up some of our technicians here, which was very kind of him. I didn't come myself."

"Oh. Then I absolve you from blame for the breaking of my favourite mug."

"A breakage? Nothing was said to me."

"I doubt if the person thought it worthwhile. I was fond of it. It was a souvenir of my first holiday in Europe. We did a cruise along the Danube. Anyway, let me show you round. That's Tim's room on the left. Jeremy lives on the other side. We have a sort of communal sitting room – that's in here." Patrick opened the door to reveal what might well have been a lounge in any suburban house, if it were not for the gigantic music centre which was at least as big as the average sideboard and the posters on the walls.

"Very nice," said Robert. Martin, he thought, would be enraged with the contrast between this and the one-room huts that the majority of the population had to live in.

"And I'm in here," said Patrick, opening another door.

"Very nice. Very nice indeed," said Robert. The only trouble with big lunches on working days is that they induce drowsiness. The only thought that crossed Robert's mind when he saw Patrick's bed was an overpowering desire to lie on it – by himself.

"I had to have a big one because of my size," Patrick explained.

"I see. What are all the caps for?"

"Rowing. School and Oxford, and those are the trophies I've got so far."

"Mmm. Quite a lot," said Robert, scanning along the row.

"Oh, other people have many more – and this is all that's left of my mug. Just the base. Father tried to stick it together, but there were two bits missing."

Robert took the fragment in his hand. He could just make out the base of a coat of arms and the end of a word. Just "au" and a full stop. "I wish your father had told me. I could have got the man to pay for it," he said.

"No point. It was the sentimental value. These things happen. I might as well sling it I suppose. It's sad, really. Anyway, this is what you've come to see."

An easel stood facing the wall. Patrick pulled it out. "This is it. What do you think?" he asked. Suddenly, Robert didn't feel tired any more. It was a pencil drawing of George and the likeness was extraordinary. The lock of hair which George was constantly shaking back was there. So was the extraordinary mixture of innocence and mischief in his eyes – made even more emphatic by the wide grin and fleshy lips.

"It's beautiful!" Robert exclaimed. "It's as if...I'm no artist, but it's as if you've caught the spirit behind the man."

"Thank you. I only did it from memory after he left. If I could get him to sit properly, I'd be able to make a better job of it. You need more than just the face to do justice to a person."

"I wonder you don't take up art as a profession," said Robert, unable to keep his eyes off the picture.

"Far too precarious. Anyway, the family need me to do more than draw pictures. Would you like to see some more?"

"I'd love to Patrick, I really would, but there's a starving sergeant six miles down the road. I really ought to go and relieve him."

"I could bring some over to your place tomorrow evening. This evening's out, I'm afraid. Father needs help in choosing a new plough."

"That would be great. I'll look forward to seeing you," said Robert and, all the way back to the caravan, he thought of the picture and of George and of a handsome young farmer with a hidden talent. Patrick was the sort of person one could like. No more than that. He was grown up in every sense of the word: the sort of person one could talk to – a bit like Raymond, really, but with

Patrick it would be a different sort of relationship altogether.

In fact, Robert need not have worried about the sergeant. Both he and the Land Rover were absent. And he'd thought to lock the door before leaving. Robert lowered himself into his chair and retrieved the crumpled paper from the basket. He spread it out on the desk. If only he had Patrick's ability, he might have been able to do it justice, he thought. There was very little in this world as a beautiful as a young man's cock, but nobody would have thought so from his crude sketches. How did one get that eagerness across? Answer: one didn't. He tore the paper into small pieces and slung them back into the basket. He had something much more important to do. From his pocket he took a broken piece of china. Finding a box to put it in was more difficult and, in the end, he had to settle for one much too big. Then came the search for packing material. The fragments of paper came out again, together with the paper from the previous day's sandwiches. Then there was the letter to write. Bruce Watts, as far as he knew, was still in Germany. Finally, the lid went on the box, Robert wrote the address and sealed it with tape.

The time? He looked at his watch. Sixteen hundred. There was still time before the mail was collected from the post office. He rang through to ATC.

"Nothing in the air and nothing in the offing, old man. I should bugger off if I were you," said the Duty Controller and, remarkably for a man who had been known to leave his mail in the box for days on end and who took just as long to get down to answering it, Robert was soon speeding along the dusty road on his way to the post office.

He sent the packet by airmail and, on the way out, opened his post box. There were just two letters: one, in a pale blue envelope and an official one. He drove down the hill, said *jambo* to Kiberech and went inside to read his letters. The official one came first. "Sir. I am commanded to inform you...transfer to the Education branch...Durham University...with effect from..." No. It couldn't be. The date given was in the following year. He read on. "...essential duties...impossible to find a replacement at such short notice..."

He dropped the letter on to the floor. That seemed to be that. Another year in Kenya.

"Shit!" he said, and opened the other letter. It was from Raymond and started off as what Robert used to call a bread-and-butter letter. "Thank you very much for a very enjoyible [sic] stay," it started. For a lad who was able to rattle out the Latin names of snakes, it was remarkably badly spelled. The entire first page was full of thanks to him and regards to Kiberech. Almost certainly someone else had been in the room with him when he started the letter. His mother, Robert guessed. The tone changed on the other side of the paper.

"Guess what. A certain MM has been seen twice by your trusty spy in company with a certain VS. I shall find out what is going on. I have not seen the other one (GM) for some days but he is around. Did you here [sic] from Durham yet? Thanks again for a great time. Your freind [sic], Raymond."

It was nice of him to have written, even though the letter had all the signs of having been composed under pressure. Raymond would be as disappointed as he was at the news from the Ministry of Defence. He reached for the phone and dialled the number printed in the top left hand corner of Raymond's letter.

"Three-nine-five-oh-six-one." A woman's voice.

"Sorry to disturb you. Is Raymond at home?"

"Who's calling?"

He told her.

Raymond's mother was obviously nothing like Catherine Marriott. She said nothing about her son's stay. Just "One moment, please" and then Raymond came on the line.

"Hi, Robert."

"Hi! I thought I'd ring to say thank you for your letter."

"Oh, you got it then? I wasn't sure about the PO box number."

"Bad news, I'm afraid. They've approved my transfer and they've put me down for Durham, but not until next year."

"Oh shit! Still, never mind. I can have a year to get things organised for us. Why won't they let you go straight away?"

"They reckon I'm essential. That's balls. I do sod-all now the strip is up and running. I think it's going to be a very lonely year and, to be honest, that's what I dread most. I'm going to miss you badly."

"I thought Martin was number one in your life."

"I think both of you are, in different ways. When are you coming up here again, Raymond?"

"Can I? You sure you want me?"

"Of course."

"Well, school is still on, but we can bunk it any time after the end of June. How about then?"

Robert said that sounded ideal and the rest of the call – which was quite long – was concerned with snakes, or so Robert thought at first. Raymond's question as to whether he had seen any trace of the mambas in the garden was genuine enough, as was his query about the snakes in the hedge.

"You remember I told you about that Indian snake?" Raymond then asked.

"No. Which one was that?"

"Yes you do. I mentioned it in the letter."

"Oh yes. I see. The brown Indian snake?"

"That's the one. Well, I think it's getting used to being handled by that friend of ours. The one I mentioned in the letter."

"Good for our friend, but wasn't it a particular pet of yours?"

"It still is, but it's good experience for our friend, don't you think?"

"Oh, sure. Providing you don't mind."

"Why should it worry me? They need to be milked as often as possible. Anyway, I'd better ring off. Dinner's ready."

"So is mine," said Robert. Kiberech had laid the table and Robert's mouth was watering – not entirely because of the smell coming from the kitchen.

Chapter Thirteen

"I'm not very happy with this one," said Patrick. "What do you think?" He took yet another large sheet of paper from the huge folder propped up against the verandah wall.

"I think it's very good," said Robert. He had to hold it securely against the evening breeze. "Who is he?"

"A first-year history undergraduate. I thought he had an interesting face."

"Yes, he does. I see what you mean."

"The difficulty is getting them to pose for me. Nobody at Oxford seems to have any time for anything but studying or sport. I've only got one regular model. I suppose I could get more if I paid them, but I'm only an amateur."

"And which one is he? Have I seen him?"

"Er...no. Not yet. He's the only one who'll sit long enough for me to do more than just a head and shoulders portrait."

"Let's have a look."

Patrick opened the folder again, rifled through the sheets and brought one out. Apart from a towel draped over his middle, the young man was naked and sitting on a river bank with one knee drawn up to his chest.

"This is beautiful, Patrick! Is he another rower? It looks as if he could be."

"No. He's a theology student, actually. They have times when they have to sit silently and meditate, so I can draw him while he does it," said Patrick. "An ideal opportunity."

"I see."

"I'm hoping to do a watercolour one day of him in his robes. Ideally I'd like to do it in the cathedral. There's a beautiful stained glass window there, and I could get a bit of colour from that on to his surplice."

"That's a nice idea," said Robert, which was a total lie. An even nicer idea would be a picture without the towel.

Yet more pictures were produced. One or two pictures would have been pleasant to look at, he thought. He must have seen at least fifty and by the look of the thickness of that folder, there were at least another fifty to go through. He'd seen students looking to the left; students looking to the right. Others seemed to stare out from the paper. There had been students with dark hair; students with blond hair. One or two had crewcuts. The pictures were brilliantly executed, but there were enough in that folder to fill a gallery. He went indoors to get another beer and an orange juice for Patrick.

When he went outside again, the folder had been closed and the strings tied – to Robert's relief.

"Father says that you were asking about the Meinerherzhagen cup," said Patrick.

"Yes, I was. I feel, as he does, that it's one of these legends that goes around and grows as the years go by."

"I'm not so sure. I think there might be something in it. I wish my grandfather had lived longer or written something down about it. Jeremy and I spent most of our holidays looking for it when we were younger."

"And you didn't find it? No. I'm quite sure I'm right. It's a bit like the Holy Grail. I'll bet you any money you like that it doesn't exist any more. From all your father said, Colonel

Meinerherzhagen was an oddity. He was desperately poor, apparently. He would have sold that cup years before and, not wanting anyone to know, he made up all that business of burying it on your land."

"Quakers don't make bets, so I can't take you up on that," said Patrick. "Oh! Father asked if you would be around in the weekend. They're giving a party and they'd like you to come. So, for that matter, would I. It would make a change from boring settler-talk."

Robert excused himself. He had to go into Nairobi for the shopping, he explained, and had already arranged overnight accommodation.

"That's a shame," said Patrick. "I shall get landed with Peter Hardwick for sure. I really don't like that man."

"So you said."

"It's George I worry about. They're as thick as thieves. It would have been much better if they'd never met. The annoying thing is that my father introduced them. Father is very friendly with Mr Glover."

"So I heard."

"I don't know…Do you mind me talking to you about this sort of thing?"

"Of course not. Carry on."

"We have a family Meeting every evening when I'm home, but you can't talk openly there. It makes a change to talk to someone outside the circle, if you know what I mean."

"What's on your mind?" Robert asked.

"Well…it's George and Peter. I think there's something going on between them."

"What sort of thing? Do you think they're having an affair?"

"Oh no! Nothing like that. That sort of thing doesn't happen out here, though…"

"Though what?" The evening was getting interesting at last.

"Well, I've never thought of it in those terms. I suppose it could be. Peter's not married and Father is notoriously bad at judging characters. But no. Not with George. George is okay."

"But Peter could be hoping?"

"I doubt it, but the other day…I don't know…They were sort of looking at each other in a funny way. I noticed it once or twice. Father would be talking and they'd sort of catch each other's eye and smile. If I thought that…what you said, I mean…I'd forget the Society of Friends' pacifist policy for a few minutes and give him the hiding of his life! Maybe I ought to fall in with the parents' ideas about getting George married off. You've heard about that, I suppose?"

"I heard something to that effect."

"Rosemary King-Masterson. She's a nice enough girl. I was dotty over her myself when I was younger, but she isn't the girl for George. George would need somebody with a bit more 'go' in her and someone interested in the countryside. Rosemary's idea of a fun afternoon is sitting on the sofa doing needlework pictures. Father really is the worst judge of character this world has ever seen. We both believe there's some good in everybody – even Peter Hardwick, I guess. Rosemary probably has more than her share of goodness, but she's not right for George."

"Don't you think he's old enough to make up his own mind?" Robert asked.

"No, I don't. George is like a very young tree. He's still green and he bends whichever way the wind is blowing."

That remark amused Robert. Green? Possibly, but there was one aspect of George that even a hurricane couldn't bend.

The rest of that week passed very pleasurably. Lunch with the Hansons broke up the day beautifully and, by the time Robert was on his way to Nairobi on Saturday morning, he felt even happier than usual.

Martin was waiting for him at the Ainsworth roundabout as usual. "Hi," he said, as he got into the car.

"Hi! What sort of week have you had?"

"Very good actually. I've got something to tell you."

"What?"

"I'll keep it for later. Have you done your shopping list?"

"Of course I have. It's in the glove pocket."

They did the shopping, loaded the car and drove back to Kenyatta Avenue where Catherine, as usual, held forth for the rest of the day. The subject of that weekend's tirade was the appointment of an African curate to St. Martin's church. "I shall still go to church," she said. "That's expected of one, but I won't go to Communion. I could never take a wafer that one of them had been holding. You never know where their fingers have been, do you? I fail to see what's so funny, darling." Martin was choking back his laughter.

Malcolm inadvertently added to her wrath by announcing, on his return from the golf club, that the new curate had applied for membership. He, Martin and Robert were all equally glad to escape to Plum's that evening.

"We won't tell her. We'll let her find out for herself that he's a Cambridge man. He's also a bloody good golfer. Cheers, you chaps," said Malcolm.

"Cheers."

"Cheers, Dad."

"So...what's been happening up in the bundu this week? Anything?" Malcolm asked. Robert told them about meeting Patrick.

"What's he like?" Martin asked.

"Six feet and three inches of muscle and, surprisingly, a very clever artist. A nice chap," said Robert. He went on to describe Patrick's plans for the future.

"Now that is a brilliant idea," said Martin, when Robert had described the proposed new plant to produce gas from animal dung. Patrick had calculated that it would supply enough fuel for the house and the farm training school. The solar water heater would effect a similar saving. "Then, with the money saved, he'll build a dispensary on the farm and that, in turn will save the money and time spent taking people down to the dispensary in the village," he explained.

"Sounds like he's got a good head on his shoulders, this Patrick," said Malcolm.

Martin agreed, but he felt that something rather more elaborate than a dispensary was necessary in an establishment where people worked with dangerous farm machinery. Malcolm was trying to bring him down to earth with the estimated salary figures for the medical personnel Martin considered absolutely necessary when Raymond strode in, as unkempt as ever and with his crash helmet tucked under his arm.

"I hoped I'd find you here," he said. "Do you mind me joining you, Mr Marriott?"

"Not at all."

"You've heard, Martin?" he said, when his crash helmet had been stowed under the table.

"Heard what?" Martin asked.

"No school next week. All the priests are tied up with some sort of meeting and that means there's nobody available for us. You can volunteer to help teach the junior kids or bugger off. Oh! Sorry, Mr Marriott."

"I feel like using an even stronger word," said Malcolm. "Honestly! That place. I presume they'll be giving us all a refund of part of the fees – I don't think!"

"How did you find out?" Martin asked.

"I met Father Cox at the snake park. He was there with some of the little kids. I've spoken to Mum and Dad, Robert. Could I come up to Kampi-ya-Moto for a week?"

"Sure. I'll need to get some extra provisions, but Viraswami's is open on Sundays."

"That's an idea. Could I go too, Dad?" Martin asked.

"That depends on your mother," Malcolm replied. "Ask her when we get home."

"I shouldn't have to ask either of you. I'm old enough to make my own decisions," said Martin, apparently unaware of having asked in the first place.

The rest of that evening was taken up with excited planning. Malcolm sat back contentedly smoking his pipe.

"I hope Ibrahim's got two pairs of clean shorts ready. He might not have done. I suppose I could ring home to get him started on them now," said Martin.

"I never worry about things like that," said Raymond. That was obvious. There was a large stain that looked like motor oil on his jeans. It would have been noticeable to anybody – especially Robert, who happened to be looking in that direction. Two of them could be rather fun, he thought. Raymond wasn't like George. The two of them would be at it like a couple of rabbits. He just hoped he might get a chance himself.

There has been enough said about Catherine Marriott to imagine the scene when they got home. The film on television was ignored that night. It would have been better if she had turned the thing off. As it was, she had to talk above the sounds of bombs and screams in what appeared to be the war to end all wars. Malcolm was ordered to phone the headmaster at home to find out if David's class would be affected.

"Yes. At this hour. If they make last-minute decisions, they must expect it," said Catherine. Malcolm returned and explained that the priests had to attend a meeting with an African cardinal.

"Oh well, that explains it," said Catherine. "They're quite incapable of planning anything in advance. Now then, where is Ibrahim? That man is never around when I need him."

Ibrahim took the news that he would be up half the night washing and ironing clothes and packing Martin's bag with his

usual equanimity. Martin, as usual, took no part in all these pro-
ceedings. Robert would have been happier if Martin had not given
the impression that the whole idea had originated from him. It
was true Robert had made the invitation, but he'd said nothing
about Raymond coming along as well. The good thing was that he
had announced it as a fait accompli and not asked her permission.
No doubt Malcolm would put things straight when they went to
bed, thought Robert.

Unfortunately, there seemed very little chance for anyone to go
to bed that night. Once or twice Martin caught Robert's eye and
gestured towards the stairs but once Catherine had got the bit
between her teeth, there was no stopping her and Martin, the centre and cause of her concern, obviously had to stay. Both Robert
and Malcolm sat by whilst she hunted through the newspaper to
find a pharmacy which would be open on Sunday, wondered if
Martin had enough clean socks and went into the kitchen three
times to make sure that Ibrahim knew what was expected of him.
They would probably have been sitting there till the early hours of
the morning had not Malcolm stood up.

"Well, I don't know about you, but I'm going to bed," he said.
Catherine protested but it gave Robert and Martin the chance they
had both been waiting for.

"We'll have to attend to the rest tomorrow," said Catherine but,
by that time, they were both halfway up the stairs. Malcolm was
already in the bathroom. "Shower later, eh?" said Martin with a
mischievous grin.

"Much later," said Robert sitting on Martin's bed. "Come here."

Martin fell backwards on to the bed and lay there with his feet
still planted on the floor. "You look nice like that," said Robert.
Martin looked much more than just "nice". He had a really beautiful face. His massive chest contrasted with the concavity of his
belly and then there were those enormous thighs, in that position
seemingly thicker than normal.

"Looking isn't everything," said Martin, again with that encouraging grin. "Father Cox says that some of the other senses are stronger. There's smelling and tasting and hearing for example. Not to mention feeling. He's a biologist, so he should know. He reckons that memory depends on all five senses. Will you remember me, do you think?"

"How could I possibly forget?" Robert was busily undoing a particularly intricate belt buckle at the time.

"Raymond says that you and he are going to the same university."

"That won't be for some time yet." The belt was undone, so was the zip, to expose an expanse of mauve cotton stretched tight over a large swelling.

"I wish Ray wasn't coming to Kampi-ya-Moto with us," said Martin. "Hang on a bit. It's sort of got twisted up." He raised himself off the bed slightly. Robert grasped the underpants and shorts together and yanked them down over Martin's knees. Martin's cock was almost upright but not quite. He breathed in deeply and the first fragrant whiff lingered in his nostrils.

"Be fair. It was his idea. Don't get me wrong. I'm delighted that you're both coming, but with me at work you'll have nothing to do." He slid one hand up under Martin's shirt and undid the buttons, one by one, with both hands.

"Raymond managed."

"He's got his snake-hunting."

"I could have a go at finding that gold cup. That would be something to do."

"For God's sake, Martin. Can't you forget the cup? It doesn't exist. It's a myth."

"I don't think so. Nor do George and Peter. They're trying to squeeze me out."

"Good. Let's hope they succeed." It was on the tip of his tongue to say "Grow up, for Christ's sake!", but the top button was undone. Martin's shirt lay open on either side of him. He might have a lot of mental growing up to achieve, but there was nothing about his body that needed further development.

"All the senses. Remember?" said Martin. He reached down and fingered his cock.

Robert stood up to undress. "All the senses," he said, unbuttoning and undoing with feverish haste.

Sight first, he thought, looking down as Martin sat up to extricate himself from his shirt and then the trousers and pants round his ankles. Martin really was an exquisitely beautiful young man. He knew, somehow, that this memory would never fade.

He was about to get on to the bed; in fact one knee was already on it when Martin spoke. "Not yet," he said.

"Why not?"

"I'm trying Father Cox's theory. At the moment I'm concentrating on sight."

"That's funny. So was I."

"Stand up close, so I can get a good look. A bit closer. That's right. Mmm. I like it when it's standing up like that. Sort of keen, if you know what I mean. Like a runner on the starting blocks..."

"Poised for action," said Robert, glancing downwards. It was a good analogy.

"We'll make it a long-distance race tonight. Not a quick sprint," said Martin.

"That suits me. Ready for the next sensual thrill."

"Not quite. Turn round." Robert did so. "I like your behind," said Martin.

"I like yours," said Robert, addressing Martin's reflection in the wall mirror.

"Yours is hairier than mine. At least I think so."

"Not much actually," said Robert. His cock, reflected in the mirror, nodded its agreement. "Are you ready yet?" he asked. "If we've got all five senses to go through I think we ought to get started."

"Sure. Which one shall it be next?"

Robert climbed on to the bed, lay down and took Martin in his arms. "Touch," he said.

"I hoped you'd say that."

That was really the first time that Martin let himself go completely. His hands and his fingers went everywhere. So, for that matter, did Robert's. He'd never fully appreciated the shape of Martin's face until his fingers were stroking it. The difference in texture between the hair under Martin's armpits and the thick bush round his now fully erect penis was a revelation. There was a difference too, in the smoothness of the young man's inner thighs and the skin of his penis. Both were silky to the touch and delightfully cool. It was probably Martin's reciprocal reaction which led his fingers to leave massive muscle and move to rigid flesh. Similarly, it may have been Martin's manipulation of his nipples that made them seem so responsive.

"You're so..." Martin breathed – and just at that moment Malcolm called.

"The bathroom's free!"

"Thanks, Dad," said Martin. Robert couldn't have spoken if he'd had to.

"And now smell," Martin said, as the door to his parents' bedroom clicked shut. He knelt and then twisted round and almost fell on to Robert so that his head was between Robert's thighs. At first his cock pressed against Robert's neck and a bit of manoeuvring was necessary before Robert's cheeks were pressed on either side by smooth flesh. Robert inhaled deeply and then put his hands round Martin's buttocks to pull him down even more. He breathed in again. Perspiration was there, quite a lot of it, but it couldn't smother that other far more delightful scent. He would never be able to describe it. All he could think was that it was like all his favourite smells rolled into one. Cool air wafted against his balls, as Martin took deep breaths down there.

The move from smell to taste was automatic. Robert couldn't remember whose tongue was the first to come into play. He only knew that the feel of Martin's lascivious licking made his own lingual foray even more exciting. He loved the feel of springy hair against the tip of his tongue. He loved the wrinkled, soft skin of Martin's scrotum and, above all, the feel of Martin's rigid cock in his mouth. He would have carried on for much longer and, indeed, Martin showed every inclination to do so. Robert had to push upwards against the young man's hips to get him to stop. Fingers, after all, are not the only parts of a man sensitive to touch.

Martin was already panting and sweating slightly. He grinned and turned over on to his front and spread his legs wide. Fingers had to be used at first, of course. It was a pity that the next stage was a one-sided affair, he thought. Martin had never – as far as he knew – experienced the delight of pushing against a tightly closed opening and feeling it relax by degrees until suddenly, and always surprisingly, the finger slid in, to be enveloped and clutched by warm, moist muscle.

"Yeah!...Mmm!" said Martin, as the questing digit slid further into him. Robert had forgotten all about Father Cox's theories by that time. It was only afterwards that he tried to remember the various sounds made by an extremely randy young man during what Father Cox would undoubtedly have described as the process of copulation. There was the louder yell as a second finger came into play. The bedsprings also added their contribution as Martin began to wriggle and then gasp as he took the last few greasy millimetres. The grip on Robert's fingers tightened hard and then slackened. Martin was ready.

More than ready, as a matter of fact. It is possible that if Robert hadn't decided to slip a pillow under him, he might have come even sooner than he did. As it was, he lay there, still writhing. "Oh, do it. Do it!" he groaned as Robert tried to shove the pillow underneath him. He felt Martin's cock on the back of his hand and knew, the moment he withdrew it and saw the viscous trail on his skin, that the ultimate pleasure wouldn't last long – not for Martin anyway. He put his hands on Martin's shoulders, felt his cock-head pressing against hard skin, adjusted his position slightly until it was pushing against knotted flesh and then by pulling on Martin's shoulders and pushing for all he was worth, he was in.

It was odd, he thought momentarily, how all young men's arses seemed especially designed to accommodate his cock. "All" wasn't really the right word. The few he had fucked had, but there was something special about Martin. Martin was active – very active, in fact. The pillow helped Martin's upward heaves and, hopefully, saved him from any discomfort as Robert thrust deeper and deeper into him until he felt Martin's balls touch his own.

"Oh! Oh! Oh!" Martin gasped. Common sense said that the moment had come to stop so that the young man could cool down, but who yields to common sense when he's fucking an extremely good-looking, extremely well-built young man like Martin Marriott? Martin gasped and then let out a long, drawn-out sigh. Robert didn't need that to know what had happened. The sudden, painful tightness that squeezed his cock was eloquent enough.

"Oh! Jesus!" Martin gasped and lay still. Robert kissed the back of his neck.

"Hang on … a bit!" Martin panted. Robert kissed him again. There was a horrible, uncomfortable ache in his groin and his cock felt as if it was on fire but he forced himself to stop and to lie still. Sex shouldn't be a selfish pleasure, he thought. Martin was too nice a person. His wishes should be respected.

It was just as well that Martin said "I'm okay now," when he did. Robert had to clamp his hands against Martin's mouth to suppress his yells of sheer pleasure. Malcolm was next door, hopefully asleep, and Catherine hadn't even come upstairs yet. It was more than possible that she had already started to pack Martin's bag, a job which should've been left to him. Left in her hands, Martin would never mature. It was as well that Martin had found Robert – or that he had found Martin. Did getting laid contribute to emotional development? Possibly. Desperate to delay the final moment as long as possible, Robert forced himself to slow down.

It would do Martin good to pack his own suitcase for once, he thought. It was funny. He always found it an easy enough job. Poor old Pat hadn't. It was always the same. The anguished "I can't get it all in". Well, it was all in now! The thought occasioned the final, triumphant thrust. Martin bit his fingers and then relaxed. Robert felt the spunk spurting and fell, sweating and panting, on to Martin's perspiring back.

They were both exhausted. By the time Robert had carefully withdrawn his extremely flaccid cock, Catherine had come upstairs, used the bathroom and gone to bed.

"The best ever," Martin murmured and kissed him gently on the lips.

"I thought so too," Robert replied, returning the kiss.

"I'll tell you what, though," said Martin. "It was Father Cox I was thinking about."

"Cox, not cock?"

"Both really. About what he said about senses. Have you ever been to the game park?"

"Just once, when we first got here."

"You ought to go in the wildebeest migration season. You sounded like a herd of them!"

"Cheeky sod!" said Robert. He reached down and playfully smacked Martin's buttocks.

That night, after showering, they slept in the same bed. Not that either got much sleep. Martin wanted to talk at length and, sometimes, interestingly. "George and Peter are as thick as thieves these days," he said. "I hardly ever see George now. I would so much like to find the gold cup before those two."

"Which you are not likely to do, because it doesn't exist and, even if it did, they've got technology behind them. Forget it, Martin." Robert twined his fingers in Martin's hair and kissed his ear.

In the very early hours of the morning, both Martin's cock and the subject of the gold cup came up again. Robert was enjoying the feel of a putty-like penis as, very slowly, it hardened in his hand. He tickled Martin's navel with the other.

Suddenly, Martin turned on to his side to face him. "Oh, it's you. I thought it was a dream," he said sleepily.

"Don't sound so disappointed," Robert whispered.

"I'm not."

"Who was it in the dream?" Robert asked.

"Doesn't matter. Mmm. I like you doing that."

"I like doing it. Tell me who it was."

"George, actually." Martin's voice changed from a sleepy slur into his normal conversational tone. "He's seems to have gone off," he said.

"Gone off where?"

"Gone off fisting. I went up there on Wednesday afternoon. The whole family were out except George. Usually he can't wait to get it out for me. Not that time, though. I had to ask him outright, but he said "No". He said he had a lot to do, but that's balls because we sat talking for about an hour."

"What did you talk about?" Suspicions Robert had dismissed as impossible were hardening at about the same rate as the flesh in his hand.

"The gold cup. He reckons it's still there. Peter reckons it's still there."

"You don't think that Peter might be using the story?"

"That sounds rather manipulative. Why?"

"Can't you guess?"

"No, I can't. Tell me."

"Peter is unmarried, isn't he?"

"As far as I know. Yes, he is. I remember. George told me."

"And one evening at a party in Eldama he meets this extraordinarily good-looking young man..."

"George?" said Martin in an incredulous tone.

"George. Now he soon finds out, as I did, that George is hard to get. But he's got a trump card up his sleeve: an aircraft. An aircraft that will encourage George in his quest for the gold cup. If he wants to make friends with George, he has to have a good excuse so he gets involved in the gold cup myth. Plus there's this idea about a private game-park, just the sort of thing to appeal to George."

"George wouldn't. I know him too well."

"I wouldn't be so sure." Robert slid his hand up Martin's thigh, found what he wanted and wrapped his fingers lightly round it.

"It's odd that he didn't want to be fisted, certainly," said Martin, "but I don't really see where the plane comes in. You couldn't do much in a plane, could you?"

The reply to that question had to be delayed. Robert had found a much more enjoyable use for his tongue.

Chapter Fourteen

"Ninety degrees of flap", a motto often applied to various officers Robert had encountered during his career, could have been accurately applied to Catherine the following morning. Ibrahim had left an immaculately folded pile of clothes on the kitchen table. Catherine unfolded each item and then folded it again. "I wouldn't put it past him just to iron the top few," she explained. "You know what they're like."

Malcolm gave it as his opinion that it wouldn't be the end of the world if Ibrahim had done so, but one glance from his wife shut him up. After breakfast they went into the lounge. As always, Ibrahim had been out early to get the Sunday paper, so Malcolm was happy enough reading that. He passed the comic section over to Martin, which irritated Robert. The whole family seemed determined to keep Martin a schoolboy for the rest of his life.

Catherine came in. "Now then, the clothes are all ready. How are you off for towels, Robert? I wonder if I should pack two."

"I've more than enough," said Robert.

"More than enough for an adult, I'm sure, but you know what young people are like and I very much doubt if Raymond will think to bring one with him. Sometimes I wonder how that family survives. They seem to live from day to day. Like this trip for example – fancy deciding to go away at the last minute like that."

Obviously Malcolm had told her the whole story of their meeting in Plum's, Robert thought.

"No thought at all for the rest of the family," Catherine continued. "Not that you could describe them as a family. They're more a bunch of individuals living under the same roof. Now, I'd better get your toothbrush and toothpaste, Martin. I've got a new face flannel in the drawer, so I'll pack that."

"Leave it," said Martin, without looking up.

"I beg your pardon?"

"I said leave it. I'll do it myself later."

"You? You wouldn't know where to start. You left your razor behind last time. Daddy noticed it."

"I used Robert's. I won't forget this time. Now leave me alone. I'll do it."

Malcolm put down his paper. It was his turn to give his wife what could only be described as a "significant look", after which he smiled and returned his attention to the newspaper. Distinctly flustered, Catherine flounced out of the room and a few minutes later could be heard venting her anger on Ibrahim, who had apparently used far too much washing-up liquid.

"Never a dull moment in this house," said Malcolm from behind his paper and then added, "Well done, son." Robert revised his earlier opinion of Malcolm.

A few minutes later Catherine reappeared. "I'm going to church," she announced. "You're not thinking of leaving early are you, Robert? You'll still be here when I get back?"

"He always leaves after lunch," said Martin. Robert was even more amazed. He'd never heard Martin talk to his mother in this tone.

"I know, darling, but he has to pick Raymond up. I doubt if that family ever sits down to lunch together. They probably send out for something when they feel hungry."

Malcolm put down the paper again. "I thought you said you

wouldn't be going to church again?" he said.

"I'll give it a try," said Catherine, "but if he's preaching, I'll walk out. I'm not having one of them tell me how to run my life." She went upstairs to change, came down again and had another go at Ibrahim.

"I've told him about lunch. Keep an eye on him though," she said. "I won't be too long. In fact I shall probably be back in time to supervise him myself." She left, slamming the front door rather more loudly than usual. "Peace at last," said Malcolm, from behind his newspaper.

"Well, I'd better get this packing done," said Martin, standing up.

"Do you want a hand?" Robert asked.

"No thanks. I can manage," said Martin as he left the room.

"He can, too," said Malcolm.

Robert phoned Raymond who, contrary to Catherine's supposition, said that they always had lunch at one o'clock and that he would be ready any time after two o'clock. They settled on two-thirty.

"Nice lad, that," said the voice from behind the paper. "I prefer him to the Glover lad. He's got his head screwed on tight, which is more than can be said of young George. Somebody ought to take a spanner to that lad."

It wasn't a spanner, thought Robert, but the screwing bit was certainly under way.

"Tell me," said Malcolm, dropping the paper on to his lap, "What do these lads actually do when they're up at your place?"

Recent thoughts discomfited Robert. "How do you mean?" he asked, hoping Malcolm wouldn't notice.

"Well, there's sod-all up there, as far as I know. Down here in the city they've got everything, but they can't wait to escape into the bundu."

"That's probably the answer. City life palls. Raymond collects his snakes. Martin is genuinely interested in the people and the history of the place. I expect Raymond will rope him into helping him catch snakes this time."

"For God's sake, don't tell Catherine that. She'd have a fit. Do you feel like a sherry?"

"That's a nice idea. Thank you. I will."

For the next hour they talked about Martin – sometimes about Catherine, but mostly about Martin. They broke off when Martin returned to ask Robert what provisions he needed from Viraswami's.

"I can go myself," said Robert, but Martin wouldn't hear of it. Robert gave him the money and the car keys.

"Are you sure?" asked Martin. "Dad doesn't let me drive his."

"Nor would I if I had a car like your dad's. Go carefully, but there's not a lot of traffic on the roads on a Sunday morning."

"That was good of you," said Malcolm and they continued their chat. Robert's opinion of Malcolm climbed higher and higher. "I think he'll cope all right at University," Malcolm continued, just as they heard the front door being opened. "I'd prefer him to be with somebody he knows – someone like Raymond. We'll have to see. Anyway, enough of that topic. She's back."

Catherine had been pleasantly surprised. Not only could the new curate read – an ability she had previously doubted – but he also appeared to be a gentleman, or at least as like a gentleman one as one of "them" could possibly be.

"I'd like to invite him round one day," she said – to Malcolm's obvious astonishment. "If he were to wear his clerical collar, that would be all right. I wouldn't want the neighbours to get the wrong impression. I thought you'd gone out, Robert. Where's your car?"

The news that her son was driving it and that he had gone shopping without a detailed list was enough to make Catherine stop worrying about the impact on the neighbourhood of a Kenyan visitor – even one with a clerical collar. Robert already knew that Martin had only held a licence for a year, but Catherine told him again nevertheless. Only slightly mollified after having been told that Robert's insurance was adequate, she took herself upstairs to change again.

"She'll stand looking out of the window till he comes back so that she can judge the distance between the gateposts and the car," said Malcolm, with a smile. "I love her dearly but there are times..." Robert nodded sympathetically.

A driving instructor might have found fault with the extreme care with which Martin drove. Two following cars had to slow down whilst he negotiated the entry to the drive. Robert guessed that he'd seen his mother at the window, an impression heightened by the fact that she was at the front door, holding it open whilst Martin took plastic bags out of the car. Ibrahim, whose normal duty this was, remained in the kitchen.

"I got a leg of lamb. They were going cheap and Kiberech is good with lamb," said Martin when he came in.

"Good idea. Thanks."

Catherine was strangely subdued for the rest of the day. That is not to say that she was silent, of course. That would have been a miracle, but there were one or two occasions when she failed to rise. At lunch-time Malcolm mentioned his new Kenyan assistant. Martin spoke of his friend the accountant whose recent pay rise meant that he could afford to send another son to school. There was obviously something on her mind and Robert had a very good idea what it was. In some ways it was a pity that Martin was going away and wouldn't be able to fight for his independence. She was almost certainly firing off the first few rounds at Malcolm as Robert drove out.

"On the way at last!" said Martin. "Thank God for that."

Raymond, as untidy looking as ever, was ready with his bag and his snake-catching stick by the side of the house. The zip on the bag had broken and it was tied round with a length of rope. Martin got out to put it into the car for him. Another piece of rope had to be found to tie the implement on to the roof rack. Robert suggested that they should change places halfway, but Raymond said he was quite happy in the back.

He didn't go back into the house at all. Robert drove slowly at first. Sunlight flashed through the thick foliage of the avocado trees which lined the road.

"On the way at last," said Raymond.

"That's what I said. What are we going to do when we get there?" Martin asked.

"What do you think?" Raymond asked.

Martin laughed. "I thought you'd brought that pole to catch snakes with," he said.

"I have, but you can't catch snakes all the time."

"What's George doing this week?" Martin asked.

"Search me. Getting laid by his new friend, I guess."

"Robert said something like that. Do you really think so?"

"Of course he is. Did I tell you about last Tuesday?"

"I don't think so. What happened?"

"Well, I was in the bugs lab with Father Cox. That would have been about five o'clock. Long after everybody had gone home, and what do we see?"

"What?"

"We see George's lover drive up to the main doors. Not the side door: the main door. He's got some car, I may say. A Ferrari, I think. Anyway, George appears as if by magic, gets in the car and off they go together."

"On a Tuesday? Where would they be going on a Tuesday?" Martin asked.

"A hotel, of course. The New Stanley, probably, for a night of lust."

"George's folks wouldn't allow it," said Martin indignantly.

"What the hell has it got to do with them? He's over eighteen."

"Your –"

"My what?"

"– imagination may be running away with you," Robert interjected. "In fairness we don't know. We may be putting two and two together and making five."

"Or three, if you take this bloke's prick as one and George's arse as two," said Raymond.

The thought, even the vicarious thought, of a night with George was an enjoyable one. Robert glanced down at Martin's long legs and the immaculate creases in his trousers. Only a few weeks ago George had been sitting in the same seat. He should have realised then that there was no chance. A two-year-old Mazda and a bungalow in the bundu didn't match up to a Ferrari and a night in the New Stanley.

The conversation turned to cricket and then to snake-catching, enabling Robert to get a grip on his thoughts and concentrate on his driving. He turned off the main road and on to the dirt road. "Nearly there," he said – unnecessarily, for they both knew the road. He stopped for a few minutes for them to watch a rhinoceros in the distance. It lifted its head and stared in their direction. Robert drove on. Mr Hanson had told him what an angry rhino could do to a car and its occupants. Martin wanted to stop and chat to a group of Samburu warriors but Raymond said that most Samburu didn't speak Swahili.

"There's somebody behind us," said Raymond when they were near the house.

"I know. I can see him," said Robert. The dust cloud in his rear-view mirror had been getting nearer for the last few minutes.

"He'll have a job overtaking us on this road," said Martin, turning to crane his neck. The dust cloud got bigger until Robert could just make out the vehicle that was causing it. It was a Land Rover: a dark green Land Rover.

"Shit!" he said.

"Why?"

"One of Mr Hanson's cars. Looks like we are going to have a visitor."

Martin laughed. "I'm glad Mum said...I mean, I'm glad I put trousers on, if we're to be surrounded by poshness," he said. "Don't worry, Ray. We'll make out that you're a servant of some sort. We won't tell him why we employ you, of course, though that would be a laugh. 'He's merely a servant, Mr Hanson. We don't spend money on his clothes. He doesn't usually wear any. We just keep him for fisting. Maybe you'd care to try –'"

"I'm older than you are, so watch out," said Raymond.

"In point of fact, it isn't Mr Hanson at all," said Robert, who had slowed down.

"That's a relief," said Martin. "You can do without visitors on the first evening."

"Oh, he's a visitor anyway. That's Patrick, the son." Robert turned down the hill. Patrick drew up close and flashed his lights and then followed them down the hill and into the drive.

"Hi! Oh, I'm sorry," he said as he climbed out of the Land Rover. "I didn't know you had company. Kiberech said you were due back this afternoon. He said nothing about visitors. If I'd known..."

Kiberech came running out of the house and a sort of melee ensued, with Robert ineffectually trying to make introductions. "This is Patrick. Patrick, this is Martin Marriott."

"How do you do?"

"Nice to meet you."

"Put the stuff in the yellow bags in the fridge, Kiberech....And this is Raymond." But Raymond was already talking in Swahili to Kiberech, who was shaking hands with Patrick.

Eventually, things sorted themselves out. Raymond and Kiberech took the shopping inside, leaving Patrick, Martin and Robert standing on the verandah.

"Grief! My grandmother once said *I* was tall for my age," said Martin to Patrick. "You're amazing!"

"I think drinks would be in order," said Robert. Martin was liable to get a crick in the neck if they stood talking for much longer. Raymond was still in the house talking to Kiberech, but Robert brought out a couple of chairs whilst Martin attended to the drinks.

"Phew. I needed that," said Robert after the first sip.

"Me too," said Martin. "You sure you wouldn't prefer a beer, Patrick?"

"No. Most Friends don't drink."

"Mine do," said Martin. Patrick explained. "Oh. Sorry," said Martin, but the faux pas didn't seem to make any difference. The two of them were soon discussing life at university. Robert was happy enough to sit there and absorb the atmosphere of a Kenyan evening. Raymond came out and joined in. Oxford and the Isis. Durham and the Wear. Ancient buildings. Wonderful facilities – none of them could possibly match Kenya, Robert thought, contentedly. He breathed deeply to inhale the smell of wood-smoke and knew, somehow, that he would never forget. It was as Martin's teacher had said, a combination of the senses. The sun was low in the sky. Crickets were chirping in the grass and the hedge. Tusker beer had a taste all of its own and the bottle felt cool to the touch. He didn't have Pat or his mother-in-law to worry about any more and he had the company of three very pleasant young men, two of whom... He pushed that thought out of his mind. It would be a disaster if Patrick were to notice the physical effect of it.

"Are you staying to dinner, Patrick?" he asked, interrupting Patrick's enthusiastic account of a new racing eight.

"May I?"

"I've already told Kiberech that you are," said Raymond. "He's doing roast lamb."

"I'd better call home to tell them – if that's all right," said Patrick.

"No family Meeting tonight then?" Robert asked.

"Oh, it won't matter just for once." He went inside the house.

"He's a really nice bloke," said Martin. Raymond agreed.

"I hope he comes round often," said Martin.

"Not too often," said Robert in a deliberately low voice. "There might be times when we don't want to be disturbed."

"Oh, yes. I see. Well, maybe we can go and visit him."

"I'm sure you can."

Patrick put his head round the door. "Can I have a word with you, Robert?" he said. Robert got to his feet and went into the house. Patrick was standing by the phone, holding the receiver against the palm of his hand.

"What is it?" Robert asked.

"Peter's flying up tomorrow with George and stopping for lunch. Dad says, do you want to come?"

"Could do, I suppose. It might be interesting."

"I don't want to meet him again. Peter, I mean. I'd like to see George again, but Peter gives me the creeps. Shall I tell him you've got guests?"

"If you do that, he'll invite them as well. I'd better speak to them first."

Patrick put the receiver to his ear again. "Robert's in the bathroom at the moment, Father. He's just coming out," he said.

Telling lies was obviously not in the same bracket as drinking, Robert thought as he went out on to the verandah again.

"Shit!" said Martin vehemently. "I told Mum to tell George I was with a friend in Gilgil if he calls. I don't want him to know we're here."

"Why not?" Raymond asked.

"Stupid question. If he knows we're here, he'll want to join us."

"So?"

Martin looked behind him, smiled and then said, in a low

voice, "I've graduated from just fisting people and that's all you get from George."

Raymond grinned. "All *we* get, you mean. I'll bet my bottom dollar Peter gets a lot more."

Robert went inside the house again. "You'd better let me talk to him," he said. He took the phone from Patrick.

"I'm so sorry, Mr Hanson. Call of nature. Probably something I ate down in Nairobi...Yes. Patrick told me. I'm so sorry. I was going to ring you in the morning about lunch anyway. I'm afraid I shan't be able to make it tomorrow...Oh. One moment." Patrick was pointing to himself and mouthing words. Robert put his hand over the receiver.

"Get me out of it as well if you can?" Patrick requested.

"Are you there, Mr Hanson? It's rather difficult. One of the lads who was here recently dug a vegetable garden and I asked Patrick to come down tomorrow to have a look at it and advise me on what to plant. Yes, of course. Here he is."

Patrick took over. "Hello, Father...Yes. I think it'll take all day. I need to do a soil test, really. He's right on the edge of the Rift as you know...Yes. Erosion...Could do, I suppose. That's a good tip. Anyway, I'll talk to you about it when I get home. I don't suppose Peter will miss me that much."

"Thanks a million," he said, when he had put down the phone. "It's a pretty weak excuse, but he doesn't seem put out. I suppose there really is a vegetable patch."

"Sure there is. Raymond will show you."

They went out on to the verandah again. It was empty. "Where are they?" Patrick asked.

Robert laughed. "That's typical of Raymond," he said. "That lad can't sit still for more than a few seconds. They're probably round the back of the house. Raymond reckons I've got a nest of snakes in the compost heap."

"Blow that. I like him. In fact they're both nice."

"Yes, they are," he said.

Robert's beer had gone slightly flat. Nonetheless he took a long swig before answering. He didn't know if historically there had been eastern potentates with all-male harems but, at that moment, he felt like one.

"Raymond is interesting, he seems to fit in with life in the bundu, if you know what I mean. Martin looks as if he's come from the city."

"Which he has, but I think I know what you mean," said Robert, envisaging the crude darn in Raymond's shorts and the dark stains on his shirt – not to mention his mop of hair that always looked as if it hadn't been combed for years.

"I'd like to draw him. Do you think he'd let me?" Patrick asked.

"I'm sure he would. Ask him when he comes back."

"I wouldn't like to do that. I've only known him for a matter of minutes."

A swishing noise came from the side of the house and then the sound of Raymond's voice. "You often get them in long grass like this," he was saying. "I'll show you tomorrow."

"No, ta very much and all that. I'll leave the snakes to you." They came on to the verandah by climbing over the side wall. "You didn't let on?" Martin asked.

"No," Robert replied. "Ray, can you show Patrick the bit of land you dug? His excuse is that he's coming down tomorrow to test the soil and give us advice about planting it."

"You can see it from here. Over there in the corner. I snipped the hedge back a bit, too."

"Better take Patrick over there."

Patrick was on his feet in seconds. "Yes, I think I'd better have a closer look. I should take a soil sample home, really. Father's got this testing kit," he explained.

"He's a nice chap, isn't he?" said Martin.

At that moment, Raymond was crouching low by the side of

the plot. In that position it was a wonder his shorts didn't split. Robert licked his lips – as his eastern potentate counterpart would certainly have done at the thought of what that taut, khaki material contained. Raymond stood up and came back, leaving Patrick standing over the plot like a colossus.

"Patrick needs something to take some soil home in," he explained. He went inside and returned with one of the newly emptied plastic supermarket bags. This time it was Patrick who crouched. Robert admired Patrick's arse.

"He must be incredibly strong," said Martin. It was almost as if he could read Robert's thoughts.

"He must be, if he's a rower," Robert replied.

"Do you reckon he fists?" Martin whispered.

"I guess he must."

"Mmm. I'll bet he's got a beauty."

It was probably as well that Patrick and Raymond returned at that moment. Thoughts such as Martin had generated had a visible side-effect. The next half hour was spent discussing possible crops. If Patrick had his way, there would be hardly any need for Robert to spend his weekends in Nairobi. Cabbages, potatoes – even endives, whatever they were – would grow in profusion. Why, if he or Raymond were to enlarge the plot, there would be scope for fruit, as well. Not only that, but he could keep chickens – even a pig, maybe. A couple of rolls of wire should be sufficient. Robert had not the slightest intention of turning into a smallholder but said nothing.

Dinner was served. "Did your father say why Peter is coming tomorrow?" Robert asked as he carved the joint.

"It's that aerial photography I mentioned," said Patrick.

"He's brought the date forward then. He said he was going to start it in the holidays when your father went down to meet your brothers."

"When did he say that?"

"Oh, a couple of weeks ago."

"That's odd. Father must have spoken to him, I suppose."

Martin frowned and gave Robert a look Catherine would have been proud of. "What time tomorrow are you coming to look at the garden, Patrick?" he asked. Patrick said he could come at any time. Raymond said he planned to do a bit of snake-hunting very early in the morning but would be free after eleven.

It was arranged that Patrick should call at about eleven o'clock. "That way I can miss the poisonous toad altogether," he said. "I just hope he doesn't arrive too early."

"Not George?" Martin asked.

"No. I like George. Peter Hardwick. I know you're supposed to see good in everybody, but that man stretches the imagination. I wish Father had never brought the two of them together."

"You think what I think," said Raymond. "He's, er...getting at George."

"Foul creature," said Patrick. "People like that should be locked up."

Once again, Martin caught Robert's eye, but this time it wasn't a glare but a glitter of amusement.

Patrick left them quite late, not that any of them minded. He was good company. Raymond and Martin plied him with questions about university life. Raymond became more and more enthusiastic about the proposed garden and let slip the news that Robert would be there for another full year to enjoy the produce. That led to a discussion of Robert's plans, with which Patrick agreed enthusiastically. "It would be better if you left the armed forces altogether," he said. "The Quakers believe that if all the countries in the world disbanded their forces, the world would be a better place altogether."

It wasn't an argument Robert felt like following up – especially at half-past ten at night. Patrick picked up his bag of Kampi-ya-Moto soil, slung it into the Land Rover and drove off.

"A really nice chap," said Martin as they watched the rear lights disappearing over the crest of the hill.

"Even if far too religious," said Raymond.

"He can't be all that religious. He didn't say a blessing at meal-time. Did you notice?"

"But sufficiently religious for you to forget about him in the carnal sense," said Robert. He put an arm round each of them.

"I didn't. Well...I might have done," said Martin.

"Forget it. Who's sleeping with who tonight?"

"Let's do it with three of us," said Raymond. "Is your bed big enough?"

"Oh, I think we can just about squeeze in." Robert's cock began enthusiastically to agree.

"A three-man spunky orgy! Great!" said Martin.

Robert slid his hands down the two boys. Martin tensed up immediately. Raymond, on the other hand, moved even closer until their sides were pressing together. It was surprising, Robert thought, how different two young men could be. Even allowing for the smooth texture of Martin's expensive trousers and the rough stiffness of Raymond's shorts, their initial reactions were different. Their arses were different. Martin's had relaxed slightly but still felt tight and delightfully round. Raymond's was broader and much softer. Robert moved his hands down a bit further. Raymond's flesh yielded like a blancmange. Martin's felt more rubbery to the touch.

"We ought to have a shower first," said Raymond. "I feel like someone's thrown a bucket of dust all over me."

"Have it later. You'll need one then, anyway," said Robert.

"I think I ought to. The dust leaves horrible red marks on the sheets and that wouldn't be fair on Kiberech."

"The sheets will be in a mess anyway, and no electricity means no hair-dryer. It's too late to stand outside to dry it."

"I can rough-dry it with a towel."

"It probably is a good idea," Martin added. "Mmm. I thought you'd get round to that."

Hoping that a little manipulation might delay their wish for personal cleanliness, Robert had transferred his hands to their fronts. Martin's cock was difficult to find at first but, after a little groping, Robert traced its soft outline as it was just beginning to make its presence known. Raymond, on the other hand, actually put down a hand and guided Robert's fingers to the right place. Something like four inches of rapidly hardening and lengthening flesh moved as if it had a will of its own under the material of his shorts.

Robert tried to locate the zip fasteners but, in that position, it proved to be impossible.

"We could shower together. That would make it quicker," said Martin.

"You might get two under my shower, but not three," said Robert.

"Oh. Pity."

It was all too apparent that they were going to have their way. "I'll use the bath and you two can shower together. How would that be?" Robert asked.

"Okay. Let's do that, then," said Raymond, whose cock had grown to the proportion of a very useful handle and ideal for holding him back – but Robert let it go. Filling the bath and running the shower at the same time needed a degree of skill and care. Once, Pat had decided to soak the curtains in the bath and have a shower at the same time. If Kiberech hadn't run in to warn her, the outside boiler would have imploded.

"You have to fill the bath first," Robert explained when they were inside again. "We can get undressed while that's happening and then you can have your shower and I shall lie back in the tub and relax – and watch you at the same time, of course."

"A regular peeping Tom," said Martin, laughing.

"You're a great one to talk. What about you and Vijay?" said Robert.

"Ah! That was different. Vijay is worth looking at. We're not."

"Don't you believe it," said Robert as he peeled off his shirt. Martin had already taken his off. One look at his pectoral muscles and his arms was all that had been needed to make Robert's voice sound breathless.

"Yes, don't you believe it," said Raymond. He was sitting on the edge of the bed, taking off his shoes.

"I could tell you something else that you won't believe either," said Martin, undoing his belt.

Robert continued to undress. "What's that?" he asked.

"You have to promise not to tell anyone. Especially you, Ray."

"I think I know what's coming, but tell us. We promise," said Ray. Robert said nothing. He was too busy trying to make out the motif of Raymond's boxer shorts, which looked as if they'd been designed by someone pretty high on a hallucinogenic drug.

"I've fisted Vijay," said Martin, triumphantly.

"Good for you." Raymond stood up and the boxers slid down. He stepped out of them. His cock was upright and at such an angle that the tip was less than an inch away from the flat skin of his abdomen.

"Where did you do it?" he asked.

"In the arboretum, actually. He said he felt randy and so did I. He said he fancied a walk and I said I'd go with him. He did me as well. He's fantastic."

Raymond grinned at Robert.

"Only you mustn't say a word, especially you, Ray. Vijay says that if his dad ever finds out, he'll throw him out of the house."

"You can rely on me to keep my mouth shut," said Raymond. "When's the next time going to be?"

Martin pulled his sparkling white Y-fronts down to his knees, stood up and stepped out of them. Once again, Robert was struck by the difference between the two young men. This time it was a matter of angles. Both cocks were eagerly erect but Martin's stood out at ninety degrees. Both were dry and that was a good thing but, if they kept talking about Vijay, anything might happen.

"I'll go and have my bath," Robert said. "You need to give it about five minutes for the boiler to fill up enough but don't make it any longer than that."

In fact, Robert had far too much bath-water. That was apparent when he got into it. His cock, stiff as that could be, was completely submerged. In fact, he thought, that was probably a good thing. A cold shower was just the thing to cool the boys' ardour and he would have the pleasure of warming them up again – bringing them both to boiling point. He washed and waited – and waited. He stood up, soaped his cock and balls liberally and sat down again. There was still no sign of them. If he sat completely still he could hear voices from the bedroom, but not what they were saying. If they were still talking about Vijay Shah, it was quite likely that Martin would come in seconds. He wasn't so sure about Raymond, who had actually had the famous Shah tool in his mouth. Anticipation was a more powerful aphrodisiac than recollection.

The boiler gurgled loudly and then stopped. "Hurry up!" Robert shouted.

"Just coming!" Martin called.

"I hope not," Robert muttered. He was plying a sponge over his shoulders when they walked in. Both cocks had gone down. Not completely, but they were certainly less rampant than they had been a few minutes previously.

"I was just telling Ray about the gold cup," said Martin.

"I think it's the funniest thing in years," said Raymond.

"Yes. It's one of those myths, as I told Martin," said Robert.

"No. That's not what I meant. The laugh is, George is letting Peter Hardwick fuck his arse in the hope of getting loads of money when they find it, and all the time it's not there. Boy! Is he going to be sore!"

"In one sense he might well be," said Robert. Raymond went into the shower. Martin followed him. Raymond made an attempt to close the curtain but Martin pulled it back again and winked at Robert. One of them turned on the water. The sound of water splattering on the tiled floor prevented Robert from hearing more than the occasional word and it was as well that his cock was submerged so that the effect of the visual delight they afforded wasn't apparent to them. Once again, his imagination transported him to an oriental palace. One needed a eunuch really, he thought – or maybe not a eunuch, but a devoted slave who would say something like 'Which one will delight you tonight?' and he would reply 'Both of them,' but he would say it in a languid, bored tone which belied his true excited state.

There was Raymond, whose hair grew darker and darker from the straw-blond shock on his head to the dark brown clump at his groin and the much blacker hairs on his legs. The effect of the cascading water made them look like pencil lines against his brown skin. Then there was Martin. He had his back to Robert and was equally sun-tanned, save for the broad white band of his arse – and what an arse! The more Robert contemplated it, the more perfect it looked. He loved the way it contrasted with the slight concavity of Martin's back. He lay back in the bath to admire the hairs on the inside of Martin's thighs and the way they faded out above his knees and then reappeared below them.

"...do it."

"Okay. Be careful, though. Don't get me going too soon."

Robert lay quite still. Raymond's left hand ran down Martin's spine and came to rest on his right buttock.

"...going to let me?"

"Sure. Not tonight, though. Tomorrow maybe."

"I'll be snake-hunting and then Patrick's coming."

"We'll find time."

"...let me fuck you before?"

"I've learned a lot from Robert."

Another hand, clasping a tablet of soap joined its partner. At that point the hot water must have given out. One of them turned off the taps. The hands began to move until Martin's buttocks were smoth-ered with suds. The soap fell to the floor. The fingers of Raymond's hands touched each other.

"You feel really good," Raymond murmured. "Sort of springy."

"So do you," Martin replied. "Hey! Be careful!"

"I was only feeling it. Is Robert the only one?"

"Yes."

"So far. I'm next. And then..."

"Then what?"

"Then who, you mean. How about Vijay?"

"Some chance! Anyway, I don't fancy letting him. I wouldn't mind fucking him, though. He's got a lovely figure. All slim and...Stop there. That's enough."

Robert got out of the bath, pulled out the plug and dried himself. Raymond and Martin emerged and flopped through the pool of water on the floor to the towel rail. Fortunately Robert had put several out, remembering the time when he had inadvertently used George's towel.

None of them spoke during the drying process and there was a tension of some sort in the air which hadn't been there before. It was as if they had only just discovered Robert's presence.

"I'll finish off in the bedroom," Robert said. "Come in when you're ready."

Both of them had wrapped towels round their middles, but they could not mask the outline of two very large erect cocks.

"You're ready, all right," Robert muttered as he stepped into his bedroom. He looked down. "And so, for that matter, am I."

Chapter Fifteen

Once again, Robert waited. He got two extra pillows out of the cupboard and slipped new covers on them before getting into bed. He lay in the middle and glanced from one side to the other. It would be a bit of a squeeze, he thought. They were both built like barns, but the three of them would manage somehow. The word "squeeze" would have been better forgotten. Robert couldn't resist the urge to slide his hand under the cover to caress his cock, which was as impatient as he was. That had to stop, of course. He put both hands behind his head and lay there. Of course, Raymond would need a long time to dry his hair. In that case, why didn't Martin come in and leave him to it? They were obviously talking to each other – but about what? About him? Giving each other little tips? That was another expression with a double meaning. Big tips possibly? Big tips, dripping with viscous fluid…

He tried to force himself to think about work. Had Peter filed a flight plan? He must have done. In that case, the details of his flight would be on the daily "mayfly" when it came through in the morning. "One Cessna Skymaster. Persons on board: two. Permitted to land on private landing area. Overflying restricted area prohibited except in case of absolute necessity." It wouldn't say anything about something else that should be prohibited and the purpose of the flight would probably not be given, either. It would be a laugh if that had to be put down on the 1156. "Type of aircraft", "Registration number", "Name of pilot", "Licence number", "Cruising altitude", "Bearings", "Beacons" – all that. Then there would have to be a big space, maybe a separate sheet for "Purpose of Flight"...

Item One: Get George worked-up in the aircraft. That should be easy enough, once Peter had achieved his cruising altitude. Stick in one hand and something similar but much more responsive in the other.

Item Two: Do the photography. For that George would have to slide a window open and lean out. One could only hope that Peter was a good pilot. Holding a low altitude with an arse like George's to admire would not be easy.

Item Three: Fly back to Mombasa. A sherry or a beer? "Did you enjoy the day, George?...Yes, they're charming people. Much more your cup of tea than railway engineers or jumped-up civil engineering clerks who think they're the cat's whiskers because they hold commissions in the Air Force. You're different. Come and sit here with me. There's not a lot of room. Why not sit on my lap? That's right. My word, you're big. Let's see if the rest of you is in proportion. It felt like it this morning. Mmm. I thought so. As for all this silly 'fisting' business you told me about, there is so much more than that. That sort of thing is all right for the working classes, but you and I are different. We can do what we like. As for sitting out on a verandah dressed in African night-wear! I never heard anything so ridiculous. A young man like you should be properly dressed until the time comes for someone of your own class to undress you."

It was unlikely that a person operating a camera in an aircraft with the window open would have worn shorts but the fantasy was so enjoyable that Robert kept it going. Raymond and Martin had not been forgotten by any means but, if the mind is fully occupied, waiting can be less tedious.

"Specially tailored for you? An excellent idea. Stand up for a moment. There! That's better! Now sit down again. Just the shirt. Mmm. A body like yours deserves good quality clothes. There! That's better. These are magnificent! I like young men with big balls, especially when they go with a cock like this. You're going to taste delicious. I know you are. You've denied yourself so much pleasure in the last few years. Your parents' religious beliefs probably have a lot to do with it. We'll start with a spot of fellatio...Yes, that's what the working classes call it. They have no imagination at all. We speak of 'dining', not 'food eating'. I prefer to think of it in terms of a flower: a particularly beautiful blossom in your case – and, I shall suck the nectar from you. And then, dearest George, after dinner we shall go to bed, but not to sleep. I shall compensate for having sipped your sweet syrup. Oh, you're as tight and as soft as a bud down there. You're going to experience such delights – and just think – we can do it as often as we want, now that we've decided that there is no point in your going to some boring university.

"If you delay going for a year, I can't see any problem. I can't tell you how I know or who told me but I happen to know he likes you and he's keen."

"Mum and Dad wouldn't mind. They've been on at me to do just that. Mum especially."

It took some minutes for Robert to snap out of his reverie and realise that Raymond and Martin had come into the room. He opened his eyes. "You took your time," he said. "I was half asleep." His body might have been, but his cock was very far from comatose.

"Sorry. I was drying my hair and we had something to talk about," said Raymond. "I see you've grabbed the best place. Who goes on what side?"

"It doesn't really matter," said Robert. They parted and approached the bed from different directions. Martin climbed in on his left and Raymond on his right.

Martin chuckled slightly as he lifted the covers to get in. Robert knew why.

"Well, now we're here, who does what?" Raymond asked.

"Let's not rush. What were you talking about?"

"I want to ask you a question first," said Martin. "Will you answer this completely honestly?"

"Sure. What is it?"

"Which one of us do you love most?"

"Oh, that's unfair, Martin. You can't expect me to answer that. I'm not at all sure that I could. I mean...you're both different."

"No. Come on. Tell me. It's important."

Robert reached out and touched Raymond.

"Then I would say you," he said, addressing Martin but tapping Raymond lightly. The intention was to get the message of "I'm only saying this. I don't mean it of course," across.

To Robert's amazement, Raymond said, "There. What did I tell you?"

"Then that settles it," said Martin. "I delay going. That should make everybody happy. You, Robert and Mum and Dad."

"And Vijay," said Raymond.

"And Vijay."

"Would one of you mind telling me what all this is about?" Robert asked. He moved his right hand down to about an inch above Raymond's navel. He moved it further downwards and put out his other hand. Martin's fingers wrapped round his wrist and gently guided him to the right place.

Once again, Robert had the opportunity to compare them. Of the two, Raymond's hair was more prolific and much coarser in texture than Martin's silky and still slightly damp bush. Raymond's balls were bigger too, but when Robert's fingers found their cocks, Martin took the lead. The swelling skin felt like satin and it was so beautifully proportioned...Robert gasped involuntarily as two hands landed on his thighs simultaneously and began to move slowly upwards.

Punctuated by the oddest sounds from right and left, the story came out.

"Vijay likes Martin and Martin likes Vijay," said Raymond.

"And if I go off to England next year instead of this year, we could...well, you know. Mmm."

"I don't want to put a damper on the idea, but where would you do it? I gather that Vijay's father is a risk and your mother..."

Putting a "damper" on things was actually a good idea, Robert thought. Their pulse rates were speeding up fast, Martin's particularly – and his own. Robert could actually hear his own heart. He spread his legs to allow a bunch of fingers to reach under his balls.

"Mum would be all right, I think. Vijay's rich and if I tell her that he's one of the people who persuaded me...Mmm."

"Have you thought about what you'll do during that year, Martin?"

"Well, no. Not yet."

"What you could do..."

"What?"

"You could probably get a job teaching at the school in the village or ask Mr Hanson if he can use you in the farm training school."

"You mean ...Oh, yeah. That's nice. You mean live here?"

"Why not?"

"That'd be great. And I can go down to Nairobi with you every weekend and see Vijay. You wouldn't mind that?"

"Not at all. I shall have you during the week."

"It's now I'm more concerned with at the moment," said Raymond. "I'll come in a minute if you don't stop." But he sounded much more calm than Martin, who was already beginning to breathe heavily.

Robert took his hand away and turned on his side to face

Martin. Starting at the young man's nipples, he stroked downwards until both hands met at the base of Martin's cock.

"Did you get the stuff out ready?" Martin asked.

"On the bedside table."

Martin turned over and raised his head. "You've got enough grease there to lubricate a locomotive," he said.

"Two locomotives, actually," said Robert.

The analogy was accurate. Martin didn't actually whistle when Robert's finger went into him, but he sounded like a whistle. He gasped and then groaned when the second digit, dripping with lubricant, came into play and – as always – he wriggled his bottom.

"Shall I turn out the light?" Robert whispered.

"No. I want to see," said Raymond, from the other side of the bed.

"Let him," Martin gasped. The hissing of the gas lamp was added to all the other sounds. There was Martin's long drawn-out groan as a twenty-nine-year-old cock which had, in the days of Robert's marriage, been so badly misplaced, insinuated itself past the tight muscle-ring and, finding itself properly employed at last, began to inch its way into Martin's soft and yielding interior.

There was a memory of Pat. Only a fleeting one. A day they'd spent on a restored steam railway. The puffing of the locomotive as it climbed a gradient really did sound exactly like a young man being fucked. But Martin was no ordinary young man. Martin couldn't be compared to the young men in the past. Martin would be with him, it seemed, for a whole year and there was no chance that Robert would ever forget his name as he had with some of the others. A whole year with Martin! A whole year doing this and then...well, that was in the future...

Another sound made itself manifest, very softly at first. Robert's hips made contact with the smooth and still slightly damp skin of Martin's rump.

"Oh yeah! Fuck him. He loves it!" That was Raymond's voice

and Robert didn't need to guess what he was doing. The mattress on Raymond's side had taken on a wobble quite different from the regular compressions of the springs.

Martin jerked convulsively. Robert pushed even harder. Martin groaned. The train was very near the summit. Just a few feet more...a few millimetres, actually. Would they make it before the boiler burst? Yes, they would. Yes...yes...yes!

"Aaah!" Martin tightened. Robert thrust and both bodies stiffened as the engine and the engine-driver – a perfect combination – spurted.

Robert lowered his head to kiss the back of Martin's head. "Christ! That was the best ever!" he gasped. At that moment, Raymond let out a cry and Robert felt flecks of moisture spatter on to his sweating back.

All three lay still for a very long time. Finally, still trying to get his breath back, Robert withdrew.

"That was good," said Raymond, patting his back.

"Your turn in the morning," Robert replied. "I just hope I'll have the energy."

"Actually, so do I," said Raymond. "Time to turn off the gas?"

"Time," said Robert reaching out towards it. "Good night, both."

"Night, Robert," said Raymond – and Martin snored.

One of the nicest ways of being woken up – even if it is still dark outside – is to feel a young man's fingers wrap round your cock. Coincidentally, Robert was dreaming about Raymond capturing a gigantic python when it happened.

"You were well away," Raymond whispered. "Ah. That's better. It's beginning to wake up. Is Martin asleep?"

"He must be."

"Make sure."

"That's a bit unfair. You wanted to watch him."

"He can wake up later. I want to talk to you first."

Robert touched Martin's shoulder. "Are you awake?" There was no answer. He touched Martin's arm. "You awake, Martin?" he asked, more loudly this time. Martin stirred slightly, grunted and turned on to his side.

"He's asleep," Robert whispered. "What is it? Me saying I loved Martin more than you? I'm sorry about that, but you see..."

"God, no! Of course you do. It was the right thing to say and if you can get him a job up here that would be perfect. You'll have him for a year and then come to England and I'll be there waiting for you."

"That's a nice idea. You can't put yours off?" Robert reached out, touched hair and then found what he was looking for. It was already in that enjoyable half-hard state.

"No. I'll have to go. It's about that, actually. Can you make sure Martin doesn't let Vijay down?"

"How do you mean?"

"Well, despite what he said, you know what his mother is like. She'll go ballistic if she finds out that he's even friendly with an Asian. I've promised Vijay that Martin will...well, sort of look after his needs when I'm not around. He's looking forward to it. I just don't want him to be disappointed. I'm actually really fond of Vijay and he won't do a bloody George on us. Vijay isn't a snob."

"Funnily enough, I was thinking about George when I was waiting for you. He'll be up here tomorrow."

Raymond sniggered. "And right now someone's 'up' him," he said. "Are you ready yet?"

"Nearly. Hang on. I'll have to reach over Martin to get the stuff."

That was easier said than done. If Robert had thought about it, it would have been much more sensible to secrete the rubber and the tube under the pillow – but, on the other hand, the tube might have burst. He struggled as carefully as he could on to his knees and leaned over. Raymond's hand left his tool and stroked his buttocks. He put a hand on the head-board to steady himself and reached over. The tube nearly fell on to the floor. He just managed to stop it in time.

"There!" he whispered. "Now then..." He lifted the covers. Raymond's cock was at ninety degrees which, for most people, would count as a full erection – but not for Raymond. A little more patience was necessary and, probably as a result of having shot his load only a few hours previously, Robert was in a patient mood.

"Tell me more about Vijay," he whispered. "What's he really like?"

Raymond took a deep breath. "Well, he looks magnificent," he said.

"I know. I met him in Nairobi when I was with Martin and George."

"That's right. Vijay said he'd met Martin and he was with a man. He wondered if...if you know what I mean."

"You'd better not tell him. Leave that to Martin. Tell me more." Robert touched the tip of Raymond's cock. Raymond didn't move away.

"Well, he says he's not gay and I believe him. George says the same thing about himself, but we know what he's doing. Martin said it until he met you. Vijay does it for kicks."

"So how did you find out?" Raymond's cock was hardening by the minute and beginning to tick, like the second hand of a clock, in an arc leading to his navel.

"He's curious. If you start talking about it, he wants to know all the details. I was talking to him about wanking and he said there was a lot of that in their religion. They have stone penises and people pour coconut milk on them and that sort of thing. Well, one thing led to another. I said one of my favourite ways of doing it is lying on my stomach and sort of fucking the mattress and he'd never heard of that before and wanted me to show him. That was a laugh. I showed him the actions down by the cricket nets when he had a free period."

"But you didn't come?" Robert asked. That was almost certainly the reason for Raymond's belly-close erection, he thought – which was imminent. He took the head of Raymond's cock between his thumb and forefinger.

"God, no. Not there. Anyway, he kept on about it. He said he'd tried it one night and it was good and then he asked if I knew any other ways so I thought, in for a penny, in for a pound, and took him home one day. That's when he told me he's engaged already. His fiancée is in India. His dad fixed it up. So...there I was thinking, 'Shit!' and he started to get undressed. Oh God! You never saw a body like his. He's brown all over – even between his arse-cheeks and he's tall and slim...Bloody hell, just thinking about him makes me randy."

"So I see – or feel," said Robert. "You sucked him?"

"Yes. That was brilliant. He tastes nice, too."

"And that's as far as you got?"

"Yeah. I asked him to let me fuck him, but he wouldn't. Then he said he'd think about it. He said that Martin and George watched him in the showers. I told him why, so he wanted all the details. There weren't that many; in those days all they did was go round to each other's houses and wank. I didn't tell him that. I told him that Martin was the most outstanding fuck and fucker I'd ever known."

"Outstanding, certainly," said Robert. "I think it's time you turned over."

"Me too," said Raymond. "Funny how talking about it gets you like this." His cock was pressed hard against his belly. He turned over and parted his legs.

Just as Robert's fingers were busily occupied again, Martin spoke. "What was that about me?" he asked.

"How long have you been awake?" Raymond groaned as Robert spoke.

"I just woke up. I just heard my name."

"Ask him to tell you in the morning. Go back to sleep."

"You must be joking!"

"Well, don't light the lamp."

"Don't worry. I'll just listen," said Martin.

He wouldn't have been disappointed. Raymond was a very vociferous young man indeed, even with a couple of fingers playing inside him. He was amazingly tight – much tighter than Martin – and, as on previous occasions, it felt as if two separate sets of muscles were working against each other. He cried out just once and then fell silent for a few seconds before yelling again and clamping tight against Robert's fingers. Then he relaxed again. The same thing happened when Robert was poised over him with the tip of his cock squeezed between Raymond's arse-cheeks and pressing against him. It seemed that no power on earth would be strong enough to overcome resistance like that and then – suddenly – he opened up and Robert's oily cock slid into him. Martin had taken it bit by bit. Raymond took the whole length with his customary "Doppler" yell. His usual tenor turned soprano as Robert penetrated him. Robert felt the hard, nut-like knob of his prostate against his cock-head. A shuddering spasm ran through him and he groaned loudly.

Raymond could never be compared to a railway engine, Robert thought. The sounds he made were far too human. Agony and ecstasy mingled. Raymond would give a loud cry one moment and then follow it with "Harder! Oh, yeah! Harder! Yeah!" He didn't wriggle as much as Martin, either. Neither did he raise his butt as Martin tried to do. Nonetheless, he was a superb fuck. A feeling of complete and utter happiness seemed to wrap round Robert just before he came. Nobody in the world, he thought, was quite as lucky as he was. He had the company and the friendship of two strong, good-looking young men. Both of them liked him. As for him? Well, it was much more than just "liking".

"Loving"? Well, maybe. Everything had worked out right.

Raymond gave another cry as the cock swelled inside him. Then he gave a long groan. Robert slid a hand under his belly and brought it out again, soaked. He licked his fingers and looked down and to his side. Martin lay with his eyes tightly closed, playing with his newly erect cock and smiling.

It was understandable that Robert was late for work the following morning. Sucking Martin to climax gave him a good appetite for breakfast and he waited around before leaving, just in case the boys should wake up. He'd had to climb over Martin to get out of bed. Neither boy stirred. Finally, after giving Kiberech directions to let them sleep as long as possible and warning him that Patrick would be down later in the morning, he got into the car and drove it, sleepily, along the familiar road.

"One light aircraft. Nothing to do with us, and nothing else," said the sergeant who, thoughtfully, had the coffee pot on the hob.

"Good. That'll be Mr Hardwick coming up from Mombasa."

"Nakuru," said the sergeant. "He's given an ETA of eleven-fifteen. Then he wants to do a series of low-level sweeps. Not over us, of course."

"Yes, I think I heard about that."

"Tomorrow as well and the next day," said the sergeant.

"That must be why he's using Nakuru. He'd need a lot of fuel for a series of low-level passes and there's none up here," said Robert, thinking aloud. Other thoughts were going through his mind, too. One could fuck a man anywhere. A luxury house in Mombasa or a hotel room in Nakuru. No doubt the desired result would be achieved. He would have preferred to contemplate further, but a cup of coffee and the process of acknowledging Peter's flight plan kept him occupied. It was only when the radar screen picked up the blip that he found himself thinking of the secrets behind that little anonymous green dot.

"There he is," said the sergeant. "Spot on time."

"Good. Once he's down, I'd like to nip off. Can I leave you in charge? One of us ought to be here if he's flying in our air space."

"Sure," said the sergeant.

The cursor located the Cessna on every rotation. It got nearer and nearer. Robert picked up the phone and tapped in the Hansons' number. "Just to let you know that your guests are in the circuit, Mr Peters," he said.

"Thank you, sir. I'll inform Mrs Hanson."

"Is Mr Patrick still at home?" Robert asked.

"No, sir. He left earlier this morning. He was going to your house, as I understood the matter."

"Yes, that's right. Give my regards to Mr Hardwick and tell him I hope he enjoyed a good night's rest."

"I'll do that, sir."

Robert left the caravan and stood outside. The sound of the aircraft could barely be heard at first, but grew louder by the minute and then appeared as a tiny glittering dot in the far distance. Peter started his descent a long way off and then made an exaggerated bank and turn. Anyone else would have guessed it was because he didn't want to be seen overflying a military area. Robert knew otherwise. George was busy with the camera. It came in towards them and made what appeared to be a perfect landing behind the farm buildings.

"Right. He's down. I'm off. See you tomorrow, sergeant." He refrained from telling the man to be careful to lock the door and switch everything off. To do so would have made him sound like Catherine Marriott. That made him wonder how the Marriotts would take the news of Martin's deferred higher education. Pretty well, he thought – providing they never learned the reason and actually...Yes. That was quite a good idea. Vijay could drive up to KYM for weekends. He would almost certainly have a licence and a car. Funny...they would probably meet on the road. Vijay going to get fucked and Robert going shopping. It was a shame that there would be nobody waiting for Robert in Nairobi and the Marriotts could be a bit of a drag. Well, he'd go back to his old routine and stay at Plum's...No. Not Plum's. That was Malcolm's local. Well...okay then...the Norfolk. Maybe pick up some local lad. He wasn't so sure about that. He'd never done it with one of them. One would have to make sure the boy had a good bath first. Maybe even put a few drops of "Milton" bleach in, like that woman Catherine had met...

He realised with a shock that he was actually thinking like Catherine. He wouldn't have believed it possible. With a feeling of shame, he also realised that he hadn't been concentrating on the road at all and had somehow ended up safely at the top of the hill. He coasted down and drove in.

Patrick, Raymond and Martin were all standing by the plot, which had been raked. Robert parked the car, got out and walked over towards them.

"Oh! Hi, Robert. I say, you don't mind me calling you by your Christian name, do you?"

"Not at all. You made a smart getaway this morning, Patrick."

"Father and Mother wanted me to stay around to say hello, but I said I was too busy. We've been working out what to plant. Martin's given me a list of the vegetables that you most often eat and I've brought down some seeds from Father's store. I can bring the rest down tomorrow."

Robert tried to show some enthusiasm, but gardening had never been a hobby and Patrick, pleasant young man that he was, could easily be a nuisance. Martin and Raymond didn't seem able to see that and even made extra suggestions. For a quarter of an hour, they discussed the properties of various kinds of cabbage. One didn't need to go to Nairobi for cabbage; they were available in the village. Potatoes, the next item on the list were similarly easy to get.

"Patrick's staying for lunch," said Raymond. "Is that all right?"

"Anything to get away from the monster. Hateful creature! Did you know he's staying at the Stag's Head for three days? With George, of course," said Patrick

"I guessed he must be, when I saw he took off from Nakuru."

"Father knows the manager of the Stag's Head. If it wasn't for that, I'd ring the man and tell him. I feel so sorry for George, being corrupted like that."

"It may be that George enjoys it. You never know," said Martin.

"Of course he doesn't. I mean…well, it's stupid!"

The discussion seemed likely to end in argument. Patrick had gone quite red. Robert stepped in. "Did you ask Raymond, Patrick?" he asked.

"Ask me what?"

"Patrick would like to do a picture of you."

"Only if you don't mind," said Patrick.

"I don't mind. What sort of picture?"

"Well…ideally, I'd like do a watercolour, but they take longer. I could do a pencil sketch."

"Do a watercolour, if you want. Can I have it when it's finished?"

"I'd like to do one I can keep. What say I do the pencil one first and then the watercolour?"

Raymond seemed more than happy with that. Robert went indoors whilst they set to work planting the first rows of seeds. Kiberech was busy laying the table. For want of something better to do, Robert sat at his desk in the corner. He felt he ought to be outside gardening but there were three of them out there already. It would not be true to say that he was planning. He wasn't that sort of person. There were things that needed to be thought through, though. In the first place, Patrick would have to be dissuaded from using KYM as a bolthole to get away from Peter. In the second place, there were two randy and good-looking lads out there and there was no way Robert could fuck both of them every night. Anyway, it was only fair to let them have a chance with each other. Some sort of arrangement would have to be reached – when Patrick was out of the way. Robert tore a piece of paper from the writing block and began to work out a complex permutation. Afternoons (minus P) would be M and R1. Evenings would be R1, M, R2 – maybe R1 + M again, at least once. Robert screwed up the paper when they came in.

"That's most of them in," said Patrick. "That's really good soil you've got there. Loads of humus. Father said the last man kept cows here. That probably accounts for it. Where can I wash my hands?"

"I'll show you. In here," said Martin. All three of them trooped into the bathroom - a reminder of the previous evening. Robert smiled.

Kiberech served lunch. Chicken casserole served on a plain white plate might not have been what Patrick was used to, but he ate ravenously and apparently complimented Kiberech, for the man smiled with delight and said something in Swahili which made all three of them laugh. Kiberech had just served the dessert when they heard the sound of an aircraft in the distance.

"There they go," said Robert. "The famous aerial survey has started. You can go home safely now, Patrick – not that you were ever in any sort of danger."

"Oh. We were going to start Raymond's picture this afternoon," said Patrick.

"I thought maybe Raymond and Martin would like a little doze. We were all up late last night."

"We're okay," said Raymond. "You doze and I pose. How's that?"

"As you wish."

"How do you want me, Patrick?" Raymond asked. "Nude, seminude? Standing or sitting?"

"Oh good Lord! Nothing like that. Heavens!" Patrick was flustered.

"Don't worry. I was only joking. How do you want me?"

"Well...er...Out on the verandah, possibly. Sort of standing and looking out over the Rift. If Robert's got some paper and a pencil. I'll bring the proper stuff tomorrow."

Robert dragged two loungers out from the lean-to for Martin and himself and put them up in the shade.

Patrick took up his position in the verandah. "How about standing on the wall?" he said. "That would look good." Raymond climbed up.

"Now if you could undo your shirt and let the wind blow it about a bit...That's it. That's perfect."

"Nude would be even more perfect," Martin whispered.

"That's why I thought to leave you two together this afternoon," Robert replied. "If he's going to come painting every day, you won't get a chance."

"Oh, he's all right. Raymond told you all about the Vijay plan last night?"

"Yes, he did."

"What do you honestly think?"

"I think it's very sensible. I was thinking about it on the journey home. What you could, perhaps do..."

Martin listened attentively. "He could do that. His dad's buying him a car this holiday," he said. "It would certainly save any problems at home. You wouldn't mind an Asian being here?"

"Certainly not. Anyway, I shall be down in Nairobi at weekends."

"What about you, though? I mean, if we are both up here you won't have any company."

"Oh, don't worry about me. I might even relish a rest. It can be exhausting, you know – even for a twenty-nine-year-old."

Martin laughed. "You didn't show it last night," he said and then, "You're a very selfless person, aren't you?"

"Am I?"

"I think you are. I love you a bit more every day."

"And me, you." Unseen by the artist and his model, their hands touched.

"And hopefully every night," Martin added.

Chapter Sixteen

The picture was a masterpiece. They all agreed upon that –
except Patrick, who felt that he hadn't "got Raymond's face
quite right" and hoped he might be able to remedy that on the
following day when he came to do the watercolour. He spent
what seemed to Robert an inordinate amount of time rubbing
out a line here and adding another one there.

"Maybe the watercolour will be better," Patrick finally said.
He laid it carefully on the passenger seat of the Land Rover; covered it reverently with a cloth and drove off. By that time it was
late in the afternoon.

"I'd like to see more of him," said Martin.

"Dirty sod!" said Raymond. "He might not be gigantic all
over."

"I actually didn't mean that," said Martin, "but it is a
thought."

The thought cropped up again several times that evening.
Over dinner when Kiberech served a long, cylindrical suet pud-
ding and again when they were out on the verandah. "It's a
shame that Patrick's religious," said Martin. "Think of all the
fun he's missing." He fingered the lump in the front of his kikoi.

"Religion doesn't seem to make any difference to George,"
said Raymond.

"George's different. He just uses being a Quaker to get out of religion lessons and chapel. I suppose he's back in his luxury hotel in Nakuru right now."

"He's bound to be," said Robert. "Peter can't fly at night."

"Just about the only thing he can't do," said Raymond, bitterly. "Rob, would you mind awfully if I didn't join in tonight?"

"You haven't suddenly got religion, have you?" Martin asked.

"No. I think it was standing on that wall that did it. Patrick wanted me to tense up. My legs feel like jelly."

"Not the only thing by the look of you," said Martin, staring down at his friend's groin. "Come on. It's more fun with three of us."

"It was worth it. It's a beautiful picture," said Robert, remembering the skilful way Patrick had portrayed Raymond's hairy legs and somehow managed to give the impression that his behind was clenched underneath the shorts. "Have a night off by all means," Robert added. "It'll look better anyway if the bed in the spare room is actually slept in." The truth of the matter was that he felt somewhat relieved.

"Do you think he really is tired?" said Martin later. He was sitting on the edge of Robert's bed and undoing his shirt.

"I'm sure he is. I've read somewhere that posing is hard work. Stand up and I'll take those off for you."

"It's a bit of a laugh really, isn't it? Tired by Patrick's pencil! Patrick's prick would be bloody exhausting! I wonder what it's like, actually."

"Raymond's theory might well be correct and it's no good speculating." For a moment Robert remembered the scraps of paper in the caravan waste-bin and felt guilty about chastening them when he too was prone to speculation – but only for a moment. "This," he said, "is for real and much nicer." He licked Martin's cock lasciviously.

"Mmm," said Martin. Robert stopped and looked up. Martin's

eyes were closed. His imagination was going again. Robert put a hand between the young man's thighs. Martin parted his legs. Robert took the other man's balls in his hand, knowing very well that, to Martin, it wasn't his hand at all. He was a funny lad. He loved Martin, and Martin apparently loved him, but yet there were these times when Martin preferred an imaginary lover. He ran his fingertips through Martin's bush.

"You could make several paint-brushes out of this," he murmured.

"Mmm!"

"As for this, it's far too thick to make a handle. It feels good, though."

"Mmm. Suck it."

"Not yet. Let's go to bed."

He had to guide Martin to the bed and sit him down again. Martin fell back and spread his legs wide.

"You don't need painting. You're a work of art as you are," said Robert. He managed to get Martin to slew round to make room for him. Robert lay alongside and gently tweaked Martin's nipples, until Martin reached over and did the same to him - still, Robert noticed, with his eyes closed.

Whether he opened them at all, Robert didn't know. Perhaps he did when his face was buried in the pillow, but by that time Robert couldn't have cared less which role he was playing. It might well have been his own imagination that made Martin's usual reaction to the feel of a cock-head pressing against his anus seem tenser than usual and Martin's groans even louder when he yielded. As always, he squirmed and Robert held him as tightly as he possibly could as he began to thrust, as patiently and as regularly as he could.

"Ah!"

Robert wondered if Raymond was awake and whether he could hear them. Probably not, he decided. He hadn't heard Martin and

George. Mind you, they hadn't been fucking. George was stupid not to have taken advantage of Martin's arse. It was so perfect, so soft and yet so tight...

"Ugh! Ah!"

...and George was well hung...That was the wrong word, if ever there was one. It wouldn't be hanging. It would be as stiff as a board...

"Ugh! Ah!"

It probably was at that moment. In a bedroom in the Stag's Head...How would one go about fucking a young man with George's physique? Peter would want to see George's club-headed cock, so George would have to be lying on his back. Yes...Lying on his back with his legs up on Peter's shoulders. That was it.

Peter's cock reaming into George's tight arse. Peter muttering promises – flights to anywhere George wanted to go. Maybe even a car. George would be able to have one now that he wasn't going to university. They were so expensive and so difficult to re-sell that only young men who intended to stay in the country bought them. That wouldn't worry Peter. 'You shall have a car, George. Any car you like, George. You deserve it.' George groaning with pleasure...

"Ugh! Aah! Aagh!"

"Ugh! Oh! Oh! Oh!"

The rapidity and the force of Martin's ejaculation took Robert by surprise. Martin's muscles clamped on his cock. Martin writhed, then heaved upwards and backwards against Robert, whose nose came into painful contact with the back of Martin's head. Martin sank down on the pillow again. Robert held on for all he was worth and gave just one more thrust. That was all it needed. Martin gave a contended groan.

"Beaut...Great!" Robert panted.

"Mmm," Martin murmured.

All thoughts of Patrick – if indeed there had been such

thoughts – seemed to have been dispelled by the early morning. Martin sucked contentedly on Robert's cock and Robert licked Martin's whilst stroking Martin's beautifully smooth arse-cheeks.

"I really do love you," said Martin after they had both climaxed again.

Robert hugged him tightly and kissed Martin's leg. "Not as much as I love you," he panted.

"How are your legs, Raymond?" Robert asked at breakfast.

"Oh, much better, thanks. I just hope he doesn't want me to stand like I did yesterday."

"Ask him to think of a better pose. Anyway, I'd better be off to work. I'll come back as soon as I can."

When he drove out they were both standing by the new vegetable patch. "Bloody amazing!" Robert muttered. His life had changed completely in a matter of a few months. He felt light-hearted and happy – so much so that he might easily have collided with Patrick's Land Rover had Patrick not flashed his lights. Patrick was obviously an early riser. He probably had to be, thought Robert. He was obviously tied up with and interested in the farm and farmers have to get up early. He drove into the airstrip and parked the car.

"Mr Hardwick's on the mayfly again, sir," said the sergeant. "ETA eleven-oh-five."

"Yes, he would be. Nothing else?"

"No sir. Just him."

"Well, it seems stupid for both of us to be here. You nip off home, sergeant. I took time off yesterday afternoon."

When he had gone, Robert made coffee. The sergeant had left a newspaper behind, so he read that, did the crossword and then had another coffee. He was busily occupied with a children's puzzle and didn't notice the time. The sound of an approaching aircraft made him jump. He glanced at the screen. Peter was already in the circuit. He watched from the doorway as the aircraft came down and then went back to his puzzle. It was obviously going to be an elephant, but he joined all the dots up just to make sure.

Corned beef sandwiches filled some more time. Then a couple more cups of coffee. Sooner or later somebody would realise what a waste of manpower this was, he thought – and then hoped they wouldn't realise too soon.

Peter took off again at two o'clock in the afternoon. Robert watched the aircraft as it banked over the farm and then flew into the sun. A few minutes later it came back, banked again and flew southwest. Watching it on the radar was less of a strain on Robert's eyes, so he did that. Young George, he thought, might easily be air-sick. Peter was flying ten miles, turning sharply and then doing ten miles in the opposite direction. Those turns would unsettle anybody's stomach – especially after one of Dorothy Hanson's "makeshift" lunches.

Robert stayed around until the aircraft turned and banked again and disappeared in the direction of Nakuru. He locked up, got into the car and drove home. It had been a total waste of time, he thought, but why worry? He was being paid for it.

Martin was standing in the drive between the gate posts. Robert stopped the car abruptly. "You'll get run over there, Martin," he called out.

Martin grinned. "I'm here to make sure that nobody comes in," he said. "I suppose I'll have to make an exception in your case." He stood aside. Robert drove into the lean-to and got out of the car.

"How did the gardening go?" he asked.

"Oh, fine. We've planted everything."

"So why the guard on the gate?"

Martin grinned again. "I'll show you," he said. "Come with me."

Robert followed him along the side of the house, past the boiler and then round the back. Martin put his finger to his lips and pointed. Patrick was standing at an easel, and had his back to them. One of the loungers had been brought out and put on the bit of grass at the other side of the house. On it, completely naked, was Raymond. He was lying on his front, with one foot in the air and apparently engrossed in a book. Robert stared – not for long, because he was so surprised. Martin tapped his arm. They turned and went back the way they came, despite the fact that it was the long way round.

"It was Ray's idea," said Martin. "It was so funny. Patrick blushed like a kid. I've never seen anyone so embarrassed. If only he knew. It's the first time he's done a nude, apparently. By the way he behaved, I don't think he's even seen anyone naked before."

"He doesn't know what he's been missing," said Robert. "Show me the garden."

Little plastic pegs along the edges of the plot were all carefully labelled in both Swahili and English. "The Swahili is for Kiberech's benefit," Martin explained.

"That was thoughtful. Where is he?"

"We packed him off home. Ray's doing the dinner tonight. I'm doing the washing up and then..."

"You think Ray will be feeling better?"

"He said he would be. Ray will feel quite wonderful. We have a little plan..."

"What's that?"

"I'll tell you about it later. Here come the artists."

Raymond, modestly clad in his kikoi, carried what looked like a small, wooden attaché case. Patrick, carrying his easel, followed closely behind.

"Oh. I heard the car. I guessed it was you," said Patrick, reaching out between the legs of the easel to shake Robert's hand. "I hope you don't mind but I –"

"He's painted me in the nude. It was my idea," said Raymond.

"You don't mind, Robert? I won't show it to anybody, of course, but I've never done a nude before. It was awfully decent of Raymond to let me."

"I don't mind at all. Can I see it?"

"Oh well. I...er...It's not awfully good."

"Let him see," said Raymond.

Blushing furiously, Patrick turned the easel.

"I think it's wonderful!" said Robert, truthfully.

"It's not quite dry yet. I wonder if I could leave it here till the day after tomorrow."

"You can leave it here as long as you like," said Robert. The likeness was perfect. Robert knew every square inch and curve of Raymond's body. Yet, somehow, Patrick had made him even more beautiful. It was on the tip of his tongue to offer to purchase it but Patrick was hardly short of money and would have been embarrassed.

"I'd better get back," said Patrick when Raymond asked if he would stay to dinner. "I shan't be around tomorrow at all, I'm afraid. Peter's nearly finished the photography and my parents have insisted I stay home and be nice to him."

"Not easy," said Robert.

"You're right there. But Father has spoken and we are supposed to be a Society of Friends so I shall have to be friendly. Just for this once."

They went to the Land Rover with him. Raymond put the painting kit in the back. "I think the pencil sketch would be the best one for me to take home to show my folks," he said.

"Oh, of course! I'll bring it down next time I come."

"That reminds me. Where is the ravine?" Raymond asked.

"The ravine? About five miles on the other side of our place. I wouldn't advise you to go there."

"How deep is it?"

"About a hundred feet, I suppose."

"The perfect place for snakes," said Raymond. "My dad said Eldama used to be called Eldama Ravine in the old days."

"That's right. It was. Father's furious about it because the government promised to settle people near there and to build housing. They didn't, so all the no-goods – the alcoholics and the people who've been kicked out of their villages – have moved there. They use the ravine as a rubbish dump. I'd keep well away if I were you. Anyway, thanks a lot for everything – especially you, Ray. See you soon." And he was off.

Raymond and Martin were busy in the kitchen that evening and Robert had to endure solitude on the verandah again. It wasn't as bad as it had been, though. In fact, the sounds emanating from inside the house were sometimes quite amusing. There were occasional crashes; apparently caused by Martin.

"Not again!" said Raymond after the third one. "Wipe it up and start again."

There was an argument as to whether Ibrahim was right or the cookbook that Raymond had at home was. "I'm sure Mum would have told him if he's been doing it wrong," said Martin.

"Too right she would," Robert murmured.

Despite the controversy, the meal was very good indeed. Martin gathered up the plates and went into the kitchen. "Reminds me of the last time I was here," said Raymond as he put the apron over his head.

"Did you do the washing up, then?" Martin asked.

"That's right."

Robert stayed in the kitchen to help. Martin dried the dishes, occasionally handing one back to Raymond to be washed again.

Robert put things away. "What was the plan you spoke about?" he asked, when they were nearly finished.

"Well, if you don't mind..." said Martin hesitantly.

"If I don't mind what?"

"Would you mind awfully if we...er...slept in the other room?"

It was a disappointment, but they were young and young people sometimes needed young company. Robert had enjoyed them both and there would, no doubt, be other opportunities. He looked from one handsome face to the other, smiled and said, "Of course not."

"It'll be back to normal tomorrow. I promise. We both do," said Martin. "It's just..."

"Twenty-nine is a bit on the old side?" said Robert.

"No way!" "Not at all!" They both spoke together.

Robert was dying to ask the details of the "plan". What exactly did they have in mind? Who was going to do what to whom? It was sheer prurient curiosity, of course, and one of those questions one did not ask. A wire kitchen sieve set his mind working on lines he later felt ashamed of. As he wiped it, he wondered what it reminded him of. He hung it on the hook. Of course! The mesh on the loudspeaker in the caravan. Loudspeaker?...Pat had bought a baby alarm in Tottenham Court Road just before they'd left for Kenya. The plan had been to use the spare room as a nursery. So where was the baby alarm now? She wouldn't have thrown it away. There was only one place it could be and that was the built-in cupboard in the spare room.

"That's done!" said Raymond, pulling the plug in the sink. "Now for a shower and then the verandah. Do you want to shower first, Rob?"

"No, no. You go first. I'll have mine later, when there's enough hot water."

He stood out on the verandah, not looking over the Rift this time but watching what was happening in the house. Raymond and Martin went into the spare room and emerged completely naked. Raymond said something that made Martin laugh and they went into the bathroom. He gave them about five minutes. The boiler gurgled. It was time. He padded into the house and nipped into the spare room. Neither of the lads appeared to have used the cupboard. Their clothes were still in their suitcases on the floor. The top shelf was choc-a-bloc with Pat's things: handbags, hats, a cardboard box full of papers. If he'd followed his instincts, all of it would have been sent to England but then, so would the baby alarm. He felt more and more guilty as he rummaged. He knew that he would be somehow relieved if it wasn't there. He was about to give up the search when he found it. The master unit worked off the mains, so that was no problem. The listening unit – a small plastic thing not much bigger than a couple of matchboxes – was battery powered and that, for a moment, posed problems. Then he remembered his portable radio. That was on the bedside cabinet in his room. The batteries fitted. The lads were almost certainly unprepared. He opened the drawer and removed the essential for a sexy night.

Back to the spare room. Every second counted. The boiler had ceased its seething. He put the lubricant on the window shelf and hid the unit under one of Pat's hats. Hoping that the sight of a cupboard door ajar wouldn't offend their sensibilities, he left it slightly open and returned to his room, closing the door behind him.

He plugged the master unit in and lay on his bed and waited. The sound of the bathroom door opening came to him both electronically and acoustically. Then came voices. It worked! They say that listeners never hear good of themselves. Fortunately, that theory turned out to be incorrect.

"Hello. What's this?" Raymond's voice. For a second, Robert panicked.

"Rob must have put them there. That's good of him," said Martin. "He must have realised."

"Of course he realised. He'd be stupid not to. It is thoughtful, though. He's a really nice guy, isn't he?"

"I think so. And it's great that we're both going to England at the same time. Why don't you wait another year?" Martin asked.

"No. I'll go this year. It's better that way. Can I have the towel?"

"Oh, sure. Here."

"It's still warm enough outside to dry off properly. I'll wait for you out there."

"Sure. I won't be a minute."

Robert switched off, undressed and went into the bathroom. Naturally enough, the boiler hadn't had enough time to heat the water. He couldn't say that he actually enjoyed a cold shower, but it probably cooled his ardour. By the time he emerged on to the verandah clad in his kikoi, the two lads were already on their second drinks.

"Er...thanks for putting the stuff in our room...er...if you know what I mean," said Raymond.

"Think nothing of it. Better safe than sorry."

"Let's hope that holds good tomorrow," said Martin.

"Tomorrow? I thought –"

"Not that. Ray's roped me in to help him catch snakes."

"I need a second pair of hands to do it properly," Raymond explained. "There's no danger. I'll look after the biting end, but big snakes can be a bit of a handful."

"Just be careful. That's all," said Robert. "Why can't you have a safe hobby?"

"I have," Raymond replied with a grin.

Martin laughed. "That can be a bit of a handful, too!" he said.

The conversation turned to future plans. Raymond spoke of the flat he would find. Martin asked questions about Durham University. From time to time Robert thought of the entertainment the two boys would unknowingly provide and then, when guilt reared its head, he determined not to listen – a resolution he didn't keep. They went to bed shortly before eleven. He said goodnight and that by itself was sufficient to make his heart beat faster. He lay in bed for some time before reaching out for the switch and then putting his hand back under the quilt without having touched it. Five minutes later he reached out again, this time to turn off the lamp and then, in the darkness, Robert felt for the listening unit and found the switch.

"Immoral. Totally immoral!" he muttered – and that reminded him of Pat's mother again, but not for long.

"Did your friend tell you if he's done it before?" Martin's voice sounded tinny but every word was clear.

"As far as he knows, he hasn't. He wants to, but he can't. They've got so many servants in the house," Raymond replied.

"We've only got Ibrahim and he's a nice bloke. He must know about me and Robert, but he never lets on. It's Mum and Dad I worry about. Dad would have a fit if he knew I was arse-fucking and Mum would go over the top at the thought of an Asian in the house."

"They must go out together sometimes, surely? Spread your legs a bit. That's right."

"Mmm. You're good at that. Not often, actually. There's the golf club dinner and dance, but that's only once a year."

"I'm sure you'll find a way. Now then, stop thinking about Vijay for a moment and concentrate on me."

"You'll tell me if it hurts or anything? I want it to be really good when it happens."

"I'll tell you. Now, I'll get you warmed up just a bit more. "

"Will Vijay, do you think?"

"Sure he will. He's dying to see it and feel it. He told my friend how he watches it grow under your towel when you and George are in the showers."

"Why won't you tell me the name of this friend? Mmm. Aaah. That's right. Tickle them."

"Because he asked me not to. Vijay wouldn't like it, either. Very careful, is our friend Vijay."

"It must be Simon Adams. He's the only bloke you talk to a lot."

"Maybe. Maybe it's Father Cox. I talk to him a lot too."

"Father Cox! Don't make me laugh! He's a priest and a teacher!"

"You really do have a lot to learn, Martin. However, you've got a good teacher in me."

"And Robert. Don't forget Robert."

"And Robert. Now then, let's stop talking and concentrate on the action, shall we?"

To detail the sounds of the next twenty minutes would entail the use of page after page of grunts, groans and gasps. Neither spoke very much.

"I'll put it on for you." That was Raymond's voice.

Then came the sound of tearing paper. Martin said, "Be careful."

"I will."

Martin gasped and there was another pause.

"Use quite a lot. Robert won't mind," said Raymond later. "You'll probably need a hell of a lot for Vijay, especially the first time."

Robert smiled. Raymond had got Martin pretty well summed up.

"I guess I will," Martin replied. "What will he feel like, do you reckon?"

"Sheer bliss," Raymond replied. "He's got what it takes. Long legs, narrow waist and a perfect little bum. You just need to be patient and stretch him a bit. That's right. Like that. Don't push too hard now. Make it last."

Robert picked up the unit and held it to his ear. Disappointingly, that made reception worse. A hissing noise masked the slippery noises he wanted to hear and, anyway, he had other uses for his hand. He put it down again.

"That's it. Yow! No, it's all right. Keep on. Go in slowly. That's it. Now run your finger round inside – like you're running your finger round a nearly empty jam jar. Yeah! That's good. Now put two fingers in. Mmmm. That's good. Careful now. Try and make a V-sign inside me. Mmm. Yeah!"

"I...can't hold back...much longer," Martin panted.

"Hang on. I want to see it go in." Bed-springs creaked loudly and Raymond said "There! That's better! Oooh! Aaah! Oh! That's great! Give it to me. Oooh! Push! Push! Ah! Oh, fuck me! Give me the fucking of my life! Ah! Ah! Ah!"

Martin panted and groaned. Raymond gasped and groaned. The bed set up a chorus of its own and there was one moment when something banged hard against the wall.

All too soon, one of them came. It was impossible to know which one. There was a long drawn-out sigh, a moment of silence and then another session of panting and squeaking.

"Fuck me!" said Raymond after a while. It was an exclamation, rather than a command or a request.

"I...just...did," Martin panted.

"Bloody well, too," said Raymond. "Vijay doesn't know what's coming to him."

"Or in him," said Martin. "Will you tell your friend?"

"It might be a good idea. Then he can tell Vijay that getting fucked by Martin Marriott is heaven."

"You'll tell me what he says?"

"Sure, but I know already."

"What will he say?"

"He'll say 'I can't wait'. That's what he'll say."

"Your turn in the morning?"

"Sure. Wake me if you wake up first. God! I love your arse!"

"I love yours, too. Shall I pull out?"

"I guess you'd better. Till tomorrow morning then?"

"You...bet!"

Chapter Seventeen

Unsurprisingly, Robert woke early the next morning. Not early enough, unfortunately. The next round – if there was one – was all over. There was no sound from the boys' room and the shower was running. Still feeling guilty, he put the listening unit in the drawer and clambered out of bed. He waited for the water to stop running, gave them a few minutes extra and then opened the door just as they came out of the bathroom.

"Good morning. Did you sleep well?" Robert then asked.

"There wasn't a lot of sleep, actually," Raymond replied. Martin said nothing.

When Robert came out of the bathroom, they were both seated at the table and dressed in shorts and safari jackets. Robert dressed for work and joined them.

"Have you got a busy day ahead?" Martin asked.

"I doubt it. It will be a bore, as usual."

"When will you be back?"

"Oh, some time this afternoon. Now, you two be careful."

"We will be," said Martin. Robert stayed around to see them off. Kiberech had made a pile of sandwiches; Robert made sure they had enough soft drinks with them and then they left. Raymond strode ahead with his catching pole over his shoulder and a rucksack on his back. Martin, unladen as far as Robert could make out, just about managed to keep pace.

"Exhausted, poor sod!" Robert murmured as he got into the car. The chances were that they would be back within the hour.

Peter Hardwick landed, as usual, at eleven o'clock. Robert noted it in the log, although there was no need to. It was just something to do. The sergeant went off to lunch. Robert stood in the open doorway of the caravan and watched the Land Rover's dust cloud gradually disappear. He was about to go inside again and wondered if Kiberech had made the same sandwiches for him as he had for the lads. Another dust cloud formed on the crest of the hill. Another Land Rover, but this time a dark-green one. Company – Patrick!

It stopped on the hard standing in front of the caravan and Patrick climbed out. "I've come to hijack you to lunch," he said.

Robert said that he had sandwiches. "Please come," said Patrick. "I can't stand that poisonous reptile alone."

"Sure. In fact, the lads are after poisonous reptiles today. Perhaps I should have brought them along too."

"I'd rather face any number of cobras than Peter. No...In fact, that's a lie. I wouldn't. Sorry," said Patrick. Robert locked the caravan and climbed into the Land Rover.

"Jeremy's out again, but he'll be back for lunch," said Dorothy Hanson. "What will you have?"

Robert opted for an orange juice and turned to Peter Hardwick who was sprawled lazily in one of the armchairs.

"Finished your survey?" he asked.

"I should be able to wrap it up tomorrow or the day after," said Peter.

"I imagine George's enjoying it. Where is he, by the way?"

"Over in my place, listening to music," said Patrick.

"And dying to get in the air again, no doubt," said Robert.

Peter frowned. "He doesn't come when I'm photographing," he said.

"So who does the camera work?"

Peter laughed in an irritatingly supercilious way. "It's automatic. It's mounted on the aeroplane... George only came once and that was more than enough for him."

"I see." Robert should have realised. A young man who has been airsick during the day might not be an ideal bed-mate.

Several times whilst they waited for Mr Hanson, Patrick caught Robert's eye. Peter seemed to make very little attempt at cover stories.

"How have you found the Stag's Head?" Mrs Hanson asked. "Jeremy knows the owners."

"Oh, it's ideal for us. George loves it and that's the main thing."

"You seem very fond of George," Patrick observed in a tone best described as "chilly".

"Oh, I am! George is a absolute delight. He has such a wonderful personality."

That wasn't the only thing about him that was wonderful, Robert thought, remembering George's huge club-headed cock and delightfully curved bottom.

Worse was to come when lunch was served and George and Mr Hanson were at the table. Peter intended to take George on a tour of the USA to publicise the proposed rare animal park. Peter asked if George might have a second helping of the dessert. Peter announced proudly that George had achieved fifty press-ups the previous evening – in Peter's room in the hotel. Patrick looked over to Robert with a face like thunder.

"You share a room at the hotel, then?" Robert asked, as light-heartedly as he was able.

"I sometimes wonder if we ought to. We're in and out of each other's rooms most of the time," said Peter. George gave a simpering smile and launched into a long-winded explanation of how Peter was teaching him the rudiments of aeronautics. "It's really all a question of thrust, lift and drag, you see," he concluded. "If you've got enough thrust, you overcome drag and you get lift." The mental image that sentence generated in Robert's mind had nothing at all to do with aviation.

Lunch finished. "Oh, well. I must leap into the sky again," said Peter. "I'll come back for you at about five, George."

"Sure," said George.

"And then what are your plans, Peter?" Mr Hanson asked.

"Oh, back to Nakuru for tonight. George wants to see Lake Victoria, so I'll fly to Kisumu tomorrow and refuel there and then it's back to Nairobi. The films should be ready in about three days."

They all stood in the porch to watch the take-off, which was actually very well accomplished. Soon it was a glittering speck in the sky. Robert turned his attention to George and Patrick. They crossed over the rose garden in the direction of the boys' house.

"They get on awfully well. We're so pleased," said Dorothy Hanson. Not knowing what to say, Robert said nothing. How did one go about explaining to a lady, a practising Quaker, that her son was gay. Robert was hardly in a position to do so, anyway. Even Mr Hanson, whom Robert had heard expressing liberal sentiments on the subject, probably thought that gay sex was a matter of holding hands and an occasional furtive kiss behind a cricket pavilion.

Not wishing to disturb Patrick and anxious to work off the meal, he walked back to the caravan, carefully noting as he did so the patches of soil, which looked as if they had been disturbed. There were just three of them and all were within sight of the house. He spent the afternoon sitting on the caravan steps. The sergeant hadn't returned and would almost certainly not turn up until the morning with a load of silly excuses.

Over in the distance, Peter was ploughing the sky in meticulously parallel tracks. Eventually he landed and within half an hour was on his way back to Nakuru. Back to the Stag's Head and the semi-shared bedroom and George doing naked press-ups. No doubt Peter was sitting on the edge of the bed encouraging him...

"Oh, yes! It's good for the muscles. Not that yours need much more exercising. Yours are perfect already, but let's go for fifty-five this time. Not so much for your benefit, as for mine. I love to see your bottom jigging up and down like that and the exercise will make you delightfully tight when I fuck you later on. Not to mention the scent of your sweat which turns me on very quickly. I shall lick every inch of you."

Robert switched everything off, locked the caravan and got into the car. He was at the top of the hill when he thought it might be an idea to call for the post. He hadn't been to the post office for some days. Once again, there was a letter from his parents, the usual RAF "bumf" and a pink card indicating that a parcel awaited collection. He went back inside the post office. The man behind the counter smiled and, without even asking if he had a card, fished a packet from the pigeonholes behind him and handed it over.

"BFPO?" Robert was mystified. He drove home. As usual, Kiberech was waiting.

"*Jambo*, Kiberech. Boys home?" he asked.

"Not come, bwana."

"Oh, they'll be here soon." He sat on the verandah and opened the package. The letter inside was from Bruce Watts. Robert had forgotten writing to him. "Dear Rob, it was difficult, but a mate of mine here is in the antiques business and recognised it. It worked out at £55, which is steep for a mug but apparently they are quite rare. Souvenirs of a pre-war cruise along the Danube from Budapest to Passau, apparently, and the gold rim is real gold...' Bruce had used several German newspapers to wrap it. By the time it was unwrapped, the verandah floor was covered in paper, which began to blow about in the afternoon breeze. Robert put the mug on the table and gathered the pieces up and then sat down to read the other correspondence.

Six-thirty came round. He opened a beer. Seven o'clock...Half past seven.

"Dinner, bwana?" Kiberech asked. "All ready."

"Give them another half hour," Robert replied and pointed to his watch. When they eventually arrived, he thought, it would be worth telling them off slightly. It was all very well to wash up and lay the table as Raymond did, but it really wasn't fair on Kiberech to keep him waiting around.

At eight-thirty, having eaten a lonely dinner, he was worried. At nine o'clock it was pitch dark. Only an idiot would try to get home in the dark. Only an idiot would remain out in the dark. Something must have happened. Something pretty terrible. Maybe Raymond had been bitten by a snake and lay dying. Martin would stay with him and try to do something to alleviate his friend's agony. They'd been attacked by a hostile animal, maybe. There were plenty of those around. He spilled the rest of his beer on to the grass. A clear head was necessary. What should he do? Well, telephone their parents. That was the first thing. He went inside and had dialled the first three digits of the Marriotts' number, but put the receiver down again. What did one say? "I'm terribly sorry, but your son is missing?" That would only make things worse. The police? The nearest police post was at Kabarnet, about thirty miles away, and what could they do? Nothing. He phoned the Hansons.

"Mr Hanson, I'm sorry to bother you, but I need your advice." His voice sounded shaky even to himself. He explained the position.

"Oh, my dear Lord! When did they set out?"

"About eight o'clock this morning."

"And you didn't ask where they were going?"

"No. I didn't think to do so."

Mr Hanson tutted. "They've been gone for about thirteen hours then," he said. "That means anything up to about twenty-eight miles in this territory. Look, the best thing to do is for you to stay put just in case they come home. I'll get Peter Hardwick on the phone and get him to fly up here in the morning. That's obviously the best way of finding them. Can you get here at about ten? Tell your man to stay there. I guess they'll sleep out in the open and come home in the morning. Silly devils. We can only hope and pray. Rest assured that we'll do both."

It wasn't exactly a reassuring speech, but it was nice of him, Robert thought. He left the light burning and went to bed. He didn't sleep well. One minute the lads were falling off a cliff and he lost his footing as well. Then Mr Hanson and Mrs Angel were telling him what a fool he was, after which the biggest snake in the world dangled from the boughs of an acacia tree holding Raymond by his cock.

Robert got up at six o'clock. One only had to look at Kiberech's face to see that he believed the worst. He put a reassuring hand on Robert's shoulder and said something in Swahili. Robert couldn't eat any breakfast. The waiting around was agonising. Every time he heard voices or a vehicle he jumped to his feet. Kiberech went off for a few moments and returned with a very large and heavily armed search party. Robert managed to persuade him that it would be much better if he stayed behind to look after the lads if they got back – "if" being the operative word. Inquests, courts of enquiry, angry parents, lawsuits, the poor lads themselves...He felt physically sick.

At half past nine, having told Kiberech to remain on the premises and not to go anywhere, Robert drove up to Eldama and, for the first time, was delighted to see Peter's aircraft parked. He didn't need to ring the bell. Peter and Mr and Mrs Hanson must have seen him drive up.

Dorothy Hanson said it was "awful". Mr Hanson felt that it would be like looking for a needle in a haystack. Peter seemed the only one who was unfazed.

"What were they wearing?" he asked.

"Khaki shorts and shirts."

"Hmm. Not the best material in the world, but we'll have a go. You have flown in a light aircraft before?"

"Several times."

"Come on, then. Let's go."

He was a good pilot. The take-off was absolutely perfect. Robert looked down as the house and his caravan became smaller and smaller until both were veiled by thin wisps of cloud.

"This is very good of you," he said, speaking into the microphone.

"No problem. I gather you haven't an idea where they might be?"

"None at all. Where's George this morning?"

"With Patrick. We haven't really got room for three. Now then, if we start over there, I'll fly in decreasing circles. That's the outer limit of their stamina I think."

"Sure. I must be holding up the development of your pictures. I'm sorry."

"No need to be. I'm meeting a friend at the airport this afternoon and I want to be back in time for her. Otherwise my time is my own."

"Her?"

"Keep it under your hat, old boy. One word would destroy me here. Winnie is a Kikuyu girl."

"And you...?"

"Cohabit. Live together. That's right. She's been in London for the last few days. I didn't want George to know of course."

"Well, I'm...I'm damned!" said Robert.

"It's not so unusual. You just have to keep your mouth buttoned up. You're married, I believe?"

"Getting a divorce," said Robert.

"Oh, great! Two social sinners in one aircraft. All it needs now is for one of us to be gay." Robert forced himself to laugh. "Not much fear of that," said Peter. "Now then, where the hell are they? I'll go down a bit. You've got nothing in the air today?"

"No, and my sergeant is down there. No worry."

Peter flew, as steadily as any RAF pilot with whom Robert had flown, occasionally coming down to a few hundred feet. A herd of gazelle bolted from the cover of some trees and a couple of giraffes stopped chewing for a few minutes and looked up at them. There were a few vehicles on the dirt roads. Otherwise, there was no other sign of life – certainly no sign of two exhausted khaki-clad humans.

"I think we have to give up. No sign of 'em," said Peter. By that time they had been in the air for over an hour.

"Just one possibility," said Robert. "Where is the ravine?" Peter had got into a climb and he had to shout over the roar of the engine.

"Over there. You don't reckon? No. They couldn't have done it in the time. Not all the way from KYM."

"Raymond mentioned it. It would be worth looking."

"As you wish, but remember – I have to get George to Nairobi and well out of the way before British Airways gets on chocks."

From the air, the ravine looked like a jagged mouth in the ground. A little group of round, thatched huts stood near one end. Peter came down and people came out of the huts and waved.

"I'll fly along it as low as I can. That'll scatter 'em," said Peter. Robert held on tight. "First pass," said Peter. Robert had rarely felt so scared. The wing-tips were about six feet above the edges of the ravine and wobbled dangerously in the rising air currents. Robert looked down. The ravine was really deep. There were three rusty lorries in there. Another vehicle lay on its back. They zoomed over a tree which grew inwards from the side of the ravine. Robert could just make out a stream running along the floor and then he spotted something else.

"There!" he cried. "Down there by the stream!"

"I'll have to do another pass," said Peter. "Are you sure?"

"Only Raymond has hair that colour. That's them, all right." He was so relieved that he actually felt sick for a moment or two.

The locals ran back into their huts, waving their arms wildly. Peter banked and turned and then flew back. For a moment, Robert thought he must have been mistaken and then he saw the lads again, running as fast as they could for the protection of the tree. It was as if they were afraid.

"Silly sods!" said Peter. "You'd think they didn't want to be rescued."

"So what do we do now?" Robert asked.

"We go back to Eldama and get Jeremy to come out with the Land Rover and some rope. This ain't no helicopter."

"Oh!"

It was a relief to fly back at a reasonable altitude. First the caravan came in sight and then the house. Once again, Peter made a perfect landing. Mrs Hanson was waiting. "Any news? Any news?" she called.

"They're down in the ravine," said Peter. "Is Jeremy around? This needs four wheels."

"Why, no. He's out somewhere. Patrick's at home. He'll go."

"I'll get him," said Robert, and he set out at a run through the rose garden. He pushed at the bungalow door, but it was locked and there was no bell push. "Damn!" he said and went round the side. The blinds were down over the first set of windows. The next windows had curtains drawn, but the blinds were up. He tapped on the glass and waited. Nothing happened.

"Come on! Come on!" he muttered impatiently.

He was about to rap on the glass again when he heard George's voice: "I'm going to miss this. When are you coming down to Nairobi?"

George's voice appeared to be coming from the roof at first.

Robert looked up. The air conditioner ventilator louvers were pointing downwards and acting as a perfect sound carrier.

"As soon as I can," a disconcertingly familiar voice responded. "Carry on. It feels great!"

'Feels great?' Robert moved to one side. There was a tiny gap, not more than half an inch between the curtain and the window frame. He peered in – and got the shock of his life. Patrick, naked save for a chain of some sort round his neck, was sitting on the edge of the bed. George, similarly unclothed but without a chain, was kneeling between Patrick's legs with Patrick's penis in his mouth. Spellbound, Robert watched the younger man's head bobbing up and down. He stopped. Patrick's cock, glistening with saliva, popped out of George's mouth.

"You make a good sex-slave," said Patrick. "You can get up now." He put his hands in George's armpits and hoisted him up as if he were a life-sized doll with a more than life-sized and extremely hard penis. "Get into position," he said. George climbed on the bed and knelt on all fours.

Patrick ran his hands over his buttocks. "Superb! I love a nice arse," he said. "I must paint this one when you come up again. I may even do a full frontal." He slid a hand between George's legs.

"Not lying on a bed reading a book?" said George, breathlessly.

"Oh, no. Something a little better than that. I've never found cocks very attractive, as a matter of fact."

"I've gathered that and I've only known you for a few days."

"They're really only useful for one thing. Two, if you count peeing."

"I would have said peeing was quite important. If you don't start soon, I shall have to go and do exactly that."

"All in good time. You're not ready yet. If I stand back a bit, I can watch your cock. That will tell me when you're ready."

Robert jerked his head back in case he was spotted but Patrick had something much more attractive on which to concentrate.

Robert pressed his head against the window frame again.

"Do it now! Peter will be back soon. He's got a business meeting in Nairobi this afternoon," said George breathlessly.

"Bugger Peter. You don't have to go back with him. You could stay the night here and I could drive you home in the morning."

"He won't like that. No. I'll go back with him."

"Peter! You'd stand on your head for Peter!"

"I'm not doing so badly for you. For Christ's sake, do something. I'll go off in a minute."

Opposing intentions were battling for supremacy in Robert's mind. Some miles distant there were two lads in the bottom of a deep ravine. Patrick and George were only a few feet away and what they were doing was much more interesting than snake-catching. Raymond and Martin were obviously not in any sort of trouble, not if they could run for cover as they had. Climbing down into the ravine was obviously a schoolboy prank, a bloody silly schoolboy prank at that. They could wait.

"...but he's a bad influence on you. Can't you see that?" Patrick was saying.

"He's not that bad."

"He's nearly old enough to be your father. It's not right."

"It will be if we get this rare-game park going. I get free housing and a free car. That can't be bad."

"There are more important things in life. You ought to be going to university like the others."

"Just so I'm around in England for you when you want me?"

"You like it. You said so."

"I said I didn't mind. That's not the same thing, but do it for Christ's sake."

"That's the second time. Now then, where did I put it? Ah! Here."

Robert hadn't noticed the cane even though it was lying on the pillow. It was a proper one with a walking stick handle. Patrick picked it up and brought it down with a soft "thwack!" on the pillow. George jumped. Once again, Patrick stroked his buttocks.

"Such a beautiful arse, so smooth…It seems a shame to mark it but it has to be done. Young men fuck so much better when they've been whipped." Patrick put his hand under George. "Ah yes! You're beginning to react nicely. You love it, don't you?"

"Not…too…hard!" George gasped.

"I won't draw blood. I promise. You're in the hands of an expert. Not perhaps up to Father's high standard, but then he's got three of us and I've only got you. Incidentally, he's going to have an aching arm when Tim and Jeremy get back for the holidays. Their school reports came this morning. Jeremy was caught smoking a reefer and is down in practically every subject and Tim's not much better. Jeremy got a splinter in his thigh last time. You should have seen Tim's face when he was brought in and saw the blood on the table!"

"Your dad's a bastard," said George.

"He is not! I won't have that said of him. There ought to be more strict parents. It didn't do me any harm and it's not doing Jeremy and Tim any harm either." Patrick laughed. "The only person who suffers is Father. Rowing has nothing on arse-whipping for making your arm ache. I shan't be doing any painting this evening. That's for sure. It'll be worth it, though."

That made Robert think. Pulling two very strong and heavy young men out of a hundred-foot-deep ravine needed strength. It was time to stop the performance. He stood back and shouted at the air conditioner. "Patrick! Patrick!"

"Who the f…hell?"

"It's me. Robert. We have an emergency. Can I speak to you?"

"Be right with you. Hang on a minute."

It was more like five minutes before the curtain was drawn back and Patrick opened the window. He had a towel round his waist and there was no sign of either George or the cane.

"I was just having a doze," he explained.

"I'm sorry to disturb you. We need your help." Robert told him about the boys' situation.

"I'll be right there. I've just got to get dressed," said Patrick. Robert wouldn't have minded waiting for him by the window. A body like Patrick's was worth careful study. His nipples were huge and as red as raspberries. A tempting line of brown hair peeped above the towel. Below it, if one cared to look downwards as Robert did, there was more hair on Patrick's legs than many people have on their heads. Robert forced himself to turn away and went to wait by the front door.

"Sorry about that," said Patrick when he came out. "I must be getting old. I seem to need more sleep these days."

"Stress of studying and rowing, I expect. Where's George?"

"George? No idea. Around somewhere, no doubt." One would have thought Patrick hardly knew the lad or was, perhaps, pre-occupied with the plight of the other two. "We need a load of rope. Fortunately, Father has some. It's going to be a rough ride, I'm afraid. There are no roads at all."

He hadn't exaggerated. When they were underway, Robert had to hang on like grim death. They lost a coil of rope at one stage. Fortunately, Robert glimpsed it in the rear view mirror, lying on the ground behind them and he ran back to retrieve it.

"I don't want to park too near the huts," said Patrick. "We might need some help though. Let's have a look first." One or two people popped their heads out to see who it was and waved. Patrick waved back and Robert followed suit. Finally, Patrick brought the Land Rover to rest at the edge of the chasm and pulled the brake lever back.

Very gingerly, Robert approached the edge and peered over. He couldn't see them, so he shouted down. "Raymond! Martin!" His voice echoed back at him. "Raymond! Martin!" he shouted again.

"Down here!" Raymond's voice drifted upwards. Robert took

another cautious step forward and then he saw them. Once again, Raymond's hair gave him away.

"Are you all right?" he shouted.

"Yeah. Sure."

"We'll soon get you out. Patrick's here with some rope."

"Oh. You don't need a rope. There's a way down to your left. You can't see it easily from the top. Come down by yourself."

"I'm not so sure," said Patrick. "Let's have a look."

They walked along the edge, following Raymond's gesticulating arm.

"Did you have to wait long for me to wake up?" said Patrick. "I was out like a light, I'm afraid."

What to answer? "No. I shouted and you woke up" or "I saw and heard everything"?

"Let's just say that I hadn't realised that you and I had so much in common," Robert replied.

Patrick had blushed when he had showed Raymond's picture to the others, but that was nothing in comparison to his reaction now. "You mean...with George?" he asked, in an unusually breathless voice.

"No. Not with George." Robert pointed down towards Martin and Raymond and then converted the gesture into an encouraging wave.

"I would never have thought..." said Patrick.

"That was one of my mother-in-law's favourite expressions. Let's talk about that later. We have to bring them out alive. This looks bloody dangerous to me."

"Just there!" Raymond shouted. "See that bush?"

"Yes." The word echoed back at him several times.

"Hang on to that and you'll find a sort of step. It's not too bad after that."

"Oh no!" said Patrick. "One of us gets roped up and goes down. The other one holds the rope."

"Well, you're certainly the stronger of the two. I'll go down," said Robert.

"You sure? I don't mind."

"Quite sure. Do you know about knots?"

"No problem. Put this end round you like this…"

Robert couldn't help remembering a night some time previously when Martin showed him how to knot a kikoi. Patrick's strong arms went round his waist twice and some sort of knot was tied.

"Okay. Down you go. Don't worry. I've got you," said Patrick.

It was a nasty descent, but got slightly easier as he neared the bottom. Patrick was able to let the rope slacken and that made it even easier. Apart from a slight scratch on his forehead, he reached the bottom safely. Raymond and Martin were waiting for him – and smiling. That was the last straw.

"I suppose you realise the trouble you've caused," he began.

"But I got two pythons – not very big ones, but they'll grow," said Raymond.

"Fuck the snakes! You've had several people worried out of their minds. Of all the stupid –"

"And there's something else," said Martin. "Come with us, but don't make it look as if we're showing you. I don't want Patrick to see."

"To see what?"

"Just come with us. Make out you're telling us off."

"I don't need to make that out. Bloody idiots. You know how I feel about you both. You could have been killed. Just wait till we get back."

Actually, Patrick would be the man for that job, he thought. To punish young men with such bad behaviour as these two.

"There!" said Martin.

"There what?"

"I don't want to point. Look to your left. See that slab?"

Through the accumulation of roots and vegetation in the side of the ravine, one could just about make out that the large stones had been cemented together. In the centre was a concrete slab about as big as a paving stone.

"We would never have spotted it, but one of the pythons put up a fight and swept all the plants away," said Raymond. "See the swastika?"

Robert's anger vanished when he saw it. Someone had drawn a swastika in a circle in the cement whilst it was still wet.

"Well, I'm damned!" he said.

"The Meinerherzhagen cup! I'll bet that's where it is!" said Martin.

"You could be right, but there's no way we're going to be able to get it out. Not without special gear."

"You could get some and we can come down one night," said Martin.

"There will be no more night-time excursions. We need Patrick."

"Do we have to?"

"Yes, we do. Patrick!" he yelled.

"What is it?"

"...it?...it?" came the echo.

"Can you get down on your own – and get back up again?"

"Sure."

"...sure...sure."

They watched him scramble down. Robert felt ashamed of his own clumsy effort.

"What's wrong?" Patrick asked when he at last joined them.

"Nothing's wrong." Robert pointed to the swastika. "The non-existent Meinerherzhagen cup, if I'm not mistaken," he said.

"Jesus Christ! Forget I said that. Hell's teeth!"

"So how do we get at it?"

Patrick peered closely and pulled a penknife out of his pocket.

He jabbed at the concrete. "A pneumatic drill job. We've got a couple and a compressor. A cold chisel - maybe two. Crowbars too. Rope is no problem. About four labourers, I should think, and Father, of course. Can you stay here? There's no need for you to come with me."

"That would be the best thing. Are you two hungry? Shouldn't you go back?"

"We'll wait with you," said Raymond decisively.

"It'll be some time. We'll have to hoist the compressor on to the back of a flat-bed."

"We'll be okay," said Raymond.

"Fair enough, then. I'll be as quick as I can." Patrick had obviously secured the rope at the top. He went up like a monkey.

They heard the Land Rover start and an eerie silence fell.

"We'll have to share it with them now," said Martin. "At least that awful Hardwick man isn't in on it."

"Actually, I have something to tell you about him," said Robert. "Promise to keep this completely secret, though the chances are that you'll hear it firsthand sooner or later."

"What?"

"You remember when you said that George was going to get fucked?"

"That's right. I was wrong, though."

"Only when you said it would be one of us. Neither was it Peter Hardwick, who happens to be straight and living with a Kenyan girl."

"So who...?"

Robert smiled and pointed upwards and in the direction of Patrick.

"No! I don't believe it!" said Martin.

"I do. He was getting quite worked up when he painted my picture," said Raymond. "Guess what? There's a chance after all. I quite fancy an oarsman."

"Whore's man is more like it, in your case," said Martin.

"I think you might not enjoy some of Patrick's more...er...outlandish ideas," said Robert.

"Such as? Come on. We've got time. Tell us everything," said Raymond.

They sat on the ground. Protected from the sun's glare by the overhanging tree, Robert told them everything.

"Of course! We should have known. George is always going on about corporal punishment in a big way," said Martin. "I wish to hell he'd told me. I'd have gone out and bought a whip for him."

"Each man to his own," said Raymond. "I don't mind being fisted. I like being sucked and I love being fucked, but I draw the line at that."

"Which brings to mind an interesting possibility," said Martin. "How long did it take you to get here, Robert?"

"Oh...more than half an hour. There's no road."

"We know that. So we have at least half an hour. We ought to do something whilst we're waiting, don't you think?"

"You mean?"

They both stood up. Two pairs of shorts slid down two pairs of hairy legs simultaneously, followed by two pairs of underpants, one sparkling white and the other a pale shade of mauve – not that Robert was much interested in colours.

A lot of dramatic events had occurred in that ravine. The wrecked vehicles attested to that, but none, surely, was so unusual as the sight of two young men leaning against the hard, stone walls whilst Robert, kneeling in front of them and moving from one rampant cock to the other, slavered over their thighs, licked their balls, inhaled their perspiration, finally bringing them, gasping with delight, to a viscous but delicious climax. Not quite finally. No doubt the drivers of the wrecked trucks had lain on the stony ground, but they would have been dead – or at least seriously injured. Robert was very much alive.

Their mouths and their hands went everywhere. His hands were busily employed reaching out to touch them, to hold them and to feel them. With one hand on Martin's arse and with the other attempting to bring Raymond's cock back to life, he shot, splattering them both.

They lay there for some time, kissing, hugging and holding on to each other as if afraid to part. Then using broad leaves and water from the brackish stream, they washed away the spots. There was still a long wait ahead.

"I wonder if Patrick's two brothers are like him," said Martin, suddenly.

"No idea. My wife met them apparently, but she didn't tell me. If you're staying on for a year and living in the area you're bound to meet them. Mr Hanson is pretty strict with them, apparently. Aha! What's that?"

It was an engine noise. Several engine noises – and it got louder by the minute. "That's them," said Raymond, pushing his shirt into his shorts and adjusting his belt so that the buckle was in the middle.

The four Kenyans came down the sides more rapidly than Patrick and without the aid of ropes.

Patrick stood on the edge. "Watch out!" he called and two compressed air hoses snaked through the air and landed with a thump on the ground.

They heard the compressor being started and then Patrick lowered the drills one by one and finally clambered down himself with some sort of tool bag slung over his shoulder. Mr Hanson came down with equal ease, which made Robert feel ashamed of himself. Mr Hanson stood for some minutes, feet apart on the very spot where Robert had lain and looked around. "This is disgraceful. Absolutely disgraceful! When I was a kid, I used to come and play here. It'll have to be cleaned up – and soon. Make a note of that, Patrick."

"Yes, Father. The stone is over here."

"This used be part of our estate in my grandfather's day. I should have realised," said Mr Hanson.

"And so should Jeremy and I. Here it is. See the swastika?" said Patrick.

"Hmm. That must be erased. Can't stand the sight of it. Now then, where are the watu? Ah! Jeremiah. *Kuja hapa.*"

"They're going to drill round the edge and then lift the stone out," Raymond translated. The noise of the drills was so deafening that the four of them had to walk away.

After overseeing the start of the operation, Mr Hanson joined them. "He made a good job of closing up after him. How did you find it?" he asked. Raymond explained.

It took an hour before the stone was free. Robert was beginning to wonder if his hearing had been permanently impaired. The ringing in his ears made conversation almost impossible. The men collected the hoses, tied the end of a rope round them and shouted up. Then the drills went up and finally, the men – again without any assistance – scrambled to the top.

"Now then. Let's have it out," said Mr Hanson. All five of them seized crowbars. All five of them were needed. It might have been the size of a paving stone, but it was about four times as thick. Raymond almost lost another toe when it fell.

"It's a cave!" said Martin, peering in. "A big one. Who's going first?"

Unbelievably, everyone hesitated. "It's on your land." "No, you go." "What about you, Raymond?" "Perhaps Robert should go." "Patrick, you're the strongest." Finally, Martin and Raymond climbed in one after the other.

"What can you see?" Robert called.

"Sod-all at the moment. Sorry, Mr Hanson. I mean nothing. We should have brought torches."

"That's what you said last night." Raymond's voice came from deep inside.

"Boxes. Crates. Wood. In pretty ropey condition." That was Martin's voice. "Hang on. What's this? Jesus!"

Mr Hanson appeared not to have heard the exclamation. "What is it?" he called.

"Hang on. I'll bring it out. I hope the bloody thing isn't loaded."

Fearing the same thing, all three onlookers stood back as Martin's hand appeared, clutching a very rusty machine gun. "There are hundreds of them," he said.

"What else? Can you see the cup?"

"I can. At least I think so," Raymond's voice echoed back at them. There was a scuffling sound and he appeared at the entrance holding a wooden box. "I'll bet that's it," he said. "It's heavy enough."

It was. It was so heavy that Mr Hanson nearly dropped it. The wood had decayed to the consistency of cardboard and had almost fallen away. Martin and Raymond looked out of the hole as Patrick tore away the wrappings.

"Well, I'll be...So he did have it," said Mr Hanson. It stood about eighteen inches high, glittering in the sunshine and coincidentally on grass that had recently been fertilised by a few drops of semen – the nearest it would ever get to the use Martin had proposed for it if it were found, Robert thought.

"How much is it worth?" Martin called.

"More than any of us have ever seen in our lives," Mr Hanson replied.

"You've seen nothing yet, sir. It would be better to form a chain to get the rest out. They're heavy, too."

The first gold bar surprised them to the extent that it was dropped twice in transit. By the time the fiftieth was brought out – Mr Hanson was counting them out loud – their arms were aching. When the final one, the hundred and fiftieth, was laid on top of the rest their senses were numbed.

There was paper money too: German Reichmarks. "Each one of those is a collector's item," said Mr Hanson. "This was all he needed to start his revolution. Amazing!"

"My dad will be thrilled. He can put it in the book he's writing," said Raymond, climbing out of the hole.

"If you'll take my advice, you won't even tell him. This amount of wealth and all those weapons would be enough to destabilise Kenya for years to come. We can give the cup to the Government. The gold had better go somewhere like Dubai to be converted in cash for you. I can arrange that. As for the weaponry, I think we'll bury it and say nothing."

"How do we get it all back, Father?"asked Patrick.

"We'll do it tomorrow. I'll bring a cattle net and we can use the front winch on a Land Rover. Now these two young heroes had better go back and get a good night's sleep. If you and Robert can stay here and keep guard –"

"We're all right," Martin protested.

"Back and bed," said Mr Hanson firmly.

"And take the livestock with you, please," said Robert. "Patrick is welcome. Pythons are not."

They watched them climb up. Once or twice Mr Hanson had to give them a helping hand.

"Whacked. Absolutely whacked!" said Patrick. "Both of them are."

"But not in the sense you would prefer, eh?" said Robert.

"Did you hear everything?"

"I heard and saw. You left a gap in the curtains."

"Bugger."

"I wouldn't worry about it. George didn't seem to be raising any objections."

"Something else rose, though," said Patrick. "He was getting near. He'd have juiced up any second. Anyway, I suppose we should get some rest. We could use a gold bar as a neck-rest. Kenyans sleep that way."

"An expensive way to sleep. It's odd. All this started with Kenyan sleeping habits. It's like coming round in a full circle. Martin and a kikoi."

"Tell me."

"Tomorrow. I'm too shattered now. Incidentally, pop round when this is all over and collect your mug."

"You couldn't have repaired it."

"I didn't. I've got you a replacement."

"Why should you have gone to all that trouble? I mean, it's decent of you and all that..."

"I somehow knew it was important to you. Don't ask me how."

"The full circle is complete," said Patrick. "Shall I tell you or are you too tired?"

"Go on. Tell me."

"Father felt I ought to visit Europe when I passed my A-levels and was waiting to go up to Oxford. Well, Jeremy and I had been hunting for this cup for ages, so I decided to try and trace von Meinerherzhagen's family and ask them about it. The German embassy here could only trace one and he lived in Passau, so I went to see him. In fact, he wasn't a lot of use. He was the old boy's great nephew. I was able to give him a photo of the grave in Gilgil and that pleased him. He invited me to stay, so I did and, er...well, you can guess the rest. He gave me that mug as a thank-you present. It commemorated the loss of my virginity."

"Then do come and collect it. Bring George, if you can. We'll have a sort of ceremony. It was Martin's idea. The real cup is rather too valuable and much too big. I presume you won't be using it for drinking from."

"I don't feel comfortable, really, drinking from a Nazi cup. And if Martin's idea is what I think it might be, I'm much more interested in drinking from the mug," said Patrick. "Are you feeling thirsty at the moment?"

"If *your* idea is what I think it might be, I could enjoy a little liquid refreshment," said Robert. "Move a bit closer."

Epilogue

"Martin and Vijay aren't up yet," said Raymond. "How the hell they can sleep through those bloody cathedral bells, I will never know."

Robert laughed. "You can be sure that they have been 'up'," he said. "Let them sleep. They're only here for a fortnight."

"It's quite like old times again, having them in the flat. We only need George and Patrick," said Raymond.

"They'll be here in the summer. They've got a lot to do."

"I know. The Marriott-Glover health centre back in Kenya. That was a good way to use the money, giving something back to the country itself. Maybe some day they'll get a chance to do the animal park, too. It was nice of Martin to let George in on it, and use his name as well. I'm rather glad that Peter Hardwick helped out. I was never very happy about that man at first, though."

"Neither of us were. I was very suspicious. Wrongly, as it turned out."

"We were both as bad as each other. When you go out, don't forget to post my letter," said Robert.

"Hey! You're not an officer any longer. Stop ordering me about. It wouldn't hurt you to post it yourself."

"I've got an early lecture."

Raymond came over and kissed his forehead. "I'll do it. Of course I'll do it. You're a year junior to me, but I'll still do it because I love you."

"Not half as much as I love you," said Robert.

Also by Peter Gilbert

Sex Triangle

Tim and Danny are furious that their friend and lover, Michael, has fallen under the spell of smooth-talking Adam. Before long, another young friend has been spirited away and our heroes must give chase towards Dubai. If they can unravel the sordid business that motivates Adam, perhaps they can save the boy.

In this exciting sequel to **On Target***, the adventurous threesome find that hunting villains is randy work.*

"And what do we do next?" he asked – as if he didn't know!

"We change positions," I said. "If we're going to do this properly, we'd better stand up."

He laughed. "I think we are both standing up already." That was true enough. If he'd shot at that moment, it would have missed his nose by inches. I took both pillows and laid them one on top of the other across the bed.

"Get over that and spread your legs," I said – as if he needed to be told. So many drenched pillowcases had gone through our washing machine at home during his stay with us that we were lucky the draining mechanism hadn't clogged.

He lay forward and spread his arms and legs. "A hot-cross bun." I said.

"What is that?"

"Something you have in England at Easter."

"I do not think I can wait until then," he said.

UK £7.95 US $12.95 (when ordering quote FIC 25)

Also by Peter Gilbert

On Target

Tim Scully is your average boy-hungry public school boarder – but he thinks it's only him and his 'friend' Adam who feel that way.

Tim wants to follow his grandmother's trade – armaments – and worries that his sexuality could ruin his career. Unfortunately, he very nearly lets his career ruin his sexuality, before coming to his senses and grabbing the love of his life.

UK £7.95 US $11.95 (when ordering quote FIC 24)

New erotic fiction by Jack Dickson

Out of This World Out Oct 2001 from Zipper Books

Hard and horny stories of sex between men in the real world, the cyberworld, last year and next century – in their own bedrooms or lost in space.

Jack Dickson's wank-worthy porno tales have been published in US anthologies and all-American magazines like *Powerplay* and *Bunkhouse*. This collection brings together the very best.

UK £7.95 US $13.95 (when ordering direct, quote OUT 634)

New erotic fiction by Sam Stevens

Boy Banned

Four young men are about to get the biggest break of their lives. In a hot new boyband, they ride into the pop charts on a wave of sex and success. But they're not like every other clean-cut bunch of cuties: they're gay, they're out and they're horny as hell.

In this fresh new erotic novel from the author of *The Captain's Boy*, fame is the biggest turn-on of them all.

'You certainly have high opinions of yourselves, I will say that. Now what is your band called?'

Joe crossed his arms and grinned sheepishly at the older man. 'The Big Boys.'

'Interesting name. What's the reason behind that?' Nick gazed unblinkingly at Joe, who returned the stare.

'Well... we liked the name, and it sounds good and er...'

'I hope you live up to your stage soubriquet.'

Paul looked puzzled. 'Our what?'

'Your band name. If you call yourselves big boys, it seems only right and fair that you should be.' A palpable tension seemed to be hovering in the air about the three men.

Joe broke the silence, shifting a little in his seat and spreading his legs slightly, easing himself forward an inch or two, his tight trousers emphasising the bulge within them.

'I've had no complaints so far.'

UK £7.95 US $12.95 (when ordering direct, quote BOY360)